Je Anne Boleyn
Book One

Sandra Vasoli

As Anne loved Elizabeth…
For Tom

STRUCK WITH THE DART OF LOVE

Je Anne Boleyn

Book 1

ISBN-13: 978-84-944893-6-5

M

MadeGlobal Publishing

For more information on MadeGlobal Publishing, visit our website: www.madeglobal.com

Anne Boleyn illustrated by Dmitry Yakhovsky, based on a miniature of Anne Boleyn, attributed to John Hoskins.

PREFACE

ANNE BOLEYN IS, without question, a historical character about whom much has been written. The writings have taken many forms over the years: biographies, fictional accounts, narratives, poetry, theatrical productions, Hollywood extravaganzas. Yet there remains something indefinable about her – and, in particular, about the nature of her relationship with Henry VIII - which compels us to delve into the facts we know, and imagine those we don't, in the ongoing efforts to explore her true nature.

There is just enough extant information about Anne to allow us a tantalizing glimpse into her heart and soul; the missing pieces are equally alluring. Perhaps this is why historians and writers, artists and actors have over the years developed their own representations of Anne and her brilliant, tragic story. I am no different. I have researched, read, dreamed and imagined, and have created an account, as I think Anne herself would have told it, of her tumultuous, passionate love affair with Henry, King of England.

In support of my project, there have been numerous people who have generously offered their time, knowledge and inspiration. I can't possibly express how grateful I am to all of them. Without them, the outcome would have been impossible. My author-mentor, Mr Brian Callison – a fine writer and even finer gentleman – has provided wisdom, patience, encouragement, and unending skill in helping me hone this product until it seemed ready for delivery. My appreciation for him knows no bounds.

As I conducted the research so critical in seeking answers about Anne and Henry, there have been individuals who took the time and interest to improve my understanding of Tudor history. They include Professor James Carley from York University in Toronto, Canada, with whom I had a dialogue about the spectacular Book of Hours containing inscriptions from both Henry and Anne; Dr Catherine Fletcher, of the University of Sheffield, UK , who enabled my knowledge about the role of spies in the Tudor court (especially with reference to the purloined love letters Henry wrote to Anne), as well as provided education about Henry's ambassador to Rome, Gregorio Casali ; the assistance of the kind Information Specialists in the Manuscripts Reading Room at the British Library as I studied the famous Book of Hours with Henry's and Anne's inscriptions. My thanks must also go to Ms Sophie Clarke, who provided a critical reference to my application for access to the Manuscripts Room – which was an incredibly important experience in making this story come alive. I am indebted to the gracious Ms Anna Spender, Deputy Head Steward at Hever Castle, who organized a private tour for me, and made herself available in later months to continue answering questions I posed. My gratitude extends in no small part to Professor John Immerwahr from Villanova University, Villanova, Pennsylvania, USA, who discussed with me the benefits of viewing original documentation, and provided documentation necessary for my admission to the *Biblioteca Apostolica* – the Papal Library - at the Vatican. There, with deep thanks to Dr Giuseppe Ciminello, Director of Admissions, and to Dr Paolo Vian, Director, Manuscripts Department, I was privileged to view the original letters which Henry wrote to Anne from approximately 1527 through 1528. This was a truly indescribable experience, and the inspection of Henry's pen strokes, the way the ink was applied to the pages, gave me a thrilling and unique insight into the nature of their relationship.

As the story took shape, there were friends and supporters who spent time reviewing my manuscript, and I cannot thank them enough. They include Cathy Howell, my dear friend who also accompanied me on the magical mission of viewing the Book of Hours at the British Library; Cathy Giannascoli, whose critique and help with French translations proved invaluable; Maria Maneos, an encourager unlike any other, whose keen reader's eye was a wonderful gift; Laurie Vasoli, whose feedback made me feel as if I had conveyed Anne's spirit; and Donna Bolno, whose insightful commentary never fails to bolsters my confidence.

Finally, I am profoundly fortunate to have the advocacy, advice, and love of my husband Tom, and my daughter Stacey. They make the seemingly impossible very possible indeed.

DRAMATIS PERSONAE

In order of appearance

Anne Boleyn (c.1501 – 1536): Marquess of Pembroke, Queen of England from 1533 - 1536

Henry VIII (1491 – 1547): King of England from 1509 - 1547

Anne Gainsford Zouche (1495/1500? – 1545?): Anne Boleyn's lady-in-waiting and companion

Katherine of Aragon (1485 – 1536): first wife of Henry VIII; Queen of England from 1509 - 1533

Thomas Boleyn (c.1477 – 1539): Earl of Wiltshire, Knight of the Garter; father of Anne, Mary and George Boleyn

Marguerite d'Angoulême (1492 – 1549): Princess of France; Queen of Navarre; French mentor to Anne Boleyn

Mary Boleyn/Mary Carey (c.1499 – 1543): sister of Anne Boleyn; mistress to Henry VIII; wife of William Carey

George Boleyn (c.1503 – 1536): 2nd Viscount Rochford; brother and confidante to Anne Boleyn; married to Jane Parker

Henry Percy (1502 – 1537): 6th Earl of Northumberland, Knight of the Garter; in love with and precontracted to Anne Boleyn

Cardinal Thomas Wolsey (1473 – 1530): Henry VIII's Lord Chancellor, and Archbishop of York

Lady Elizabeth Howard, Lady Boleyn (c.1480 – 1538): Countess of Wiltshire; wife of Thomas Boleyn, Earl of Wiltshire; mother of Anne, Mary and George Boleyn; mistress of Hever Manor

Margaret Wyatt, Lady Lee (1506 – 1561): sister of poet Thomas Wyatt; wife of Sir Anthony Lee; friend and lady-in-waiting to Anne Boleyn

Anne (Nan) Saville – mentioned in primary documents as lady-in-waiting to Anne Boleyn; very little known of her

Thomas Howard (1473-1554): 3rd Duke of Norfolk, Knight of the Garter; married to Elizabeth Stafford; uncle of Anne Boleyn

Charles Brandon (c.1484 – 1545): 1st Duke of Suffolk, 1st Viscount Lisle, Knight of the Garter; married to Mary Tudor, sister of Henry VIII

François I (1494 – 1547): monarch of the House of Valois; King of France from 1515 until 1547

Sir Henry Norreys (c.1482–1536): courtier and Groom of the Stool to Henry VIII

Thomas Wyatt (1503 – 1542): courtier, ambassador, poet; introduced the sonnet as a form of English poetry.

Emporer Charles V (1500 – 1558): ruler of Spain; crowned Emperor of Holy Roman Empire by Pope Clement VII in 1530; nephew of Katherine of Aragon

Bess Holland (d. 1548): mistress of Duke of Norfolk from 1526; daughter of Norfolk's chief steward; maid of honour to Anne Boleyn

Margery Horsman (died c.1547): maid of honor in the household of Katherine of Aragon and Anne Boleyn, possibly to Jane Seymour as well

Lorenzo Campeggio (1474–1539): an Italian cardinal and statesman; cardinal protector of England; legate assigned to oversee the proposed annulment of the marriage of Henry VIII to Katherine of Aragon

William Sandys (1470 – 1540): 1st Baron Sandys of the Vyne, Knight of the Garter; diplomat; appointed Lord Chamberlain in 1526; a favourite courtier of Henry VIII

Mary Tudor (1516 – 1558): daughter of Henry VIII and Katherine of Aragon; Queen of England and Ireland from July 1553 until her death

Francis Bryan (c.1490 – 1550): courtier and diplomat; became Chief Gentleman of the Privy Chamber to Henry VIII; cousin to Anne Boleyn

Henry Fitzroy (1519 – 1536): 1st Duke of Richmond and Somerset, Knight of the Garter; illegitimate son of Henry VIII of England and Elizabeth Blount; married Lady Mary Howard, daughter of Thomas Howard, Duke of Norfolk

Thomas Cranmer (1489 – 1556): Fellow of Cambridge University; humanist and leader of the Reformation; appointed Archbishop of Canterbury in 1532 by Henry VIII

Thomas Cromwell (c.1485 – 1540): 1st Earl of Essex, Knight of the Garter; advisor to Cardinal Wolsey; member of Henry VIII's Privy Council and chief minister from 1532 to 1540

Guillaume du Bellay (1491 -1543): Seigneur de Langey; diplomat and ambassador from France under François I

Thomas Cheyne (1485 – 1558): Knight of the Garter; Constable of Queenborough Castle; married to Anne Broughton

Gregorio Casali (c.1500 – 1536): Italian diplomat; Henry VIII's representative in Rome and at the Vatican

Anne Savage (c.1496 – 1546): Baroness Berkeley; lady-in-waiting and friend of Anne Boleyn; one of the few documented witnesses to the wedding of Anne Bolen and Henry VIII on 25 January 1533

Rowland Lee (c.1487 – 1543): Bishop of Coventry and Lichfield; supporter of Henry VIII's annulment; possible officiant at the marriage of Henry VIII and Anne Boleyn

Greenwich
November 1525

I will admit it to be true.

WE GALLOPED FULL out across the rutted, frozen November fields, foam flying from the horses' mouths and clods of deep-chilled earth from their hooves. Thundering headlong behind the bellowing hounds I glanced up and became utterly transfixed watching him lead the field. The supple strength of his commanding figure: the ease with which he controlled his huge bay gelding - his image held me captive! I was completely absorbed in the scene played out before me. Too late did I realize I had committed a most flagrant breach of hunt formality. Protocol did not permit me to ride to the head of the field, yet there I found myself, forging towards the front like a novice. And worse - that my mare, unchecked, had run right up on his hunter's hind end, precipitating an angry backlash from its left rear hoof which narrowly missed my own mount's head.

Scrambling to a desperate halt, I swiftly became all too aware of where I was, and of what had just happened. With a forcible drag on the reins, he pulled his steaming horse up, and whirled about in annoyance to find us standing there, my horse and me heaving with exertion. I, for my part, wishing I were anywhere else in the kingdom.

We stood together silently, enshrouded in the swirling, cold grey mist, streams of white vapour blowing from the horses' nostrils. Expressionless, he observed me for a very long moment. Then, though I may well have imagined it, just the very corners of his mouth crinkled upwards, nearly imperceptibly. My breath caught in my throat, and I am certain my heart ceased beating.

God's blood! What came over me at that moment?

I had scarcely a chance to recover, much less mumble an apology. The intensity of his gaze never wavered. Only at long last did he nod slightly.

"Greetings, Mademoiselle Boleyn."

Abruptly then, the King reined his horse about, spurred him to a gallop, and followed the master huntsman into the woods.

•

For the remainder of that long afternoon in the field, my distraction was such that I am not even sure if we brought down the stag we pursued. At last, we clattered back into the stable yard at Greenwich. Never had I been so glad to hand my mare's reins to the stable boy before running back to my room where I found my chamber mate, Anne Gainsford, curled comfortably by the fire, reading. I pride myself on a cool sense of composure, but as I entered the chamber my breath was quick and shallow, my heart pounded, and my mind was completely flustered. Sinking to a stool, I remained motionless for what must have been minutes. Finally, Anne glanced up from her book and said "Zounds, Anne! Was it that exhausting a hunt? You look as though you've been out there for days!"

I didn't even think to reply, confounded as I was by the extraordinary encounter with the King. Recalling his expression as we stood face to face, I tried most anxiously to interpret it. Surely it must have been one of amused indulgence, like the attitude one would adopt with a precocious child who had overstepped her bounds. But those vivid eyes fixated on mine? What of the fact that I could not draw a single breath while he stared at me? Had he experienced that, too, perchance? Suddenly I wondered how I had appeared to him. Eyes unblinking, wide with surprise? Or, even more awful - might my mouth have been agape?

I then became aware of the many dishevelled strands of hair which had come loose before the whip of the wind and turned to the mirror to remove my riding hat - and promptly burst out laughing. Other than give way to hysterics, there seemed ought else I could do. Attached to my forehead and looking for all the world like a third eye neatly placed above and between my own, clung a huge splat of dried mud.

•

During the weeks following that unsettling event, I went about my routine, trailing after Queen Katherine, conscientiously fulfilling my duties as a maid of honour in her court. December had brought a hard freeze, and hunting had ceased for the year. The temporary denial of such heady diversion during those dark, chill winter days afforded me ample time to contemplate my situation.

As a daughter and the middle surviving child of a nobleman, holding a position in the Queen's court was something of which to be proud. My father, Thomas Boleyn, Viscount Rochford, was pleased with the rank he had achieved as well as the places he had secured for me, my younger brother George - also a courtier, and my elder sister Mary. As far as I was able to observe, no one at court worked harder than my father to support, organize, negotiate, and barter on behalf of his sovereign. Still, it was alleged by some, not without an element of jealous spite, that my father had been appointed viscount only because Mary had been mistress to the King for a time. Regardless of whether or not that was true, the family Bullen had most certainly benefited by Father's elevation to the peerage.

I was exceedingly fortunate in having received an outstanding education in my youth, most especially for a girl. I was sent abroad at twelve years of age and was well schooled in the conventions of the elegant courts of France and the Low Countries. In 1522, when I was twenty-one and of a very marriageable age, I was summoned back to England, and was at intervals present at the English court, or in Kent, at the manor of Hever. Once happily back at home, the only cloud on my horizon was the ongoing negotiation between my father and the Irish Earl of Ormonde to contract a marriage between me and his son, James Butler. Although I had no rights to resist a marriage with Butler, I was not at all enamoured by the prospect. I dreaded the thought of spending my entire life in the backcountry of Ireland, a most desolate place full of bogs, hamlets, and wretched tribes. Furthermore, I resented being used as a prize in a game of familial bartering, but, being a woman, decorum forbade me from having a voice in such matters, so I reluctantly abstained from expressing my opinion.

At this most dreary time of year, the ladies to Queen Katherine were mainly occupied with sewing projects and embroidery, both of which I loathed. To me, there was nothing more deadly boring than sitting by the window stitching mindlessly, feet and hands demurely positioned to steal the warmth from the fire. Of course, the main distraction while doing such mundane needlework was the gossip amongst the ladies in waiting. I listened, certainly, but had my own ideas about how to conduct myself while in the company of the ladies and maids of the court. In the cultured, aristocratic Habsburg Court of Archduchess Margaret of Austria in Brabant, a young lady learned the art of discretion. At court, in and around the thriving cities of Ghent, Bruges, and Brussels, I had been schooled with other children of the great houses of Europe, learning French and the rules of continental behaviour. The Archduchess, a woman of exquisite taste and noble bearing, insisted upon impeccable conduct among the girls who served as her *desmoiselles d'honneur*. Gossip was not permitted, no more than was loose talk or impulsive action, especially in the presence of gentlemen of the court. Later, when I had been sent to France to serve under Mary Tudor during her brief marriage to King Louis XII, I had continued to mature, to absorb, and become finely attuned to the ways of courtly demeanour.

Above all, I learned early in my tutelage to listen discerningly. During my time at the French court, and to my great good fortune, I had become a *protégée* of sorts to François' brilliant sister, Marguerite d'Angoulême. A woman of fiercely independent ideas and the courage and finesse to apply them in the male-dominated political and theological arenas, she took a liking to me and my obvious interest in every aspect of my surroundings, and became my unofficial adviser. Oh, how I looked up to her and wished to mimic her worldliness and poise! She taught me many things, but one concept, especially, proved key to the rest: '*Savoir, c'est pouvoir*'. 'Knowledge is power'. With a meaningful glance she had the ability to instruct me when to keep my mouth firmly closed and my ears open. I learned by observing her ever so carefully as she sat with her ladies, surrounded by members of the court. I watched her decide when to speak and what, then, to say. I witnessed her covertly but intently regarding others, listening to the idle conversation taking place while feigning absorption in sewing or reading. The habit of actively observing and selectively conversing I quickly adopted when I returned to England as a maid of honour to Queen Katherine of Aragon.

Such seeming reticence was to prove a most useful artifice. It never failed to surprise me what interesting and pertinent information could be gleaned by merely watching and listening.

While dutifully completing a chain stitch in crimson on a background of white satin, I followed one particular discussion with interest which revealed that there would be no court celebrations for Christmas this year. It was said that the King planned to leave for Eltham Palace within the next few days, taking the Queen and the Princess Mary. Plague had persisted throughout autumn, and there had come reports of cases being on the rise in London. It was well known that His Majesty would move from location to location constantly to diminish the risk of the great scourge entering his household. As a consequence, he intended to spend a quiet Christmas season at Eltham with just a few courtiers. While I was disappointed there would be no court festivities, the King's decision would at least allow me to spend Christmas at Hever manor with my family, and that prospect brightened my mood considerably.

While her ladies stitched, attempting to muffle their amused whispers, Queen Katherine was in her chapel at prayer: a situation which I must confess to liking because it was at such times, while she was absent, that the most titillating discussions took place. Elizabeth Stafford, Lady Fitzwalter, was speculating on how well the Queen would cope with the appearance at court of young Henry Fitzroy, the newly ennobled Duke of Richmond. It was said that King Henry had brought Fitzroy to London from his childhood home in Yorkshire to have him at court throughout a good part of the year. It was obvious to all that the King adored his son, whose mother was Elizabeth Blount. Fitzroy was a handsome child, robust and fair of face, and Henry proudly intended to show him off at court, no matter his illegitimacy. This beauteous son of Henry's, misbegot according to the Queen's very vocal judgement, was naught but a slap in her face. For years, she had yearned to give her husband the King a lusty, healthy son. But her pregnancies had aborted, her children had died at birth, and she was mother only to her daughter Mary. Oh, she had most demonstrably expressed her displeasure at the King's having bestowed upon his blond, six-year-old son the titles of Earl of Nottingham and Duke of Richmond and Somerset in an elaborate and beautiful ceremony this June past. But the Queen's objections to the young Duke mattered not to His Majesty, who wouldn't be deterred – and this only added a giggling frisson to our stealthy conversation.

It was inevitable, then, that the discussion would move to an even more engrossing topic - the obvious ageing of the Queen set against the enduring virility of the King - and how that contradiction would affect their relationship as time passed. All of the ladies stopped sewing and leaned forward to listen while Joan Vaux, Lady Guildford, archly reported catching His Majesty casting a most appreciative eye over Mistress Joan Champernowne the previous evening.

On this subject, though, we were not all in accord. Katherine's most beloved lady in waiting, Maria de Salinas, disliked it intensely when anything was discussed which implied her lifelong friend and mistress was in danger of losing her hold over King Henry. She rose, gathered her sewing and rustled off in a huff, saying in her still-thick Spanish accent that she would look in on our mistress the Queen; the tattle continued nevertheless, conjecturing on who would be the next object of His Royal Highness's attention since it was well known that his affair with my sister, Mary Boleyn, had ended some time ago.

As the gossip became evermore lively, peppered with names of the most beautiful ladies in and around court as conceivable mistresses to the King, it became my turn to shift about in my seat uneasily. Since that unusual day several weeks ago on the hunt field, I found that the mere mention of King Henry's name caught my most rapt attention. How curious this was! I had heard the King's name uttered thousands of times, and never had it struck me in just this way. I found myself breathlessly wanting to hear any scrap of information about him and clinging to it with a delicious satisfaction.

This preoccupation concerned me. Always had I been surrounded by men of power - handsome men, those possessed of great charm and gallantry towards ladies - yet I was not the kind of young woman who swooned and fawned over a man merely because of his wealth, position, or even his flirtatious attentions, as did so many of the simpering, vacuous beauties who populated the high places of England and France.

I had, in fact, spent some hours - all too many, were I to be completely honest - thinking about the unexpected interaction the King and I shared. At times I felt rather ridiculous, catching myself reliving the moment over and over. Nevertheless, my daydreams dwelt on that afternoon, whether I willed them or not. I wanted so desperately to know what he had felt. Had his breath caught in his throat for a moment, as mine had done? I could not determine it, no matter how many times I replayed the scene in my mind.

As the December days passed, I caught only infrequent glimpses of him as he swept through the palace chambers followed closely by his eager retinue, but there had been no proximity: no signal between us. Clearly the matter was closed, and my immature silliness exposed for what it was.

So why, then, did I continue to brood as I stitched absently? I chided myself sharply, admitting the futility of even another moment spent fantasizing about a romantic connection which, I was certain, was of my own imagining.

Hever
Christmastide 1525

I RECEIVED PERMISSION FROM Queen Katherine to travel to Hever for the holiday season, and anticipated my visit most keenly as my chambermaid, Charity Dodd, and I packed my things. The trip home was well-timed. It would be good to escape awhile, for of late it seemed every time I turned around, Henry Percy's mournful gaze was fixed on me.

As we packed, I thought over the previous months. My Lord Percy was the son and heir of the Earl of Northumberland, in attendance upon the Lord Chancellor, Cardinal Wolsey. When the Cardinal was occupied with matters of business, Lord Percy would visit the Queen's chambers to partake in the pastimes there. One could see he enjoyed his dalliances amongst Her Majesty's maidens. I knew he watched me closely, but furtively, during his visits, until at last he approached me hesitantly, and started a conversation. It was acknowledged that several other maids of honour were enthralled by his youthful and attractive looks and his ability to entertain: not least by making us laugh. I, for my part, enjoyed talking - no, flirting, quite frankly - with him. Some of my saucy precociousness was motivated by the other maids' jealous glances, and soon Percy paid attention only to me. The looks of longing and lust he cast in my direction were evidence that the elegant young lord nurtured rather more serious intentions than mere whispers and hands held when no one was about.

The opportunity he sought presented itself one morning while his master was in conference with the King. There were few people in the Queen's Presence Chamber, and all engaged in private discussion, reading, or other distractions. As we talked, Percy glanced about, then quickly pulled me around the corner into a small closet. There he wrapped his arms around me and kissed me with an earnest vehemence.

"Anne, sweet Anne, I must marry you! Will you have me?"

He scanned my face with such a desperate candour that I felt a sharp stab of emotion. What if Percy was to be my destiny? The proposed marriage with James Butler, my father's preoccupation, had never been perfected - or brought to an approved fruition - by Cardinal Wolsey. And no mention of any other marriage prospect had been made to me since. Northumberland was a powerful and wealthy earldom, which would, no doubt, please Father. Perhaps a union with Percy would be acceptable, after all. I allowed Percy to kiss me again, and told him his proposal would be in my thoughts, and I would give him my answer soon.

During the days, then weeks which followed, I carefully considered my response to Lord Percy. All the while, even though I did not provide him with a clear affirmative answer, I did little to discourage his ardour. This was to prove a great mistake. At length, by virtue of the fact that I had not turned him away, Percy concluded I was in agreement to our betrothal. Still, I had little will to deflect his advances, yet I could not bring myself to commit to him by word or by deed. Shortly thereafter, the young and inexperienced Lord, in his overabundant enthusiasm, blurted to the Cardinal that he held me in great affection, and intended we be married. In fact, he completely overstepped his bounds by telling Wolsey we were betrothed, already having promised each to the other. This, I swear, was not true! Nevertheless, Wolsey, taking his responsibility of being an informant to the King very seriously, promptly reported the news to His Majesty, who was sore offended.

The upshot followed swiftly. After departing for his palace in Westminster, Wolsey angrily summoned Percy to the gallery at York Place where, in the vicinity of servants and nobles alike, the Cardinal chastised the boy most harshly. I was told he came nose to nose with Percy, spluttering - spittle flying, shouting that he marvelled not a little at Percy's peevish folly, entangling himself with a foolish girl, a mere maid in the Queen's court. He had continued to rant at Percy, reminding him he was heir to one of the richest earldoms in the realm. Raising his voice to screech, he demanded, "Would it not have been courteous to seek the opinion and consent of your esteemed father?" And yet more shrill: "Would it not have been meet to make such a request known to the King's Grace, seeking his advice and approval, thereby allowing His Grace to provide an appropriate match in accordance with your estate and future title?"

Percy's father, the Earl of Northumberland, was next called to London by Wolsey for the sole purpose of correcting his son's impertinent behavior and berating him publicly. This the young Lord's father did with zeal, to his eldest son's great abashment. Upon hearing of this, I seethed with anger. What an exceptionally cruel man he must be! I could not imagine any parent wishing to see his child disgraced and humiliated, much less to be the perpetrator of such pain. I felt terrible for Percy, who later cried bitterly in my arms and told me that our precontract was broken.

As for me, I was infuriated with Wolsey! How dare he imply that I - or worse, my family's lineage - was anything less than noble and that I was an unsuitable bride for the son of an earl? This coming from him of all people: the overbearing son of a common butcher and nothing more.

I was indignant when Wolsey told all and sundry I was not worthy to marry into the Percy clan as the next countess. However angry I was at Wolsey's insult, though, the loss of Percy as a marriage prospect did not leave me broken-hearted. I was not keen on the prospect of banishment to the freezing, wind-swept wilds of Northumberland, nor of being affiliated in any way with a man as mean and uncaring as Percy's father. And, most importantly, I was not in love with Percy although I knew he worshipped me. Oh, I was attracted to him, yes. His boyish face was expressive, his eyes so blue with a disarming appeal, and while it was undeniable that he had the lovely, lithe physique of youth, I felt no passion for him. He was just that - a boy. One who had never been away from England, and who had little knowledge of art, of music, of philosophy. He also possessed little insight into women and how to woo them. At first, I had felt sorry for him - for myself, too, in some ways - but after two months of his seemingly relentless infatuation I had grown weary at the sight of his moping, lovelorn face.

•

When I finally arrived home after a long, tedious journey, I tore off my heavy cloak as I raced through the front hallway and up the narrow staircase to see my mother. She was in her dressing chamber, and I rushed to hug her as tightly as I could.

"Mother, I am so delighted to see you! How wonderful it is to be home for Christmas with our family! It will be a Christmas just like those when I was a little girl at Hever."

The Lady Elizabeth Boleyn, Viscountess Rochford, was not only my beloved mother, she was my best friend in the world. It had been terribly difficult being away from her for so long while at the French Court, and I was happy to be near her again.

I pulled at my traveling bonnet while chattering excitedly. "Has George arrived home yet? Is he bringing his wife? And what about Mary - will she and William be joining us for

Christmas …?" Finally, I stopped, caught my breath, and Mother and I both burst into laughter at my prattle.

"Your brother arrived this morning, along with Jane. And Mary, William and baby Catherine will be here on Christmas Eve to stay with us for a week." Mother's lovely face brightened with an amused smile. "I am as excited as you are, Nan. We will be sure to have a lively time together!"

Oh, how I loved it when my mother called me by the affectionate name of Nan. Hearing it instantly made me feel loved and protected, as I did when a child.

•

Christmas Eve and Christmas Day were merry in our house that year, and indeed, they were filled with the warmth I remembered from Christmases of my girlhood. Catherine, my two-year-old niece, was a joy. She was beginning to talk, and her babble entertained us all. Mary was with child again, and she and her husband, William Carey, appeared content.

I thoroughly enjoyed my time with both my brother and sister. I cannot say the same for Jane, George's wife, however. I found the former Jane Parker, now Lady Boleyn, to be - at its most charitable - prickly. Whenever a story was being told, it seemed to me she always had to interject a tale that would best it. Nor did I like the way I would catch her inspecting me when she thought I was unaware. Most annoying, the way she carried herself – her gestures and her clothing – all seemed to mimic mine. She seemed quite a jealous girl in my view. I was not at all sure how George was getting on with his marriage to Jane, but hesitated to bring up the subject, considering it rude.

If anyone deserved domestic contentment, though, it was surely my sister Mary. She was a lovely woman, honey blonde like my mother and more delicate looking than I. Nor was her constitution as strong as mine. Mary had always been somewhat naïve, and in my opinion, far too easily persuaded to enter into situations which were not advantageous for her. Her relationship with the King had been disturbing to observe. She had performed like his puppet, obediently dancing whenever he operated the strings. Knowing her as well as I did, I saw that there was no spark of life about her when she was in his company, yet she always managed to keep a smile on her face. I had heard the rumours, the continuous speculation that Catherine was the King's child, and I did not hesitate to ask Mary directly when she was first pregnant if it were true. She confided in me that she knew the child was not Henry's, but instead her husband William's. Furthermore, she said the King knew and accepted this as well. She also made it quite clear to me that even though she had been favoured, given gifts, and treated well and kindly by His Majesty the King, she had never loved him.

Of this, I was certain.

•

Throughout the days following Christmas, my mother and I spent much time together. In the evenings after supper, we gathered in the cosy parlour chamber in front of a crackling and popping hearthfire. Often George would join us, whereupon the conversation and gossip became evermore lively and infused with laughter. On occasion, my father sat with us, and I took the opportunity to teach them several new card games I had learned at court. During the day, when the weather permitted, Mother and I walked in the gardens to gather the few herbs not yet withered by frost. It was so good to engage with the person who knew me better than anyone else. She offered sympathy for the thwarted marriage plans with Lord Percy, but I confided in her that I didn't mind: instead I sought a match made for love - for passion - and he had not been the one.

Mother cast me a look of both admiration and pity. "Oh, how I would wish that for you as well, my girl. But I am your mother, and I am obliged to discourage you from the notion. You are twenty-four years old, Anne, and the truth is many men are seeking brides who are much younger. We both well know that nobly-born women from households of means have little say in selecting husbands. It is strictly a matter of creating lineal and financial arrangements. Anyway, I'm confident that your father will yet find you a desirable match."

I sighed and thought of my father. Unquestionably, he was highly intelligent. Widely recognized as a consummate negotiator, tactician, and a courtier's courtier; a warm and caring man he certainly was not. Based upon my mother's comments, I was sure the match would be beneficial for him and the family Bullen, first and foremost.

"I know that, of course, Mother, but what if the arrangement just *chanced* to be one of love and advantage both?"

"Well then, Anne, you would be a most happy woman, would you not?" she said and put her arm around my shoulders as we crossed the bridge spanning the moat and walked through the courtyard back to the house.

•

One late afternoon just before the New Year, my mother called me to her chamber. The twilight reflected a deep indigo on the glass panes of the windows: the candles and warmth radiating from the large fireplace making me feel safe and content as I perched on the edge of her bed.

"Nan, I have something for you," Mother said, handing me a big and most beautifully presented parcel wrapped in gorgeous crimson and gold Florentine paper. "These items were ordered some time ago for you, my darling. I had intended to save them to give you upon your betrothal, but I have changed my mind. I want you to have them now."

My eyes suddenly brimmed with tears so profuse that I had to blink fiercely to see as I unwrapped the gift. There was a large package which contained fabric … oh, such beautiful fabric! The softest velvet, it was the unusual colour of new moss in the springtime - green with a golden sheen to it. Beneath that, a bolt of satin of a deep wine colour, like the richest claret. What an enticing gown this would make! The smaller package I opened with bated breath to discover a red leather box covered in Italian goldleaf scrollwork. Slowly I lifted the lid and froze. Nestled on a bed of black satin was a magnificent collar of large, radiant pearls. From this circlet hung a rosy gold 'B', beautifully crafted. And dangling from the lower loop of the 'B' were three pear-shaped pearls, striking for their size and great lustre. As if that were not enough, attached to the circlet was a longer strand of equally captivating pearls, meant to be draped over my shoulders and tucked into a bodice. I could not believe what I held.

"Mother, these gifts are remarkable – gorgeous… and certainly much too costly."

"I want you to have them and to wear them in good health and fortune, darling Anne. A gown made in those colours will flatter you such that everyone will take notice of the extraordinarily beautiful woman you are. And the necklace… treasure it, Nan, and remember me always by it. Let us hope that perhaps, someday, you will be blessed by having a beautiful, accomplished daughter who will wear this very necklace with pride in her Boleyn heritage."

She fastened the piece behind my neck, and we both gazed at its reflection in her mirror.

Oh, I just loved her so.

Greenwich
Winter 1526

BY EARLY IN January I was back in residence at Greenwich where the entire palace, it seemed, was caught up in the preparations for a masque and banquet to celebrate a belated New Year and the King's and Queen's return from their self-imposed isolation at Eltham. I looked forward to the entertainments which were planned, especially anticipating the banquet to be held in the Great Hall.

Much to my delight I located a dressmaker in London with the ability to transform the fabric my mother gave me into a splendid gown, in short order. The finished piece had been delivered, and it was perfectly fitted. In addition to its unusual design, its colour would be, I was sure, unlike any of the other ladies' attire on that evening.

Maggie Wyatt and I strolled through the Great Hall on the way to our chambers in the afternoon before the celebration. It was a sight to behold as yeomen stewards balanced precariously on scaffolds to hang heavy tapestries while others carried tall silver urns filled with branches that had been dipped in silver and gold to be placed about the room and on the dais where the King and Queen would sit. The fireplace was being laid with massive logs: the tables already spread with gleaming white damask cloths.

Maggie nudged my arm as we gaped at the preparations underway. "Well, are you going to wear your brand new gown to the envy of all, Anne? It is a bit unfair to those of us who have no idea what you might unveil tonight."

Maggie Wyatt was my lifelong friend. Her family lived at Allington in Maidstone, just a short distance from the Manor of Hever. Her brothers were George's friends, and her sister a friend of Mary's as we all grew up together. She had always been 'Maggie' to me, although her Christian name was Margaret. Maggie was a few years younger than I, but she had attached herself to me from an early age, following me about across the fields and lawns which joined Hever and Allington. A plucky child, she kept up with me till the difference in our ages no longer mattered, and we became fast friends. It was because of her dedication over the many years that I so valued her company when she came to court. I hope she did mine, as well, because it was a relief to have a friend one could trust and confide in at close hand.

While she was at Greenwich, we'd spent many an hour chattering and laughing about nearly everything under the sun, including our childhood together. But there were two subjects I dared not broach. The first was the fact that her brother, Thomas, had quietly yet consistently been paying me attention. A poet growing in renown, he had composed two very beautiful sonnets and sent them to me. I found his attentions charming – even a bit intoxicating, true – but I was uncertain of how I felt about Thomas Wyatt, and thus had not given him any indication of reciprocal interest. Had I been even somewhat inclined to provide him with a favourable response, the situation would have been further complicated by the fact of his marriage to a girl called Elizabeth Brooke. While I'd heard their marriage was not a happy one, made notable by Mistress Brooke's habit of coquetry with men who were not her husband, I was not sure if it had been dissolved. Maggie had not mentioned Thomas's interest in me, and I wondered if she was even aware of it.

The other subject I carefully refrained from mentioning was my encounter with the King this November past.

Some things one must keep to oneself, no matter how deep a friendship.

"Yes, Maggie, I intend to wear the new gown," I replied, "and while it's kind of you to imply that mine will be special, you know as well as I that there will be many stunning women adorned in magnificent attire in attendance tonight - you not least among them."

I took her elbow and steered her purposefully toward our chambers. "We should tarry no longer, or neither of us will have any hope of being ready in time."

My preparation for such a special evening would be painstaking in its detail, and I was especially glad to have Charity assist me. Charity had been assigned as my personal chambermaid by Sir John Gage, who was presently the Vice-Chamberlain of the King's household. She was new to court, and a bit nervous, but she was a sweet girl, and as it turned out, most talented in styling hair.

She had laid out for me my petticoat and bodice, kirtle, and sleeves. The sleeves had been tailored in my favourite style, narrow at the top, widening below and ending in long, trailing points. I'd created a unique design in which the shortest part of the sleeve ended just above my knuckles. This exposed my fingers, which allowed me to feature rings to complement the gown, and I thought it made my hands look very graceful. The flowing, trailing sleeves were beautiful, falling to just above floor-length when my arms hung straight at my sides. Not only did they waft as I moved, but their linings were exposed, which I'd specified should be made from the same burgundy satin as my petticoat. I also had the dressmaker lower the neckline just a little, and create a tighter bodice. Often I intercepted wry glances being exchanged between the master tailor and his apprentices as I informed them of the modifications I desired in my particular designs. When the garments were finished, however, and I'd tried them on, they looked well: so well that the master tailor beamed with satisfaction at having taken part in a creation of *le style nouveau.* On a less pleasing note, once clad in my finery, my ability to draw a breath would be compromised. It would not be the first, nor the last, time that a lady of the court's comfort was to be sacrificed on the altar of image!

After Charity had cleared away the remnants of my bath, I sat, folded into a deliciously thick robe, before the chest which held my personal items. Between two lanterns, my mirror had been ready placed at an angle which allowed me to see my face clearly enough to complete my *toilette.* I was indebted to my education at the court of François I. The noble Frenchwomen were so very clever about the rituals of beauty and how to create its illusory magic. As a matter of course, the young women of high rank at court were taught to appreciate what looked best on them and how to contrive their own personal style. I had learned most assiduously and, for this evening's celebration, intended to exploit that invaluable knowledge to its fullest.

While Charity brushed out my hair, I lifted from the chest the beautiful enamelled porcelain powder jar I'd received as a departure gift on leaving Paris. In it, I kept a special blend of powder with a soft puff of lamb's wool. I applied it to my face, neck, and *décolletage.* A soft brush blended the powder until it made my skin glow, with a faultless finish. I then removed from a wooden case a very fine painter's brush and a small ivory cask of black kohl powder. Dipping the brush into a tiny amount of egg white, then carefully into the kohl, I drew the finest line above my eyelashes. I had become quite steady-handed at this, though my initial efforts had been comical. Once the lines had been traced, I selected another short but, this time, wider brush. Dipping it into the egg white, then the kohl, I brushed it upwards against the underside of my lashes, adding an extra dimension to their thickness. For the next few minutes, I sat wide-eyed, desperately trying not to blink until the egg white had set, or the kohl would end up on my cheeks. Next, out came a silver jar which, when opened, revealed ochre powder pressed into a cake. Using another exquisitely soft lamb's wool puff, I applied just a touch of the ochre to each cheek, carefully blending it in with my fingers. Most English women used a pale crimson rouge made of cochineal, but I had learned that ochre was just the right shade for my skin, which already had a golden cast to it. It lent my cheeks the colour of rose brick. I used the same pigment on my lips, blended with a bit of an ointment the apothecary had made for me. Finally, from a dainty perfume bottle, I dabbed the scantest amount of fragrant oil about my neck and chest. That evening, I wore a special mixture of patchouli with an essence of apothecary's rose.

My hair had now been brushed, with just a touch of oil applied to the bristles, till it gleamed, silken and flowing in the candlelight. While it appeared very dark - almost black - in the evenings by candle or firelight, in fact, it was shot with auburn and ginger tones which were visible when the illumination was right. I chose to wear it loose under the short veil attached to the back of my hood. I did this often, even though I knew it drew disapproving looks from some of the older women of court ... or, perhaps, because of such pettish disapproval. To their disfavour, I gave little regard: unmarried girls were permitted to wear their hair unbound, and I was, after all, unmarried. The fact that I was no longer considered a girl was a minor detail I steadfastly overlooked. I was not one to let an advantage like my long, glossy hair be hidden.

Cosmetics complete, it came time to dress. Charity first helped me on with my chemise, and then the successive components of my gown. She laced the petticoat, stomacher and bodice tightly at my back, not without some tight-lipped discomfort on my part. Carefully she lifted the kirtle over my head and settled it in place, arranging the folds and the opening in the front to expose the burgundy satin of the petticoat. Finally, she attached the sleeves with lacings and pins while I studied my reflection with, I confess, a self-satisfied smile. The dressmaker had done excellent work. But it was the colours which pleased me so much. The mellow golden green velvet was beautiful against my skin and hair. The rich golden edging applied to the neckline matched the gold embroidery on the bodice as well as the small French hood Charity had pinned to my hair, while the facing satin of the deep wine hue afforded just the right counterpoint.

From my small jewellery casket, I selected a ring of gold set with a small, deep red ruby and placed it on the middle finger of my left hand. It glimmered and winked, just exposed by the sleeve as I'd intended. Finally, I held my hair forward as Charity clasped the necklace that my mother had given me around my neck, arranging the 'B' so that it hung in just the right spot before tucking the longer string of pearls into the bodice.

I was well pleased with the overall result.

•

I slipped just inside the entrance to the Great Hall and gazed about in wonder at the room's marvellous transformation. The imposing space glittered as if with an alchemist's magic touch. Aware of someone approaching, I turned to see Maggie, who looked striking in an embellished, tawny-velvet gown with silver and gold embroidery accenting her kirtle and gable hood. For a brief moment, we observed in silent awe as the resplendent lords and ladies of the court assembled to celebrate the beginning of that year, 1526.

Maggie and I wandered through the crowd, having selected a goblet each of French wine from a liveried servant's silver tray. As I raised the cup to my lips, I felt a penetrating stare from my left. Seeking its source, I caught the King, eyes focused directly on me from across the room, while he conversed with Lord Suffolk. The moment my gaze met his, he quickly drew away and continued his conversation. The company as a whole approached our respective places at the table, and when the

King and Queen were in seated in place on the dais, the rest of the court and guests sat as well. A parade of servants in their finest Tudor green and white livery entered the hall and began serving the guests while, at the King's and Queen's table, their personal ushers were placing platters of steaming and fragrant roasted veal, mutton, and venison before them. Only after they had taken their first bite did we begin the feast.

The meal was well underway; the wine was poured ever more abundantly and the noise level in the room increased as merriment ensued. In between courses I was acutely aware of the King, even though I was not seated in his direct line of vision. I tried to snatch covert glimpses of him without his noticing. When I succeeded, I was taken with the comeliness of his appearance. His attire was, of course, magnificent; all gold and black velvet which provided a backdrop to the glitter of his richly coloured jewels. But far more captivating was his expression. He fairly beamed with pleasure and imparted the fresh-faced radiance of a boy. His red-gold hair shone in the light of the candelabra and the broad smile and ebullient laugh revealed even white teeth.

As I watched - furtively, I thought - he looked up and caught me out. Our eyes met, and instantly I was drawn to him, consumed by our mutual gaze; unaware of anything or anyone else. For that moment, there was only the King and me. At last, I looked away, lightheaded, and managed to excuse myself to escape the crowded hall. I needed to hide my stunned confusion and take some much-needed air.

Standing by a window in the watching chamber, I looked through the open casement to the courtyard below, gratefully inhaling the cooling night air. What was that extraordinary communion we had just shared? I had no experience with which to compare it. There was no denying the feeling stirring in me, yet it took me by complete surprise. I had been at the English court for almost four years and had often been in the company of the King over that time. Indeed, I admired him and most surely thought of him as handsome, but never had

I been subject to such a state of excitation in his company. I turned away from the window to return to the hall - and there he was. We stood inches apart. He leaned down to speak in my ear. He was so close that his scent surrounded me, and I found it to be profoundly alluring.

Quietly, he murmured in my ear, "*Bonsoir, Mademoiselle Anne. Vous êtes magnifique ce soir*. I wish you and your family great happiness in the new year." And then he was gone.

I returned to the hall as soon as the pounding of my heart had subsided, laughing at myself shakily. I concluded that my reaction must surely be the beginnings of a galloping infatuation; of the sort I had experienced in France as a girl of thirteen or fourteen years of age.

I was not alone for long. Within moments, a smiling Thomas Wyatt appeared at my side and led me forward as his dance partner. He steered me to the very front of the room; in fact, we were directly before the King and Queen, who sat in their chairs of estate to enjoy the dancing. As luck would have it, the next piece played by the musicians was suitable for the Volt, a dance in which partners held each other closely. Couples assembled on the dance floor; Thomas put his arm around me as we began. I enjoyed dancing with him: there was no doubt that Thomas was exceptionally attractive. He had matured into a strong, physically handsome man, but with an appealing sensitivity about him. And because of that, I knew he loved me. His feelings were plain when we were in each other's company. But I could not escape the fact that we had practically grown up together. Perhaps that was why I seemed unable to turn the deepest affection I held for him as a lifelong friend into the romantic love I so desired in a suitor or husband. So while I danced closely with him, I could not fully return the pressing warmth of his embrace. And, as we twirled and spun around the candlelit room to the sounds of music and laughter, there were two additional pairs of eyes which never left me: King Henry's, from the front of the room, and Henry Percy's, aft.

•

The following week was one long entertainment as the King and his comrades enjoyed being together again. The masques were clever, with fabulous costumes and sets. The dancing was very gay, as everyone tried to master a new version of the *saltarello,* a lively folk dance which had been refined at the Neapolitan Court. It was quite challenging, because the music was played in a fast triple meter, and it featured a difficult leaping step for which it was named, from the Italian word *saltare* - 'to jump'. There were musical interludes, with instruments played by members of the court, and I ventured to play several pieces on my lute. And throughout the festivities, I frequently encountered the King, who always smiled directly into my eyes with a familiar warmth which never failed to induce a blush in return.

I noticed, as did almost everyone else, that the King kept company with Queen Katherine less and less frequently. When the occasion called for them to be near each other, I watched the way his eyes narrowed and his face stiffened, which I read as his effort to maintain an air of nonchalance. Meanwhile, I could not help but wonder why Katherine insisted on spending so much time in her private chapel, and away from most all the events she and the King had always enjoyed in the past. Her ladies and I all knew she passed many hours on her knees praying in supplication to the Blessed Virgin that God might grant her a son, even in this, the late autumn of her childbearing years. But would not some of that time be best spent in the companionship of her husband? I thought it highly unlikely that God would give her a son if she and her husband were never together! And I privately thought how unappealing Katherine had allowed herself to become. Her gown colour of choice was almost always black, and on her, served only to accentuate the deep folds which had formed from her nose to her mouth, and between her eyebrows. Her now constant expression was one of long suffering, as I suppose it might well be after having endured so many pregnancies which ended tragically. So in total, along with the greying of her hair, her appearance spoke of advancing age. In contrast, Henry's masculinity radiated in a glowing aura. It was clear to all observers that he was at the peak of manhood while poor Queen Katherine had lost all the lustre of her vivacious youth.

I did not feed the gossip. I kept my observations to myself as I watched them grow more and more distant from each other. This knowledge, along with the continuance of Henry's piercing gaze and most warmly spoken pleasantries, compelled me to wonder what might lie ahead for the three of us.

•

February 1526 was surprisingly mild, with day following day of fair weather. Enough so that the lists were quickly being readied for a jousting tournament, and we all spent time outside, wandering the lawns and enjoying the wintergreen gardens in the pale sunshine. I longed to hunt, but the grass season would not start for some weeks yet. Instead, I took frequent walks to the stable to visit my lovely chestnut mare, Cannelle. I was even able to ride out a few times, and there was no question that this was when I was happiest. I adored the freedom of being on horseback, the physical effort and strength it required, the always present sense of risk, and the glory of wind and sun against my face and hair. And how I loved horses! Strong and powerful; graceful beyond measure, yet with the softest brown eyes and even softer muzzles.

One afternoon, my brother George rode with me as we crossed the fields in Greenwich Park skirting the Duke Humphrey Tower.

"So tell me, Anne, what exactly was going on last evening during our game of Prime in the Queen's Chamber, when I saw the King scrutinizing your every move? At first, I felt sure he was trying to gain a glimpse of your cards, but then I realized that *you* were the object of his close inspection."

I sighed. George's adorable, dimpled face always belied his penchant for pestering. With a glance, I saw that he had adopted the wry smirk which I had come to know so well when my younger brother wanted to cause mischief. Especially when the irritating beast added, "… might you have become his mistress without my knowing?"

"Absolutely not!" I sniffed with a little too much indignation. "Why would you think it any of your personal concern, George? But, for your information, your suggestion is simply implausible. I would never permit it."

"Well, Sister," he chortled unrepentantly, "you may not have the luxury of choice in the matter. And methinks you well know it; that is, when it comes to our King and his, ah … interests."

"You are being absurd. It was abundantly clear that his interest was in my cards, and nothing more. I did win the first three hands if you recall. What I do well know is how he hates to lose – and, did I not, by the way, beat you as well as the King?"

Forcing a laugh I pressed Cannelle's sides with my boots to canter off back toward the palace stableyard so George couldn't see my burning face.

•

It was Shrovetide, and a joust was about to take place in the tiltyard at Greenwich. I believe the entire court planned to be present since everyone was appreciative of having a rousing outdoor activity to attend. We looked forward to the excitement of the tournament, especially since on the morrow we would commence the sacrifices and solemnity of the Lenten season.

I shifted about in my seat in anticipation of the start of the competition. I was positioned in the very front row of the *berfrois* between Maggie Wyatt and Honor Grenville. We chatted animatedly while the competitors lined up to parade before the spectators and pay homage to the ladies of the nobility. First into the arena rode Nicholas Carew, followed by

Charles Brandon; next came Henry Guildford, and then the King. Not yet having donned their armour, all wore jousting costumes which were elegant by design and decoration. I smiled a pleasant acknowledgment to the King, and he returned the greeting with a nod and a saucy grin. It took me a few moments before I became aware that on his tunic was a motto in brilliant red and gold. It said '*Declare Je Nos,*' while, embroidered above the words was a scarlet heart streaming with flames. As he approached the spectators, and everyone read his device: *Declare I Dare Not,* there arose a perceptible ripple of curiosity among the crowd. But there was more to come.

As his horse passed in front of me, he doffed his cap and made it quite plain he had eyes for one person only - his pointed, smiling gaze never left my face. Whereupon the lords and ladies of the court looked open-mouthed from the King to me, then back again while I, for my part, felt I couldn't breathe at all. My composure was further tested seeing both Honor and Maggie wearing expressions of slowly dawning realization.

I lowered my eyes and acknowledged that the previous few months had not, indeed, been the figment of my overly active imagination.

His Majesty, King Henry VIII, had quite openly revealed himself to all as my courtly suitor.

•

As the damp chill of early spring slowly warmed toward the full, luxurious flourish of May, I thus found myself engaging in a thrilling new game of romance. The King never failed to pay me special attention when we were in each other's company. He greeted me with a charming nod and always asked after me and my family's welfare in beautifully spoken French, complimenting me on my costume of the day, or the jewelry I was wearing. With every encounter, I felt a charge of excitement. It was delicious – and dangerous. Oh, but I had been well schooled in the behaviours of chivalric romance in the court of

François. It was naught but this training which prompted me to reply with gracious appreciation, yet never permitting my suitor to come too close or become overly familiar.

More and more, though, did I find that I *wanted* him close - very close.

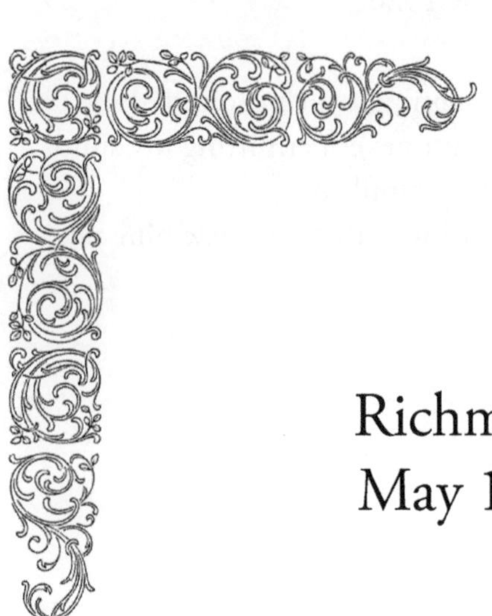

Richmond
May 1526

THE MAY DAY festival was in full measure, and Anne Saville and I crossed the brilliant green gardens of Richmond Palace to join the court for a picnic, which would be followed by sporting competitions, dancing, an abundance of wine, and a masque later in the evening. It was warm - a perfect day, really - with bright sunlight washing the fields and riotously blooming flowers; the velvet lawns gently sloping toward the river. It was an excellent day for the flirtatious abandon which was always a feature of the spring fête. We had barely arrived amongst the picnic guests when we were approached by Thomas Wyatt.

"May I join you exquisite ladies?" he bowed.

I could see Anne was quietly thrilled to have Thomas be a part of our group. She had told me recently that she was completely enamoured with his poetry, and with him. We sat on rugs laid on the grass for the afternoon, and I watched Anne fix her eyes on his handsome face as we laughed, joked and nibbled at the delicacies provided us. I knew Thomas had not yet given up on the prospect of winning me, however. I could feel his attention on me while he sat just a little too close. Idly, I reached for my silver pomander and brought it to my face. I did love the scent of lavender and had stuffed it full of fresh flowers that very morning. The amber stone embedded in the silver glowed warmly, and my initials engraved on its surface glinted in the sun. I took a deep breath of the delicate, powdery fragrance. I looked up when Thomas said, "Milady, if you will give me, or merely lend me, your jewel, it will provide me with just the inspiration I need to write my next verse. My ability to create has been so stifled lately; now I realize that what I need is a beautiful token from an even more beautiful lady, combined with her heady scent to stimulate my mind and my pen."

I shifted uncomfortably and was unprepared with an adept reply. He had caught me totally unawares, and thus did I give him the pomander without much protest. Anne appeared crestfallen. I felt terrible and dearly wished it had been Anne he had asked, so, glancing over at her apologetically, I jumped to my feet to leave them together and made my way over to join the game of *boules* just getting underway near the hilltop.

Of course, the King was at the centre of the teams being selected. As I joined the group, he took my arm to guide me to where his team stood. Wyatt and Anne had followed me, so Suffolk, who captained the opposing team, selected Wyatt next. There was much ribbing amongst the competitors and laughter as the rest of the teams assembled, and then the jack was set in place, and the competition began. At my turn, I heartily propelled my ball forward, and to my delight, had great success in hitting the jack. Next was Henry's chance, and he expertly rolled the ball, his knocking mine out of the way before coming to rest perfectly nestled against the jack. Throughout the competition, which was great fun, Henry and I played as if all England depended on our individual successes. I would have been very happy to have had a better end score than the King's, but I did not, even though our team won. As we walked back over the lawn to the palace at the conclusion of the game, the King accompanied me, and slipped his arm about my waist, smiling down at me with the most winsome eyes.

"You are quite the competitor, Mistress Anne. I had no idea you were of such an athletic nature. I admire your dedication to winning and I was fortunate to have you on my team."

"Thank you, Your Grace. I was, in fact, born with an exceptionally competitive spirit. I know that it is an uncommon trait for a woman, perhaps a not entirely attractive one, and I suspect I should be better advised to hide it. I find myself not a little embarrassed ..."

"Not at all, Milady," he said, with a perceptible squeeze of his arm about me. "I admire the quality greatly, being, as it is, a huge part of my essential nature also."

He smiled then: an impish grin. "I seem to recall that you are also an avid huntswoman, am I not correct?"

I flushed and dipped my head, recalling his introduction to my hunting skills, but said, "It is true, Your Majesty. I love riding and hunting more than anything else in life."

"More than anything in life, indeed?" His amusement was noted by that irresistible crinkle at the outer corners of his eyes. "Then why not join me tomorrow morning in the stableyard for the opening hunt of the grass season? I would have you ride with me at the head of the field."

"I should be delighted to, Your Grace," I curtsied. "I will see you tomorrow morning, then."

With that, we parted ways, and once alone, I skipped back to my chamber, beaming to myself.

•

After I sent Charity to give the stable boys instructions to have Cannelle groomed, braided, saddled and ready for me to ride in the morning, I sat at a small wooden table, propped the mirror against the wall, and, resting my chin in hand, studied my reflection thoughtfully. While my looks appeared at odds with mostly all the girls and women at court, they were not so different from many of the Frenchwomen I had known, or even some of those at Mechelen, at the Margaret of Austria's court. In England, however, the women selected to serve were almost all blonde, fair complected, and blue eyed. Even the Queen, herself, had been a honey blonde in her youth, with blue eyes. I, on the other hand, was distinctly *brunette.* I do not know from whence those looks came, because my mother had been fair-haired, and my father's locks had been light brown before they turned grey in early manhood.

I knew that I was attractive to men. This had become evident to me when I was no more than 15 or 16 years of age in France. But I often wondered how I appeared to others.

I carefully assessed my features in the mirror. I was happy with, and felt grateful for, my abundant hair of deep brown which glinted red and gold when touched by the sun. I sometimes liked to allow its natural curl to be seen, peeking from beneath veils or hoods. But with brushing, and the sparing application of a drop or two of perfumed hair oil, it could equally become sleek and straight, with a burnished gloss. I felt it to be my one of my greatest physical assets. My eyes were middling brown, with both darker and golden flecks throughout, if studied closely. They tilted up just the slightest bit at the outer corners, and my lashes were thick, long and dark, and curled up at the ends. This was why I had learned to enhance them with the egg white and kohl mixture. When augmented with carefully applied cosmetics, I knew them to be a great attraction. I had learned to express myself with my eyes when I wished to be noticed, leaving speech for the more mundane. My nose was a strong one: no tiny upturned button on me. Beneath that nose were ample lips, with the top lip as full as the bottom. They were usually a nice rosy colour unless I became very chilled, and then they became quickly tinged with blue. With great good fortune, my teeth were even, and pale ivory coloured. I took exacting care of them, brushing, wiping, and picking them every day, imagining how terrible it must be to suffer the scourge of revealing bad teeth. My skin might best have been described as fawn-colour, with a pleasing satiny sheen. My complexion, also, I looked after as taught by the beautiful women in France. I washed frequently and used a specially concocted oil to smooth and soften the skin of my face and hands, and also the rest of my body. Not for me, the alabaster-fair hue flaunted as the height of beauty at the English court. The activities I loved - hunting, riding, hawking, playing with my dogs in the garden - all had the tendency to imbue my cheeks with a russet tone. I even had some freckles across my nose and cheeks. My cheekbones were set high on my face, and I was blessed with a strong, if somewhat pointed chin: the overall shape of my face thus presenting a slender oval, which I felt was pleasing. My build was slight, yet I was quite strong from so much riding and walking. I was not very tall; in fact, the King towered more than a head above me.

My second favourite feature was my hands. They were narrow and graceful: my fingers long and slim. I did my best to protect them when I was outdoors at sport, and almost always wore kidskin gloves. My nails were well shaped; I kept them buffed and groomed, and had learned to use my hands expressively when I spoke. This was why I took such pleasure in designing the sleeves to my gowns. I had not many rings, but the few I possessed were indeed beautiful, I considered, and accented my hands nicely. Good fortune had endowed me with a long, slender neck and a smallish but adequate bosom, and both looked fine in deep, square necklines. All in all, while I did not consider myself a great beauty, I did have confidence in my appearance once a selection of gowns, jewelry, and hood or hat was made to accentuate my best features.

I hoped for fair weather on the morrow and was determined to show off my abilities riding to the hounds. Charity helped gather my riding ensemble, sending my boots out for a polish while making certain that my deep green velvet riding jacket was brushed and immaculate. I wondered if Queen Katherine would accompany the King. She used to enjoy hunting, although she was not a very skilled rider and usually remained timidly at the back of the field. Recently, though, I had not seen her ride out at all.

Daybreak revealed a soft, peach-coloured sky with a cool breeze which promised to warm as the sun rose. As dew evaporated, the soft smell of honeysuckle and roses, clambering on the stable walls, suffused the yard. The cobbled stable yard was alive with sound and brilliant colour as some twenty riders arrived assembling for the hunt, and to my relief, I noticed that the Queen was not amongst the company. I spied the King; he was at the centre of a throng of riders awaiting the arrival of Master Rainsford with his greyhounds. Henry was taller than all the rest, and was mounted on his big gelding, Governatore, who had been groomed and brushed to a gleaming bright bay, his black mane and tail neatly braided. His Grace looked compellingly handsome in his hunting attire, topped by pheasant feathers which adorned a stylish green cap. I watched him from afar, and once again, liked very much what I saw. He was distracted by the assemblage, which fluttered and hovered about him like hummingbirds drawn to a gorgeous flower. Soon, though, he noticed me and called me to him, whereupon the other riders reluctantly moved aside to allow me to ride up next to him. Their glances of envy were plain, but I was afforded little time to concern myself with them because Henry blew a sharp blast on his heavy silver hunting whistle and the entire pack of greyhounds, Highland deerhounds, and riders moved as one, out of the yard and toward the open fields.

We were but minutes into the King's private hunting grounds when the huntmaster cast the hounds in search of quarry. I situated Cannelle closely behind the King as the hounds gave voice, and the field was off in pursuit of a large hart. We tore over the countryside after the hounds. Loose strands of hair whipped against my face, and I sat in my saddle as tightly as I could while the King and the huntmaster flew across hills, scrabbled down rocky paths and splashed, spray flying, through streams. My determination to stay at the front never ebbed, and I kept pace with the best of a field of men.

More than once Henry turned to see if I had fallen back, then grinned and shouted out to me in encouragement when he saw I remained close behind.

We approached a stream so wide and deep that I knew the horses would jump rather than cross, and my heart pounded as Cannelle made a mighty effort and jumped ably enough to well clear the banks. I clung on, and gasped in relief, not having wanted to end up unseated in the stream, awkwardly soaked to the skin. I was proud of myself and my mare and hoped Henry would notice my performance this outing, and that it would trump my seeming lack of horsemanship during our last hunting encounter. Finally, the hounds, bellowing wildly, circled the hart and brought it to bay. The huntmaster leapt from his horse. Using a spear, he quickly inserted it between the hart's ribs to dispatch the thrashing animal. Henry jumped down from Governatore, and using a shorter hunting knife, also stabbed it into the hart's body. Quickly, the huntsmen lashed the feet of the carcass to poles brought for that purpose, and the field turned toward home, with the hart as our prize.

Henry and Governatore fell in step beside my mare and me.

"Please, have some refreshment," the King said while handing me a silver hunt cup of ale. Gratefully I took a deep draught while he watched with shining eyes and a face flushed with exercise.

"Mistress Anne, my admiration for you grows steadily. You are an accomplished hunter, and fearless at that. Do please ride along with me on our return to the stables. What an impressive young woman you are! Where did you learn to ride so well?"

"Thank you, Your Grace," I replied with a respectful nod. "My father and brother taught me when I was just a girl growing up in Kent. I rode often, and then while I was away in France I did have some chance to hunt, though more often I just rode out on my own or with friends whenever I could. I have a passion for horses."

"As I do, my lady," agreed Henry, stroking Governatore's neck, sleek with sweat. "They are God's glorious creatures, are they not? Your mare is quite lovely and held her own in a field of bigger geldings. Would you be interested in trying one of my new Barbary hunters on our next outing?"

I gave him my warmest smile, clearly showing him my pleasure at the invitation both to ride one of his prized horses and the implication that there would, indeed, be other outings.

"Oh, I would enjoy that greatly, Your Majesty."

We continued our ride back to the palace, chatting and laughing amiably all the way.

Greenwich
June 1526

DURING THE REMAINDER of spring and the beginning of summer, I rode with the King's hunt quite often. Predominantly we stayed at Greenwich and hunted the woods and open fields which surrounded the palace. As we rode alone together one afternoon, returning from the chase, the King leaned in towards me and said quietly, "Mistress Anne, I would be greatly honoured if you would consider joining me this evening for supper in my privy chamber."

My mind raced, but I did not hesitate before saying "Your Grace, the honour would indeed be mine. I will look forward to it."

"I shall see you this evening, then." He smiled with obvious pleasure, then, nodding a courteous farewell, rode off to converse with my uncle, the Duke of Norfolk.

I found myself to be unsettled while preparing for the evening ahead. I was eager because I very much wanted to spend time with the King by myself - yet I could not shake a vexing feeling of guilt as I dressed. I would not be in service of the

Queen this evening, of course, but still, I was one of her maids of honour. And I planned to have a private supper with her husband. I concentrated instead on my toilette and did my best to put the contradictory nature of the coming evening from my thoughts. I wondered what kind of gossip might result from my dining with the King, and if Queen Katherine would hear of it.

Nevertheless, I took particular care with my appearance, and selected a gown of deep violet silk, with sleeves trimmed in grey velvet. My pearl necklace, with its golden B, looked beautiful against the unusual colour of my gown. Charity had loosely woven a violet satin riband through my hair, which was topped by a grey velvet and pearl hood. I added a ring of silver set with an aquamarine to the first finger of my right hand.

The Lord Chamberlain led me through the presence chamber filled with courtiers eating supper. Each and every eye followed me closely as we proceeded to the King's privy chamber, where my arrival was announced before entering.

As I stepped over the threshold, I looked about in awe. His chamber was fantastic in its elegance, with tapestries and arras of a perfect quality covering the walls. The room was bathed in the amber glow of torch and candlelight. The table had been set with a pristine white damask cloth, and upon it was silver plate, shining in the warm light. But most radiant of all was Henry's expression as he watched me enter. I dropped into a deep curtsey, and he rose from his chair and came to my side to guide me to the seat next to him at the table. Quietly, he said to the Lord Chamberlain, "Thank you, Your Grace. You are dismissed for the evening. I will summon you if needed."

The only ones remaining in the chamber in addition to Henry and I were two discreet Esquires of the Body, who stood guard by the door and pointedly did not look our way.

"I am so very pleased that you agreed to join me this evening, Mistress Anne," Henry said as he poured me a goblet of wine. "I have wanted to share a private conversation with you for some time."

"I feel likewise, Your Majesty."

I sipped my wine, and closely studied him in a more deliberate manner than I had yet the opportunity to do. He was gorgeously clothed in a doublet of deep tawny velvet with gold brocade sleeves and wore several rings of gold set with diamonds and emeralds. Yet it was his countenance which was truly arresting. Although his masculinity was undeniable, his face had an ethereal beauty about it. His eyes were golden brown; clear, intelligent, and were capable of a keen gaze. He possessed a straight, strong nose with a defined jaw and strong chin. His skin was ruddy from so much time spent outdoors and his hair, cropped short under a black velvet cap, was the colour of russet leaves in autumn. It was his mouth, however, which demanded my attention. It was so expressive, the lips so sensual, that I could not drag my eyes from them.

Perhaps it was as well, given my blatant fascination, that I was startled by a knock at the door. Into the chamber came ushers bearing platters piled with roasted capon; serving vessels filled with poached mullet, and brimming with chestnut purée. After we had been served Henry asked, between bites, "So, *Mademoiselle*, tell me something about the time you spent in Paris at François' court. Did you find it a pleasant experience?"

"I did indeed, Your Majesty," I replied. "By the time I arrived in Paris from the Habsburg Court, I had long overcome my homesickness and found interest in everything which took place around me. I was accorded excellent tutors, and as a result, my French became quite fluent: so much so that I was honoured to have been asked to be a translator for your sister, the Princess Mary while she was being prepared to wed King Louis XII and become Queen of France. Subsequently, when King Louis died, and she was widowed, I remained in her service. Then, of course, Her Royal Highness decided to marry Charles Brandon, Duke of Suffolk. I was no longer required as her maid, and when she and her new husband departed to return to England, I was requested to remain in France in the service of the new Queen, Claude, wife of King François I."

Too late I realized that I had stupidly stumbled upon an old, but sensitive subject. Hesitantly I added, "My apologies, Your Grace. I know your sister's decision to marry Brandon was without your consent, and I heard you were most grievously offended. I was foolish to mention it. I do hope you will forgive my rude error."

Although I'd seen his face briefly cloud over at my mention of Mary and Brandon's elopement, he graciously replied, "All is well, Mistress. They have been forgiven, and it is in the past."

It came, then, as a blessed relief that his pursuit of our conversation never faltered. In fact, at his encouragement I continued my narrative, doing far more talking than eating while the King listened intently.

"After your sister and her new husband sailed for Dover, Your Grace, I commenced my duties in the newly formed court of Queen Claude. She was so kind - such a dear soul - I cared for her greatly. I came to love the countryside surrounding the Château Royal of Blois in the Loire Valley, where Claude was most often in residence. It was at Blois that I learned to dance, and to play the lute passably well. I was often called upon to be an interpreter when English envoys were presented to the Queen. And I was selccted as one of the *filles d'honneurs* who would be introduced, along with Claude's ladies-in-waiting, at the Field of Cloth of Gold. I clearly recall that what thrilled me most about attending that extraordinary event was being one of the *desmoiselles* selected to greet you ..."

I looked at him purposely, then added with a flippant grin, "... though you probably do not remember me, Your Grace. Am I not correct in my assumption?"

By his slightly embarrassed look I could see he harboured no recall of a simple nineteen-year-old English girl amidst such magnificence, and in the company of stunningly beautiful Frenchwomen, but he did not respond directly to my most forward challenge.

"And what did you then do, *Mademoiselle*, following the Field of Gold?" he queried.

"When we returned to Paris, my acquaintance with Marguerite d'Alençon - François's sister - grew, and she befriended me which honoured me immensely. Madame Marguerite seemed, to me, as thoughtful and intelligent as François was impulsive and capricious. I learned so much from her, too."

At my description of François, Henry chuckled with amusement. "And what was that, primarily?" he asked as he selected strawberries from a silver bowl.

"It was she who shared with me writings of the great humanists. She was a scholar, and discussed with me readings from the Greek philosophers and religious evangelicals like Jacques Lefévre d'Ètaples."

Henry's eyebrows raised slightly, and he leaned back in his chair in thoughtful surprise. There had obviously been a point to his courteous inquisition. "So then, *Mademoiselle*, apparently you are as well read as you are skilled at sport. My esteem for you grows every time we encounter one another. Pray, tell me: would you consider yourself a Christian humanist?"

"I would, Your Grace. Though I have much to read and learn, I am intrigued by the humanist approach to some of the theological views debated at the French court. I dare say it is a radical way of thinking, but the tenets expressed by Lefévre and the court poet Clement Marot have made an indelible mark on the way I view religion. I have also read some of Sir Thomas More's *Utopia*, and find it quite interesting, albeit, in parts, perplexing."

Just then one of the esquires discreetly approached the King to tell him that Cardinal Wolsey wished to see him. Henry seemed annoyed, and waved him away, indicating that Wolsey should return in the morning. A moment or two later, the esquire was back, saying the Cardinal insisted that it was an urgent matter which could not possibly wait. Henry paused, and I saw the muscles along the side of his jaw tighten in irritation. He looked at me and said, "I beg your pardon, *Mademoiselle*.

May I take your leave for a few moments while I attend to some - apparently - pressing business?"

"Why, of course, Your Grace," I said, feeling quite foolish that the King thought he needed to ask my permission to handle a matter of state, but appreciating his sarcastic edge nonetheless.

Into the chamber trundled Cardinal Wolsey, still projecting a pronounced air of self-importance despite Henry's initial rebuff. His gaze idly cast across the table before finally alighting on me. Clearly it took him a moment to become aware of who I was. He blinked. His astonishment at finding me supping with the King was plain to see, but he attempted to conceal his surprise, at least from the King. Not without some difficulty caused by his exceedingly large girth, he bent to speak close to the King's ear while handing him a document. As Henry perused the letter, the Cardinal seized the opportunity to regard me openly: peering bird-like down his long, beaked nose, nostrils flaring delicately as if having detected an unpleasant smell and thus clearly indicating a distaste for what he had observed. With a few more whispered words to the King, he retrieved the document, bowed to the extent he was able and retreated with a smug look of satisfaction.

My opinion of thc great Cardinal Wolsey had never been a good one. At that moment, I decided him to be insufferable.

As soon as Wolsey left the room, the King leaned across the table toward me. "*Mademoiselle* Anne, I depart in a week's time on Summer Progress for the next two months. A few of my trusted courtiers and I, along with the Queen, will travel northward through small towns and villages, visiting local townsfolk and staying at the manor homes of nobles for the remainder of the summer. I am looking forward to enjoying the beautiful hunting grounds in those counties; at least the sport they afford helps relieve the tiring routine of giving audience to every merchant, landowner, and burgher in each town north and wide of London. Exhausting as it may be, though, it is necessary. Those subjects would never see their King were we not to go to them."

He looked keenly at me then, narrowing his eyes in contemplation, and in the shifting candlelight, I once again was flooded with the strange sensation of knowing him in a way that was altogether impossible considering the brief amount of time we had spent together. I wondered if he was experiencing that same uncanny feeling.

"I will miss seeing you during my time away," he said simply.

"And I you, Your Grace."

"If…?" He hesitated, then continued. "If I were to send you a message while away, would you feel inclined to reply?"

"How could I ignore a missive from Your Majesty, my King?" I asked with frankness.

"But, *Mademoiselle* - that would not be the intent with which I would write," he insisted, and I perceived in him the young, hopeful and surprisingly vulnerable boy. "You know that, do you not?" he asked, so quietly I had to strain to hear the words. "What I wish to know is whether you would reply, of your own accord, because you wanted to?"

We regarded each other for what seemed like an aeon.

Finally came my answer. "Indeed, I believe I would, Your Grace."

Slowly a smile spread across his features, and I saw in that smile both delight and relief. Then it seemed as if he had unexpectedly remembered something. Affecting an air of royal command, he said, "Oh! - And *Mademoiselle* - was I mistaken earlier today, or did I see a silver pomander worn openly about the waist of Sir Thomas Wyatt? A pomander which, I suspected, had at one time belonged to you? It seemed as if it must have been yours, for it had 'AB' engraved plainly upon it."

I flushed and replied awkwardly, "Yes, Your Grace, it was in fact mine. Sir Thomas compelled me to give it to him, avowing that he was unable to write unless he could have it and breathe in the scent of lavender. Truly, it had no other meaning."

"Is that so?" He looked at me sharply. "Well then, that being the case, I feel it only fair you should offer me a token of equal sincerity. Would you not agree?"

Caught off guard yet again, I could only nod acquiescence, and cover my confusion with a bow of the head.

"Your ring will do nicely," he pressed. "When I weary of progress: of trailing from town to town, visiting my subjects and listening to their many complaints and requests, it will inspire and refresh me by reminding me of this special evening which we have shared."

What else could I have done? I slipped the silver and aquamarine ring from my finger and handed it to him. He promptly placed it on his left little finger, where it flashed as the light caught its facets. He stood and took both my hands as I rose from my chair.

"Bonne nuit, Mademoiselle." His mouth curved into a sweet smile which could only be interpreted as intimate. "*Et dormez-bien.*" I curtseyed, eyes downcast, then left his chamber.

Hever
Summer 1526

I ACCOMPANIED MY FATHER on his return to Hever in July. He would customarily spend at least a month or two at home in the summer, ensuring all was well with the estate, taking care of matters of business pertaining to the property and staff, and overseeing the harvest. Only George remained with the King, as part of the small retinue who would accompany the King and Queen on progress.

I truly loved being in the country in the summertime. Being at home allowed me to live more slowly and deliberately than the frenetic pace kept at court. I was glad, also, of the chance to remove myself from the gossip I knew had resulted as word of my private supper with the King found its way from mouth to ear.

One oppressively hot afternoon, while walking with my father in the gardens, we sat on a stone bench in the shade to cool off. He turned to face me. "Anne, tell me, please - what is the nature of your relationship with the King?"

His expression was tightly controlled: he might equally have been a merchant negotiating the price of wool as a father asking his daughter about a possible suitor. I was not surprised he questioned me, having probably heard rumour of the evening I spent with the King, even though I had never even hinted at it. And of course, he would be acutely interested. This I knew, especially after observing Father's reaction to the success he enjoyed as a result of the affair between the King and my sister Mary. It was, after all, in no small part due to Mary that my father was now Viscount Rochford.

But I felt obstinate and waved away his inquiry. "Why does it concern you, Father? There is nothing to tell. Nothing at all, other than a few meaningless flirtations the King and I have shared."

"Really, Anne? And do not gesture at me so insolently, Daughter. I hear quite to the contrary. I have my sources, as you are more than well aware, and am informed, most reliably, that the King entertained you to a private supper before he left on progress. His Majesty would not consider such a dalliance were he not thoroughly captivated by his guest: I know him well, and of this I am certain. Plus, Anne, I have seen the way he looks at you. You cannot pretend with me – I do not make my living as a courtier by being oblivious to what goes on around me."

I hesitated a moment then replied with some reticence, "Then you will also see that it is clearly a courtly romance and nothing more."

He raised a derisive eyebrow. "And why do you assume it to be nothing more?"

"Because that is all I intend it to be, Father!" I retorted, setting my jaw and defiantly returning his steady gaze.

"You are an intelligent girl, my Anne, but that does not necessarily make you a wise one," he countered, equally sharply. "I will remind you that it is your responsibility to the Boleyn family to refrain from jeopardizing our prosperity and standing in the peerage. And since I have raised you, nurtured you, and educated you, you will accord me the respect I deserve and fulfil that responsibility. Is the point understood?"

"That it is, Father. But, as we are both well aware, there is simply nothing else to be done but to graciously respond to his gallantries. The King already has a wife and Queen. And as for matters of the heart – mine will be decided by me."

I rose from the bench and purposefully walked the gravel path back into the manor house.

•

The remainder of the summer passed languidly. We were most fortunate not to have experienced any sign of the plague or the sweat within miles of Hever. As the late summer waned, I looked forward to early autumn, which was my favourite season of the year. I loved the warm, golden days, and the nights which brought a pleasing chill. And hunting was superb in the autumn, it being cooler to ride at mid-day.

On an afternoon in mid-September, I returned home from a visit to the neighbouring estate to find the kitchen in an uproar. My mother caught up with me as I sought the cook to find out what had caused all the excitement.

"Anne, a royal messenger arrived earlier this afternoon," eagerly she handed me a beautiful cream-coloured document made heavy by a crimson waxen seal. Pretending to be mystified I inspected the seal, even though I knew it must be the King's.

"And what's more," Mother finished triumphantly, "the accompanying servants delivered a magnificent buck to our kitchen!"

I took the envelope from her, saying, "Mother, will you excuse me please?" even as I hurried upstairs to my chamber to open it privily.

Once in my room, I cracked the wax seal imprinted with the King's standard and slid from its covering a parchment, delicate and of high quality. The writing was carefully penned, the letters small and neat, though the precise lines of script began to slant upwards by mid-page. The message was written in French. My heart beat rapidly against my chest.

I read aloud in English:

> Although, my Mistress, it has not pleased you to remember the promise you made me when I was last with you - that is, to hear good news from you, and to have an answer to my last letter; yet it seems to me that it belongs to a true servant (seeing that otherwise he can know nothing) to inquire the health of his mistress, and to acquit myself of the duty of a true servant, I send you this letter, beseeching you to apprise me of your welfare, which I pray to God may continue as long as I desire mine own. And to cause you yet oftener to remember me, I send you, by the bearer of this, a buck killed late last night by my own hand, hoping that when you eat of it you may think of the hunter; and thus, for want of room, I must end my letter, written by the hand of your servant, who very often wishes for you instead of your brother.
>
> H.R.

A peal of laughter escaped me on reading the last sentence. Then I was stabbed by a mite of remorse. I had neglected to reply to the message Henry had sent me just after my arrival at Hever, asking if my travel had been safe. At the time, I had felt it unnecessary to answer. After all, what was I to say – 'Yes, thank you, Your Grace, I am indeed alive and well?' It seemed trite. Now, however, I must respond, for how rude it would be to ignore such a generous gift. I determined to compose an appropriate acknowledgement the very next day. In the meantime, I emptied a small but sturdy coffer, and carefully placed the letter within before locking it and hiding the key.

My reply to the King was brief. It was well thought through, however, and I made sure I fully expressed my gratitude for such a lavish gift: one that my family all found quite delicious at dinner earlier in the day. I added that I was enjoying my summer at Hever, but indeed did miss being at court, then ended by saying I looked forward to seeing him again once I returned to court - as his most loyal servant.

I felt the message sufficient. I sealed it and had the courier take it to Windsor, which was where the King and his company were lodged.

A scant two days later, a messenger from the King arrived with an enormous, brilliantly coloured bouquet of summer flowers, the stems bound in a swath of purple silk. The courier refused to leave the flowers and the message with the house steward, instead insisting upon delivering them to me personally. He bowed low, and presented me with the posy as well as a further letter, with the information that both were from the King's Grace, and that the King looked forward to my reply with great anticipation. He then asked if he might remain until I had crafted my return letter, but I courteously declined. I took note of the slight nervous tic the poor man assumed when I told him there would be no reply for him to deliver just then. Hesitantly he bid me good day, and then bravely set off to break the news to the King that the eagerly awaited response would not be forthcoming, after all. I couldn't help but giggle devilishly at the thought.

After I had sent the flowers inside to be placed in an urn, I hastened to my favourite spot under a spreading pear tree in the orchard and unfolded the parchment. Its length and tone implied that Henry had been disappointed by my previous, rather impersonal letter. He wrote that he considered me his lady, but if it would make me less uneasy, he would reluctantly grant me the place of '*servaunt*'. He also added, somewhat dryly, that he was at least glad of the mere fact I remembered him!

Remembered him, indeed! Over the next days, as I went about my business, the King was rarely far from my thoughts. Finally, admitting to myself that my mind was constantly preoccupied with images of him, I decided to spend some time alone in my chamber attempting to sift through my sentiments for the truth.

I sat quietly, looking out the window at the lovely landscape below. Suppressing my tumultuous emotions, I pictured Henry and instead willed myself to allow logic to direct my thoughts. I determined that I was extremely attracted to him - in a way I had never experienced with any man. And there was no denying the mysterious feeling I had when I was near to him: that of knowing him so familiarly, which, especially, haunted me. I felt almost certain the King's interest in me was his sophisticated version of courtly romance, and in that game, I played the role of his beloved. Even though it was apparent Henry was no longer in love with Katherine as he once had been, still she was his wife, the mother of his child, and the crowned Queen of England - a princess of the blood - and that was unalterable fact. So, knowing that, we must either continue a chaste game of courtly romance, or if his suit was of a more serious nature, I would be pressed to become his mistress, exactly as my sister had done. Contemplating the latter choice prompted a visceral, negative reaction. I was instantly certain that no good – no good at all – could come from my acquiescence. I resolved never to give in. The consequences of my refusal would not matter to me. No, I had not come to this point in my life merely to become someone's mistress, even if it were to be that of the King of England! I also sensed that somehow, such a relationship would sully the deep esteem in which I held the King.

I vowed never to allow that to happen.

I would remain his friend, servant, admirer - his chivalric lady - but his mistress? Never.

•

The leaves were delicately traced with russet, and the air fresh and crisp on a late September Tuesday when two liveried equerries clattered across the drawbridge and into the courtyard of our manor house. I peered, unseen, through the open casement window overlooking the scene, and from above, listened intently to their conversation with my mother in which they announced an impending visit from the King. We were informed His Grace would very much like to visit the manor of Hever on Thursday.

Mother sent the gracious reply that His Majesty would be warmly welcomed at Hever, and please to inform His Grace that his visit was eagerly anticipated.

I well knew that my mother was aware the King had been paying me particular attention but had so far, unlike Father, been too discreet to pry. She thanked the gentlemen messengers and escorted them to the gate to see them off, then headed back toward the house, and while doing so, caught me eavesdropping from the window above. When our glances met, she subtly raised a single eyebrow in my direction. I returned the look with a secretive smile, removed myself from the open window, and went about the business of readying for our illustrious visitor.

As I discussed with the gardener which flowers would be cut and brought into the house for decoration and planned my attire for the visit, I mulled over how I should present myself when I met Henry. After some thought, I made my decision and felt confident that I had the situation well to hand.

Thursday arrived, and the house and kitchen staff and my mother and father were prepared for the visit. In the early afternoon, a lone herald rode in and informed us that the King and several of his courtiers would arrive in two hours' time. Those hours seemed to me longer than any others I can remember. Finally, though, the castle yard was filled with horses and men as the party arrived. From my vantage point at the mullioned window above, I watched Lord Suffolk and Sir Henry Norreys doff their caps to my mother and thank her for her offer of hospitality. My heart skipped when I saw Henry. He leaped easily from his horse and went straightaway to my mother, kissed her hand and bowed in a chivalrous gesture of appreciation.

I paused for a moment to gather myself, then, tucking a loose tendril of hair under my hood, descended the staircase to greet our guests. The King and the others were gathering in the hall below. Henry's attention was caught by my footfalls, and I stopped on the landing as we beheld each other. I was intensely aware of his strength and virility, and he appeared to me more attractive every time I saw him. I felt the resolve I had so carefully planned slipping from my grasp.

"Mistress Anne! How very delightful to see you again," the King called out with a jaunty lilt to his deep voice.

"And I you, Your Majesty," I replied as I approached him and slipped into a deep curtsey.

Henry looked meaningfully at Norreys, then Suffolk. "You gentlemen have pressing business to discuss with Lord Rochford, do you not?"

"Indeed we have, Your Grace," Norreys replied. He nodded solemnly and followed my father and Lord Suffolk to a small office chamber.

Turning to my mother, the King said, "Madame, would it be acceptable for your daughter to show me about your beautiful gardens before the light fades?"

"Why, of course, Your Majesty. I do hope you enjoy them!" she curtsied, then, before departing to oversee the preparations for supper.

I saw her cast a collusive glance in my direction.

Henry took my arm, and we strolled through the courtyard, across the bridge spanning the moat and into the walled rose garden. Once concealed from prying eyes by a turn in the path, we took a seat on a stone bench with a view of the lavender and roses. Henry sat unsettlingly close to me. We were closer than we had been at any time, save that evening after the banquet at Greenwich when he had followed me into the watching chamber and wished me good night. As I remembered vividly from that evening, I was once again acutely aware of his scent. Not merely the scent of musk or ambergris. Not a fragrance or expensive perfume, it was his personal scent which drew me. It was very male and pleasing to me in a way I cannot describe. He searched my face, and I felt myself flush. I knew he was aware of it, and he warmed in response.

"*Mademoiselle*, I see your blush. It is incredibly becoming on you. In fact, I can see that the summer has enhanced your beauty greatly, though I have no idea how that could be possible. You look enchanting." His voice was deep and resonant, and the way he formed his words cultured and so appealing.

"Your Grace is far too kind," I replied, but my expression gave away my pleasure at his comments. "How has your summer been? How was the hunting? Exciting, I hope, and fruitful?"

"In fact, Milady, exciting it has certainly been. François has recently given us a gift. He sent us a shipload of the most ferocious wild boar this country has seen in many years. He recalled my complaint to him that boars were now scarce in the English countryside, and to continue to foster our good relations, sent us a sounder to repopulate our forests. They are mighty foes on the hunting field, with fearsome tusks."

"I'm sure they must be, Your Grace. I imagine boar hunting has provided you with great entertainment. You probably have very little to interest you in returning to court, with such excellent sport available in your forests," I replied. I confess that I played the hunter in our discourse, baiting him just a little bit.

"Mistress, I hope you know that is quite to the contrary," he said and moved even closer to me with his arm tightly about me and his eyes locked on mine. We were so close that our noses almost touched and I could see the green and amber flecks in his eyes. "I have missed you beyond my expectations, and want nothing more than for us to be near to one another again."

I didn't move, or try to pull away. I couldn't! I was captivated.

"Did you, by any chance at all, miss me?" he murmured, and that tender, inquiring look of a young boy transformed his face. My intention to maintain an appropriate distance was well-nigh forgotten; I could not resist him when he appeared this way. The contrast between his strength, his power, and magnificence, and that almost plaintive vulnerability affected me too greatly. "In truth, I did, indeed, Your Grace," I replied quietly, and as I lowered my eyelids slightly, he kissed me.

It was a gentle, heartfelt kiss. His lips were as soft and sensual as they appeared, and I melted into him. We gazed into each other's faces, and I felt deeply the connection between us. The look he returned to me was unmistakably a look of love. I have seen that look before, yet on the King, it was complete, mature.

With some difficulty, I roused myself and stood up. "Your Majesty, we must return to the house. I would prefer if no undue suspicion were raised."

"Of course, Mistress, but first you must promise me you will return to court as soon as you possibly can. I would wish that you never be such a distance from me again."

"I will do so, Your Grace. Just as soon as I am able," I said, and we walked back to the house to join the others for supper.

•

My mother allowed almost a week to pass without asking me anything at all about the King's visit. Only eventually, while we were in the herb garden one afternoon gathering plants to be hung and dried for the winter, did she break from adding rosemary to her basket, rise and, with hand on hip, look directly at me.

"So, Anne, are you going to tell me nothing at all about what is going on between you and the King?"

"Well ..."

I stumbled in momentary confusion. Once set on course, the maternal inquisitions of Lady Elizabeth Boleyn, Viscountess Rochford, were not ones to be evaded lightly by her offspring – and of a sudden I became a little girl again.

"I am sorry, Mother," I rejoined somewhat awkwardly. "It's not that I don't trust you or want to share information with you. But I have been so accustomed to maintaining my privacy from my time spent in France that it's become a habit. I didn't mean to exclude you. Anyway, there is nothing much to tell."

She afforded me that penetrating look that only passes between mothers and daughters.

"Nan, I know you too well to believe that to be completely true."

I resigned myself to the inevitable.

"Alright, then. I would, in fact, welcome your advice. I find that I have developed an affinity for the King. It is clearly not love. At least I do not interpret it that way - but I am powerfully attracted to him, and it is plain that he is to me, as well, yet I have absolutely no idea of what to do about it."

There! I had shared my burden. Her response was direct and unequivocal.

"Anne, do you intend to become his mistress?"

"Never, Mother - that is not at all what I want! Hence my great dilemma. I do not wish to be a mistress and never a wife. I am fearful I will be asked – even commanded – to consent, and become Henry's short-lived *chatelaine* just as Mary was. I am so unlike Mary, and it would kill me."

Her response was softer than expected. "I understand, Nan. I really do. But you are in a precarious situation."

I could sense her concern as she looked out across the umber fields of waving grass. After a minute, she added, "You might consider remaining away from him for a time. At least until you have had a chance to determine your course of action."

I agreed. After that lingering kiss in the rose garden, I wondered if I could trust myself in the King's proximity. I had not expected to be so unable to resist his advances. There was no question about it; I needed to remain at Hever although I realised I would still have to write to him, at least to offer some excuse.

"Mother, please explain to Father why I will not be returning to court for a while. I cannot think clearly with the pressure he places on me!"

"I will, Anne, but I am certain your father will want you back at court for Christmas. So you will need to prepare yourself to see the King again by December."

"I know, Mother. I hope I will be of a more decided mind by then.

•

I wrote what I thought was a perfectly lovely letter to the King, thanking him profusely for his visit to our manor, and politely inquiring after his health, as well as that of the Queen, his son Richmond and the Princess Mary. I told him I planned to keep company with my mother during the autumn, at Hever, while my father and brother were at court. I wrote that although I still went out riding most days, I missed the excitement of following the royal hunt. I did not give any indication of when I might return but kept the tone of the letter warm yet not too familiar. With satisfaction, I sealed and sent the letter off with the courier. A week elapsed, then a messenger arrived at the portcullis gate one morning, with a gift of oranges and dates in a beautiful basket, and the request, as sent directly by His Grace, that I return to court. With an expression of thanks I accepted the gift and asked the messenger to return on the morrow as I intended to have a reply ready by then.

Once again I composed a letter full of appreciation for the delicious gift of exotic fruit. I expressed my concern for his health and well-being and informed him that, much as I missed being at court and desired to see him, which was true, I simply must stay with my mother, who was suffering from a chest cold. I wished him well but offered no indication of when I would return. As I sealed this latest letter, I considered how much I yearned for the excitement of court, and with some surprise, how very much I missed Henry.

•

The weather became progressively raw and the landscape ever bleaker as December moved into its second week. There had been no further communication from the King. My perspective on his silence varied wildly. At times I felt, surely, his annoyance with my failure to return to court must have dampened any affection he held for me. In fact, I rationalised, certainly he must have found a pretty dalliance to occupy him. At other moments, I replayed that exquisite kiss in my mind and yearned to be near to him, and was altogether convinced he felt likewise. My emotions ran chaotic, and I had all but decided to resolve the situation by avoiding the Christmas celebrations at court entirely when another messenger from Greenwich arrived.

The royal courier was thanked and sent on his way, and I flew through the great hall, up the staircase, and into my chamber. Firmly closing the door, I sat on my bed, cracked the seal, and smoothed open the parchment.

There was no formal greeting: in its place at the top of the sheet was a splatter of dark brown ink, the droplets smeared by his large hand. The letter was written in French and a full page long, while, at simply a glance I could discern the fervour with which it had been written. The large, bold, well-spaced writing was in stark contrast to his previous letters, which had been closely and elegantly transcribed.

I began to read:

En debatant d'apper ... On turning over in my mind the contents of your last letters, I have put myself into great agony, not knowing how to interpret them, whether to my disadvantage, as I understand them in some places, or to my advantage, as I understand them in some others, beseeching you earnestly to let me know expressly your whole mind as to the love between us two. It is absolutely necessary for me to obtain this answer, having been above a whole year stricken avec du dart d'amours -with the dart of love ...

I stopped reading, startled, and reprised the past months in my memory. I recalled in vivid detail the moment when we encountered each other on the hunt field in late November – just over a year ago! - and my clumsiness caused us to come into such close contact that an exchange of looks left me breathless.

Long had I wondered how he felt at that moment. Written here was the answer - right before me!

> ... and not yet sure whether I shall fail of finding a place in your heart and affection, which last point has prevented me for some time past from calling you my mistress; because if you only love me with an ordinary love, that name is not suitable for you, because it denotes a singular love, which is far from common. But if you please to do the office of a true loyal mistress and friend, and to give up yourself body and heart to me, who will be, and have been, your most loyal servant, (if your rigor does not forbid me) I promise you that not only the name shall be given you, but also that I will take you for my only mistress, casting off all others besides you out of my thoughts and affections, and serve you only. I beseech you to give an entire answer to this my rude letter, that I may know on what and how far I may depend. And if it does not please you to answer me in writing, appoint some place where I may have it by word of mouth, and I will go thither with all my heart. No more for fear of tiring you. Written by the hand of him who would willingly remain yours,
>
> H. R.

It took me but an instant to decide that I would, after all, reply to King Henry. And more -that I would reply in person. I called for Charity to begin packing to return to court for Christmas.

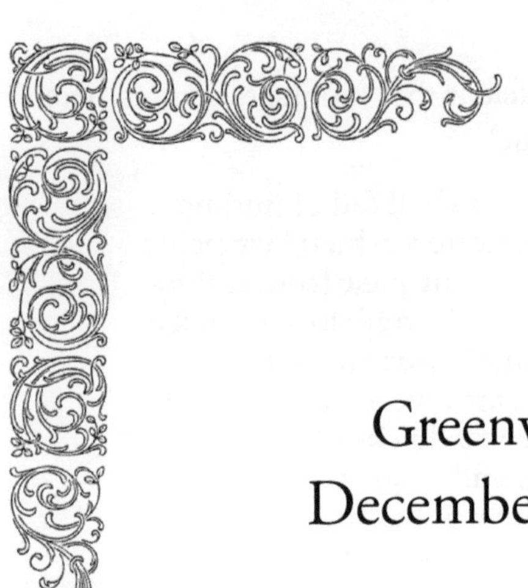

Greenwich
December 1526

"HOW DO YOU think this looks, Anne?" Maggie asked, holding a bodice and kirtle against herself while squinting at the mirror.

We were in her chamber at Greenwich. How content I felt, being in her company again! I sat on a stool near the hearth and watched her while she busily moved about the room, gathering items which would comprise her attire for the Christmas banquet. She had wanted my opinion of her choice of gown, headpiece, and jewellery. It was a great relief to feel completely at ease, finished with my duties in service of Queen Katherine for the evening.

Mon Dieu! What a burden it had become to serve the Queen and pretend to care about her daily needs. I had no idea whether Katherine was aware of the King's attentions to me, but I certainly hoped not. The situation was proving difficult enough without having to endure her retributions if indeed she did suspect there to be something between her husband and me.

As children, both Maggie and I had loved to run wild outside on long summer evenings, doing our best to keep up with our brothers. We had, somewhat disapprovingly, been called 'tomboys' and would much rather have been outdoors, romping in the fields than learning how to embroider or manage a household. Neither of us had cared a fig for our clothes then, or how we'd looked. All that, of course, changed for me during my stay at the fashionable French court, whereas Maggie had not been afforded such opportunity and, as a consequence, was now possessed of much less confidence than I when it came to assembling attire to complement her looks.

The gown she held up was a becoming shade of deep green, with sleeves trimmed in gold. It would look beautiful against her dark blond hair. I had finally convinced her to wear a French hood rather than a bulky gabled one. That way, enough of her lovely hair would be uncovered to be seen as an asset.

"I adore that gown for you, Maggie. It is such a festive colour and green looks well on you. I think you should wear it, and you can set it off with the emerald necklace."

"Oh Anne, it just gives me some extra certainty when you approve. Thank you, my friend. And what will you wear? Have you decided?" she asked, sitting down in the chair across from me, rubbing her hands together to warm herself by the fire.

"Not yet. I am the indecisive one, it seems," I shrugged. "Maybe the indigo blue brocade which just arrived from the dressmaker? Do you think that would be a good choice?"

"Indeed. Its colour will look splendid on you." She gave me an impish little smile. "You will have at least three specific pairs of eyes riveted on you in that!"

"What do you mean?" I asked, pretending to be piqued. "I hope there will be lots of eyes on me, because why spend so much time and effort getting ready if not to be admired?"

"Undoubtedly you will be the object of attention, Anne, but there will surely be three in particular. Those of Lord Percy, my brother Thomas and, most significant of all - the King's ...!"

She grabbed my hand and squeezed it. "My dearest Anne, I am aware of the attraction between you and His Majesty. It is not my business to know anything more than that. But I will say this - when the two of you are together, the radiance you emit is unmistakable. You are similar to His Grace in many ways, and you both shine brightly. In truth, Anne, you would make a formidable twosome … or formidable foes, for that matter!"

She fell quiet for a moment just watching the flames, and I was thinking about what she had said, when she added, "My poor brother Thomas. He is so in love with you. You know that, do you not?"

I nodded slowly as she continued, "Thomas is a wonderful man, Anne; handsome and so accomplished. Fortunately, he was able to leave behind that misguided marriage to Elizabeth Brooke, but I fear his hopes will never be fulfilled. He pines for you, yet I know he will never be able to compete with the likes of our King."

•

The approaching twilight deepened the shadows in my chamber, and I was engrossed in preparing for the Christmas celebration. I had decided to wear the deep blue gown. Its sleeves were lined with a gold tissue, and the hood edged with gold embroidery. I had borrowed a necklace from my mother, a circlet of gold links studded with three sizable sapphires. I stepped into my satin slippers and sat before the mirror so Charity could arrange the hood far back on my hair which was how I preferred to wear it. I stood then and tugged at the bodice to lower it a bit while frowning at the mirror to study the result. All seemed satisfactory, and I finally permitted myself a smile, pleased with my choices.

Hurrying through the torch-lit gallery, I headed for the Royal Chapel, where I was to sit with the Queen's ladies for Evensong. A celestial beauty filled the chapel as the slanting light of late afternoon illuminated the stained glass, spilling pools of vibrant colour across the stone and dark wood. I slid into my seat while glancing covertly along the pew, past the other maids and ladies in waiting, to observe Katherine. She looked drawn and tired. Gowned in dark crimson, the colour of oxblood, the tone accentuated the lines etched on her face. I felt a twinge of compassion - indeed, guilt - as I observed her melancholy. Even as Mass began, I continued to muse. Guilt was not warranted, I concluded. I had done nothing overt to encourage the King's attentions. Compassion, however, was something else again. I did feel pity for Katherine, who had endured so much sorrow with failed pregnancies and stillborn children, and whose anguish over aging must not be limited to her waning beauty, but surely for the demise of her fertility.

I wondered what would become of the three of us. I had not yet permitted myself any conjecture on my prospects with Henry. In so many ways, our affinity seemed to me a chimera. My fascination with him was undeniable, but despite his letter I was not at all certain that his for me would endure.

My reverie was interrupted as the congregants began to file forward to receive communion. The Cardinal progressed through the rest of the Mass without delay; he likely anticipated the awaiting feast, as did we all.

The Great Hall at Greenwich, bedecked and aglow for Christmas of 1526, was an incredible sight. It had been said that the King wished to have a special celebration this year since last year's Christmastide he'd spent away from court, and as a result, the Lord Chamberlain and his staff had outdone themselves. Gleaming silver candelabra, placed on every table and buffet, held tall, flickering white candles. The chandeliers were ablaze. Astonishingly beautiful new tapestries, which King Henry commissioned from artisans in Brussels, hung on every wall: their Old Testament stories depicted in brilliant colour, shot throughout with threads of silver and gold. The spectacularly carved and gilded beams of the ceiling high above were festooned with boughs of pine, holly, and English ivy. Entwined throughout those boughs were silvery branches. The musicians played merry French *chansons* and traditional carols while the guests entered the Hall and mingled, greeting each other and sipping spiced wine from silver and golden goblets. An entrancing fragrance filled the air from censers which smouldered with frankincense and rosemary. And at the center of the room, the great Yule log blazed. I roamed through the crowd, offering Christmas wishes, and unawares, turned to find myself confronted by the King. He squeezed my arm with a warm grasp then, lowering his head so he could speak closely to me, whispered, "Be certain to dance with me, *Mademoiselle*. I will await that moment."

I smiled up at him, filled with happy anticipation for the evening ahead.

•

As it turned out, Thomas Wyatt was my dining partner. I took note that, this time, my place was in full view of the King and Queen, and I had been positioned upboard, much closer to the dais. Wyatt paid me continuous attention throughout the evening, keeping his face close to mine when he spoke. As soon as the dancing began, he steered me to the floor, and we danced the first galliard while the King watched, his eyes piercing and his features peculiarly devoid of expression.

The evening became ever merrier, and I danced often. The King, however, had yet to approach me. He kept a close watch, though, even while he talked and laughed with his many guests, all manoeuvring for a private moment in which to wish the King and Queen a happy Christmas.

So many courses were served that I lost count. Midway through the feast, there arose an audible gasp from the guests, as brought to the table was an immense roasted boar's head – likely one of the ill-fated boars sent to us by François. In its mouth was an apple, and its curved tusks gleamed fearsomely. I did not intend to eat any of that beast. Instead, I would await my favourite dish, 'Christmas Pye', which the baker concocted of neat's tongue, eggs, sugar, flour and many spices, raisins and orange peel. So very delicious!

A hand on my shoulder caused me to look up to see King Henry. He had wedged himself between Thomas and me and was offering his arm. I laid my hand atop his jewelled sleeve, and he led me to the dance floor where courtiers were assembling for a pavane. The King and I assumed our places at the head of the formation. Master Taverner, conducting the musicians that evening, announced that the piece we were about to hear had been composed by His Royal Majesty. I smiled up at Henry while the guests applauded, and the music began. It was an enchanting melody, played well - indeed, he was a most able composer - and Henry and I danced as if we had been partners all our lives. I knew we were the centre of much interest, but I could pay attention to little else than the thrilling sensation of dancing with the King. Never had I encountered anyone so skilled. He was graceful and strong all at once, and our steps were in perfect cadence. When we faced each other, his pleasure was evidenced by his shining eyes and broad smile. The dance concluded, there came more applause - and it was clearly intended for us both.

As midnight approached, the King was handed a lute. He positioned himself where all could see. He began to play, and the clear notes of the eloquent and moving piece resonated in the room which had quickly stilled: the captivated assembly silent. As the final note sounded, then faded away, there arose a burst of genuine acclaim. Gracefully, Henry bowed to his audience, telling them he had titled the piece '*If Love Now Reynyd*.' I, along with others in attendance, marvelled at the many talents possessed by this magnificent man.

Along with the midnight chiming of the clock, my heart beat rhythmically. All present began to sing '*Gloria, Gloria in Excelsis Deo*!' and I sang too, the words more meaningful to me than I could ever have imagined. For – at long last, and for the first time in my life - I had fallen boundlessly in love

•

The endless winter was so confining. I hated being constantly indoors, but the thick shelves of ice which coated the ground and covered the pathways around the palace prevented any of us from venturing out. The physical limitations imposed by those coldest and darkest months gave rise to an increased interest in gossip and speculation amongst members of the court. I had begun to notice curious glances and delicately probing inquiries from the other ladies when we were together. Many of them were now aware that I was the object of the King's affection. While nothing was asked of me directly, it was easy to detect their change in attitude. They were more cautious around me – and more deferential. While as for Katherine herself? I would say that when we were in the same company, there were no obvious signs of discord between us.

Yet, unmistakably I sensed her uneasiness and realized that in truth, she knew.

Hampton Court
January 1527

ON A FRIGID morning in January, the Queen's ladies and I huddled in her apartments at Hampton Court, where we did our best to stay warm near the hungry braziers being continuously fed logs by the servants. Thinking it better to move about, I walked to the window and idly watched particles of sleet and snow pelt the leaded panes of glass. The tree branches in the orchard laboured under the accumulated weight of ice. Sighing, I warmed my stiff fingers near the brazier, then returned to my seat and worked at my piece of embroidery awhile, listening to the conversation. The political discussion had been especially lively in recent weeks. There was a great deal of debate concerning the marital prospects for Princess Mary, and, since the King was inclined to ally with France and ensure the favour of François, some predicted that Mary might become betrothed to François I himself, although there was a diversity of opinion. Many thought she would be wed to François' son, the Duc d'Orléans. For Mary's sake, I hoped it would be the young Duke, for I could not fathom the naive and inexperienced princess becoming a wife of the libertine François. I had observed how badly he had treated poor Queen Claude. She was constantly with child, and even though the pregnancies took an enormous toll on her already frail health, it apparently caused him no concern whatsoever - worse, it was as if her condition gave him open license to lasciviously entertain himself elsewhere. Placed in Claude's position, I could imagine myself humiliated, and it would no doubt prove that much worse for a young foreign bride.

The discussion then turned to the imminent departure of Thomas Wyatt and Sir John Russell for Italy on an extended diplomatic mission. The conflict between the Emporer Charles V and the Italian monarchs had become a topic of some concern. It was Charles's great desire to subjugate and rule all Italy. Thomas and Sir John were instructed to monitor the situation and provide regular reports to His Majesty. This assignment did indeed provide a sound rationale for Thomas's extended absence from court although I suspected the truth was rather more material: Henry had specifically arranged Thomas's removal to ensure there could be no further distractions between the two of us.

The winter months were made bearable only by the diversion of organized pastimes. No one surpassed Henry in making sure there were activities available which could be enjoyed by all. In fact, though I may have been mistaken, it seemed to me as if there were events planned which enabled Katherine's ladies to mingle with the King and his coterie more often than usual. We watched matches of tennis which the King often won in his inimitable style. There were games of shovel board, which I enjoyed because women were permitted to participate, and they afforded me a physical outlet for my competitive spirit. And of course, in the evenings, there were masques and plays, music and dancing, and games of cards accompanied by fierce wagering.

And thus, it was that a group of us, the King's favourites, were seated in the library around his polished card table on a February evening while the wind moaned about the eaves and flailing tree branches scraped relentlessly at the windows. It felt secure and comforting to bask in the warmth of our surroundings with the lambent flames from the hearth dancing against the dark wooden wall panels, and the thick carpet soft beneath our feet. Candlelight illuminated the faces of the players: the King, my brother George, Charles Brandon, Francis Bryan, Anne Gainsford, and me. The Queen had played the first two or three hands but then had retired to her chambers for the night. We played Prime, laying down money on each round, and I was even with the King on winnings. I thoroughly relished matching wits with him, although I weakly attempted to disguise my desire to win. I rather enjoyed giving the King a run for his money and did not feel that I should arrange a loss to preserve his dignity. It was my turn as dealer, and I placed cards in front of each player. When I came to Henry, I looked directly into his eyes. His lips curved in a subtle smile and with an almost imperceptible lift of his eyebrows, he silently questioned me. I understood clearly. I had not yet addressed the query he posed in the letter I received before Christmas.

"'Mistress Anne, are you as accomplished at cards as you seem to be in so many other endeavours?" Henry asked.

"I would wish to be, Your Grace," I nodded demurely.

"Then you intend to win this hand?" followed the droll question and the crinkle at the outer corners of his eyes. The innuendo was clear.

The others paid little attention as they organized their cards, and had not a clue to what Henry referred. I, however, understood precisely.

"Your Grace, it will depend on the hand I am dealt and whether it will be an advantage to me, or a detriment," I responded pertly, smiling back.

Cheeky witticisms aside, I was acutely aware that I must give him an answer in some fashion, soon. And I needed a strategy - a good one - because I was in love with him.

London
February 1527

THE RUTS ALONG High Oldbourne Street caused the carriage to rumble so viciously that Charity and I nearly finished the journey with mouthfuls of chipped teeth. We were glad to step down and walk quickly along toward Ely Place. Nestled next to St Etheldreda's Church stood a small timbered building. We entered, welcoming the opportunity to step in out of the biting cold. The moody grey sky had begun to spit snow, and I wanted to take care of the business at hand and return to the cart which waited for us well around the corner, out of sight. The intent of my errand was exceedingly private.

"Master Phenwolf, it is a pleasure to meet you," I greeted the small, wiry man seated behind the worktable. He stood up and came toward me, and I was surprised to see that he was younger than I had anticipated for a master goldsmith of his renown.

"The pleasure is, of course, mine, Mistress Boleyn," and he offered his hand, which was rough and worn, and discoloured from his metalwork. "Please come by the stove to warm yourselves, and do show me the drawing of the piece you wish me to make for you."

I sat down and took a paper from a small bag I carried. I smoothed it on the table, and we scrutinised it together.

"I wish for the piece to be made from a very fine gold – Welsh gold if possible. I would like you to depict a ship listing in the waves as if in a storm. On the deck of the ship, there must be a lady. And fixed between the two masts, I would like you to place a diamond. Are you able to create such a jewel, Master Phenwolf? The quality must be of the highest order," I said, searching his face for reassurance that he would create a masterpiece. "This is a very important ornament."

"Mistress, I would not accept the commission if I were unable to do it justice," he said simply. "You will be most pleased. I will begin tomorrow and will contact you as soon as it is ready to be collected."

"Thank you, Master Phenwolf. And please remember that discretion is paramount."

Charity and I hurried down the street and around the corner to our waiting coach as the snow swirled thickly, and deepening twilight veiled us.

Hever
March 1527

I DID NOT KNOW what to do.

The enigma caused me great agitation. I admired decisiveness, yet my mind continuously sought a way forward, and nothing came. I knew the King wanted me - but what was the true nature of his heart? Of that, I could not be certain. I longed to be his – a desire greater than I had imagined possible for any man. My determination to avoid becoming his mistress, though, was at war with my yearning for him. While the role of *mâitresse* would fulfil my need to be with him, I feared that in the very briefest amount of time the lustre would fade, and the relationship cheapened in a way I could not tolerate. Hence, there seemed no possibility of anything more between Henry and me, since the Queen, although ageing, still appeared healthy and strong.

Around and around ran my thoughts 'til, in an effort to seek some peace, I decided to ask permission to go home to Hever for a while.

As always, my lady mother was there for me; a support and friend when one was needed most. I held my mother in great esteem and hoped that I had inherited at least a few of her fine qualities. She was an elegant woman, now forty-two years of age, and in good health. This was somewhat surprising, considering she had withstood so many difficult pregnancies in succession, and endured the heartbreak of several children's early deaths. She was nobly born, having been a daughter of the Duke of Norfolk - my grandfather, Thomas Howard - and was descended from 13th century English royalty. As a girl, she had served in the court of Henry's mother, Elizabeth of York, and then had spent considerable time as a lady-in-waiting to Queen Katherine. It was through these experiences that she'd adopted the grace and poise for which she was known. She carried herself with an aristocratic air and great dignity, no matter the circumstances, and I admired this attribute greatly. Her features had a delicate beauty, with enviably smooth skin. It was a face I loved very much, and nothing in the world could replace the comfort and reassurance I felt when I looked upon it.

While the cold rains of March fell, I busied myself with the daily tasks of helping to run the large household at my parents' estate. My father was not present, being one of a diplomatic envoy recently departed for France. The King was in pursuit of a treaty which might pave the way for the marriage of the Princess Mary to the Duke of Orléans, and there was much to do to achieve that objective. So my mother and I had time to ourselves, and I leaned on her to listen and to give me her advice.

"Mother, I am in a predicament from which I see no apparent way out," I lamented, letting out a groan as we sorted and organized linens for the bedchambers. The weather was utterly dreary, raw and chill, and I felt the same way. "I may as well remain here for the long term, and not return to court at all because it is simply too trying when I am in the company of the King. And, oh, it is even worse when I am near the Queen! She has turned very sharp with me, and there is such tension between us. It is clear she suspects an affair is taking place behind her back … yet the irony of it is that her suspicions are completely unfounded. Here I am at Hever while the King is at Greenwich, and there is nothing - nothing at all - taking place between us."

My mother allowed me to twaddle on, patiently tolerating my inclination to unload all my imagined troubles. I grant this tendency sometimes got the best of me. It seemed especially rife at certain times of the month, between my monthly course. I do not know why, but when the headaches came upon me, and I felt awful, it was almost impossible for me to keep my mouth closed and my peevish reflections to myself. I tried to contain those impulses but was all too often unsuccessful.

"Anne," she hurried to interject during a brief pause in my grumblings, "all I can tell you is that you need to be honest with yourself. You must do, as concerns the King, what your true heart and your conscience tell you. You know I would not say such a thing in earshot of your father, but I firmly believe that women must do whatever they can to assert their rights. Discreetly, yes - but do their best to live a life which will be meaningful and gratifying to them."

"Mother! I know you have a mind of your own, but had not realized you were quite so progressive in your thinking!"

"For me, that opinion has become stronger with age, my daughter," she said ruefully. "Women have so much to offer, yet very little of it is ever allowed to be expressed. My talents might have served to accomplish more than just the management of this house, but there was no opportunity for me to exercise them. Perhaps it will be different with you, Anne. Your intelligence and accomplishments are prodigious."

"What high praise indeed, Mother." I was touched by her generous compliment. It served to banish quickly my grumpiness. "You know that your advice means a great deal to me. I will take it to heart, I promise. And I could not agree with you more – in my reasoning, there is no validity to the perception that a woman cannot govern a city, a country … even an empire if she possesses the wit, courage, and desire to do so. I am keenly interested in what goes on at court. I do not mean the idle gossip and uninformed speculation. No, I find myself more intrigued by the political complexities, and the debates and decisions which result. The important decisions! The ones which affect not only England but the entire world. I find the intrigue fascinating. Oh, how I would welcome the chance to express my opinions on matters of such consequence."

Deliberating further, I glumly concluded, "Sometimes I think I should have been a man! Life would have been so much easier."

•

One of the King's couriers arrived the next morning, with a parchment to be delivered directly to me. Simply the sight of the royal messenger caused my heart to beat rapidly in anticipation. I made a hasty exit to my chamber to open it:

> A ma mestres -To my Mistress - Because the time seems very long since I heard concerning your health and you, the great affection I have for you has induced me to send you this bearer, to be better informed of your health and pleasure, and because, since my parting from you, I have been told that the opinion in which I left you is totally changed, and that you would not come to court either avec madame votre mere -with your mother, if you could, or in any other manner: which report, if true, I cannot sufficiently marvel at, because I am sure that I have since never done any thing to offend you, and it seems a very poor return for the great love which I bear you to keep me at a distance both from the speech and the person of the woman that I esteem most in the world: and if you love me with as much affection as I hope you do, I am sure that the distance of our two persons would be a little irksome to you, though this does not belong so much to the mistress as to the servant.

Consider well, my mistress, that absence from you grieves me sorely, hoping that it is not your will that it should be so; but if I knew for certain that you voluntarily desired it, I could do no other than mourn my ill-fortune, and by degrees abate my great folly. And so, for lack of time, I make an end of this rude letter, beseeching you to give credence to this bearer in all that he will tell you from me.

Escrit de la main du toute votre serviteure,

Written by the hand of your entire Servant,

H. R.

It was thus clear that Henry was suffering as much inner turmoil as I.

I went to the locked chest I kept in my chamber, the one that held Henry's letters, and from within it, I removed a pouch of black velvet. Releasing the drawstring, I spilled into my hand the jewel which had been crafted by the goldsmith Morgan Phenwolf, upon my commission. It was unique – astonishing, really. The artistry demonstrated in fashioning a ship tossed about by waves of gold with a lady on its deck was inspiring. To set off the piece, the diamond fixed between the two masts was both stunning and significant.

•

When a January snowstorm had us all housebound, I had pulled from the library shelf a copy of *Roman de la Rose*, the French epic poem written in the thirteenth century as a dream- induced homage to courtly love. My first encounter with this literary work had been confusing – its poetic meaning had eluded me. This reading, though, due perhaps to the maturity I had attained since my initial translation as a girl of eighteen years, I found memorable. I'd become fixated on a particular passage:

Although he chastice thee without
And make thy body vnto hym loute
Haue herte as hard as dyamaunt
Stedefast and nought pliaunt
In prisoun though thi body be
At large kepe thyne herte free
A trewe herte wole not plie
For no manace that it may drye
If Ielousie doth thee payne
Quyte hym his while thus agayne

The thought of somehow sharing these lines with Henry had captured my imagination: the lyric verse with its intriguing symbolism. While dozing, just before drifting to sleep one night, the perfect idea occurred to me – what if I was to commission the making of a jewel representing the sentiment in the passage? I'd jumped from my bed, and drawn a ship adrift in a stormy sea, with a lone woman aboard desperately seeking a port. I knew Henry would, were I to present him with such a piece, understand the question it posed: would he be my harbour in the storms of life? The diamond, glittering and hard, supporting the masts swaying in the gale, represented my steadfast love were we to commit to one another.

I held the ornament, turning it about; feeling its weight in my hand for what seemed a long while, deep in thought as daylight faded. I stripped bare the personal façade I had learned to maintain so carefully and forced myself to explore the depths of my heart. I was a woman of twenty-six years, now well beyond the age most suitors desired. I had neither money nor land as a dowry. I was unproven when it came to the ability to bear children – forsooth, I was yet a maid! I stood and went to the mirror. Its reflection revealed a face with a proud, high forehead, glittering, dark eyes which spoke the truth, and a distinct chin unaccustomed to trembling. Not beautiful, but by God's blood, strong and fearless! A face which was loved - no, adored - by one of the most powerful men in the world.

I pushed aside the mirror, lighted a lantern against the gathering gloom, and took up parchment and pen.

My most noble Sir: I hope you will accept the gift I respectfully send, and be mindful of its genuine meaning and sentiment. You shall see I am but a maiden in the heart of a storm, a maid who seeks refuge. My greatest desire is that you will be my harbour, and if you agree, you will find my dedication to you as resolute as the diamond is hard, never to waiver. I send this token praying for your health and happiness and that you wish to see me as I do you; I send it, also, with the most sincere feelings of love and loyalty.

A. B.

Once written, I did not hesitate. I sealed the letter with wax, found a ribbon with which to bind both the folded letter and the velvet pouch, and called for our head steward to have it delivered with all haste and great care to His Majesty, the King.

As the steward hurried away, I muttered aloud, "Well, Anne, there you have it… your die has just been cast."

I will not deny I was unsettled that evening and found I was in just as much distress throughout the next day. I moved from room to room restlessly, unable to concentrate on anything at hand. As we sat to supper late in the afternoon, a loud rap at the door was answered, revealing a messenger, bedraggled from having ridden hard from Greenwich, bearing a letter for me from the King. He handed me the roll containing the parchment, and I took it, bemused by the fact that my missive must not have been delivered more than twenty-four hours previously. Perhaps our respective letters were written independently and had merely crossed paths?

Scraping my chair back clumsily in haste, I excused myself from the supperboard, ignoring the questioning glances, and fled to my room. With trembling hands I cracked the great seal and removed its covering. The fine parchment slipped free, and smoothing it before me on the surface of a table under the dancing flames of candlelight, I exhaled softly, breathing an 'Ohhh' at the sight of it. Before reading even a single word, its poignant message spoke to me. It was exquisitely inscribed: no smears or smudges on this page. The first letter of the first word, "**D**", was black and dramatic and scrolled with a fine edge, as if it were the first letter in an illuminated manuscript. The deep ink against the stark, pale sheet made a formal and very decisive statement. The letters themselves were each distinct: sharp and close. My eyes dropped to Henry's signature and widened in utter amazement. There, oh so carefully drawn, was a heart which encased my initials!

Delaying no longer, I read:

> De l'estrene si bel que rien plus (notant le toute) je vous an marcy tres cordiallement - For a present so beautiful that nothing could be more so (considering the whole of it), I thank you most cordially, not only on account of the fine diamond and the ship in which the solitary damsel is tossed about, but chiefly for the fine interpretation and the too humble submission which your goodness hath used toward me in this case: for I think that it would be very difficult for me to find an occasion to deserve it, if I were not assisted by your great humanity and favour, which I have always sought to seek, and will seek to preserve by all the kindness in my power, in which my hope has placed its unchangeable intention, which says Aut illic, aut nullibi.
>
> The demonstrations of your affections are such, the beautiful mottoes of the letter so cordially expressed, that in vos lettres

… here he had scratched out 'in your letters' – I wondered what he had intended to say? …

> they oblige me forever to honour, love, and serve you sincerely, beseeching you to continue in the same firm and constant purpose, assuring you that, on my part, I will surpass it rather than make it reciprocal, if loyalty of heart and a desire to please you can accomplish this.

I beg, also, if at any time before this I have in any way offended you, that you would give me the same absolution that you ask, assuring you, that henceforth my heart shall be dedicated to you alone. I wish my person was so too. God can do it, if he pleases, to whom I pray every day for that end, hoping that at length my prayers will be heard. I wish the time may be short, but I shall think it long till we see one another. Written by the hand of that secretary, who in heart, body, and will, is,

Vostre loyal et plus assure serviteure

Your loyal and most assured Servant

H. aultre AB ne cherse R.

Henry Rex seeks no other than Anne Boleyn

The royal H R were beautifully embellished, the heart so lovingly inscribed, and the words 'aultre' and 'ne cherse' impossibly tiny; the whole device making a pretty picture at the bottom of the page. There was no mistaking it. This was a love letter, fervently composed, and written with ardour by a man whose size did not easily enable small, delicate script. I understood its intent. It was meant to embrace me, oh so tenderly, in his absence.

I would go back to court as soon as I was packed and ready. Not one moment longer would I wait to see him.

Greenwich
April 1527

I ARRIVED AT GREENWICH on 1 April to find the King and Cardinal Wolsey intensely involved in final negotiations to betroth eleven-year-old Princess Mary to the Duc d' Orléans, the son of François I. The details of the 'Treaty of Eternal Peace' between England and France were being finalised. There was much anticipation that this diplomatic strategy would unite France and England through a fruitful marriage and hence a loyal, lasting friendship. Although there was critical business to hand, as soon as the King was informed of my return to court he sent me a message asking that I join him for supper in his privy chamber on the morrow. This invitation I accepted with pleasure and great expectancy.

As was my way, I gave my attire much consideration: finally deciding upon an ivory satin gown with pale yellow silk sleeves and insets. I knew ivory and yellow looked striking with my colouring, and I fully intended to make an impression. This was an important rendezvous, and as I dressed, I was not without trepidation. Did Henry understand the motive in my letter?

Did I over scrutinize and misinterpret his? I wished I was able to share my thoughts and anxieties with a friend, but there were none close enough. My mother had remained at Hever, and I missed her because she was the only ally who was trustworthy with such private confidences.

I expected Lord Chamberlain FitzAlan to call for me at any moment. My *toilette* had been meticulously completed, and the yellow silk hood was being placed on my hair, which had been brushed to gleaming. My hands quivered as I selected a ring of gold with a large pearl and placed it on my finger, and Charity fastened my pearl 'B' necklace. She gave me an encouraging smile and shyly said, "You look wonderful Mistress. His Majesty will be ever so happy to see you."

Just those simple words of confidence allowed me to pause, take a deep breath, and gather myself. I hugged Charity with gratitude, dabbed the merest trace of rouge to my lips, touched scented oil to my neck and *décolleté*, then left my chamber to join the waiting Lord FitzAlan, who was to escort me to the King's chambers.

Hesitantly I stood at the open door to His Grace's privy chamber. The King stood before the fireplace, his back to me, engaged in reading a small book. As Lord FitzAlan announced my arrival, Henry turned about; a broad smile creased his face. To FitzAlan, he said "Thank you, Your Grace. No further service is required at the moment."

With a low bow, the Lord Chamberlain backed out of the room, and quietly closed the door. I took notice that this time, there were no esquires of the body standing guard inside the doorway. Henry and I were alone.

He rushed to me, took my hand and fervently kissed it, then continued to hold it in his warm grasp. He looked deep into my eyes, and said, "You cannot have any idea how much I missed you, my lovely Anne."

I replied that I did, for I had missed him just the same. He never took his eyes from my face as we approached the table which had been set for us. Henry gave me a sweeping glance from head to toe, and, standing back, said, "*Tu es magnifique! La plus belle femme du monde.*"

I replied with a curtsey. "*Merci beaucoup, Majesté!* But I must beg to differ. There are many – so very many – beautiful women in your court." I was flush with pleasure at such a lavish compliment, yet nevertheless a bit flustered.

"*Au contraire, Mademoiselle.* How you do shine more brightly than all the others! Your beauty and grace are unparalleled, and I am almost afraid to believe what I read in your note." He paused, then asked, "Anne, was I mistaken, or did you indeed agree to be mine and mine alone?" His eyes earnestly searched my face, and I felt my anxiousness depart to be replaced by a surge of tenderness, heightened by the extraordinary familiarity we shared.

"Henry," I whispered, venturing to call him by name without his title, "I am yours. I feel, inexplicably, as if I have somehow been yours always. I do not know how else to describe it, but I cannot but sense we are joined by some unusual and powerful bond, and that we have known each other forever."

"My beautiful lady," he said with evident awe, "it is totally fitting that you would confess such a thing because I too feel that way. I do not know what it is, or why it is so - but I *do* know, Anne, that it can no longer be ignored. We are meant to be together, and, I commit to you, we will remain together always."

How marvellous that sounded! But I braced myself to pose the question which must be asked.

"Sir, and what, precisely, do you say to me? My letter and gift told you I seek safe harbour. That can only mean with you as my husband, Henry. Nothing else. Is this your understanding?"

His steady gaze was guileless, showing his most honest and true self. *Mon Dieu* but my heart nearly stopped! He was either about to reject me - or promise me the impossible.

King Henry VIII of England said slowly and deliberately, his eyes never leaving mine, "I promise you, Anne Boleyn. You shall be my wife. We will eclipse any royal couple known before or after us. Our love will bind us and etch our place in history."

It was then that he gathered me into his arms, no longer only my King but the love of my life - my destiny - and kissed me over and over.

For the very first time, I did not resist.

•

In the days following that evening with Henry, I drifted about, dreamlike. Never had I imagined such a feeling! I excitedly anticipated our next meeting, yet needed the time to myself to comprehend what had happened; to think about that which had been said, and to come to the full realization that the King and I were betrothed.

A great concern, though, cast its shadow. I still did not know how Henry intended to rid himself of Katherine: only that he had promised to do so, and with haste. Occasionally, a trace of remorse would breach my joyful fantasies, when I pictured Katherine receiving the harrowing news. But I was completely entranced with new love, and forced such discomfiting thoughts aside, at least for the time being.

In spite of the fact that I was now a woman betrothed, and secretly deliriously happy, the affairs of state carried on. And they did so in grand fashion, as was Henry's way. It was the final day of April 1527, and the gentlemen of Henry's court who had travelled to France some weeks before along with my father - the Duke of Suffolk, the Duke of Norfolk, Sir William Fitzwilliam and Chancellor More - had proved successful in negotiating the *Treaty of Amiens* which would lead to an Anglo-French alliance, and furthermore clear the way for the marriage of the Princess Mary with Henri, Duc d'Orléans, François' son.

The preparations currently in train for the celebration to mark the event were unlike anything I had ever seen, save, perhaps, those for the Field of Cloth of Gold some years ago.

The grounds of Greenwich were teeming with craftsmen and labourers rushing to finish the construction of a new banqueting house. I had peeked within the structure, and was informed by Sir Henry Guildford, who managed the project, that it was designed as a basic building but ingeniously constructed with the flexibility to accommodate stages, props for masques, a special location for musicians and minstrels, various types of wall and ceiling hangings, and everything needed as an advanced centre for dining and entertainment. Across the tiltyard, a proper disguising house was being fabricated, which would feature mummeries and masques. In the disguising house, a spectacular ceiling had been painted by Master Hans Holbein, representing the universe and its astrological bodies. It was surely a work which would mark Master Holbein as a painter of unsurpassable skill since it was most splendidly accomplished with gorgeous blues and yellows, stars and constellations of silver and gold leaf.

Everyone at court was readying for the celebration to commemorate the signing of the Treaty, which would take place on Sunday. For this event, especially one in which my father had played a key role, my mother had come to court. With her, she had brought a glorious gown as a gift for me. It was a most unusual colour - a fascinating peacock blue silk - and I was so grateful; for the gown, but much more so for her companionship.

On the morning of Sunday 5 May, the French envoy arrived to hear Mass said by the Bishop of London. Afterwards, the King and some of his ministers, as well as the French Bishop of Tarbes, Monsieur Grammont, and the Viscount of Turenne, retired to the chamber just outside the Chapel Royal. Here, King Henry signed the Treaty of Eternal Peace between England and France. The bishop and the viscount, as François' proxies, were duly warned that unless François himself signed the treaty within a reasonable period, England would not be obliged to observe it.

With the serious business accomplished, everyone then hastened to prepare for the grand *soirée* to be held that evening in the new banqueting house.

There were audible exclamations of amazement as the company entered the building. Guests passed through an enormous, carved and ornately gilded triumphal arch. Once inside, above the arch reaching to the ceiling was painted a huge and realistic image of the English victory over the French at Thérouanne. I wondered which advisor had persuaded Henry this was a good idea, especially when I saw the French ministers shift their glances in discomfited embarrassment when it was pointed out to them. Once inside, the building revealed itself as an architectural marvel. A complex network of beams created the ceiling, and entwined throughout those beams were branches fashioned from iron. Such was their intricacy that it gave visitors the sense of being in a forest; a mystical forest lit by hundreds of twinkling lights. Metal cups forged to the branches held candles, each aglow. The branches trailed carved vines from which roses and leaves, created in vivid detail, hung. As if this display were not impressive enough, high above the beams and branches billowed a canopy of red buckram imprinted with marvellous patterns of gold, reflecting the light of the candles. When one finally tore one's eyes from staring heavenward, another astonishing sight awaited. Aglow throughout the room were silver candle staffs fashioned as fanciful beasts, lions, dragons, and greyhounds. Draping the walls were the most amazing tapestries, lustrous in colourful silk weave and shimmering with liberal use of silver and gold thread. Against one wall stood an immense buffet, the largest I had ever seen, groaning with gold and silver plate, laden with what appeared to be all manner of choice dishes, staged and ready to serve to the guests.

Amid the preliminary turmoil of guests seeking to find their places at tables, the French ambassadors were seated on the dais, along with the King, Queen Katherine, and Princess Mary, who looked quite grown up in a silver gown. The musicians began playing, and the jolly sound of lutes, shawms, sackbuts and tambours filled the air and invited the guests to dance even while the food was being served. The wine flowed freely - the finest vintages imported from the Burgundy region of France to honour the French dignitaries. The Princess danced gaily with her father, whom, it was obvious, she adored. One could see he was proud of her that night and delighted in showing off her talents in dance and language to the ambassadors. When, finally, the sweets were served, along with small silver goblets of hippocras, the King made his way through the crowded room, and I saw him whisper in the ear of select individuals. He approached me and, hidden by the masses of people, slipped his arm about my waist, giving me a gentle squeeze. "Mistress Anne, meet us for dancing in the Queen's Apartments once we adjourn."

His lips brushed my ear as he spoke. I shivered with emotion and longing.

•

When the banquet had concluded and the sated guests dispersed, those singled out by His Grace headed to the Queen's Presence Chamber. Minstrels awaited, we assembled, the music began, and I was approached by Monsieur de Turenne. He inquired, "*Mademoiselle, vous parlez français, n'est-ce pas?*"

I replied with a curtsey and a sweet smile, "*Oui, monsieur, j'ai vécu en France!*" As we danced, I told him that I had been a member of the court of François, in the service of Queen Claude, and I had loved her very much. He seemed pleased, and we danced together several times that evening.

I knew Henry had kept close watch while I danced and conversed with the French ambassadors. He appeared satisfied to note the attention I received from them. Then, when the musicians had been successful getting every guest to the floor, the King and I partnered for several dances in a row. We delighted in being closely entwined while dancing the Volt, and the implication as we held each other was clear to us and us alone.

Or so we thought.

•

The following day was clamorous with a jousting tournament attended and loudly cheered by many enthusiastic spectators. In the evening, the new disguising house was introduced in all its glory, with a masque featuring roles for both Princess Mary and the King. The entire company then enjoyed music by the Royal Choir, and while they sang, sounding like a host of angels, the guests craned their necks to peer skyward and were entranced by the wondrous and sparkling images of heaven and earth on the ceiling; designed, decorated and painted by Master Holbein. Considering the new and lavish settings, the fascinating entertainment and the rarest and most tempting food and wines, it was no wonder that people spoke of it being an event not to be rivalled.

But such carefree revelry was not to last.

The delightful party came to an abrupt, horrible end when we were informed by messengers that an Imperial army - some twenty thousand German and Spanish troops led by the bold and brazen Charles, Duke of Bourbon, had invaded Rome. The Pope had been frantically transported to the safety of the Castel Sant'Angelo along with as many panicked Roman families as could gain access. According to the messengers' accounts, the situation became dire when the Duke was shot and killed by an enemy arquebus while scaling the city walls. Enraged at the loss of Bourbon, the brute foreign soldiery took swift and vicious revenge, running rampant through the city - murdering, raping and plundering, totally out of control.

In the following days, we heard the news that Emperor Charles V had not intended his troops to cause such devastation. But we were told that Rome lay littered with precious art and statuary which had been dragged into the streets, broken and smashed till it became refuse. The Tiber stank with bodies floating and bobbing downstream and the *palazzos* of the wealthy had been pillaged and destroyed. It cannot have been a proud moment for Katherine, hearing what disaster her nephew's army had wrought.

•

Henry and I supped together in his chamber one late April evening. We had not been alone since the joyous night several weeks prior when we had promised ourselves to each other. I was eager to be near to him, to touch him, and to talk with him privately. After we embraced for what seemed like forever, we finally sat at the table and shared wine and cheeses and fruit.

"Henry, I have thought continuously about our promise to each other. You feel the same way now as you did some weeks ago, do you not?" I looked at him with hopeful anticipation, tinged by a certain shyness. I had no idea whether or not his feelings had shifted and he would resume his request that I become his *mâitresse.*

"Of a certainty, Anne, I feel more strongly than ever that we are meant to be united, and I fully intend that to happen. I have wanted to talk with you because we did not speak of this when we last met. For some time now I have been ill at ease concerning the validity of my marriage to Katherine."

I leaned forward, genuinely surprised. "But how could that be, Your Grace? You and the Queen have been married for so many years."

"I have been reading, studying, and reflecting on the topic, almost incessantly. I pray, and my prayers seek a sign that I may know the truth. Time and again I ask why Katherine and I have not been granted the blessing of even one living son. It has troubled me for long - for many years - and as the Queen is now too old to bear children, the reason for this failure has at last become clear to me. God is angry with us – with me! I should not have married my brother's wife. The marriage was never a valid one in the eyes of the Lord God."

While I was flummoxed by this revelation, I did not doubt his sincerity. His expression was too grave; too full of regret and remorse to be misinterpreted.

He pushed his chair back and strode quickly across the room, picked up a Bible, and brought it back to the table. A ribbon marked a spot, and he opened the book to that page.

The passage he pointed to was in *Leviticus 20.21.* Written in Latin, it read '*If a man shall take his brother's wife, it is an impurity: he hath uncovered his brother's nakedness; they shall be childless.*'

I read along with him, and sank back in my chair, thoughtful. He continued. "Anne, there are plans underway to examine this premise in the courts of canon law. I have appointed Dr Richard Wolman, the Archdeacon of Sudbury, to gather evidence in support of my theory. And, along with the facts he has been assembling, tomorrow Cardinal Wolsey will commence a secret trial to assess the validity of my marriage."

"Henry!" I was astounded. The concept of an invalid marriage between the long-espoused King and Queen of England was almost too provocative to comprehend. If I found it radical, how would others in the Church and the realm view it?

A loathsome thought slithered to the fore. Through tensed lips, I asked, "Does the Cardinal know of us - of our promise?" I awaited Henry's response with dread. If that serpent was to know about our plans – surmise my happiness - he would subvert them using any conceivable method, I was convinced.

"No, he does not. And I feel it best we keep our betrothal secret between us for now. I have yet to inform Katherine of my views, and what that will mean for her," he said quietly.

I breathed a sigh of relief. "I agree fully, Your Grace. It is sure to be an extremely difficult message for the Queen to hear and accept. When do you intend to tell her?" I asked uneasily, thinking how zealously the court gossips would latch onto the rumour of a secret trial and spread the news far and wide.

"I will tell her within a few weeks, at latest," he said, and by his tone I could tell it was a task he dreaded and would put off as long as he could.

I took his arm as we walked his private hallway to exit the palace and enjoy the spring evening in his Privy Garden. "It will be a difficult conversation; that is certain. But," I gave him a reassuring squeeze, "the rationale you state is solid and underlined by Scripture. I know you will be eloquent and compassionate, and I hope and believe that she will understand and agree."

I confess to saying this while knowing, in my heart of hearts, that under no circumstance would she offer her agreement and consent.

•

Oh, how I wanted to tell my mother that I was betrothed! Yet I had promised Henry I would not, and felt honour-bound to keep my promise. I hoped once Katherine was informed, he would grant me permission to at least tell Mother. The ladies who waited on the Queen were clearly aware that the King had a particular affection for me, but beyond that no one, I believe, suspected any deeper relationship. Nevertheless, it was proving ever more difficult to maintain an air of normalcy as I went about my duties attending to Katherine, all the while wondering what she knew. I suspected she believed I might be another occasional mistress of Henry's, granting him favours when he asked. The days passed, and I waited to hear from Henry about what had transpired when he told Katherine. Or I thought that perhaps I might detect some change in her attitude once the blow had been delivered: the bitterly unwelcome news of their marriage's nullity.

Finally, in the first week of June, Henry sent for me. We rode out together in the soft azure afternoon, at first accompanied by others but soon after that, when Sir Nicholas Carew led the rest of the party ahead, Henry and I lagged behind and rode in tandem, close enough to talk easily, clasping each other's hand.

"How beautiful you are in the sunshine, sweetheart," he said with a look of longing. "See, your hair is almost the colour of copper when the sun hits it just a certain way." And he leaned across to brush a strand from my face. He regarded me without saying anything for a moment or two - and then the news I had been so anxiously awaiting came. He told me he had visited Katherine and had informed her he was seeking a divorce.

My stomach churned. I swallowed hard, then calmly asked, "And how did she respond, Your Majesty?"

Henry looked away. "Not well, I fear. She was utterly shocked and began to cry. In her disbelief, she accused me of never having loved her … but worse, Anne, she claimed that the passage in the Scriptures was invalid as far as she and I were concerned because she had never fully known Arthur. Katherine's contention that the marriage was never consummated provides her with all the ammunition she believes she needs to disprove me."

I looked at him incredulously. "And she expects all and sundry to believe they never knew each other as husband and wife?" I asked.

"Apparently, yes," his voice revealed his dismay. "Furthermore, the trial I had requested has been suspended."

"On what grounds?" I asked sharply; forgetting my place and apprehensive of what I might next hear.

"Because the Cardinal feels the case is so complex, and the verity of consummation so difficult to prove, that he has referred it to a panel of theologians and lawyers for their review," Henry replied somewhat forlornly.

His disappointment was evident. As for me, I seethed with resentment. God's eyes, I would have known better than to trust Wolsey with this matter! Yet it was not my decision to make, so with great difficulty, I summoned her image in my mind's eye, and heard the wise Marguerite's voice utter a subtle *tsk tsk,* which I knew meant to bite my tongue. I forcefully clamped down on the inside of my cheek and kept silent.

"Anne, I leave on progress as soon as we are packed and ready. Katherine will accompany me, as she always has done. I would rather not provoke her animosity right now, so I believe it is wise for you to go to Hever, and trust in me to advance our issue with all required attention and speed. By August, I intend to stay at the Palace of Beaulieu, in Essex. I shall send Katherine back to Greenwich then, and would like you to join me after that. Will you do that?"

I reached out and touched his cheek with a soft sigh.

"Of course, I will, Henry," I said.

The thought of the two of them, together on summer progress, rankled. Katherine would have a perfect opportunity to ingratiate herself with her husband, while I had no recourse but to remain in Kent, alone. I could only pray that time and distance would not affect his feelings for me.

Hever
June 1527

I ARRIVED HOME ON 8 June. The manor's gardens were unfurling in all their resplendence. The roses, oversized blossoms nodding in colours ranging from white and the softest blush pink to the deepest velvety crimson, were fantastic that year, and when walking in the arbour, the heavy fragrance suffused one's very soul. The peonies bordering the walkways were still in bloom and bestowed upon the ancient brick walls of the garden a drooping, ruffled pink beauty. But my favourite flower called me to ramble in the woods adjoining the estate. Masses of bluebells carpeted the ground in the dappled shade, filling the air with their scent, and creating a deep blue cloister which stretched on and ever onwards.

The weeks passed, and the summer turned hot and dry. I was restless, and instead of enjoying the long days as I usually did, I spent too much time indoors, reading and writing, but mostly missing Henry.

July had commenced and still I had not received any specific instruction about joining him at Beaulieu, and I wondered if he'd even remembered. I certainly could not just show up there, even though I knew it well. The palace once called New Hall had belonged to my paternal grandmother, Lady Margaret Butler, and its ownership then passed to my father. Father sold the big estate to the King eleven years ago, while I was away in France. Henry had carried out a complete refurbishment of the old but beautiful buildings, and I wondered what it now looked like.

Much to my cheer, on a suffocating July afternoon, a royal courier arrived in the manor courtyard with a parchment, a package and - joy of joys! - a message for me. I was requested by His Majesty, the King of England, to arrive at Beaulieu Palace on the 24th day of this month, and was informed we would remain there or in the local environs until we returned to court in September. I whispered a prayer of thanks heavenward that a message had finally arrived and returned to my room to open the package. Fumbling in my anxious haste, I slid the thin parchment from its covering. The now familiar writing, with the lines crowding each other, pressing toward the top of the page, greeted me.

Ma Mestres et Amye, it began … My Mistress and Friend,

> My heart and I surrender ourselves into your hands, beseeching you to hold us commended to your favour, and that by absence your affection to us may not be lessened: for it were a great pity to increase our pain, of which absence produces enough and more than I could ever have thought could be felt, reminding us of a point in astronomy which is this: the longer the days are, the more distant is the sun, and nevertheless the hotter; so it is avec nos amours - with our love, for by absence we are kept a distance from one another, and yet it retains it fervor, at least on my side: I hope the like on yours, assuring you that on my part the pain of absence is already too great for me: and when I think of the increase of that which I am forced to suffer, it would be almost intolerable, but for the firm hope I have of your unchangeable affection

> for me: and to remind you of this sometimes, and seeing that I cannot be personally present with you, I now send you the nearest thing I can to that, namely, my picture set in a bracelet, with the whole of the device, which you already know, wishing myself in their place, if it should please you. This is from the hand of your loyal servant and friend,
>
> H.R.

The tender, transparent message brought me near to tears. How I missed him! I tugged at the white lambskin in which the package was wrapped. A red satin box, long and slender, held a delicate bracelet of finely wrought gold links, and attached to the bracelet by a gold clasp was a locket. The locket smoothly clicked open to reveal a striking portrait of Henry against a royal blue background. The likeness was remarkable. It captured his essence, with a temporarily stern expression which was about to break into that special grin, his cheeks rosy and his handsome visage set off by a black velvet cap. The portrait must have been painted by Master Lucas Horenbolte, the miniaturist new to the King's court. No one else known to the court could create such masterful likenesses in tiny paintings. I gazed at the face for a while, pining for its owner, then turned the gold locket over in my hands. Artfully engraved there were the entwined initials H and A. Henry and Anne. I sat bolt upright in astonishment, being only accustomed to seeing the official cipher: HK I inspected the monogram more closely. There was no question, HA looked infinitely better!

•

The remaining weeks at home were spent preparing for my trip. I ordered colourful new fabrics, silks, lawns, and sarcenets, while putting numerous dressmakers and seamstresses to work, creating a wardrobe of new summer gowns and riding clothes. My mother and I made plans to meet at court upon our return from Essex, once I knew where the King and his courtiers would be spending the autumn. I was thrilled that she would be nigh, for I suspected I would need a confidante more than ever.

Beaulieu
August 1527

CHARITY'S MOUTH FORMED a perfect "O", with eyes equally wide as we approached the massive brick gatehouse to the reconstructed New Hall, or Beaulieu Palace. Certainly she had never seen anything comparable, and I don't believe I had, either. It was gigantic; imposing in every aspect, and formed an appropriate setting for what was to come once its threshold had been crossed.

I rode, along with Charity and a bevy of the King's guards and stewards, through the archway of the gatehouse. As we entered the estate beneath its shadow, I perceived quite clearly that my life would never again be the same.

In the elegantly appointed main courtyard, water splashed from marble fountains and flowers and vines tumbled from huge urns. We were relieved of our horses by stablehands, and the house steward led me to my apartments. No longer did I have merely the use of a bedchamber and nearby garderobe. I was to be accommodated in an apartment suite comprising a lovely sitting room, a large privy chamber with a beautiful tester bed, and my own *bayne*, or bath. Master Steward informed me that, once I had taken the opportunity to refresh myself after the hot and dusty journey, I was requested to join the King and others in the King's presence chamber for supper.

Can I possibly express how delightful it was to have a private room in which I could bathe and take care of my *toilette*? It was a luxury I would become accustomed to quickly. I relaxed in my bath while Charity unpacked my clothes, and laid out a gown of pale yellow silk. My pleasurable bath complete, I made some haste, not wanting to keep the King waiting. I now smelt refreshed, and my mood matched the sun-coloured, lightweight gown.

With a carefully controlled eagerness, I entered the presence chamber, whereupon the King rose from his chair, hurried to my side and kissed me warmly before leading me across the room to greet the other guests. My uncle, Thomas Howard, Duke of Norfolk, was the first to approach and kiss my hand. Behind him, I was somewhat surprised to see his wife, Elizabeth Stafford. My mother told me they were exceedingly unhappy together, and I was not surprised. I had never found Lady Elizabeth to my liking. It seemed to me that her only talent was ingratiating herself to the Queen. Henry Courtenay, Marquis of Exeter, Henry's first cousin, and his wife, Gertrude, greeted me courteously. John de Vere, the Earl of Oxford, bowed in acknowledgement, and I recognized the Earl as having been one of the esquires who had stood guard in Henry's chamber the first night we supped alone together. I was introduced to Henry Bourchier, the Earl of Essex, and Thomas Manners, the Earl of Rutland. A polite acknowledgement was offered by Charles Brandon, the Duke of Suffolk, and, standing behind the others, I saw my father beaming proudly. There was a palpable air of deference directed toward me which I found quite curious. I wondered what the King had told them before my arrival.

We were seated, and Suffolk was adjacent to me. He turned and said, "Mistress Anne, it truly is our pleasure to welcome you to the gathering here at Beaulieu. I hope you are looking forward to some lively hunting and other sport during your stay."

"I most certainly am, my Lord. I know that the hunting grounds surrounding the estate are excellent. And I have heard that the King has just completed construction of a tennis play on the site. I look forward to seeing some skilful displays! So, do you think there will be a chance that you will be able to prevail over His Grace? I know the two of you are mighty rivals at tennis …" I looked at him steadily, but did little to hide a sly smile, "as well as at other endeavours?"

He chuckled with good-natured amusement and replied, "I can tell you this much - I will give the matches my all, Mistress. Though it is never an easy business, nor often a wise one, to outplay the mighty Henry!"

As we supped and conversed, the King stood. He raised his silver cup and announced, "I would like to propose a toast to our delightful and very accomplished guest, Mistress Boleyn. I welcome her with great affection and respect for her skills on the hunt field, the card table, the dance floor, and the many other goodly pastimes we will engage in while staying at this magnificent estate. All raise your cups!"

I nodded a slightly abashed thanks to the King. And all present toasted me.

"As most of you know," the King continued, "there is a further reason you have all been invited to this gathering. You are among my closest friends and most trusted companions. As such, you have been made privy to my urgent need to obtain the dissolution of my marriage to Katherine. While some efforts are underway, they have so far proved inconsequential and ineffective. I wish to ask all of you to work with me in determining the best way forward with this, my confidential matter, to achieve the result I require in the shortest time possible."

He met each individual's gaze one by one and was answered with expressions in accord with his – determined and assured.

With a start, I realized who was notably absent from the company. Cardinal Wolsey was at that very moment on assignment in France, and not privy to this gathering. As I studied the faces both up and down the supperboard, my understanding grew. It was evident that most, if not all of those present harboured a distinct dislike for Wolsey and how his power and wealth had corrupted the office of Lord Chancellor. This promised to be quite an interesting visit, indeed!

The remainder of the meal was punctuated with laughter and companionship as the guests anticipated a working holiday among close friends. Before any others had excused themselves, and feeling quite tired from my journey, I made my apologies and stood to retire, to a disappointed look from the King.

The next morning a fresh, pearly mist filled the stable yard as we gathered for the hunt. Henry had a beautiful sorrel mare saddled and ready for me. She was an Arab–Barbary cross recently imported from Italy, and she proved a dream in the hunting field, impeccably behaved and agile. By late morning, the mist had burned off, and the sun lit the rolling green hills. We had quite a civilized ride, and even though we did not overtake our quarry, enjoyed a wonderful afternoon. Late in the day, as we returned home, Henry asked if I would join him privately for supper. I agreed to, most gladly.

Charity helped me select my apparel for the evening: a bright green satin gown, the dramatic green sleeves set off by gold embroidery, with a thin double chain of gold to drape around my neck

I could not wait to spend time alone with Henry, and as soon as I was ready, I hurried to his chambers. It was a relief to have a respite from the formality of court, and following a discreet knock at his door by the house steward, I was inside, we were alone and I was finally in his arms. Our kisses were divine, and clearly conveyed our yearning for one another. The feeling of being enfolded in such a strong, protective embrace was something I had not experienced before, and it felt as if that was where I was meant to be. When we eventually drew apart,

Henry had me sit on a bench near the window. He went to an ornately carved chest and withdrew a small box of crimson velvet. He came back, sat beside me, and handed me the box. My fingers quivered as I held it, and he said gently, "Open it, Anne."

Ever so slowly I lifted the lid, and as I did so, Henry slid to his knee on the floor before me. Now we were face to face, and I saw that his eyes were earnest and full of love. Quietly he said words which touched my soul and filled me with joy – words I had thought never to hear from a man I loved - and most surely never from the King of England.

"Anne Boleyn," he whispered. "I humbly ask if you will be my wife. I will love you and cherish you with all that I am, and all that I have, forever, if you will but give your consent."

Through a blur of tears, I saw, resting in its box, a magnificent emerald ring of a size and brilliance I had never imagined existed.

He placed the ring on the third finger of my right hand, and, trembling, I looked directly into his eyes and replied, "Henry Tudor, I will be your wife. I promise to be your loving, loyal and trustworthy wife - as long as God allows me life and breath."

And I threw my arms about him again and kissed him with every ounce of the passion I felt.

•

What a magical evening we had together! Never had I envisioned a betrothal as enchanting as mine was, even though it was secret. When I finally left Henry's apartments later that evening to return to my chambers, I was flush with happiness. I did spend some considerable time, once by myself, admiring the beauteous ring, and how well it looked on my slender hand.

The very next day Henry called a council meeting of the guests after the morning meal. Not one to waste a precious moment, he provided an account to everyone concerning the actions which had already taken place in the quest to nullify his marriage. He then opened the floor for discussion about the existing plan conceived by Cardinal Wolsey, and its merits - or lack thereof. It quickly became all too apparent that Wolsey himself had dedicated very little time to the matter, and had, instead, passed off the fact-gathering, planning and execution to Dr Stephen Gardiner, his Secretary. Henry fumed, having been previously unaware of this fact, and paced back and forth in agitation. He decided to have Sir William Knight, his personal secretary, take dictation for a letter, and wrote to Wolsey demanding that Gardiner appear for questioning. A courier was then summoned to deliver the letter promptly to Wolsey in Paris. As the meeting continued it became increasingly clear that the individuals in the room on that morning held little respect or friendship for the Cardinal.

As for me, again I invoked the wisdom of Marguerite and kept my council, holding my tongue and my opinion for the present.

•

We enjoyed a magnificent sojourn in Essex that August. The dry and dusty heat of July had yielded to more temperate, yet still sunny weather. Frequent, short bouts of showers turned the landscape brilliantly green once again, and we spent almost all our waking hours outdoors. Henry and I both particularly enjoyed activities which took place outside and we were in high spirits when we were able to spend a good part of each day sporting. But I think my favourite thing to do in those early weeks following our secret betrothal was to walk with Henry and our greyhounds through the verdant, blue-green woods on the estate. It was during those strolls, nurtured by the cool and quiet of the forest, that we spoke of many things, planned our future together, and deepened our relationship with mutual respect.

One afternoon several of us had returned from a long and strenuous hunt, and we were filthy and ravenous. We agreed to meet for an early supper after we had washed and prepared for an evening of singing and dancing.

I revelled in the bliss of my private *bayne,* and used Marseilles-made olive oil soap scented with lavender to wash, including my hair. The weather was so fine, even in the late afternoon, that once combed out, it dried quickly in the warm air. In the more relaxed surroundings of court in August, personal preparations were much less involved, and I loved it. I dressed in a gossamer gown of pale blue lawn with sleeves that felt loose and comfortable. My small blue French hood was simple, and my hair tumbled free beneath it. The intimacy of the occasion, and indeed of the company, permitted us to dress much more informally, and what a welcome change it provided for those few weeks of summer. My cheeks were by now so naturally rosy that I needed no rouge. That evening, I wore one piece of jewellery only: my emerald ring. It commanded attention against the cool hue of my gown and was all the more pronounced by the absence of another adornment. It was simply magnificent, set in the finest yellow gold, flanked by two diamonds, and of a size which covered my finger from knuckle to hand. It was the most entrancing, alluring deep green, and it must have cost a fortune. When I glanced down and caught its gleam, I felt about to burst with pride.

After a most agreeable supper of roasted capon, baked sturgeon, and *salatt* of lettuces, spinach, and beetroot grown in the estate gardens, we took up various instruments to begin the music. I was surprised to learn how many of our company had talent at playing one or more instruments. For example, Lord Oxford, John de Vere, proved excellent on the recorder while Brandon, Lord Suffolk, showed himself able to beat the tambour as well as any travelling minstrel! Gertrude, Lady Exeter, had a lovely singing voice and announced that she, Oxford, and Suffolk wished to perform a new tune, the lyrics of which were composed by Will Somers, the King's fool.

I knew Somers was very clever at reciting witticisms but did not know that he was a composer of songs as well. The piece was called *The Hunt Is Up*, which seemed quite fitting for today. They began a ramping melody, with the tambour maintaining a cadence which made everyone want to tap their foot along as Lady Gertrude sang:

The hunt is up! the hunt is up
And it is well-nigh day:
And Harry our king is gone hunting
To bring his deer to bay.

The east is bright with morning light,
And darkness it is fled,
And the merry horn wakes up the morn
To leave his idle bed.

Behold the skies with golden dyes,
Are glowing all around:
The grass is green, and so are the treen
All laughing at the sound.

The horses snort to be at the sport
The dogs are running free
The woods rejoice at the merry noise
Of hey tantara tee ree!

The sun is glad to see us clad
All in our lusty green,
And smiles in the sky as he riseth high
To see and to be seen.

Oh, how we all laughed and clapped and cheered when they finished and, though we danced and sang for the rest of the evening, it was that tune which ran through my head all the next day.

•

There was a cluster of us who met on a daily basis to discuss the King's situation, and how we might best plan for the required outcome. I attended these meetings, although it was never openly stated that Henry and I were betrothed and intended to marry as soon as his divorce from Katherine was finalized. It soon became evident, however, that everyone present during the August gathering surmised the truth.

We received a response from the Cardinal earnestly refuting Henry's assertions; describing in detail the great flurry of activity which he claimed was underway in support of the King's case. I was not to be fooled. On hearing the letter read aloud, his contrivance was as plain as his long beak of a nose. Henry recognized the same, I believe, although I noticed that as soon as the group began to claim Wolsey's deficiencies and his unsuitability to direct the matter, the King proved most loath to denounce the man. Although clearly unhappy about his chancellor's negligence, whenever others commented upon the lack of attention Wolsey paid to matters important to the King, Henry visibly disengaged from the conversation, sometimes rising from his chair and wandering about the room fitfully. I wondered why.

Later that same day, I walked and talked with my father in the gardens. I recalled, with some contrition it must be said, the terse conversation he and I had shared some months ago in the gardens at Hever; the one in which I denied any involvement with the King, and testily informed Father that *I* would decide my matrimonial fate. We settled in an alcove, and Father turned to me and said, "Anne, I am aware of the promise between you and His Grace."

In complete astonishment, I asked, "How is that, Father? Henry and I agreed to keep the news private!"

"He is the King, sovereign of us both, but that does not exempt him from the courtesy of involving his beloved's father in hopes and plans for a betrothal. He sought my approval before he ever spoke with you."

Apparently, there was much yet for me to learn about my intended. By God's eyes, he was a study in contradiction! Powerful and utterly commanding, yet tender and sentimental; quick to raise a temper, but very sensitive and forgiving. I loved him all the more for it.

"I assume, then, you approve of this match! If I may ask, Father, why do you believe the King to be so tolerant of Wolsey's foibles? We can all see how frustrated he is with the obvious mishandling of the nullity suit. I find it hard to justify. If the bloated Cardinal were *my* chancellor, and I were to find that he gave a matter important to me such short shrift, he would have been dealt a vicious tongue-lashing. And he would quickly find himself lighter of a great deal of his cherished wealth!"

"Do I approve? My Anne, the fact that the King reveres and loves you so gives me great joy. I am made happier still by your obvious return of those feelings. I can picture a bright hereafter for you and the King, and the creation of a noble dynasty for the Boleyns. But make no mistake, Daughter: there are challenges ahead. It is an exacting path you must walk, fraught with peril - and the rest of us with you. You must keep your wits about you at all times, Anne. There will be many, both male and female, who will become insane with jealousy over your position and influence with Henry. It will be difficult to know whom to trust. Your mother and I are, and will be, there for you always, but take care in selecting others for sharing confidences. And you must learn to read the King as you would a very familiar book. His grand qualities are many, but he is mercurial, and his mood can change like the wind."

I nodded in agreement, but swallowed hard, thinking more circumspectly about my position.

My father continued, "In response to your question about Wolsey, Daughter, keep in mind the extent of his influence over the King. The Cardinal has ever been a mentor, servant, assistant, and in a way, a father figure. He was at court during the King's father's reign and was well in place as a key figure when Henry's father died, and young Henry ascended the throne in 1509 as but a lad. They have been together for some eighteen years, and, Henry has come to depend on Wolsey almost like a second father."

"But, do you not see how Wolsey plies the King to his advantage?" I asked.

"Of course, I do! As do many others who are close to His Grace. But such a revelation would fall on deaf ears, and most likely incite wrath in rebuke. That is unless the King sees it clearly for himself. Do not overstep your bounds with this, Anne. You best be patient and allow Wolsey to place the rope around his own neck."

Intuitively, I felt that outcome unlikely: Henry may never be completely aware of how subtly the Cardinal played him. It did not appear to me that Henry realized just how cleverly Wolsey had learned to serve his own needs and desires, and all through the *largesse* of the King. But I resolved to allow the situation unfold as it would.

Henry replied to the letter, graciously wishing the Cardinal well, and thanking him profusely for the good work he was doing, both on his Matter, and for managing the increasingly tricky diplomacy between France and the Empire, on England's behalf. The praise was deceptive; our meeting then resumed, devising the replacement of Wolsey in directing the King's Matter.

•

Those late summer days flew by, but I did my best to enjoy each one and keep it tucked safely in my memory. The King and I delighted in each other's company.

We had just finished dinner when Henry beckoned. "Anne, come with me. I have a surprise for you."

I followed him through the door and around the north side of the building, across the expansive lawns until we reached the mews where the royal falcons were housed. Henry disappeared inside for a moment and emerged with a small leather-wrapped parcel which he presented to me. Curiously, I eased the drawstring of the pouch and withdrew a fine pair of white leather gloves, embroidered in gold and lined with velvet. In the packet also was a white doeskin hawk's hood, embellished in gold. I glanced at Henry uncertainly, not knowing quite what he expected me to say. Excitedly he ducked inside once more, and, after a moment, reappeared with a beautiful grey bird on his gloved hand. "This peregrine falcon is for you, Anne, so we may go hawking together."

"Oh, Your Grace!" I dropped into a curtsey. "I thank you with all my heart. What a beautiful creature - and such a thoughtful gift! But … I am not very skilled at hawking, and wish you would teach me. Will you?"

Henry replied, "Of course, *Mademoiselle*. There are not many sports, it seems, in which you require much instruction. But I do indeed relish the opportunity to be the only man to instruct you in any sport we have yet to play!"

And he gave me a bold wink as we proceeded to the fields with the hawk.

•

Oh, I will say this - it was not easy resisting Henry. During that special time, with less staff about and court protocol eased, and in Katherine's absence, he and I spent much private time together. We were fervent about one another. Our kisses were perfection, and I cannot express how much I longed to lay with him, body to body, unfettered by clothing. I knew, though, that unless my head prevailed, all would be lost. So using all of the cunning and discipline I could muster, somehow, I managed to escape his lustful embraces before I lost all composure and completely surrendered. I hoped against hope that, wondrously, the divorce would be attained. But I remained too much a realist to delude myself with the belief that it would. I knew restraint was going to be required, but, God's eyes! Over that lush summer break, I wanted to release all self-control and live passionately! I knew, also, that I had better contrive a plan by which I could be close to Henry in private without compromising my virginity and, ultimately, the chance to bear his child – his son - within the confines of marriage.

As day followed day, I learned a great deal by having the uncommon opportunity to watch the King and some of his chief courtiers at work. What perplexed me most was the nature of their interaction. It was soon apparent that Henry vacillated between acting the all-powerful commander and a man who craved validation in his role. As we sought the ideal plan to convince Pope Clement to allow Henry a divorce from Katherine to marry again, I silently wondered why Henry was so wanting of approval. Most often, he desired corroboration from his council members and preferred not to stand alone in his decision-making. And he was anxious – almost desperate – for the Pope's assent in this situation. I knew his strongly entrenched Catholic roots drove him to seek the Church's approval, but so were we all brought up as Catholics in a Church-dominated world. More and more I felt that the paradox of ultimate authority between the Church and the monarchy was reinforced unnecessarily by the Vatican. It seemed to me that the King of England, whose motto was *Dieu et Mon Droit*, God and My Right, should simply assert that it was his God–given right to do what was best for the future of his realm.

But then, I was a mere woman …

•

We were to depart Beaulieu the next day. I was sorry to leave because it had been a time of closeness between Henry and me, with that delightful informality that I would much miss when we all returned to court. Resulting from the discussions, the decision was taken that Dr William Knight, the King's secretary, would be sent to Rome with direct instructions from Henry, instead of receiving them from the Cardinal. I felt more satisfied with this approach, which effectively removed Wolsey from the subsequent negotiations. I could only imagine - indeed, relish - the thought of Wolsey's chagrin when he learned of this dissolution of his authority!

I remained cautiously hopeful that Dr Knight would have some success on his mission to the Vatican. As a counterthrust to that strategy, though, Queen Katherine had implored her nephew, the Emperor Charles, to help in what she deemed a disgraceful affront to her integrity and her position as Henry's rightful wife.

This, in its turn, represented a considerable setback to our plans, particularly as Pope Clement, still imprisoned and with Rome remaining in turmoil at the hands of Charles, was unlikely to align himself with Henry and thereby risk angering both Charles and his aunt.

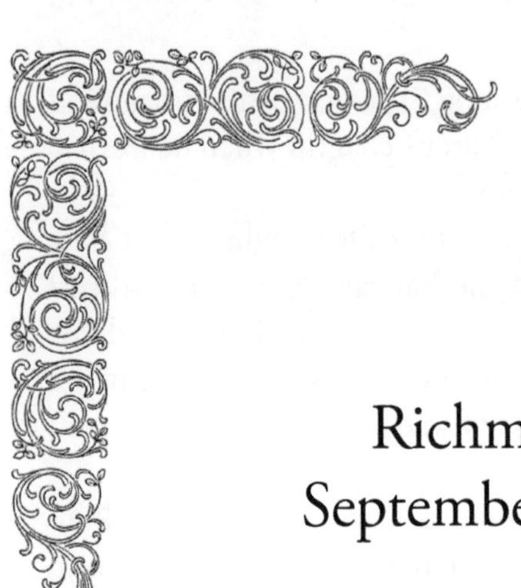

Richmond
September 1527

I TRAVELLED WITH MY father and a few other members of the Beaulieu company to Richmond, where Henry intended to hold court for the coming month or two. Katherine would not join him for a few weeks yet, so I looked forward to spending what time with him I could. We hunted and hawked, played games of cards and chance, and discussed what had commonly become known as his 'Great Matter'. We were anxious to have Dr Knight reach his destination in Rome and make positive impact on the King's behalf. Henry had received another letter from Cardinal Wolsey, who was plainly distraught about his waning position of control. The letter was an entreaty to his King for renewed confidence in his commitment and abilities, and I could tell, had been laboured over by Wolsey to create the desired result.

As we supped in Henry's chambers one evening, I ventured to ask, "Do you feel the Cardinal's influence and standing with the Pope are sufficient to gain the end you desire, Henry?"

He replied without hesitation. "No, I am not certain of that at all. I will have to follow the situation with great vigilance. God's blood! He surely should have influence and access after all the time and money he has spent there!"

I replied, "I am but an inexperienced woman, Your Grace, and cannot advise you on matters I know nothing about, but at the least I will provide all the encouragement I can, and be a support to you whenever possible."

The King turned to look at me in disbelief, then roared a mighty laugh as only Henry could. "You …? You are anything but an inexperienced woman, my Mistress Anne! Your intrinsic knowledge could be well deployed to rule nations! I would not want to go head to head with you on any matter. No, my dear, I both solicit and respect your views."

Oh, when I was with Henry, he made me feel as if I could accomplish anything - anything at all. At that moment, I happily envisioned us as a loving royal couple, married for many long years, surrounded by our children. Our sons!

•

On 30 September, Cardinal Wolsey arrived at Richmond upon the King's command. Henry and I were in the music room in the late afternoon, working together on a new composition. An esquire announced a messenger, and the young man entered and stood before us, sodden from his journey in the steady rain, and dripping freely on the Turkish carpet.

"Your Majesty," he said, bowing low. "I am sent by Cardinal Wolsey, who wishes to meet with you to provide you a report of his travels. The Cardinal wishes to be advised of the hour at which he should report to Your Grace's privy chamber for the meeting."

Upon hearing the wording of the message, my ire rose. I was quick – perhaps too quick - but could not restrain myself.

"You may remind the Cardinal," I snapped succinctly to the messenger, who blinked at me incredulously, but had the sense to keep his tongue – hence possibly his head – "that no one joins the King in his privy chambers unless expressly invited." With that I smiled and extended my arm graciously to encompass the King, saying, "His Grace the Cardinal shall report here where the King be already," as if it were the most obvious thing in the world. The messenger peered uneasily at Henry for some sign of confirmation that these orders were, in fact, valid, whereupon Henry, straight-faced, acknowledged agreement with an emphatic nod. The already-flustered messenger thanked the King, then, uncertain of what was expected of him in this unusual situation, afforded me a respectful bow and hastily retreated from the room.

I quickly placed my hand on Henry's arm.

"Henry, I am most sorry! I should not have jumped in as I did. But you must know how much it irks me when the Cardinal – when *anyone*, for that matter - presumes to tell you what you should do!"

Admittedly, it did not occur to me that perhaps I had just committed the selfsame offence.

I gave Henry an apologetic look … then started giggling uncontrollably. "I am sure that poor messenger had no idea at all what was happening, or from whom he should receive his orders. His head was spinning to and fro as if watching a play of tennis, trying to work it out!"

Henry chortled along with me. "Your invective was well worded, sweetheart. I am sure I would have said mostly the same thing. That is, had I been given the chance…" He raised an eyebrow in my direction. We burst into laughter together. My Henry was beginning to learn his betrothed was no wilting flower. "On the contrary, I am glad we have made a start at having you recognized as someone of great importance to me, even if at the expense of a soaking young page!" And he continued to chuckle good-naturedly.

Shortly after that, a crier heralded the Cardinal's arrival, and following a nod from Henry, Wolsey entered the chamber. At a glance, I could see he did not look well. His skin was pasty, and his face and hands appeared puffed and swollen. He lumbered over to Henry, bowing as low and deferentially as he could manage - only raising himself with difficulty when Henry spoke his name.

"My dear Thomas, how very good to see you again," Henry began kindly while I looked on pleasantly from my position at Henry's side.

The Cardinal's response came only after a perceptible hesitation: preoccupied as he'd so often been in the past, with looking down his sharp nose at me. This time, however, his expression was not that of haughty superiority. With a start, I recognized it.

It was the look of fear.

•

For several more weeks, we remained at Richmond, where Henry and I continued to enjoy competing: at bowls when the weather permitted or, when it did not, at shovel-board or cards. I never held back and put all I could into each game. I knew he loved that about me; our sport invariably providing us with great fun and jollity. At times, we wagered on the outcomes of our games.

Of course, I knew the supreme wager Henry longed to make above any other, but I did my best to redirect him.

But inevitably the day came when it was decided that Henry and the court would go to Greenwich, and there spend the remainder of the autumn and the Christmas season. Katherine would be joining him there, and I dreaded having any contact with her. For that reason, and because Henry and I felt it would be best for me to remain out of immediate view while we waited for a hopefully positive answer from Rome, I planned to retreat to Hever.

On our final evening together, I determined I would leave Henry with an image of me at my best. I donned a gown of russet velvet, beautifully accented with emerald green flowing satin sleeves. My headpiece was of gold tissue covering a crescent-shaped hood and adorned with several stones of topaz. On this evening, I wore a long, delicate golden chain about my neck, from which hung a sizable topaz. My hair was brushed straight and silken, and my complexion positively glowed. I added extra kohl to my eyes and lashes, planning to adopt a dark and mysterious look. I had smoothed my hands with oil, and buffed my nails earlier in the day, and now my emerald ring was eye-catching with the deep green satin of the sleeves. I added scent, feeling melancholy that this was the last time I would prepare myself to see my beloved for a while.

Henry's stare as he watched me enter the chamber made my heart ache with love for him. His expression was one of rapture and, as his gaze travelled my length from head to toe, his adoration was plain. My happiness at being by his side was mitigated by the knowledge that we must separate. I felt a vicious prodding of resentment against Katherine, wondering why she could not simply accept that her husband was hers no longer, obey him as she had once promised to do, and retire quietly to some distant abbey. But even that thought was banished as Henry gathered me in his arms and gently traced my lips with his finger, then kissed me ardently and with great emotion.

Hever
November 1527

MOTHER AND I passed the remainder of the autumn together at Hever, with an occasional visit from my sister Mary and her two children, little Catherine and baby Henry. It was a welcome diversion, their coming to stay, since I loved caring for and playing with my niece and little nephew. Oh, how such vicarious joy made me long for children of my own.

The weather, already dismal, became progressively colder, much more so than was typical for late November. I did my share of pining and sulking, I'm sorry to admit, but it was difficult being apart from Henry after we had spent every day in each other's company. I missed him mightily and thought of him constantly. How much I concurred with the painful truth in the motto '*Always toward absent lovers love's tide stronger flows.*' So I bore my heartache with conviction.

The separation also precluded me from attending a grand event held at Greenwich in mid-November - Henry's investiture in the French Order of St Michel. This, and François' equivalent initiation into the English Order of the Garter, further sealed the alliance between the two monarchs. It was celebrated by a tournament, a grand banquet, and masque at the banqueting and disguising houses at Greenwich, and, as was Henry's custom, no expense was spared to mark this event in grand style. I desperately wished I had been there.

In Kent, we made merry as best we could at Christmas, but it was so bitterly cold that we even limited the number of rooms we used in the house to conserve wood and maximize heat. On the day following Christmas, a courier arrived, practically frozen, with a package for me from His Majesty the King. While the pathetic, shivering man sat by the fire, eating and warming himself to prepare for the return trip to Greenwich, I ran to my chamber to compose a short message to be sent along in reply. I scribbled a note of thanks for His Grace's kindness in thinking of me and promised to compose a longer letter on the morrow.

Once the messenger was sufficiently revived to be sent back out into the grey, frozen landscape, back to my chamber I went and settled myself next to the hearth to open the parcel. I peeked inside the leather pouch to find a long narrow box of deep green velvet, tied with a scarlet riband. I held my breath as I untied the riband and opened the box to reveal a breathtaking bracelet of some twenty-five diamonds, large and clear, set in gleaming silver. Looking at it in disbelief, I did not know whether to laugh or cry! Also inside the leather bag was a small scroll of parchment. Unrolling it, Henry's strong script greeted me. It merely said:

To be worn by my dearest love, the most beautiful woman in the world.

I missed him so very much, and I longed to be his wife.

I found it terribly hard to be patient: to wait passively to hear some news of what was happening in Rome, when instead I wanted to be planning my wedding celebration and *trousseau.* It was all too frustrating to learn finally that the efforts of Dr Knight had not been as significant as we had hoped. I now knew that I would have to stay ever more closely in touch with how this campaign was being waged if I were to look forward to a successful outcome and any hope of becoming a bride.

It seemed Henry next intended to send Stephen Gardiner, Wolsey's secretary, along with Edward Foxe, Bishop of Hereford, to Rome with a new strategy to convince Pope Clement that his marriage was unsanctioned by God. This I knew because Henry had written me a letter in which he described the mission of Foxe and Gardiner, painted in a very positive, hopeful light. In fact, to keep me fully briefed, he had them deliver the letter to me in person at Hever before they set out for Rome. While the two statesmen waited, I carefully read Henry's personal assurances that everything possible was being done to move the matter toward a favourable conclusion.

•

Sitting as close as we safely could next to a sparking fire, my mother said to me one evening, "Anne, as often as we have talked about your hope and plan to marry the King once he is awarded a divorce from Katherine, we have never discussed the fact that the marriage would make you Queen Consort."

She did not look up from the tiny stitches she was making to seam a linen shirt for my father. She hesitated for a few minutes, then stopped her needlework and fixed her direct gaze on me. "Well, what think you on that? Is it the hope of being Queen which motivates your desire to marry Henry?"

I put down the embroidery I was working on and returned her uncompromising look.

"Mother, you are the only person in the world to whom I could say this with the chance it would be believed. A crown is not my reason for wanting this marriage, though I am no fool and know full well what it would mean for the Bullens and Howards. I am now twenty-seven years old. I have maintained my virginity, though only God knows how difficult that has been – and all because I have valued my maidenhead enough to resist the men who wished to take it from me. I have waited long for the great love of my life, and now he is within my reach! Never would I have expected this love would be for the King of England, nor could I have planned it. Yet I do love Henry with all my heart, as do I believe we are destined to be together. It is only that desire - to be a wife and, above all, to be the mother of the sons and daughters we will have together which motivates me."

I paused. It was so important that she of all people understand.

"In my heart and in my mind, to be a Queen without the true love of a husband is but an entrapment in a life of unhappiness. Do not forget, at a tender age I had the opportunity to watch closely the fates of both Mary Tudor, the French Queen, in her marriage to the ancient and ill King Louis XII, and then poor Queen Claude to François I. Both were Queens - yet neither was happy."

"I do believe you, Anne, of course, I do. Because I know you so well, I do not doubt that the love you bear Henry is the root of your desire to be his wife. But are you truly aware of how your quest will be viewed by others at court? Not only the English court, but as far away as Rome? And in France and Spain? You will not be regarded as simply a girl who wishes to marry a man she loves! Yours will be a complicated life: you will be the object of backbiting and calumny … and in that way, I do worry for you, Nan."

I went to her and hugged her close. "I know you do, Mother. And indeed, I know there are those who already resent me, even though Henry's intent has not been made public. But as I see it, there is little I can do except to walk the path which is laid before me. I love Henry and, God willing, I intend to be his wife. And if God's plan is that I become Queen, I will rule with every scrap of ability He has given me."

"Then, in that case, my daughter," my mother announced, and kissed my cheek, "I will be there for you, to support and defend you always. You may come to me with any confidence you wish to share, and it will be kept. And when and if I can, I will advise you if asked."

She stood back from me then, still holding my hands in hers.

"I do have one certainty: should God Almighty place you in the position of Queen, together you and Henry will create a magnificent destiny for England."

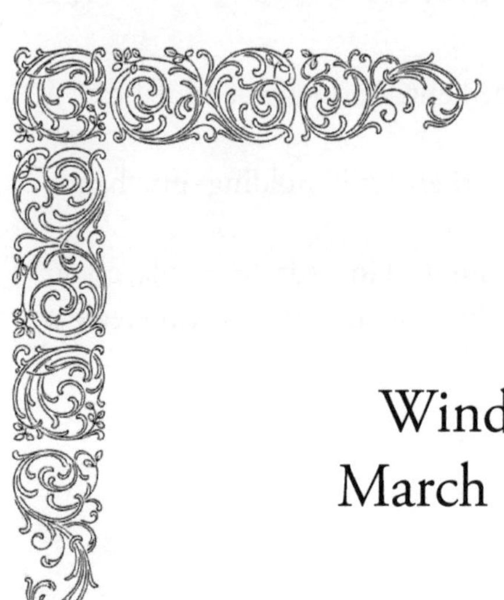

Windsor
March 1528

AT LAST, AND after what felt like an eternity, two things improved my life immensely. First, the numbing winter finally relinquished its grip on the English countryside. The second, and by far the best, was the invitation from Henry for my mother and me to come and stay with him at Windsor.

My excitement knew no bounds as Charity helped me pack gowns, riding and hunting clothes, articles for the toilette, and jewellery.

"Milady," she said with nervous excitement in her voice, "then we truly are to stay in the King's lodgings?"

"Yes, Charity, that is what the King's message to me said. The note read that he would have me, my mother - and, of course, you - join him at Windsor in the royal lodgings to celebrate the end of winter."

I looked at her with fondness. "I know – I am excited too. As much as I love Hever, I shall not be at all sorry to be in new surroundings after being closed up in this house all winter long."

•

We were warmly welcomed by the staff at Windsor Castle upon our arrival, and shown to lodgings in the tower adjacent to the great gate. The tower had beautiful floor to ceiling windows in the base court area, and hallways fanned from this room, each containing chambers. My mother's lodging was halfway along the gallery hall, mine nearer the King's, and both had stained glass windows which opened on one side to the lovely courtyard, and on the other, windows which afforded views of the massive round tower. At the foundation of the tower were the tennis courts Henry had built. My sequence of chambers included a sitting room, a large and well-furnished bedchamber, a small chamber for Charity, and a large *bayne*. When I saw it, my lips curled in a smile like a cat which has got the cream. After having experienced life with one's own personal bath, it is most difficult to do without!

We had only just settled in when a discreet knock at the door brought a note from the King.

> Milady, will you join me for supper this evening at 8 of the clock in my Privy Chamber? I wait with great expectation to see you.
>
> H. R.

The prospect of renewing our heady romance was ever so enticing. With a sigh of contentment, I turned to the agreeable task of choosing my gown and readying myself for the reunion ahead.

On that evening, we behaved like two giddy young people in love for the first time. We hugged and kissed constantly, giggled at trifling jokes and danced. Henry lifted me as if I were a mere child and swung me around till I collapsed in a dizzy, laughing heap at his feet. I had never had such a wonderful time with anyone in my life. We so enjoyed being together, and put great value on every private moment we shared, since they were but limited.

Later I revealed, "Henry, there is something I want desperately to try."

"And what might that be, my love?" he replied, cupping my chin in his hand and smiling down at me.

"Tennis! I want to learn how to play tennis! It looks such fun …" I put on my prettiest pout. "And it is so completely unfair that women are denied the chance to play!"

Henry exploded in laughter. How I loved hearing his roaring, mirthful laugh – it sounded like no one else's and was completely catching. "Well then, I shall teach you," he said, adding in a clandestine tone, "We will sneak into the tennis court at night when no one is abroad."

"You really will?" I was elated at the prospect of such an adventure after the confinement and boredom so recently escaped. "But what shall I wear, though? I will have a terrible disadvantage in my petticoats!"

"Perhaps the tailor can make you a petticoat of light fabric, which is divided in the middle as if it were to be worn for riding astride a horse?" he suggested, ever the innovator.

"That is a wonderful idea!" I agreed and determined to place my order for such a garment the very next day. "And because you are so kind as to teach me, I promise not to beat you - or at least not in the first few games!" I teased with a wink. At this, he grabbed and kissed me.

•

The weather's transformation was well-nigh to miraculous. It was as if the harshness of winter had laid the groundwork for an early and particularly lovely spring. The air was warm, and the sun gently gilded the damp earth. The grass quickly began to green, and crocus was everywhere, blooming in profusion. Daffodils had poked through the crusted ground, and in areas kissed by a steady sun, had begun to unfold in their gorgeous yellow cheerfulness.

It was a special time. Henry and I were able to ride out almost every day, alone together, only followed in the distance by his mounted guard. We explored Windsor Great Park, riding across broad meadows and lawns and into the wooded byways which I loved so much. To me, there was something very mystical about riding along trails in those hushed, deep evergreen forests. The sun cast motley shapes on the budding leaves of the trees and across the *sous bois,* the mossy, living floor under the forest canopy. The muffled thud of the horses' hooves released the sharp, clean scent of pine as they stepped on the carpet of needles. While we quietly walked our horses, my gaze swept the woods from side to side, on the lookout for wildlife of the forest: baby fawns, squirrels, an occasional bright red fox and, if we were lucky, an elusive owl.

During these rides, Henry and I had some of our best, most interesting conversations. We spoke about the Great Matter, of course, and I encouraged him to trust his instincts and be less dependent on the opinions voiced by Wolsey. We talked about religion, and I described my puzzlement as to why any educated English person should not be able to read the Bible for him or herself. I asked Henry if he knew why Arundel, the Archbishop of Canterbury, had forbidden the translation or reading of an English Bible as a matter of law over 100 years ago. Henry agreed with me in principle, but maintained his allegiance to the Catholic doctrine which prohibited such practices. We also enjoyed discussing the theories of humanism, and Henry told me that he had always been fascinated by the works of Aristotle, especially his writings on logic and ethics as a basis for humanist precepts. While I had read some Aristotle as a part of my early education, I admit I had never been an accomplished student of his work, and recognizing his evident interest in the subject, I determined to refresh my knowledge.

One afternoon as we rode our horses nose to tail on a narrow woodland path, Henry turned in his saddle and said to me, "Anne, on the morrow I wish to show you a special place.

We will leave early and have a supper outdoors there if the weather is fair."

I agreed with alacrity: intrigued to discover what he had planned.

•

At sunrise next morning, Charity awakened me from a sound and dreamless sleep. I was to meet Henry, and we would go to the docks, where the rowers were to take us on a barge down the Thames. We were to ride once the river journey was complete. It all sounded most enchanting.

While I stirred and rose to wash and prepare my *toilette*, Charity selected for me a riding kirtle of cream with a forest green velvet jacket and velvet cap trimmed with pheasant feathers. She laid out a short broadcloth cloak in case the weather turned chill. I was dressed and ready to run out the door of my chamber when, "Mistress …!" Charity called to me and hurried over to give me my leather riding gloves which I had left behind.

I met Henry just outside the tower door, and we walked through the gate and down to the banks of the Thames. There, a liveried boatman greeted us with a deep bow and assisted us on to the royal barge. We sat on soft cushions under a tented covering and listened to the music of several minstrels as we were rowed downstream. When we reached Laleham, the barge docked, and I was helped out by Henry. Raising my eyes from stepping onto the dock, I saw two horses saddled and ready for us. We mounted and set off, following two equerries who had brought an additional steed packed with supplies. We rode 'til we came to a wooded area near the old Priory of Ankerwycke. There I found myself facing the most impressive tree I had ever seen. Its branches sprawled and reached for the clouds floating above. Its massive, ancient trunk reminded me of a wizened, but kindly old face. Certainly, this was a tree which had overseen the events of centuries.

We dismounted while the equerries unpacked leather sacks which held blankets for us to sit upon and baskets of food and ale. The blankets were laid on the ground beneath the great yew, the foodstuffs neatly laid out, then the equerries bowed to the King, remounted their horses and rode off to a respectable distance. Henry and I settled under the boughs of that incredible tree, and he poured me a cup of ale. As he unwrapped cheeses and slices of meat from several parcels, he told me that this tree was witness to events which had shaped the history of England, and of the world. He said the tree was believed to be almost two thousand years old. I marvelled that this living thing had been in existence before the time of Jesus Christ! Henry continued, saying at this very spot, King John had signed the *Magna Carta* in 1215. I shivered as I listened, thinking about all the history this tree had seen. It was a place steeped in antiquity; entwined with destiny. I found it to be one of the most idyllic settings I had ever experienced.

•

The first weeks of spring were spent thus at Windsor, and again we enjoyed some freedom, since Henry had only his riding household with him in residence, and that party did not include Katherine, much to my gratification. We hunted almost every day when the weather allowed, and I used the new saddles Henry had given me. They were beautifully fashioned from supple leather with saddle blankets made of black velvet with silver tassels and fringes. I now had my own stable of five excellent horses from which to choose when we rode. We hawked in the Great Park, and in the evenings, played cards with the friends we now shared. And, true to his word, Henry and I would often sneak over to the tennis court late at night, with torches to light our way, where he taught me how to swing the racquet, and hit the ball with aim. I thought it a great amusement, and we did share much hilarity as I did my best to deliver a series of devastating blows to the little ball. But after all, it became obvious to us both that Henry should have no fear of being beaten at his sport. I had nary a chance!

We enjoyed our idyll in Windsor, but the Matter being debated in Rome was never far from my mind, nor from Henry's, I could tell. We both held to the hope that this latest advance, spearheaded by Masters Foxe and Gardiner, would yield a positive result. By the end of the month of March, we had received from Wolsey an early, promising summary sent by the two ambassadors in Rome. It was Henry's intention to have them report directly to him as soon as they returned to England in the coming weeks.

The Cardinal seemed convinced that a redoubling of his efforts on behalf of the King would pay off; his conduct concerning Henry and his Matter became exceedingly attentive. I took note that his behaviour towards me had become much more prudent as well, and it was this observation which caused me to think afresh upon my personal scheme concerning the Cardinal. I decided that, as much as I instinctively disliked him, it would behoove me to appear to put this feeling aside, and instead demonstrate my support of him and his efforts. I concluded that little good could come from an open disagreement with Cardinal Wolsey.

Such charitable interpretation was to prove a distinct misstep.

Greenwich
May 1528

COURT HAD RESUMED in full at Greenwich, and I was back in my previous placement, as a maid of honour to the Queen.

It took all my will to assume an appropriate demeanour in Katherine's household. It was by now apparent that I featured foremost in the King's desire to have his marriage annulled, and it was evident who were my allies, and who were Katherine's. Katherine and I said little between us and did our best to avoid each other. One afternoon, however, she and her ladies were assembled in the Queen's presence chamber, since she planned to receive visitors. I was seated before her, and it was almost impossible not to look at one another. I raised my eyes to find her staring at me. She did not bear an expression of anger or enmity; instead, she purposefully looked at me, or should I say through me, with an air of *hauteur.* In that instant, I decided to return her gaze measure for measure. We spent what seemed like minutes staring at each other, unblinking. Then I raised my chin almost imperceptibly. I knew she understood.

With that subtle gesture, I had thrown down the gauntlet.

•

On the first Sunday in May, after dinner, Cardinal Wolsey arrived to meet with the King. They retired to His Majesty's Chambers, and I, since it was raining, to mine. Henry had removed my lodgings from the royal gallery, where many of the Queen's ladies were in residence, to one nearer the tiltyard and adjacent to the banqueting house. Several of the ladies-in-waiting had been stricken with smallpox, and, never having had the pox, I had no wish to be exposed to its ravages. I remained in my chamber, reading, when a knock sounded, and Charity opened the door to reveal Bishop Foxe, newly arrived from Rome.

Flustered but thrilled to see one of Henry's ambassadors unexpectedly arrived at Greenwich, I mistakenly chirped "Master Stephens! How excellent to see you! Please do come in …do please sit and partake of some wine." In my elation at the potential of receiving some long-awaited good news from Rome, I had confused Foxe with Gardener, and he politely overlooked the error.

"I thank you heartily, my lady," he said with a bow and seated himself before the fire. "I have sent word to His Majesty that I've arrived, and was informed that he wished to meet me here in your chambers as soon as he could finish his meeting with the Cardinal." Taking note of the fact that Wolsey was not to be included in this debriefing, I handed Foxe a cup of wine, but even as he took his first sip, I couldn't contain myself a moment longer.

"So, Master Stephens, what news do you bring from Rome and His Holiness as regards the King's Great Matter? What are the opinions of the Pope and the clerical scholars? And the lawyers - what was their view?" The Bishop again very kindly did not embarrass me by correcting my error.

"Mistress, His Holiness the Pope was well inclined to have sympathy with His Majesty's written opinions on the Great Matter. He was intrigued by the study which supported the proposal that a papal legate be named to decide finally on the Matter in conjunction with Cardinal Wolsey. He also expressed his confidence that the King's integrity was well represented in his argument."

"And what of it, then, Sir?"

"His Holiness has requested that the legate be Cardinal Campeggio, the Cardinal-Protector of England."

I was pondering the value of such an appointment, when another knock at the door heralded the arrival of His Majesty the King, who entered, beaming.

"Your Highness," I offered with a low curtsey. Foxe leaped to his feet, and bowed to the King, who clasped him by the shoulders with a warm and hearty "Foxe! Welcome home. Do sit, have some refreshment and tell me how you fared."

I poured wine for both, and with a quick curtsey, backed from the room to leave the men to their discussion, when I realized how often I had called the Bishop 'Master Stephens'. Shaking my head at my folly, I retreated, closing the door behind me.

I was not gone but a few minutes, when Charity came running to find me, to say that the King wished me back in the chamber with him and the Bishop. I hurried back, and sat by the King's side, as together we questioned Foxe and heard him recount the entire mission, beginning to end.

When finally the exhausted Foxe was permitted to depart, Henry lingered with me in my chamber. He gushed with excitement: obviously feeling that we were finally on the correct path and that Campeggio and Wolsey together would provide him with the formal support he needed to move forward and finally rid himself of his vexing marriage to Katherine. I was, as always, swept up by Henry's enthusiasm, and demonstrated my joy by sitting on his lap and covering him with kisses.

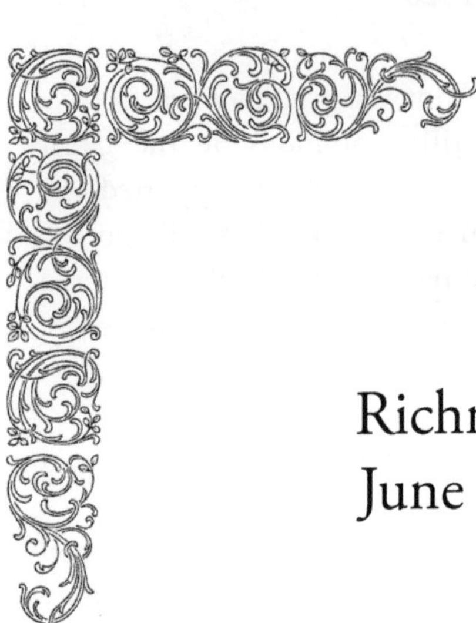

Richmond
June 1528

THE WARM AND fragrant breezes of a fine June morning floated into my bedchamber through the open casement. Charity was helping me unroll several bolts of silk, given to me by the King, to determine which I would use for new gowns. I was admiring the colours spread before us and glanced up to ask Charity which she liked best. With a shock I saw that her face was pallid with a yellow cast, and her hands were trembling.

"Charity, what is wrong? Are you ill?" I asked, alarmed.

"Mistress, I am not feeling at all well," she whispered faintly before sinking to the floor. I quickly helped her to the bed, loosened her bodice and removed her cap. Her face had broken out in sweat, so I ran to the pitcher of water, snatched up a linen towel, dipped and wrung it out, and wiped her face. I rinsed and wrung it out again, then placed it on her forehead while instructing her to keep it there while I went for the physician. Rushing from the chamber, I ran panic-stricken to the hall in search of Lord Sandys, to see if he might locate a court physician for me.

With one look at my agitation, Sandys went in search of a physician to send to my chamber. As quickly as I could, I returned to my room, and was aghast to find Charity only partly conscious, sweating profusely, and burning with fever. Her breath came in sharp rasps. Wiping tears from my eyes, frantically I applied cool cloths to her head, then lifted it to give a sip of water, but she could barely swallow.

A single rap on the door preceded Master Cuthbert Blackeden's rushed entrance. The King's Chief Apothecary, he quickly strode to Charity's bedside, and pushed me away, his expression grim.

"Mistress Anne, please keep your distance. You must already be aware there is little we can do for your chambermaid. I will offer what help I can, but she has the sweat, a bad case it appears." Turning back to Charity, he said over his shoulder, "I am sorry to tell you it is likely that she will be dead within the hour."

Stunned, I paced back and forth while he had her drink a concoction he had made. He wiped her face as I had done, and we waited. Charity's breathing grew more and more shallow, and finally, it barely raised her chest. Eventually, even the rasping slowed, and then it stopped. My sweet Charity had slipped from life, into the arms of our Lord God.

My tears flowed unchecked as Master Blackeden covered her with a sheet.

"Mistress, this poor soul is the third person in the palace who has succumbed to the sweat this day. The King is preparing even now to leave court for St Albans, where he will stay at Tyttenhanger briefly before moving again. May I suggest that you, too, depart Surrey and the London environs as quickly as you can? This epidemic will grow."

He looked at me with concern, but repacked his bag and hurriedly left, having others to care for.

I was in utter shock, not only grieving for the abrupt loss of my dear friend but further stunned by the disclosure that Henry was preparing to leave and had not contacted me!

Feeling as if the wind had been knocked from me, I mindlessly grabbed a few random trinkets from my chest, stuffed them in a travel sack, and with one last, unutterably mournful glance at Charity's shrouded, lifeless body, fled the room.

Even as I did, the porters were coming to remove her corpse. Running heedlessly through the hallways I grabbed one of the guards near the King's chambers, asking if he knew whether my father was in the vicinity. My near frenzy startled him, but he steered me toward the Chamberlain's offices. I found Father there and, sobbing, relayed what had happened. He told me to wait for him just outside the entrance to the building. Within minutes, he returned with a coach and pulled me in.

Amid a thunderous clatter of panic-urged hooves, we set off for Hever.

Hever
Summer 1528

I CONTINUED TO WEEP copiously as the cart lurched and rattled over bumpy roads on the way from Richmond to Edenbridge while Father sat across from me, staring fixedly from the small window although, at one point he did reach across and take my hand in his. It was not a gesture I would have expected from my father, but it was needed, and I clung to him for a while. I do not know what was worse: the dreadful impact of what had occurred so unexpectedly, or the ache of loss for my Charity, who had become, in a way, my most intimate *confidante*. After all, though I rarely spoke of my personal feelings about the King, it had been impossible to keep the truth from such a close personal servant. Charity had been utterly discreet, yet encouraging and excited for me in her special way. I would miss her more than I could imagine.

I was fraught with worry about whether my own time was measured as well. I had touched her, bathed the sweat from her face - slept in the same chamber all in the day of her death. What could that possibly mean for me? And if I were to come down with the contagion, would it spread to Mother? My father? And what of Henry? He, too, had been subjected to those who had come near to the contamination. I was desperately hurt that he had not been in contact with me, and instead planned to leave London with Katherine. I tried to create a rationale in which I believed he did exactly as he should have done. After all, I was neither his wife nor a member of his family. I was still only his unofficial sweetheart: a position not sufficient to gain me access to the royal family he would move from place to place to ensure their health and safety. This reasoning only served to make me throb with misery. At that moment, I felt completely abandoned and more like a fool than I had thought possible.

•

My relief at arriving home was immeasurable. Exhausted, I kept to myself in my chamber, falling into an uneasy sleep early, tossing and turning till dawn. The instant I awoke, I was forced to relive the shock and pain of Charity's loss. I arose, dressed listlessly, and meandered about the house and garden all day with little purpose. At least I had not yet been felled by the fearful illness, nor had Mother or Father. I went to bed the second evening, feeling hopeful that the country air of Hever would be our defence against the sweat.

The following morning upon awakening, I felt a strange tightness in my head and my throat. Convinced that my overactive imagination was in control, I dressed and went in search of Mother. No sooner had I stepped outside the house into the bright daylight than I was stricken with a blinding headache. Within minutes, my entire body felt as if it had been run over by a wagon. I ached everywhere and desperately sought a bench to sit on, calling weakly for one of the kitchen boys passing by. He took one look at me and raced to fetch my mother. She came running, along with her maid. Together they helped me return to my chamber, laid me on my bed, and undressed me to my shift. I shook violently with a chill and was covered with a blanket. Distantly I could hear Mother's voice, tremulous with concern, giving instructions to summon a physician. I fell into a dark, dreamless, and fitful sleep.

Time passed – I knew not how long. At intervals I became vaguely aware of my surroundings, and recalled various people administering to me with cool cloths, sips of water and other bitter concoctions which must have been medicinal; sometimes spooning broth into my mouth. I alternately sweated, then became chilled 'til my teeth chattered in my head. Finally, I woke from sleep, looked about, and knew I was in my bed, in my chamber at Hever. Slowly coming to consciousness, I realized that not only was I alive, but the heaviness in my head and limbs seemed to have lifted. Very tentatively, I drew myself up in bed, and at that moment, Mother walked into the chamber. When she saw me awake and sitting up, she ran to me with a cry and hugged me to her and would not let go.

"Oh Anne, my child! I thank God you have recovered." Her voice was thick with tears. "I have feared so many times that you were lost. I am so relieved and so very grateful!"

"Mother, for how long have I been sick?" I asked, and was surprised at how weak I sounded.

"Four days hath passed since you collapsed, Nan. You drifted in and out of consciousness for the first three, and then you slept. We did not know if you would awaken, or pass from life in your sleep."

I could see the toll my illness had taken on my mother. She looked pale and thin: it was evident that she had eaten little, if anything, nor slept at all.

I took her hand and said "Thank you, Mother, for not giving up on me, and for doing all you could to save me. I love you so much."

"I love you, too, my Nan. As does your Father for all his seeming callousness. It was fortunate that we had the King's physician, Dr Butts, who arrived at His Grace's instruction to attend to you at a vital moment. Dr Butts was very able in providing you the best care possible. We have been instructed to send a message without delay to the King to let him know your condition if it were to change. I will have the kitchen send up some meat broth for you, and then perhaps we will prepare a warm bath. In the meantime, I will bring you the two letters which arrived from the King's messengers while you were so ill."

I was surprised that Henry had sent letters to Hever, but was not at all sure whether that news pleased me. I bitterly recalled how distressed and forsaken I felt when I had been told - by a member of his staff, no less - that he was taking his family and departing for a different location.

With a sense of misgiving, I unrolled the parchment which had been delivered first.

No greeting met me, just a dark smudge where his palm had smeared the first application of ink to paper. He expressed immense relief that I had not come down with the illness as yet. The small page was splattered throughout with droplets of ink, and they appeared to be byproducts of an anxious hand. The words did not flow artfully. Instead, they were cramped and slanted sharply toward the top right of the page. It looked very much a letter written in haste. He mentioned that he, Katherine, and a few others had been at Walton and there several people, including my brother George, had fallen ill but had recovered. Thanks to God for sparing George's life! I wondered how my mother had possibly coped with the illness of both George and I. Henry then added that they had travelled to Hunsdon, and everyone there remained well. He reassured me, saying fewer women than men were succumbing to the sweat. Finally, he ended with:

> For which reason I beg you, my entirely beloved, not to frighten yourself nor be too uneasy at our absence: for wherever I am, I am yours, and yet we must sometimes submit to our misfortunes, for whoever will struggle against fate is generally but so much the farther from gaining his end: wherefore comfort yourself, and take courage and avoid the pestilence as much as you can, for I hope shortly to make you sing, la renvoyé. No more at present, from

lack of time, but that I wish you in my arms, that I might a little dispel your unreasonable thoughts.

Written by the hand of him who is and always will be yours,

Im- H. R. -muable

'Immuable?' The French word for 'enduring', or 'abiding'… Lying abed at Hever having been so near to death, with the letter-writer ensconced with his family miles away, such a presentiment seemed as preposterous as did a fire-breathing dragon. Henry and Katherine, his wife and Queen, were safe and sound at Hunsdon, along with his children. I, on the other hand, was banished to Kent to get along as best I might.

How I did feel sorry for myself! I heaved a great, pitiful sigh, then unfolded the next letter.

I was stunned by the sight of it. Before me was a page that had certainly been written with the greatest urgency. The quill had jabbed at the parchment, frantically grabbing ink from the well every few strokes. Blotched, scratchy and smeared, it was unmistakably rendered in terror. I translated the French, reading aloud in my hoarse voice:

There came to me suddenly in the night the most afflicting news that could have arrived. The first, to hear of the sickness of my mistress, whom I esteem more than all the world, and whose health I desire as I do my own, so that I would gladly bear half your illness to make you well. The second, from the fear that I have of being still longer harassed by my enemy, Absence, much longer, who has hitherto given me all possible uneasiness, and as far as I can judge is determined to spite me more because I pray to God to rid me of this troublesome tormentor. The third, because the physician in whom I have most confidence, is absent at the very time when he might do me greatest pleasure; for I should hope, by him and his means, to obtain one of my chief joys on earth – that is the care of my mistress – yet for want of him I send you my second, and hope that he will soon make you well. I shall then love him more than ever. I beseech you to be guided by his advice in your illness. In doing so I hope soon to see you again, which will be to me a greater comfort than all the precious jewels in the world.

Written by the secretary, who is, and for ever will be, your loyal and most assured Servant,

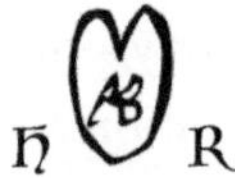

Tears welled and slipped down the sides of my face to soak the pillow. His pathos was real, and one didn't even need to read the content to see it writ large on the page. I ached to be near Henry's strength, to draw from it and to be cared for by him, as he had promised he would do. I desperately wished myself in Katherine's place.

•

The very sad news arrived that my sister's husband, William Carey, had succumbed to the sweating sickness. We were grief-stricken because we were all so fond of William. He had been a good husband to my sister. Poor Mary and her children mourned his loss, and we longed to be with her to comfort her, but she did not come to the manor house at Hever lest the disease be further spread by her travel.

I spent the next weeks slowly recovering from my illness. Realizing how close to death I had come, I repeatedly prayed, spending time at devotions clutching my favourite Book of Hours, the one made in Bruges, which I brought with me from France. I loved it – it had always comforted me; it was a beautiful book, and one I treasured. The prayers within were simple and heartfelt, and they seemed fitting as I thanked God for sparing my life.

I also spent restless hours contemplating the reality of my situation and my relationship with Henry. I was candid to the point of harshness and cruelly forced myself to face the truth. In spite of the desire we held for one another, it appeared that nearly insurmountable odds stood in the way of my becoming Henry's lawful wife. Not only was the Pope resistant, but there were many people at court and elsewhere about the realm who were now aware of Henry's wish to supplant Katherine with me, and they were quite openly opposed to it. And, in my heart of hearts, I knew that Henry had convinced himself of the logic and soundness of his argument – that he and Katherine had never been legally wed. But did he truly believe this to be a justification which would stand under the scrutiny of canon law? I thought not. And that was bitter medicine, indeed. If this be the case, he would needs resort to the only approach which might, in the end, succeed: the sheer brute force of his will.

Katherine had a committed following; she was a princess of the blood and had been Henry's beloved, respected wife and pious Queen for these many years. I, on the other hand, was seen as a usurper, and a commoner at that. In the opinions of naysayers, only a princess royal would suffice as a fitting consort for their King, and if not Katherine, it was certainly not to be me. In their eyes, I was but a scheming wench, conspiring to gain access to the crown.

I became ever more filled with despair and a deep sense of hopelessness while my ragged thoughts and emotions held me in their ugly grip during that long recovery. But the days slowly passed and as my moods varied, a persistent notion flickered like a tiny flame in the darkness which grew slowly but steadily brighter; its reassuring glow gradually penetrating the surrounding gloom, and finally blazing forth with an insistence not to be ignored: my love for him. My devotion to Henry had crossed a boundary from which there could be no return.

•

As my strength returned, my attitude rallied; I found that I looked forward to going back to court, and being with Henry again. The period of deliberation had left me with the hope that together, Henry and I were possessed of an uncanny strength - far greater than the sum of each of us alone. I prayed to God to show us the way, and one afternoon, I turned to a favourite page in my devotional– the one with a beautiful illumination of Jesus, his hand extended in a blessing. Under the illumination, I wrote:

Le temps viendra

Then signed my name and drew an armillary sphere, a symbol which I knew implied wisdom.

Je Anne Boleyn
The time will come
I, Anne Boleyn

I sent a message to Henry, confirming that I was getting better day by day, and wished nothing more than to be with him again. I told him I missed him greatly and constantly prayed that his health remain strong. Then, after considering for a few moments, I chanced to ask on behalf of the family of my deceased brother-in-law, William Carey, that his sister Eleanor Carey be considered for an appointment to the newly open position of Abbess of St Edith at Wilton. Dared I ask a political favour of Henry? The request certainly represented a new perspective in our relationship, and I had no idea how he would react.

Promptly, I received in return a long letter from Henry, this time neatly written with well executed script. It appeared almost businesslike as if he had written it while he was overseeing and signing the many documents which made up his daily routine.

Since your last letters, mine own darlyng, Walter Welsh, Master Browne, Thom. Case, Urion of Brearton, John Coke the apothecary be fallen of the sweat…

But, it continued, somehow they had all recovered, and he was hopeful it would yet pass him by. Concerning my request, he wrote, Cardinal Wolsey had looked into the matter and had discovered that Dame Eleanor Carey had borne two children by two different priests. Even worse, that she had also been intimately involved with a servant of Lord Broke. These unfortunate facts obviously rendered Dame Eleanor unfit to hold the position but, in order to please me, he offered his assurance that the other candidates under consideration would not be selected by Wolsey alone, but instead they would search for a '*good and well-disposed woman*' not affiliated with the Cardinal or any other political ties. What was most important to me was that Henry had accepted my suggestion with credence, and did not chastise me for speaking beyond my station.

While, as for Dame Eleanor? With such a scurrilous background, she had best find a new patron …

Following this letter of Henry's, in rapid succession came three further missives, each bemoaning the fact that we were still apart, and promising his efforts on the Great Matter to be unrelenting.

I felt well enough by the beginning of August to send word to Henry of my hope to return to London by the end of the month. In quick reply, I received a page covered with a light scribble:

Myne Own Sweetheart,

This shall be to advertise you of the great elengeness that I find here since your departing: for, I ensure you methink the time longer since your departing now last, than I was wont to do a whole fortnight. I think your kindness and my fervency of love cause it, for otherwise, I would not

have thought it possible that for so little a while it should have grieved me. But now that I am coming towards you, methinketh my pains be half removed: and also I am right well comforted in so much that my book maketh substantially for my matter: in looking whereof I have spent above four hours this day, which causes me now to write the shorter letter to you at this time, because of some pain in my head: wishing myselfe (specially an evening) in my sweethearts arms, whose pretty dukkys I trust shortly to kyss.

Written by the hand of him that was, is, and shall be yours by his own will,

H. R.

Ha! I laughed aloud with delight at this letter. I knew well how Henry disliked spending long periods of time bent over his desk writing, and I could only imagine the headache he had developed from four hours discoursing on the Matter. His aching head may have kept him from writing a longer letter, but it plainly did not constrain him from vividly imagining me wrapped in his arms, stripped bare of my bodice!

•

We impatiently awaited the arrival of Cardinal Campeggio, the Papal Legate designate, as we had been assured he was expected soon. There were numerous reasons, we were told, why he had not made better time, including poor weather, poor health, poor roads, and so on *ad infinitum*. How disheartening this situation was proving to be. Ever more did I wish to vent my growing frustration and resentment on the great Lord Chancellor, and oh how I could think of many ways to do so. But then a more rational judgement prevailed, and I reluctantly surrendered the idea.

Henry had written to let me know he and my father had secured and renovated lodging for me in Durham House on the Strand, and it was there I was to stay upon my return to London. Seemingly it had been the cardinal himself who had suggested perhaps it was not best for Katherine and me to be under the same roof. Thankfully, I was no longer required to provide service to Katherine as her maid of honour and, instead, was to have a small household of my own. This knowledge gave me great peace of mind, and I could not wait to return to the city and become settled near to Henry. I provided an answer to his letter, expressing my most heartfelt thanks for his generosity, and importantly, to inquire about the latest status of the Matter.

A royal messenger arrived to deliver a prompt response. A fine leather wrapper protected the thin parchment which had been folded twice. Carefully I opened it and was greeted with a smudged scrawl. It began:

My darlyng

The reasonable request of your last letter, with the pleasure also that I take to know them true, causeth me to send you these news. The legate which we most desire arrived at Paris on Sunday or Monday last past, so that I trust by the next Monday to hear of his arrival at Calais: and then I trust within a while after to enjoy that which I have so long longed for, to God's pleasure and our both comforts.

No more to you at the present, mine own darling, for lack of time, but that I would you were in mine arms, or I in yours, for I think it long since I kyst you.

Written after the killing of a hart, at eleven of the clock, minding, with God's grace, to-morrow, mightily timely, to kill another, by the hand of hym which, I trust, shortly shall be yours.

Henry R.

I carefully refolded the parchment, held it to my heart for a moment, then locked it carefully in the coffer which held his other letters.

Durham House
London
September 1528

THE STEADY THRUM of rain on the steeply pitched slate roof did not dampen my mood one whit. I was back in London, and tonight, after what seemed like an eternity, I was finally to be reunited with my love! Even as I dressed, Henry was on his way to Durham House from Greenwich by barge, and I readied myself to greet him. We planned to have time together privily, then dine with my brother George, Thomas Heneage, who was a new appointee to the King's privy chamber, and my good friend Anne Gainsford.

My mood was buoyant as I finalized my apparel for the evening. Despite my enduring grief for the terrible death of Charity, I felt joyful, for my dear Anne was to become a part of my household, and I was happy for this beyond words. She and I giggled like young girls while we looked over the gift of jewels Henry had sent to my new residence, in celebration of my return to court. That evening, I was to wear a gown of Tudor green silk, with white French lace adorning the bodice and sleeves and petticoat. The Flemish silk was matchless, and the design of this gown included a train which trailed as gracefully as did the sleeves. True, I had lost some weight during my illness, but the gown had recently been sewn, so it fitted me well, and I had the bodice and stomacher laced extra tight to create a greater swell of my bosom at the neckline.

I now had in my chamber a large and wonderful glass mirror before which I was able to complete my *toilette*. My face seemed a bit thin, with my cheekbones rather more prominent than before. But a generous flush applied artfully with ochre and soft brushes, and the accenting of my eyes, already bright with anticipation, with a generous application of kohl, allowed me to achieve the look I desired. Anne and I selected an enamelled gold chain carcanet with an emerald and pearl pendant to wear around my neck, and the gown's colour was the perfect complement to my betrothal ring. My hair was woven into a long dark cascade with a green satin riband which trailed from the hood. Finally, I touched essence oil of *muguet des bois* to my breasts, neck, and wrists, and I was ready.

Thomas, Lord Heneage, escorted me through the panelled and torch-lit hallway to the chambers which had been redesigned especially for the King. Before we reached the door, I turned to him and said quietly, "Thank you, Thomas. I would prefer to enter and greet the King myself if you do not mind."

He hesitated only a moment, then bowed. "Of course Mistress, I fully understand," whereupon, with a perceptive smile, he stepped discreetly away.

I drew an expectant breath and stood alone before the entrance to Henry's apartment.

Just as I raised my hand to knock on the heavy carved door, it opened abruptly, and Henry and I were face to face. It took but a heartbeat for me to throw myself into his arms, tears flowing down my cheeks. The intensity of such emotion took me by surprise, and Henry lifted me and carried me into his chamber, closing the door with his foot. Once inside, I looked into his face and saw that he, too, was weeping.

It was in that joyous moment that I knew I would not question the strength of Henry's love for me again, as we desperately clung to one another, infinitely thankful we had both survived and were together once more. After a time, we were joined by Sir Thomas and Anne, followed by George. Sitting at the dining table, sipping a most delicious spiced wine and gazing upon the beloved faces before me, I whispered a prayer of thanksgiving to God for such blessings. Throughout the evening, Henry held and stroked my hand, and looked upon me continuously with adoration.

That night it became evident to all present how strongly the King of England felt about me.

•

Anne Gainsford and I had been taking a stroll through the gardens several days later, when she said, "Anne, did you know while you were at Hever there was a mighty row between the King and the Cardinal?"

At this, she had my undivided attention.

"No I did not, and you simply must tell me! What caused it, do you know?"

"I was told it concerned the appointment of a new Abbess of St Edith's in Wilton."

At this announcement, my curiosity knew no bounds although I tried to disguise my avid interest for she was unaware of my earlier request to the King.

"Well," Anne continued, lowering her voice to a covert whisper, "… apparently, while His Grace had decreed that a broad constituency of women were to be considered for the position, Wolsey went ahead and appointed his own selection - Dame Isabel Jordan - in direct contravention of the King's wishes. I was told His Grace flew into a rage, ranting against Wolsey in the presence of a number of courtiers. They said it was unlike any exchange anyone had previously seen or heard between His Majesty and Wolsey."

I took her arm. "Anne, I am so glad you told me about this! What a scene that must have been! What you do not know is that I recommended a woman to Henry for that very position, and though she was not selected, Henry promised me the appointee would not be Wolsey's choice. Yet the Lord Cardinal went ahead and did exactly as he intended, anyway." I lowered my voice further. "That wretched cleric acts as if his power is fully equal to the King's."

"Oh, how I do agree with you, Anne," she said with a shake of her head. "I cannot help but dislike the man, hard as I try otherwise."

"I have felt that way since I first met him. And now he insists on directing the plans to have Henry's marriage annulled. I know he distrusts me as much as I do him, and there is nary a chance that he is truly applying himself to finding a solution. Yet still the King depends on him."

We both fell silent, then I added, "You know, this is a very delicate situation for me, Anne. I am attempting to align myself with Wolsey's decisions - I have even written him several times expressing my commendation and support. I wish I could feel confident about his intentions but, as it happens, I do not. It would not surprise me at all if he were secretly supporting Katherine."

"Do you really think so?" My friend stopped walking and turned to face me, shocked. And then, in a whisper, "If he were found to subvert the King's efforts, it would be seen as treason. Surely he knows this?"

I nodded, and distinctly replied, "Arrogance is a dangerous vice, Anne. And Wolsey is an arrogant man. I think it will be his downfall."

We turned the final corner of the maze and headed back to the house.

•

The cool, shorter days of autumn had arrived, always my favourite season. My situation had changed so greatly since last autumn. Life, even with all its new advantages, was proving to be quite complicated. While I enjoyed my temporary residence in Durham House, I often went by barge to hunt with Henry at Greenwich. Whenever I appeared outside the gates of the house, I could not avoid the conspicuous stares of the townspeople. It had become common knowledge that I lodged in Durham House, and everyone, it seemed, wanted a look at the King's paramour. It soon became obvious that the curious looks and whispers were often not supportive or friendly ones. I must admit this bothered me considerably, although I hid my dismay. Although I placed great value on my ability to appear self-confident, still, I had always cared very much what others thought of me. I did sincerely view myself as a kind and considerate person. But now I realized that my position – my relationship with Henry – had created a view of me which was distasteful.

I longed to enjoy simply my days and evenings with Henry and my friends and companions with carefree abandon. Reflecting on what both my mother and my father had told me, I saw the plain truth. Coexistent with my presumed position as the King's courtesan, that privilege was gone. The envious schemers were many; the advocates few. No longer could I allow the tenderhearted, trusting aspects of my true nature to drive my thoughts and actions. I must be on guard, must plan and contrive for my fate using every shred of cunning God had given me.

•

On the morning of 2 October, I was informed that, finally, Cardinal Campeggio had landed in Dover.

The crossing had been difficult, and his health so precarious that he had been forced to take up residence at Bath Place, where he was to recuperate. This meant we would not gain any significant information until he was well, but I was at least relieved he was in England. Perhaps when he and Henry were face to face, the legate's opinion would match the King's, and he would persuasively represent that argument to Pope Clement, thereby gaining the Pope's agreement.

There was always hope.

But then again - there was also Cardinal Wolsey.

The Isle of Dogs East London October 1528

I WATCHED HENRY STAND at the prow of the barge as we were rowed east along the Thames. I never tired of looking at him, especially when he was unaware of my gaze. He was the finest man I had ever seen, and I allowed my admiration to show as he turned back and caught me staring. He returned a broad smile, and my heart turned over as I motioned for him to come and sit next to me on the cushioned bench, which he did. I nestled into him and linked my arm with his. I was looking forward most keenly to our outing this morning, headed as we were for the royal kennels on the Isle of Dogs at Stepney Marsh. Henry had established a small, specialized breeding kennel at this isolated location to ensure purity of the strains. The dogs kept and bred there were primarily his most prized greyhounds, the very elegant harthounds, and some mastiffs. A new litter of greyhounds had been whelped a few weeks ago to one of Henry's best bitches, sired by a favourite hunting hound. I looked forward to the prospect of seeing the pups.

As we disembarked and began walking the path toward the kennels, I said, "Henry, do you have any idea when you and Cardinal Campeggio will meet? Have you had word from him?"

"No, I have not. Yet Wolsey has already met with him on several occasions. Anne, would you believe Campeggio had the audacity to suggest that Wolsey should convince me to reconcile with Katherine?" He shook his head in disbelief. "Thus far, that has been the sum total of his advice on how best to resolve the matter."

I felt as if the wind had been knocked from me. "Oh, Henry - no! What can that possibly say, then, about how skewed Campeggio must be in representing our case to the Pope? This is so terribly disappointing!"

I found myself struggling to keep my emotions in check. I wanted to cry - nay, to scream - in vexation!

"Sweetheart, do not upset yourself," he soothed in an attempt to comfort me. "I have instructed Wolsey to tell Campeggio I will not entertain any such discussion. And when we do meet, by God's blood, that damnable Italian best have a real solution, or his time in England will not be a happy one."

My silence spoke volumes. It amplified the sound of our feet, which crunched as we walked, wordlessly, on the gravel pathway.

Master Rainsford showed us to the whelping shed in which the bitches with new litters, or those about to deliver, were kept. Every dark, anxious thought escaped me when I looked into the pen which held the beautiful hound Gracieuse and her three-week-old brood. There were four soft, round, adorable greyhound pups, crawling and bumping all over themselves in a pen filled with hay and soft blankets. Gracieuse looked up at us with her soulful eyes as the pups climbed on her. There was a dark brindle pup, two which appeared fawn coloured, and then there was the white one.

That little white pup, though slightly smaller than the others, kept pushing its littermates aside to secure the best spot next to its mother and be well positioned for the next meal. With an inquiring glance at Master Rainsford, who nodded, smiling, in return, I leaned in to pick up the white puppy. The only female in the litter, she strained toward me. I was completely smitten! Her little belly was round as a pumpkin and soft pink, with liver coloured spots. Her ears were a fawn colour, as were two symmetrical markings on her back and a sweet round spot on the very top of her head. The rest of her was milky white. She squirmed and made puppy grunting squeaks as she fought to get close enough to lick my face.

"Henry, I am in love! I can't possibly give her back," I looked at him imploringly.

"Well, Mistress, since I have apparently been displaced by another for your affections, we best have her around so I can keep an eye on my competition," Henry smiled at me with that roguish look I loved. "Would you like to have her for your own?"

"Oh, that I would, Your Grace! But I would not want to keep her in the kennels with the other hounds; I want her for my companion. Does that meet with His Grace's approval?"

He came close, kissed my cheek and said quietly "Of course, my Mistress Anne. For you, anything. As I hope you rightly know."

I gave my pretty pup one more cuddle, stated that henceforth she would be called Jolie, and placed her back in the box next to her dam. Promptly she wriggled her little self back into the prime nursing position she obviously felt was her right. In a strange way, she reminded me of myself!

Master Rainsford said that Jolie could join us in another four weeks, when she would be weaned. Henry and I thanked him kindly, and after inspecting the remainder of the whelping barn, headed back to the barge to return to Greenwich. I was already anticipating the day when Jolie would be delivered to me and become the canine version of my trusted friend and confidante.

After all, the way events were setting against us, I was going to need all the support I could get.

Durham House
Autumn 1528

I THOROUGHLY ENJOYED MY stay at Durham House. Though I wished it were a bit nearer to Greenwich, which was where Henry spent much of his time, it was close enough by river transport, and Henry had made sure I had a barge at my constant disposal, waiting for me at the wharf. Having a separate residence from Katherine was a blessed reprieve. At that point, I would have found it well nigh impossible to maintain a civil manner in her company. My frustration with the lack of progress in gaining any accord with the Church, coupled with Katherine's obstinacy, incited my temper and encouraged my attitude toward her to vary from disdain to outright contempt. Perhaps I had no right to feel as such, but it could not be helped. I did my utmost to keep my thoughts to myself, however, though I was not always successful.

On 22 October, Henry, accompanied by Wolsey, met with the Pope's Legate, Cardinal Campeggio, at Bridewell Palace. I wished I could have been witness to the meeting, but it would have been unseemly. As a consequence, I depended on Henry to provide me with a detailed account. That he did, with all of the animation he must have displayed while pacing and arguing with Campeggio and Wolsey themselves, first describing how he had begun the meeting with an explosive outburst of displeasure at the two cringing clerics. Oh, how I would have liked to have been privy to that most satisfying curtain-raiser!

As the meeting progressed, Campeggio had apparently done his best to mollify Henry's anger with an assurance that the Pope intended nothing but good feeling to be conveyed on his behalf. Campeggio then reported that contrary to Henry's bleak expectations, the Pope had indeed suggested there be a unified effort to convince Katherine to disengage from the marriage. If she could be persuaded to go to a respected abbey, the Pope had suggested, Henry might assure her that she would be well cared for, and her daughter, Mary's interests, would be protected in every case. Campeggio, with supreme satisfaction at his success in acquiring this agreement from the Pope, said if Katherine agreed of her own free will to retire to a nunnery of her choosing, the Holy Father would be willing to dispense of Henry's marriage, thereby allowing him to wed again, with all hope for a son as the fruit of the new union.

Henry talked on, relating this discussion to me. I saw how truly optimistic he was that Katherine just might, in fact, agree to this alternative. After all, she was inordinately pious, was she not? If the convent were to be of her choice, how could she object? His idealism was apparent - too apparent. With a flood of tender feeling for his ingenuousness, I hastened to embrace him and reassure him he had done well with Campeggio. I even told him I felt sure we would have our hoped-for answer soon.

Privily, though, the commonality of sentiment God gave all women afforded me insight to the more likely truth: the prideful Spanish Princess would never willingly leave court, her husband, her daughter and her position as Queen of England to live out her days in a nunnery whilst a younger woman replaced her as her husband's consort - and bedmate.

•

One evening late in October, I hosted a party of games and cards in my apartments at Durham House. I had pleasingly discovered how much I enjoyed planning entertainments and small parties. Members of the court, friends of Henry's - and, I believed - mine as well, made frequent visits to Durham. It had become á *la mode* to do so, as Durham House, recently redecorated, was very beautiful as well as much more comfortable and intimate than the large gatherings of court. And, of course, most evenings the King was at Durham with me.

The guests, in addition to the King, were to include Charles Brandon, Sir Frances Bryan, Sir Thomas Heneage, Anne Gainsford, my uncle the Duke of Norfolk and his lady, Bessie Holland, whom I liked very much. We would have a light supper, then move to my well-appointed gaming room for cards and dice. I had arranged to have some excellent musicians play for us during supper and the rest of the evening. Of course, refreshment would be served throughout. I had asked the kitchen to prepare an arrangement of good cheeses, along with fine white manchet and marmalade, and a selection of fruits, pastries, and marchpane. We would be drinking spiced ale and French wine.

Outside, a blustery autumnal wind whistled around the corners of the house: inside the room was warm and the hearth burned brightly. I checked on preparations as ushers hurried about, setting tables and arranging the buffet. I was instructing the musicians where they should be positioned when I felt a hand caress the small of my back and turned, startled momentarily, to find the King behind me. The yeoman ushers all bowed and quickly moved aside so Henry and I could inspect the buffet laden with food for the evening's supper.

"What a wonderful hostess you are, darling," Henry said warmly. "I expect this will be a special evening."

He was so becoming - so suave - I was hardly able to breathe sufficiently to reply.

"I am deeply honoured, Your Grace, to have you as a guest in the home which you have so generously supplied for my use. The very least I can do is to provide hospitality befitting Your Majesty."

His purple doublet, slashed and lined with cloth of gold surmounted by the thick golden chain about his broad chest, afforded his strong features a glow of health and virility surely unmatched by anyone else. He smelled wonderful, of fine soap and expensive masculine scent. I prayed he found me as desirable as I did him that evening. The look in his eyes as his gaze devoured me from head to toe confirmed his yearning.

For my part, I wore a midnight black velvet gown, with the bodice cut provocatively low. My sleeves were black velvet as well, but the fore-sleeves were red fox fur, glossy in the firelight. The fur set off the ginger tones in my hair, as did the bodice outlined in gold braid and seed pearls. My hood was black velvet edged in pearls, which had been gifts from Henry. My perfume was a seductive blend of patchouli and bergamot.

Abruptly Henry took my arm and pulled me from the chamber into a side common room which was, at the moment, deserted. I was startled by his roughness and wondered if something had upset him. He steered me around the corner, and once out of the sight of others, his face came close to mine, and I saw the smouldering light in his eyes. My heart pounded against my chest, and I held my breath.

"By God, Anne, I can't be without you! When you are near me, I cannot think clearly. I adore you, and long to spend the night with you. *S'il vous plait? Voulez-vous me laisser entrer dans votre chambre?"*

His expression had softened to one of longing.

Frantically, my heart and head waged war. He wrapped his arms around me, and I felt his strength and warmth, and then I surrendered, and whispered, "Oh Henry, I cannot resist you. Yes, yes, you may join me in my bedchamber tonight."

He kissed me, so softly, and with a look that left me weak, released me and led me back to the reception room which was by then beginning to fill with guests.

We ate, drank, laughed uproariously and thus made merry throughout the evening. Anne won at cards, Brandon and Bryan sang and, all the while, I felt Henry's eyes on me, his heat radiant next to me. Betimes I nervously wondered what would transpire that night, but I returned to the laughter and gambling, and simply indulged in Henry's nearness.

When the evening's entertainment had drawn to a close, and my guests had dispersed, Henry dismissed Sir Edward Bayntun, thanking the chamberlain for his evening's service. It was late, and the house quiet and shadowed as Henry and I walked arm in arm through the hallway 'til we came to the door of my apartments. I opened the door motioning for him to enter. My chambermaid was stoking the fire in the hearth. She had lighted candles around the room and had sandalwood incense burning, which I loved in the evening. She looked up at me, then Henry, and dropped into a low curtsey and asked if there was anything I required of her. With a smile, I told her she would not be needed for the rest of the night. She discreetly bowed and left the room, quietly closing the door behind her.

Henry came to me and turned me around, so my back was to him. He carefully removed the pins which held my hood and lifted it from my head. He then loosened my hair, enabling it to tumble unfettered down my back, and stroked it softly. He hesitated for a minute but then untied the laces on my bodice. I turned to face Henry and unbuttoned his doublet, pushing it from his shoulders and arms to fall to the floor. He stood before me in his white linen shirt, the deep opening at the neck revealing his chest, broad and muscled, with red-gold hair exposed. Silently he watched me remove my bodice, then undo the laces of my French gown and smock. I snuffed most of the candles and went to him. Slowly and deliberately, his hands and lips explored the whole of me: delicious and, oh so long-awaited.

We lay together on my bed, and I whispered to him that we could not afford to compromise our hope for a legitimate son, so we must not have intercourse. Henry kissed me and said he agreed but did not know how much longer he would be able to wait.

Once again I valued the education I had been given by the French courtesans.

I proffered an alternative that seemed to please him greatly.

•

As I had expected, Katherine contemptuously refused to consider the proposition to join a convent. I was told that when Campeggio and Wolsey met with her, she proved obdurate, instead reiterating that she and Arthur had never consummated their marriage; thus, she had not been wedded to Arthur at all, but to Henry, and hence she would die the King's wife. She must have driven Wolsey to distraction with her stubborn refusal to discuss any other options, because he ended the interview by uttering a warning to her that, for her well-being, she best comply with the King's wishes. Obviously, he was at a complete loss in knowing how to influence this most inflexible woman.

I confess to having felt some small sympathy for my gross adversary, the Lord Cardinal. Indeed, his travails afforded me a certain insight into why he had been so tardy in acting for the King. I was certain he profoundly regretted having to be involved in the Matter at all. My empathy for him was short-lived, however.

From that point on, enhanced by the increased closeness Henry and I now shared, it became ever more difficult for the King to feign goodwill toward Katherine. He told me she constantly played to the gallery: drawing attention to herself whenever possible and thereby encouraging her subjects' sympathy and support. Her stubborn Spanish pride had become a source of such exasperation that I was surprised Henry had not exploded in rage at her.

In his frustration, though, Henry did feel driven to lodge a formal complaint against her on the grounds of suspicious political affiliations and her unsuitable behaviour with his privy council. The council, at his bidding, wrote Katherine a letter advising her to come to terms with the King's will, lest she be sent away and separated from the Princess Mary. Even at this, which must surely have instilled in her a great fear, she refused to obey. Whenever she and Henry met, he told me they did nothing but argue.

Still, she would not be swayed.

Oh, indeed there were times when I felt so completely perturbed that, had I been in her company, I would have wished to tear the very hair from her head! How her air of self-righteousness provoked me! But instead, I determined to play a much more cunning game.

Tit-for-tat.

I would make a very visible - and very grand - appearance at Christmas Court in Greenwich this year

•

By early November, the conversations amongst London's wealthy and powerful swirled with rumour. Everyone had their opinion of Henry's now conspicuous desire for a divorce. In an attempt to quell the tide of gossip, and upon the advice of his closest councillors Henry decided to address the city's most influential citizens in person. Courtiers, judges, lawyers, and other officials were invited by the King to come to the Palace of Bridewell on the afternoon of 8 November. They jostled and crowded into the Great Chamber, each and every one of them possessed of a keen curiosity to hear their King discuss so private a matter quite publicly. I was positioned with an excellent, albeit hidden, view of the entire assembly from an interior window overlooking the hall.

An expectant hush descended when Henry took his place on the raised podium, and as he stood before the gathering and drew himself to his full stature, he looked every inch the most august King in Christendom.

Eloquently he began by expressing his appreciation for their attendance. With a look of significance missed by no one, he disclosed his great distress in having discovered he had been unwittingly living in sin with the woman he believed to be his rightful and true wife these twenty years past. His voice rang out strong and deep, yet touched with humble regret as he told his listeners how, although he had indeed been blessed with a fair daughter born of this noble woman - indeed, a daughter who had given them both great comfort and joy - he had been recently informed by clerks of the realm that neither was she his lawful child, nor her mother his lawful wife.

He had paused then, to allow the gravity of his words to take full effect. Henry had always been the consummate dramatist. Only when he had squeezed the last juice from that shocking revelation did he carry on, telling the crowd that although he was appalled by this realization, he had come to know it had been a most grievous, but unwitting mistake to have fathered a child by his brother's wife. Now, he stated, he was left with little choice but to call on the greatest minds in the Church to advise him as to his course of remedial action. He went on to carefully describe how wonderful and noble Katherine was, and to assure them that his dilemma was not caused by any lack in her person.

Listening to this last comment, up in my perch above the crowd, I took spiteful satisfaction in reciting under my breath, 'other than in her constantly gloomy expression, her never-ending, self-righteous devotions, her stodgy Spanish *entourage*, that greying hair and ponderous gait.' I sniggered to myself and felt momentarily better.

Nevertheless, the impression the King's well-edited humility had on the assemblage was quite profound, and I could see he was becoming caught up in the credibility of his performance. Continuing his theme of lauding Katherine's many virtues, in a magnanimous gesture, he stated that were the marriage to be declared good, surely he would choose her again above all women.

At that, I rolled my eyes and loudly snorted with indignation! As his oration drew to a close, I looked about at the faces below. Most were sombre and silent. As Henry's speech concluded, while some spoke up to express their regret at the King's dilemma, two in the crowd, though I could not see whom, loudly offered their support and great admiration for the queen. A murmur of … was it agreement? … rippled through the assemblage.

I slumped back in my chair and exhaled. Had Henry done the right thing?

Finally, the group dispersed, swollen with their own self-importance at being privy to such personal insights: each no doubt hastening to chronicle the King's speech far and wide before others beat them to the line.

Greenwich
Christmastide 1528

I TOOK MY LEAVE of Durham House and established myself at Greenwich, nearer to the King, for the duration of the Christmas celebrations. My family would be together at court for the season, and I was glad to have my lady mother close by. Henry had provided me with beautiful lodgings which were, thankfully, some distance from Katherine's, so I need not feel as if I might run into her at any moment.

I intended to play a high-profile part in the most important festivities, in spite of Katherine's role as Queen – more truthfully, it was *because* she would be present. The house buzzed with activity during that exciting precursor to Christmas Eve, which I loved so much. On the day before, Maggie Wyatt, my mother, and I were wandering through the gallery and ended up stopping in the Great Hall to watch the house servants hang decorative greens and ready the chamber for the banquet the next evening. I marvelled as ever at the agility of those men who climbed the scaffolds to drape the beamed ceiling and the chandeliers in holly, laurel, and ivy. The pungent smell pervading the large room was wonderful and made it seem as if we were in a fragrant pine forest while abundant boughs of laurel accented by the red berries of holly branches were being arranged liberally in porcelain urns and silver vases.

"What gift have you planned to give to His Grace at the New Year, Anne, if I may be so bold?" Maggie asked.

"It seems silly, really, but I am having a miniature painted of me by Master Horenbolte, while I have a beautiful locket prepared in which to mount it when it's completed," I replied. "If it were left to me, I would never have thought to give a gift of one's own face! But that is what Henry requested - and who am I to deny him?"

"Who indeed," Mother interjected dryly.

I threw her a glance of mock sarcasm, then said, "in any case, Master Horenbolte seems to be doing a superb job. Thankfully the painting, or what I have seen of it thus far, seems to flatter rather than have me appear as some troglodyte." At that, we melted into a flood of giggles.

I gave my friend a playful nudge. "*Quid pro quo*, Maggie. Now you must reveal to us what gift you propose to give to the handsome Lord Lee?"

She had recently become betrothed to Sir Anthony Lee, of Burston and Quarrendon. I was very happy for Maggie. She seemed pleased with this match, and Lord Lee struck me as a proper gentleman.

"Well," said Maggie, flushing a little, "For Anthony I have acquired a beautifully illuminated devotional which was painted in Ghent. The artwork is magnificent."

"Then my Lord Lee is a very lucky man," I replied fondly.

My mother looked at me questioningly. "Do you think Katherine will give the King an elaborate gift this year? Or might she be upset enough to gainsay gift-giving altogether?"

"I wager that she will give him the largest, most costly, and most personal gift her courtiers can unearth, Mother," I quickly replied. I was aware that my voice had a rough edge to it. I felt a momentary annoyance with Mother for her comment, but I hadn't meant to snap.

I chose not to pursue the topic, and we walked on.

•

As one might well have expected given the circumstances, the Cardinals Wolsey and Campeggio were guests of honour at that great Christmas Eve banquet, sitting to the right and left, respectively, of the King on the dais. Surprising to all, the Queen made only the briefest of appearances at the celebration. It was apparent that she took no joy in the occasion: her expression was pinched and unhappy. From what I was able to observe, she rarely spared a glance in the direction of the King, keeping her arms stiffly pressed to her sides as if protecting herself. I was astounded to see how much older she appeared. I had not seen her for several months, and she looked to me to be a woman of advanced age, yet I knew her years to be only forty-three. Her hair had greyed while deep crevices now ran from her nose to the corners of her mouth. What a contrast she made with Henry, who radiated like the very sun!

There were furtive remarks made by many when Katherine did not appear at all at Mass on Christmas Day, instead sending word that she was unwell and would hear Mass in her chamber. The court, almost in its entirety, was present at morning Mass, and there was audible whispering when her seat remained empty.

•

A small gathering of important peers and esteemed guests had been invited to the King's presence chamber for Christmas supper. I was about to enter the room, already alive with the company, but paused for a moment at the threshold to gather an air of confidence. The opulent silk of my gown rustled as I swept into the room and approached Henry to curtsey, and greet him with a kiss before being seated in the position of honour, closest to the King at the head of the table. That evening, I had taken exceptional care with my clothing and jewellery, and my crimson silk gown with white silk kirtle, heavily embroidered with silver and gold vines, was the object of admiration. I wore a necklace of woven gold from which hung a stunning ruby given to me by Henry. At my wrist was the diamond bracelet he had gifted to me, and, as nearly always, the emerald ring was on my finger.

We ate, drank, and toasted the birth of Christ, and all the while, Henry's eyes rarely left me. I noted the wizened Cardinal Campeggio, though old and seemingly infirm, astutely observing the interaction between Henry and me. Once the gingerbread, comfits, and Christmas Pie had been served, Campeggio rose from his chair, bowed and thanked Henry effusively, saying he would retire for the night. He made his way through the guests, speaking with many of them. When he reached me, he took my hand and kissed it, bowed courteously, then looked searchingly into my eyes. I returned an unflinching gaze, sensing I was not being scrutinized by merely a man of the cloth, but instead by a charming, calculating and crafty statesman.

"*Buona notte*, *Signorina* Boleyn." he murmured in his heavily accented English. "May you have a most blessed Christmas."

I curtseyed graciously in reply, knowing that, this evening, the Pope's Legate, who would pay a considerable part in deciding my lot, had been enlightened as to Henry's true motivation for seeking a divorce.

The banqueting was frequent during the week following Christmas, along with several masques, tourneys, and even a joust which a mild spell of weather permitted. We saw little of Katherine. I was told by friends close to her ladies-in-waiting, that she was disconsolate, especially because she and Henry rarely saw each other or spoke. Once again, I wished she would simply accede, take up a position as a respected abbess - and save all of us the grief which undoubtedly lay ahead if she remained invariant.

Henry and I decided we would exchange our presents with one another privately, after the New Year celebration which involved the annual gift giving between Henry and his entire staff and court.

Because Katherine had unexpectedly announced that she would oversee the New Year's festivities, I avoided the formal banquet that night. Instead, I enjoyed an evening of music and had supper in my apartments, along with some of my closest companions. My mother and father were both in attendance, although George had felt it best he dine with the King and Queen. Henry Norreys was with us, along with Thomas Heneage, Anne Gainsford, Sir George Zouche, Lady Bridget and Sir Nicholas Harvey. We toasted the coming year, 1529, and all around the table expressed their conviction that it would undoubtedly be a very good year.

My guests had begun to depart once midnight had passed, and the merrymaking waned. A messenger entered the chamber and quietly told me the King had requested the honour of my presence in his privy chamber. I was summoned at last! I had so missed Henry this evening.

As quickly as propriety allowed, I escorted my remaining guests to the door and went to the large, ornately carved wardrobe in my bedchamber. Inside was a wooden coffer. Unlocking it, I retrieved two small boxes, each wrapped in soft white kidskin. I hoped Henry liked the image of me now mounted in its locket. Gathering a few personal belongings into a satin pouch, I hastened through the dimly lit corridors, accompanied by an esquire, to reach Henry's chambers.

Once we were alone, I flung myself into his arms. We had not had much time to ourselves during the past week due to all of the activities at court, and I missed his closeness, the feel, and smell of him. I buried my face in his neck, savouring the scratch of his beard on my cheeks and forehead. We held each other silently for a time, each fervently hoping this would be the year we would wed, and conceive a child together. Finally, we drew apart and, with a kiss, I said, "I cannot wait to give you your gifts, Your Grace. I hope you love them!"

"From you, Nan, I will love anything, even the smallest token. Just as long as your heart comes with it … with your body soon to follow." His low chuckle filled me with happiness.

With evident bated breath, as excited as a child, Henry prised apart the kidskin wrapping to find a golden hawk's hood, garnished with six rubies and seven pearls, enclosed within. I had had this hood fashioned for his new white gyrfalcon, a bird he treasured. His eyes shone as he made to kiss me his thanks, but I held up my hand, urging him instead to open the other one.

He opened the locket slowly, then carefully studied the image within before looking up at me with awe.

"Anne, my love, this miniature of you is so beautiful, and such an incredible likeness. Master Horenbolte has indeed done himself proud. I am overjoyed that I can now have you next to my heart at all times/"

He carefully pinned the locket to his doublet so it hung against his left breast. "Thank you, darling."

And then he did indeed kiss me.

It was my turn to open two packages. First, I untied the drawstring of a black velvet pouch, and into my hand tumbled a brilliant, weighty jewel: a ship of diamonds, with a fair hanging pearl, and then, from the second pouch of scarlet, a heart of gold, with a hunter and an antelope engraved on one side, and a gentlewoman on the obverse. I looked up at Henry, once again not believing my great fortune for loving this great-hearted man. Of course, I knew that the meaning behind both glittering tokens was to reassure me that he would be mine, never otherwise, and we would be united soon.

I moved toward Henry, intent on thanking him with an embrace for such remarkable, such costly, gifts, but he stood and motioned to his esquire. His gentleman handed Henry a lute, and he settled himself on a stool, indicating I should sit directly across from him. I could not imagine what he had planned, but

I was enthralled as he began to play and sing a haunting, heart-rending melody. His eyes never left mine as he sang, thus:

'Alas, my love, ye do me wrong,
To cast me off discourteously
And I have loved you for so long,
Delighting in your company.

Greensleeves was all my joy
Greensleeves was my delight,
Greensleeves was my heart of gold,
And who but my lady greensleeves

I have been ready at your hand,
To grant whatever you would crave,
I have both wagered life and land,
Your love and good-will for to have

Greensleeves was all my joy
Greensleeves was my delight,
Greensleeves was my heart of gold,
And who but my lady greensleeves

My men were clothed all in green,
And they did ever wait on thee;
All this was gallant to be seen,
And yet thou wouldst not love me

Thou couldst desire no earthly thing,
but still thou hadst it readily.
Thy music still to play and sing;
And yet thou wouldst not love me

Well, I will pray to God on high,
that thou my constancy mayst see,
And that yet once before I die,
Thou wilt vouchsafe to love me

Greensleeves was all my joy
Greensleeves was my delight,
Greensleeves was my heart of gold,
And who but my lady greensleeves

I sat in marvel, tears welling and spilling over. I knew not how to react to such an overture. His astonishing creation was for me alone - a theme which would become a legacy of our love, epitomizing gallantry and courtly romance. It touched me more profoundly than I could express.

"My Henry, when did you compose that piece?"

"Most of it while you were at Hever, recovering from your illness. There were times when I feared I might never hold you in my arms again, Anne. I pictured you, so vividly, in the magnificent gown with the emerald green sleeves you wore before we were parted, and this composition came forth, as if on its own."

"It is so personal, darling, and I wish it could remain for me alone. But it is so very beautiful. It is unforgettable! You must play it so others can hear it. And henceforth all who do will know the true nature of your love for me!"

I had scarcely recovered from that emotional scene when Henry was on his feet. Motioning me to remain, he whispered something quickly to the guard, and as the esquire stepped out of the chamber, Henry turned back to me. "There is something else, Nan. Close your eyes."

I closed them, not at all sure what might follow. When Henry said "Now you may open them," I did so only to see him standing before me holding a squirming, wriggling, spotted white greyhound pup – Jolie!

How I squealed with joy! I took her from him and could barely contain the excited mite as she wiggled to lick whoever was closest. I had made arrangements to have her delivered once I returned to Durham House, thinking she would be a burden at Greenwich over Christmas, but Henry had collected her for me and taken care of all the details. I was so happy to have her with me. She sported a beautiful green satin collar and leash, which looked most elegant against her white and fawn coat. Once put down, she ran to and fro in Henry's chamber, sniffing everything she could. And, of course, she squatted to pass a little water on the Turkey carpet. Henry laughed out loud, as did I, and a steward rushed in to clean it. One of the esquires on duty said he would take her outside to relieve herself – I would have done so myself had it not been so frigid – then return her so she could sleep in her new, soft velvet-covered bed.

Once Jolie was brought back, we played with her a while longer, then put her on her bed for the night in the small closet adjacent to Henry's bedchamber.

As for us, we retired alone to the inner suite.

And snuffed all of the candles but one.

Durham House
Greenwich
January 1529

HENRY AND I settled into uneasy waiting as an icy, raw winter gripped London and the surrounding countryside. We received reports that many subjects in both the city and the towns and villages suffered great hardship due to the brutal cold and deep freeze. Royal instructions were delivered to local officials to do whatever they could to alleviate the worst of the need, and to this end Henry provided alms for foodstuffs and tinder, yet the winter took a toll on much of the populace. As fortunate as we were to be warm and well-fed, still we sought activity which would keep us distracted. Meanwhile, in Rome, Clement had taken to his sick bed yet again, and we knew not when we would receive the next scrap of news on that issue which mattered to us most.

Patient endurance was not a virtue that Henry or I exhibited very easily.

The stakes in the Great Matter escalated, and Henry's tolerance was tested until it was nigh to breaking. Sir Francis Bryan was instructed to compel the Pope, at any cost, to agree with the King's wishes to grant the divorce. Henry had made it clear to Sir Francis he was not to mince words in conveying to the Pope that he must accede, and since Francis was possessed of a particularly sinister edge, we felt he could apply a fitting pressure to those who needed it most.

We had received two updates from Bryan since his departure. Neither was particularly promising. But he remained committed to swaying the opinions of those most reluctant. The second letter stated *'We trust that if fair words, large offers of money or pension, or bishoprics, or if all this will not serve, with some bold words we shall win these men.'*

Katherine, it seemed, had launched her counter- offensive to thwart Henry's plan. Just before Christmas, she informed him that she had specific knowledge of a brief which would prove her claims to be surely truthful. Upon Henry's insistence, she revealed it to be a written dispensation from Pope Julius II, created in 1503 after Arthur's death, which permitted her marriage to Henry even though she and Arthur *may* have consummated their marriage. Both Henry and I found the entire concept preposterous! How, indeed, did she come upon such a document, and why had it not been revealed until now? And, most absurd was Katherine's deception – did she, or did she not consummate her marriage to Henry's brother?

In the weeks following, the situation became more and more of a muddle. There was a mad scramble to locate the original of this brief which Katherine insisted was real. The Emperor contended he owned it, and then sent a copy of the document to London with an affidavit confirming his custody of the original. Henry did not trust Charles's claim, so Wolsey dispatched a group of ambassadors to Rome to seek the original there, if indeed it did exist. All the while, the days slowly churned into weeks, and no advance whatsoever was made toward releasing Henry from his marriage to Katherine. I strained to be a model of forbearance, though God knows, at times it took every shred of self-control I could muster.

•

On a ferociously cold afternoon, while a piercing wind howled about the corners of Durham House, Henry and I sat in the library reading and talking by a blazing, snap-crackling fire. Durham House, by virtue of its smaller size, seemed more welcoming and protective from winter's harsh bite than did the cavernous palaces. At least it felt warmer to me. Henry enjoyed it as well, and took opportunities whenever he could to be rowed across the Thames from Greenwich, or downstream from Richmond to spend time with me there. We were certainly gladdened by greater privacy at Durham than we had at court.

As he crunched on an apple, Henry thoughtfully put down the book he had in hand. He had been reading Aristotle that afternoon not only because he found the writings to prompt deep thought, but also because he now constantly sought material which might substantiate his case against Katherine. I looked up to see him peering intently at me, brows knit.

He picked the book up again and said, "Anne, listen to this."

Turning back a page and following a passage with his finger, he read aloud:

> '... for the good man's opinions are harmonious, and he desires the same things with all his soul: and therefore he wishes for himself what is good and what seems so, and does it (for it is characteristic of the good man to work out the good), and does so for his own sake (for he does it for the sake of the intellectual element in him, which is thought to be the man himself): and he wishes himself to live and be preserved.'

Glancing up, he said, "this is from the Seventh Book of Aristotle's *Nichomachean Ethics*, by the way," before reading on:

> '... and such a man wishes to live with himself: for he does so with pleasure, since the memories of his past acts are delightful and his hopes for the future are good, and therefore pleasant ...'

Henry paused a moment, then continued to read the next passage slowly, with great significance.

> 'Perfect friendship is the friendship of men who are good, and alike in virtue: for these wish well alike to each other qua good, and they are good themselves. Now those who wish well to their friends for their sake are most truly friends: for they do this by reason of own nature and not incidentally: therefore their friendship lasts as long as they are good - and goodness is an enduring thing.
>
> Therefore, since these characteristics belong to the good man in relation to himself, and he is related to his friend as to himself (for his friend is another self), friendship too is thought to be one of these attributes, and those who have these attributes to be friends.'

"Anne," he said, with dawning realization, "this is precisely what I have sensed about us. You are, in every way, my other self – my second self! You and I share all that is good, all that is spiritual and mysterious, all that is virtuous and profound. We are one and the same soul. You know this to be true because we have both perceived it."

He paused then, before stating, "As long as goodness prevails, we will be as second selves to each other; upon this foundation, together we will create greatness."

He came to me and encircled my waist with his arms. "Is that not extraordinary, my Anne? Aristotle perfectly predicted our unique and miraculous union. He banishes all doubt. According to history's greatest sage, our intention to create good for one another will be our triumph. It will empower us to bring forth a son whose radiance will be felt by the entire world!"

I looked into his intelligent face, pondering what he had said. I, too, felt that Henry and I were 'second selves', exactly as Aristotle had described. This passage finally explained the almost mystical sense of knowing him which had been a part of our relationship since that November day in the hunt field, which now seemed like years ago. I was filled with awe at the concept.

Absently, I reached to stroke his hair as I thought about what this revelation might mean for us.

•

That evening, after Henry had departed for Richmond to attend to business the next day, I retired to my bedchamber with the copy of the *Ethics* Henry had been reading earlier. I settled into a chair by the fire, several lanterns providing additional light, and, with Jolie curled at my feet, read the excerpts Henry had notated in the page margins:

> 'Friendly relations with one's neighbours, and the marks by which friendships are defined, seem to have proceeded from a man's relations to himself. For (1) we define a friend as one who wishes and does what is good, or seems so, for the sake of his friend, or (2) as one who wishes his friend to exist and live, for his sake: which mothers do to their children, and friends do who have come into conflict. And (3) others define him as one who lives with and (4) has the same tastes as another, or (5) one who grieves and rejoices with his friend: and this too is found in mothers most of all. It is by some one of these characteristics that friendship too is defined.
>
> Therefore, since each of these characteristics belongs to the good man in relation to himself, and he is related to his friend as to himself (for his friend is another self), friendship too is thought to be one of these attributes, and those who have these attributes to be friends. Whether there is or is not friendship between a man and himself is a question we may dismiss for the present: there

would seem to be friendship in so far as he is two or more, to judge from the afore-mentioned attributes of friendship, and from the fact that the extreme of friendship is likened to one's love for oneself.

I considered this passage for some time. It felt real to me: the notion of Henry and I being 'second selves'. We shared so many of the same ideas, desires, views and opinions. We were a remarkable match in pursuits of skill and mental ingenuity. We felt connected as if we had always known one another. And, it was not to be denied – we shared a passion which was unmatched in any pairing I had ever experienced or otherwise known of. His joys and sufferings were mine, and mine his. Together we felt invincible. And by virtue of this confidence, I knew that we would emerge victorious in the Great Matter and be united; and just as Henry had stated so assuredly, together we would beget a son who would fulfil England's hopes and dreams.

•

By March, the Pope was well enough to conduct business again, but the indications we received from Francis Bryan were dire. By then I was quite convinced that the approach we had employed would never succeed. Despite the odds, however, Henry remained optimistic, believing Pope might yet be swayed. At times, I thought him utterly naïve, though I would never have dared say so. Instead, we looked forward to the hearing, which would be held before Cardinal Campeggio and the Legatine Council, with the intent of gathering all existing evidence, evaluating it, and thereby passing determination on the case.

By this time it was all too apparent Cardinal Wolsey would have liked nothing more than to provide Henry with the answer he desired so as to put the issue to rest. The Cardinal badly needed a victory, no matter how small, for the anti-Wolsey movement was growing, and it had become tangible at court. As for Cardinal Campeggio – his character I still found difficult to read. He seemed a kindly man, and my connection with him felt sincere. But after all, actuality would prevail. Campeggio's mission was to serve his master – and that master was Pope Clement VII. So I had no sense of assurance about the upcoming hearing, yet I remained cautiously hopeful.

With the emergence of the first delicate crocus, I walked in the garden of Durham House, wrapped in a warm cloak of black velvet lined with fur of lynx, another gift from Henry. When the weather was fair, I enjoyed sitting in the sun on a carved stone bench facing the awakening rose beds, to read. I was absorbed in reviewing some of the works of Jacques Lefévre, a French humanist whose writings were introduced to me by Marguerite d'Angoulême. I found his ideas to be both progressive and sound. I especially liked his *De Maria Magdalena,* which postulated that Mary Magdalene, the sister of Lazarus, and the woman who washed the feet of Jesus were three separate people. I had heard that this work had the Church in France in a frenzy, and that it had been banned at the *Sorbonne*, Paris's edifice to conservative Catholicism. I found it to be bold and stimulating, and I admired Lefévre's courage and creative thinking. I also spent hours reading Erasmus, though admittedly, such reading went more slowly. Not only did he write in Latin, but Erasmus regularly assigned double and triple meanings to his phrases.

The more I read, the more I was unable to suppress the thoughts which continued to demand exploration. Why, indeed, were ecclesiastics held separate from the rest of mankind? Why were they permitted the pretence of determining who was morally right and who wrong? I thought carefully about Cardinal Wolsey, and of other clerics I had known. Of course, there were members of the clergy who were upstanding, and sincerely devout. I considered Sir Thomas More among those numbers, though at times it seemed to me that More's singular devotion was peculiar in its austerity. But it was not the pious priests who assumed roles of power and wealth. No, it was those who slyly contrived to wrest control of privilege and influence; whose great personal wealth was subtly displayed for all to see; those who carelessly hid their mistresses and bastards; who presumed to have the power to direct the lives of others ... why, then, must Henry – a prince and monarch born, truly responsible for the well-being of an empire and its people – be subjected to the poorly made decisions of these corrupt men who hid beneath their vestments? The more I reflected on this concept, the more illogical it seemed.

But again - I was only a simple woman, and there were few, if any, intellectuals in my female circle with whom I could discuss these ideas.

Henry and I lived a double life that spring. There was the daily occupation of pursuing a resolution to the Great Matter and all the political frustration which went with it - then there was our love affair.

Henry rarely, if ever, arrived at Durham House without an extravagant gift for me. He always had his footmen deliver his favourite marchpane and puddings, claiming that his master baker was far better than the French cook I employed at Durham House. But in addition to sweets, he delighted in surprising me with an embroidered satin pouch, a box, a parcel; always gorgeously wrapped. His eyes would twinkle merrily as he watched me ferret out the treasure inside the wrapping. One evening, an especially large package was handed to me by a beaming Henry. He was like a child who could not wait to receive a gift, yet he delighted even more in being the giver. I turned back the satin-lined velvet wrapping to behold three fantastic jewels: a diamond heart with a central sapphire to be worn on a hood, a brooch in the shape of a heart set with diamonds and rubies, and a bracelet of rubies with a diamond clasp.

Looking up at Henry from the desk on which lay the veritable trove of gems, I went to him, wound my fingers into the slashes on his doublet and slowly pulled him to me. Cradling his face in both my hands, I drew him closer and kissed him, taking my time.

When I finally allowed him to be released, he looked into my eyes and said softly, "For you, my Nan, nothing will ever be fine enough. I would give you every jewel in existence to buy time 'til I can give you myself."

I prayed it would be soon.

Hampton Court
May 1529

GEORGE SMILED AT me tentatively from across the table in the small, but beautiful library Cardinal Wolsey had built for himself at Hampton Court. His smile did not help one jot as I was in a foul humour, with an aching head, cramping stomach, and feeling just generally pitiable. On this occasion, my poor brother was the victim of my wretched mood.

"I am at my wit's end, George - and don't you dare laugh at me! You have no idea how awful it is, watching the drama play out and having no direct way of influencing it! Campeggio, Foxe, Gardener, Bryan... they are all the same. Oh, they appear so sympathetic, so encouraging. But do they care? No! After all, it is not their life which is at stake – the outcome has little bearing on their personal happiness and fulfilment, as it does mine!"

"I know, Nan," he said, hurriedly losing the smile, "I can only imagine how frustrating it must be to watch an array of old men dictate your prospects. If you want, you can vent your anger with me whenever you need to. But you best not let His Majesty see you thus."

I stood and went to the window. I drew a deep breath and willed the grim humour to leave me upon exhale. "Thank you, George. I'm sorry; I know you are my most ardent supporter, and I am so grateful for that. And you are right to warn me not to forget my place. When these moods come upon me, I either avoid Henry entirely or else I must bite the insides of my cheeks raw to keep my mouth closed."

Curled in a corner, clearly keeping a safe distance, Jolie opened one soulful amber eye and surveyed me reproachfully. For such a mite she wielded an awesome power: she could blunt the edge of my temper without moving one lazy little paw.

"Anyway, I know it is not Henry's fault," I continued somewhat less petulantly. "He is doing all he can to move things along but, unfortunately, he is still much too dependent on Wolsey. It is what he has always done; how he has always made his decisions - with Wolsey at his shoulder closely directing every move, although I must say the Lord Cardinal is not quite as cavalierly sure of himself as he was just a few short months ago. No, the time has clearly come for Henry to pry himself from that deceptive, clutching grasp. To trust himself and the advice of those councillors who are loyal, and devoted to his best interests. And I intend to do whatever I can to nudge him toward this realization."

"Certainly you're the one best placed to do so, Nan," George's tone was edged with respect. "It is apparent that the King's Highness takes close account of every word you utter. It is what I am certain of, having observed the two of you, together. Yes, I do think you are perhaps the only one who can open His Majesty's eyes to the Cardinal's connivance."

I thought on George's comment. I did value his opinion and looked to him for support. Aside from Mother, I was keenly aware that no one knew me better than George. I focused on my plan.

"Well then, I have made up my mind. I will find just the right time to have a discussion with Henry about my Lord Cardinal Wolsey. I will lead him to admit Wolsey's failure to make any headway on the divorce. And I will cleverly hint at the idea that his trusted Cardinal may, in fact, be clandestinely serving not his, but in fact the Pope's, interests. As for when the conversation must take place: soon. One way or another I must make my position clear well in advance of the Legatine hearing. Oh, Henry may not like what I have to say, but he will hear it nonetheless!"

"You will handle it well, Nan. But keep your calm. Just promise me you will keep your head about you as best you can."

He risked an impish grin. And then could not resist adding, "… rather than risk losing it altogether."

I shot him a withering look, followed by a laugh. "I shall, my darling brother, have no fear of that. Now - will you be coming to Hever at all this spring? I am going to stay there while the Legatine Hearing takes place, though I would infinitely prefer being at Bridewell, nearer to the business itself. I will have to wait for news by courier, and you know that will not be easy for me."

"Then I shall come when I can, to provide you with information and keep you company, Nan."

I pushed back my chair and went to George to hug him. One could not ask for a better brother or more trustworthy friend.

Hever
June 1529

BEAMS OF EARLY morning sunlight played across the arched half dome ceiling of my bedchamber as I lay abed, postponing arising to dress. The light suggested that a beautiful day had dawned. I remained curled under my covers for a little while longer, until finally plucking the courage to swing my bare feet to the chilly floor. From the back of a chair, I hastily recovered a wrap, pulled it about my shoulders, and went to the window. I unlatched and pushed open the leaded glass casement to view the orchard below. It was indeed a lovely late spring morning, and there was no more beautiful place on earth to appreciate it than from the heart of the Kentish countryside. The night-time mist, billowing over the lawns which sloped downward toward the river, was beginning to dissipate. Beyond I could make out the stone spire of St Peter's, the old Norman church in Hever, piercing the fresh, early blue of the sky. The apple trees were coming into bloom, their pink and white blossoms sparkling with drops of dew reflecting the sun's increasing warmth, and the swans and their cygnets glided on the castle moat. Such a wonderful day – yet it would be difficult for me to enjoy.

I had been informed that today the Queen was expected to appear before the Legates at the trial to present her testimony. I had hoped that by now, some weeks after I left court for home, there would have come a decision. But, as usual, the preparations for the hearing had moved ponderously, and the official business had just gotten underway.

Reluctantly, I was beginning to recognize that God's great plan for me included mastering the art of patience. It was proving a difficult lesson, to be sure.

The serenity and peace of home, of being in Edenbridge as opposed to the noise and clamour of court should have offered a welcome respite. But it did not. I could not concentrate on anything, being concerned as I was about the legal proceedings at Bridewell. I pictured scenarios in which there was great support for Henry's argument, rapidly followed by imaginings of a disastrous outcome. Wishing for something to lift my spirits, I was thrilled when the King's courier arrived unexpectedly. I met the equerry inside the castle courtyard and gratefully received the package he delivered. Returning to the house, I sat at a desk in the small room which served as the estate office, and cleared a spot on a desk piled with bills of lading and ledgers to open the thin, crackling parchment. Greeted by the familiar hand, I smiled fondly, almost as if I were faced with the man himself instead of the writing I had come to know so intimately. I found his letters especially touching because I knew how much he disliked writing – mostly because he hated sitting still for the length of time such labours took.

I took note of the easy scrawl: the degree of familiarity with which he now wrote. This letter was in English, not the more formal French. His penmanship was less proscribed, the messages more quickly composed; just like our relationship. He was comfortable with me now, as I was with him. Still, his care and affection for me were instantly apparent - a sweet song on the page.

> To inform you what joy it is to me to understand of your conformableness with reason, and of the suppressing of your inutile and vain thoughts with the bridle of reason.

I assumed George had reassured the King all was quite well with me while at Hever, not letting on the truth of my agony at being so far removed.

> I assure you all the good in this world could not counterpoise for my satisfaction the knowledge and certainty thereof, wherefore, good sweethart, continue the same, not only in this, but in all your doings hereafter: for thereby shall come, both to you and me, the greatest quietness that may be in this world.

His words were so encouraging, and I longed to believe them. He continued:

> The cause why the bearer taketh so long, is the bysyness I have had to dres upp ger for you: and which I trust, ere long to to ... here, he must have been distracted, not realizing he had written the word twice! ... see you occupy and then I trust to occupy yours / whyche shall be recompense enough to me for all my pains and labors.

A peal of laughter escaped me. He had commissioned for me some beautiful clothes, which in his man's parlance he referred to as 'dress up gear': and not just that – but he wished to see me in them … and then - better yet - out of them! How I loved Henry's lusty wit! He was never one to miss an opportunity to remind me how eager he was. As if I needed reminding.

Henry then mentioned that Cardinal Wolsey had not been well, but as soon as he recovered, would most certainly resume efforts on our behalf and wanted to assure us both that under no circumstances should we think him inclined to be imperial - aligned with Katherine's nephew, the Emperor Charles.

... Thus, for lack of time, sweethart, farewell.

Written with the hand which fain would be yours, and so is the heart.

R. H.

Unwrapping the parcel which accompanied the letter, I found three bolts of marvellous fabric. A soft, creamy white velvet - very rare and costly; a roll of white silk so fine as to be almost translucent, and a brilliant purple satin.

The gift of deep purple satin, reserved for royals only, spoke volumes. I recognised that these were fabrics Henry was offering as samples from which I should create my wedding gown. My heart swelled with love and gratitude. How extraordinary it was to be adored so – to be the darling of the most esteemed man in the world.

I occupied myself until dinner by sewing with my mother in the morning room, then had my Neapolitan mare saddled and readied to ride out for the afternoon. I walked Tempesta through the poppy fields and down the trails by the River Eden. As always, the ride relaxed me and allowed me to think of matters other than the hearing and its outcome. Yet it followed me doggedly - that unrelenting desire for Katherine to remove her peevish self from the scene and allow Henry and me to proceed with our lives.

I was acutely aware of my own age, and of my monthly flow, which seemed such a sorrowful waste with its every appearance.

To my dismay, days passed before I was able to hear a full recounting of the results of the Legatine Court proceedings at Blackfriars. I was notified by the King's couriers that Katherine had refused to appear when called. God's wounds! What an imperious martyr she had become!

Finally, though, she relented, and both Henry and Katherine were present, together, in the courtroom. My brother, who had been in attendance, left the proceedings to come to Kent and provide me with news. We settled in the orchard under a cherry tree, while George described how Henry had persuasively addressed the court from his Chair of Estate. With great respect and deference, Henry described once again how their inability to produce a male heir was clearly a punishment from God exacted on both him and Katherine for their marriage, which was unlawful. He continued, George had recounted, by declaring the great love and respect he held for Katherine, who had been a noble and most excellent queen. He implored the Legatine Court to relieve him from the Matter, which so greatly vexed his mind and troubled his spirit, and allow him to disassociate himself from the marriage to remarry and ensure the succession.

At that point, Katherine had risen abruptly and stalked from the chamber with the departing reaffirmation that she had never carnally known Arthur, so in fact, it was no marriage according to God; thereby her only true husband was Henry.

My jaw tightened with an involuntary clench. Seeing this, George attempted to reassure me by describing how the concerns and determinations of the council seemed to weigh in Henry's favour, as the members of the court and council discussed in detail Katherine's claim that she had not consummated the marriage with Arthur.

The mood lightened, and George and I could not help but giggle uncontrollably when he told me that a member of the court had loudly called out, saying he had been witness those many years ago when, on the very morning after their wedding night, Arthur had called for drink, loudly acclaiming 'he had been in Spain that night, which was a hot country!' The implication was obvious.

Even more startling was the testimony that at the time of Prince Arthur's death, Katherine herself indicated she might be with child! It was for this very reason that Henry had been deferred from his creation as Prince of Wales for more than six months until it was clear that there was no pregnancy. Undoubtedly, the Legates were as confused by Katherine's divergent claims as was I.

At that point in his story, George did warn me what he was next to say would likely send me into a paroxysm. I prepared myself as he described the moment when the court crier called for Katherine to enter, whereupon instead of taking her designated seat, she had approached Henry wearing a face of humility worthy of the finest actor. When she was carefully positioned directly before him, she fell to her knees and, in a loud and supplicating tone, beseeched him for justice, describing herself as but a 'poor woman and stranger' who had remained far from her homeland to be a good wife to him all their years together. She begged him, with the entire court as witness, to be compassionate and to accept her as his true wife, unless he should find her dishonest in any way.

As George spoke, my eyes grew wide in shocked disbelief. How, then, had Henry responded? George did his best to stifle his amusement at the recall of Henry, face growing ever more purple as she persisted, quite pointedly refusing to look at her during her speech. George was sure the King did all he humanly could to hold back the mighty explosion which appeared likely to erupt at any moment.

I was thoroughly perplexed. How could this woman have thought such a tactic would have had any chance of winning Henry? It was hard for me to believe she had been married to the man for over twenty years. Apparently she knew him not at all! Did she not recognize that the embarrassment she caused him in front of the peers of his realm, legal clerics, and most respected councillors would have made him her enemy for eternity? As I pictured the scene, I determined that any remnants of my sympathy and regard for Katherine must thenceforth be snuffed out, as is a tiny sputtering flame on the stub of a candle.

And equally with Wolsey. I knew then unless I found a way to counter the self-serving Cardinal's deceit, this court hearing would prove yet another wild goose chase, and it would only end for naught.

•

The substance of my life lay spread before me like a fallow field, ready for planting yet seemingly abandoned. I was a woman of twenty-eight years. I was unmarried, childless - and desperately in love with a man I believed to be my destiny. At this point, there would be no turning back, nor stepping aside. I would have to use every bit of guile and cunning I could muster to secure the desired result.

The only possible outcome for both Henry and me.

•

With wearisome predictability, the court hearings dragged on throughout the remainder of June and well into July. I could not imagine, from my remote location, what there could be to discuss day in and day out. But then, I consoled myself, what did it matter as long as it resulted in the desired conclusion?

Unbelievably- quite intolerably - on 23 July, the Papal Legate Campeggio addressed the court and informed them he was suspending all further deliberations until early October. He stated he could not proceed until he had time to consult with the Pope. At this Henry grew ominously quiet; somehow, he managed to maintain his control though he must have been seething. Not so for Lord Suffolk. I was told that he stood and slammed his fist on the table, shouting that there was 'never a Cardinal nor a Legate that did good in England!'

With Henry admonishing the Cardinals to make all haste to Rome, the trial to determine the validity of Katherine's and Henry's marriage was thus adjourned.

•

The clatter of hooves on the cobbles brought me running through the staircase gallery to the windows overlooking the courtyard. My father, accompanied by George and my Uncle

Norfolk, were dismounting and handing their reins to the stableboys. My father grabbed his leather travel sack and headed through the arched doorway and into the house. I hastened downstairs to greet them with a curtsey, and a kiss on my father's cheek.

"What news, Father?" I asked as I helped him remove his cloak, stiff with dried mud.

"We have much to discuss, Daughter! I will inform you when we sit down to dinner. Now I must bathe and rest, for it was a tiring journey from London by horseback. I am surely too old to ride for days like I used to." He stretched his shoulders, saying "I will have to call for a carriage to ease my aging bones!" He gave his steward instructions to have a bath drawn for each of the three weary travellers as I hurried to the kitchen to check on preparations for dinner.

We sat at the long table in the great hall, with my father at its head, and George and my Uncle Thomas at the first two seats along its length. My mother and I sat across from each other. As the ushers served a veal stew heavily scented with rosemary, Father said "Yesterday, the King and Katherine departed for Woodstock, where they will remain for some weeks. The events since the conclusion of the hearing have been interesting, to say the least." Norfolk nodded as he raised a piece of buttered manchet to his mouth. "Indeed, they have, indeed, they have!"

"In which way, Father?" I asked, hating that I had to learn of these events second-hand.

"Things do not bode well for Thomas Wolsey," replied my father with a grim prescience.

I froze in mid-bite then turned incredulously to both my father and uncle. "But what has caused the shift in His Majesty's opinion?"

George cut in. "Anne, after the great disaster of the hearing was over, the King discovered that a letter had arrived for Campeggio, which commanded him to return to Rome post-haste, leaving the proceedings unresolved. Most damning was the fact that the letter had been received during the hearing and that Wolsey had been well aware of this summons throughout. His Highness realized both Wolsey and Campeggio had deceived him by continuing the discussions and arguments even though they both knew no decision was to be made at their conclusion."

I felt my stomach churn with the bitter gall of anger. Damn Wolsey! How dare he cross the King that way! Henry had been so good – far too good – to this despicable man.

"Then are you saying His Majesty at last sees Wolsey's disloyalty? Does he understand that his Great Matter might have been well and truly resolved by now had an honourable, dedicated man presented the case before the Pope?"

"Yes, Anne, he does, and there is better to come," my uncle confirmed emphatically and with obvious satisfaction before continuing. "As the opportunity seemed ripe, the King's council compiled a record of the known deceptions and offenses which have been carried out by Cardinal Wolsey. They all signed the book and gave it to the King. There were thirty-four of us united in confronting the King's Grace with the truth about his Lord Chancellor. When His Majesty reviewed the book, he admitted his surprise and hurt at the degree to which Wolsey had defrauded him. There is now no question that he views Thomas Wolsey with new eyes."

"Wolsey's behavior has been shown to be no less than that of a man guilty of *praemunire*," added Father solemnly with George nodding in agreement. "We must ensure His Majesty the King sees it as such."

The late spring and summer had brought a significant changing of the guard arguing the Matter in Rome. Following the failure of Dr William Knight, a now frantic Wolsey sent Stephen Gardiner for the second time to try his luck with the immovable Clement. Gardiner, upon his arrival at the Vatican, promptly positioned himself to curry my favour and wrote eagerly to me several times, reassuring me he was totally dedicated to my cause, and that he would stop at nothing to gain the end Henry and I most desired.

While I liked Gardiner, and was certain he would do his utmost, by then, I had lost all faith in the Papacy. I harboured few expectations that it would provide a way forward for Henry's and my union. In what I believed was a futile move, Henry dispatched his lifelong friend Suffolk to Rome, knowing he could be trusted to work in the Crown's best interest. All well and good, yet I had predicted the outcome before it arose.

I received word from Henry to meet him at Grafton at the Nativity of our Lady to accompany him on Progress for the remainder of September. I could not wait to see him and to spend a month hunting, laughing, and loving. It had been too long since we'd been granted any carefree time together. Indeed, we would have important matters to discuss, and critical plans to make, but I would make sure there would be plenty of merriment between us, in sharp contrast with the past two painful, dour months he had spent with Katherine.

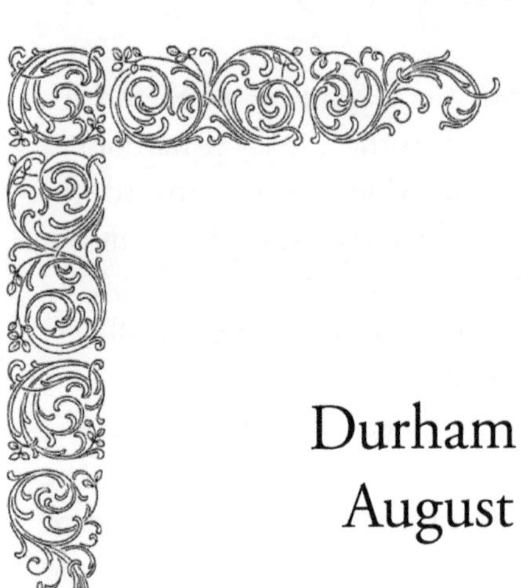

Durham House
August 1529

IN AUGUST, I returned to London from Kent, wishing to order new riding habits and pack certain books to take with me when I went to Grafton to go on progress with Henry.

The city was stifling but had remained relatively free of the sweat this summer, a blessed relief for which we were all thankful. I enjoyed walking down by the banks of the Thames and had found a spot under some willow trees which seemed to catch the cooling breeze coming off the river. I sat there, with royal guards nearby yet not too obvious, reading my copy of the French translation of the New Testament by Jacques Lefévre d'Ètaples. I read and re-read other papers which had been smuggled to me at Hever over the summer, including a pamphlet of Lutheran writings which I found quite convincing. How completely logical it seemed to me that man answers directly to God, with the singular intervention of Jesus Christ. It rang true that God alone could determine the vindication of sin, forgiveness and salvation. Such profound principles of life and hereafter were certainly not appropriated by clerics who were appointed by man; it was well known that many were corrupt, sinners of the highest order.

I could not wait to discuss these concepts with Henry. In my heart, I believed this thinking could provide the answer we had been seeking.

I gathered the final items I wished to take with me for my stay at Grafton, and for the remainder of the autumn. Henry had promised I would travel with him as he moved about the countryside before ending up, most probably, back at Greenwich for Christmas, and it was quite a task to ensure I packed all I would need for the autumn months.

As I moved from chamber to chamber in my Durham apartment, Jolie followed me. There were times I forgot she was so close on my heels, and I would step back and almost trip over her but her sweet, soft face and brown eyes looking to lure me into frolic always melted any momentary irritation. I could never be angry with her. She had been with me at Hever and had learned to be a well-behaved house dog. I now had a wonderful companion to whom I could tell anything I chose without fear of judgment. She was the perfect friend. Except for her penchant for stealing my shoes!

Jolie and I went around the corner from my bedchamber and into the adjacent sitting room. There I nearly fell upon Anne Gainsford and one of the equerries of my household, George Zouche … they had been locked in a passionate kiss. We all stumbled apart, apologizing to one another, with the colour of Anne's face beginning to resemble a ripe strawberry.

"Oh, my Lady, I am most sorry!" she blurted. I looked uncertainly from Anne to Zouche, never having realized there had been anything between them before that awkward moment.

George however, and quite unrepentantly, grinned in my direction, then at Anne. "Mistress, I do wish I could say that I am sorry, but in fact, I am not. My crime was well worth any consequence."

There was a momentary silence, then all three of us fell out laughing, with Jolie's tail wagging joyfully.

"Anne, you'd best attend to the packing, and allow Sir George to ready the horses. If our departure is delayed, I will not be so cheery. It is now *my* turn to be caught kissing my love, and no one dare stands in my way!"

Curtseying, Anne left the room, but not before tossing Sir George a significant look. I was happy for Anne. She was a friend, and I had found that because I was in love, it was easy to wish that same good fortune for my friends.

Anne busied herself gathering the remaining items on my travel list. The trunks holding my clothing and other belongings were being placed in the centre of the chamber. When all was assembled, we would call for the porters to load them onto the carts. I was sorting my hoods and headwear when I registered a sudden cry from the bedchamber.

Instantly I recalled sweet Charity, and that moment of horror - so many long months ago, now - when the poor child had succumbed to the sweat.

"Anne, what ails you?" I called in considerable alarm.

"Milady, please come!"

I hurried into the room where Anne was standing before the large wardrobe. "Milady, did you move the coffer which holds your private belongings?"

"I did not. Why?"

"If this is where it had been, then it is here no longer." Her distress was evident.

Hastily she stood aside while I searched the wardrobe, though no searching was necessary. The coffer was gone. I could see the evidence because the area where the box had previously been was dust free while surrounding its former outline was a fine film. My heart was pounding, and the blood rushed in my ears. In the coffer I had kept my fine kid gloves, a brooch or two, linen handkerchiefs ... and Henry's love letters.

I rushed to the desk in which a secret compartment held the key to the coffer. The key remained in its place. We looked at each other in disbelief. Very few people knew what was contained in the coffer, and fewer still about the secret drawer:

only Anne Gainsford, my mother, and my trusted friend Maggie. I was mystified. My breath came shallow as I thought of the implications of the box's theft. I treasured those letters and thought I had most fastidiously kept them from view.

As I began to grasp the enormity of what had happened, I searched my memory to identify anyone else who may have been aware of their existence, apart from my closest confidantes. Almost immediately I thought of a recent situation. My uncle's wife, Elizabeth Howard, Duchess of Norfolk, was aware I was in need of a personal maid and had contacted me to say she knew of an excellent lady's maid who was seeking a position. Even though I did not have a close or particularly warm relationship with my aunt, I had agreed to a trial period with Agnes Graeme. I recalled how intently observant Agnes was. She had an uncanny, almost unnerving ability to anticipate my every need, and made herself familiar with my belongings so as to provide me with the best possible service.

All in all, she had proved a skilled maid to be certain, yet there had always been something about her I could not quite identify. It made me ill at ease. I felt she was overly solicitous, almost scheming, and so after a few weeks, I dismissed her - but not before a then-seemingly innocuous event had occurred.

I had returned from an afternoon out, and upon removing a diamond brooch from my bodice, placed it back in the coffer. While it was unlocked, I had seized the opportunity to re-read one of Henry's early letters. Absently I had settled in a chair and pored over the letter while Agnes busied herself in the chamber, straightening and brushing my discarded clothes before hanging them back in the wardrobe. Upon reflection, it seemed certain she saw the letter with the royal seal, slyly observed the open coffer and from whence it had come and saw that there were other letters within.

After I'd finished reading, I'd replaced the note in the box and locked it again, never suspecting she had been watching me so carefully. I had not returned to the coffer since that day, and Mistress Graeme left my employ one week ago. She was to return to work for the Duchess of Norfolk, who would create a place for her at Kenninghall. With a sickening feeling of violation, it now made sense. I just knew she must be the offender.

… she was a spy! And my aunt, Elizabeth Howard, must have been the instigator.

I went directly to my writing desk to pen a scathing letter to the Duchess. I called for a courier to stand by to take the message directly to Kenninghall, but as I sat at the desk with quill in hand, I stopped short. I realized that the whole ugly business must be revealed to Henry first. My anger bubbled and sputtered, and I itched to vent it on the Lady Norfolk, though I was filled with remorse at my stupid oversight in allowing a veritable stranger to observe the location of my most treasured possessions. My regret was matched by a growing consternation. Was it she who had them, indeed? If so, what did she intend to do with them? And what trouble might the letters cause in the pursuit of an annulment?

I was furious with myself for having been so careless and was heartbroken at their loss. They documented our love affair from its very inception until now. With just a glance I had become able to read into the heart and soul of the writer. I had valued them, and it made me physically sick to think of anyone else reading what had been written for my eyes only. I knew I must talk with Henry about what to do at the very first opportunity.

We set off for Grafton Manor, planning to stop twice along the way, staying for a night in St Albans and once at Grevel House in Chipping Campden. Anne Gainsford was to join me on progress with Henry, and I was glad to have her company as we rode toward Worcestershire. But although we talked and laughed along the way, even that distraction could not distance me from the anxiety caused by the missing letters.

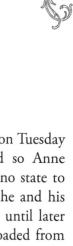

Grafton Manor
September 1529

I WAS A BEDRAGGLED sight when we arrived on Tuesday 10 September. It had rained all morning, and so Anne and I rode in the cart, but I was still dirty and in no state to be received by Henry. I was relieved to learn that he and his retinue – minus Katherine – was not due to arrive until later in the afternoon. Hastily I had my belongings unloaded from the wagons and delivered to my chambers. I left a message for Henry that we had arrived, and then took advantage of the time to unpack, bathe, and prepare a *toilette* which would remind him of what he had missed while we were apart.

A small group gathered in the hall that evening for supper. Lords Suffolk and Norfolk were present, along with Henry Norreys and a few others. Anne Gainsford was not joining us, so I was the only woman at the table. I had staged my entrance most precisely. Knowing Henry was longing to see me, I certainly was not going to let such an opportunity catch me unprepared.

As I glided into the hall on the arm of my uncle, Norfolk, all heads turned. I knew the deep yellow satin of my gown reflected the candlelight, and the fit of my bodice, laced almost unbearably tightly, would afford me an impossibly slender waist - and Henry a surge of manly desire. I wore a small, black velvet hood trimmed in pearls, and left my hair to tumble free. Loosened hair was unusual for a woman of my age, but since it was deemed acceptable for young unmarried women to do so, I intended to invoke that rule as often as possible until the day I uttered the vows of matrimony. That evening it cascaded all the way down my back, accenting the black velvet trim on my gown. As a final touch, I wore the emerald betrothal ring and a set of emerald drop earrings given to me by Henry.

Henry was in conversation with Norreys when my uncle and I entered the chamber. He looked up in mid-sentence, ceased talking, and followed me with his gaze. He sat motionless while absorbing every detail, then slowly and deliberately rose and walked toward me. Instead of an embrace, which is what I wished for, he took my hands in his and held them to his lips for a very long time. When he raised his eyes to mine, everyone else in the room faded away, and I felt the communion between us. Its intimacy caused me to flush, and in response, the curl of his lips told me how much I had been missed.

I sat next to Henry, and supper was full of wine and jovial spirits. There was a palpable relief now that Katherine had returned to London. We all looked forward to a month of fine hunting and hawking, taking advantage of the September weather which we hoped would be warm and dry. The conversation remained lively, but I knew Henry held the same thought as I; we could not wait to be alone.

When finally, the last goblet was drained, all excused themselves from the table. Henry and I strolled regally, arm in arm, through the hallway to the stairs which led to his chambers. From his pocket, he took an elaborate brass key and fitted it into the ornate, sturdy lock which kept his privy chambers free from unwanted visitors. Once within, we dissolved into each other's arms and kissed for an eternity. My world spun about: the sweet exhilaration of that reunion only emphasizing how wrenchingly I had felt his absence from me. I knew then I could not endure such misery again.

Only eventually could we bring ourselves to draw apart.

"My Hal, I have missed you so much, so very much! Please don't send me away from you again. I cannot do this any longer! I simply cannot abide being without you."

His cheek against my hair felt warm as his arms encircled me yet again. "Anne, you are my angel, and I promise you we will not separate anymore. I ached for you as well. My mind and body are incomplete without you by my side: indeed, there is no greater comfort known to me as when I am with you. Only then do I feel as if I am myself, with never a worry about what I should or should not say or do. With you, I am the man I was meant to be – the ruler I was born to be. We will be together, sweetheart, no matter the cost."

I delighted in the sheer strength of him as he lifted me and carried me to his bedchamber. Only by the greatest act of will would I maintain my virginity that night, but I ran my hands over his body, and allowed him to do the same with mine. I kissed and teased, then satisfied him in my special way. I guided him to do what I longed for. We loved one another, but we would save our most intimate lovemaking for our wedding night when, I felt certain, we would conceive a son.

For a glorious fortnight, we remained at the hunting lodge at Grafton. Indeed, the weather was perfect, and we rode out into the surrounding countryside to the chase almost every day. It was the end of summer, and my face had taken on a golden hue from the warm sun, the glorious inheritance of having spent a great deal of time during the past weeks hunting and riding. Henry told me he loved it when I looked that way. My colouring, especially at the height of summer, was so different from the pale, delicate ladies who populated court. I knew how to enhance my allure, though, and would no sooner give up hunting, hawking, and outdoor sport than become a nun.

•

It was late afternoon, and the mellow amber light deepened the green of the trees surrounding a meadow near the manor. We had come out hawking, and this was my favourite time of day to do so. The sun, lower in the sky, caused no glare, and one could more easily follow the soaring hawks as they sought their prey. Henry and I were met by Sir Robert Cheseman, the master falconer, and his assistants. They had brought with them several birds, transported in their crates.

As the yeomen falconers removed the birds from their crates, Henry said, "Well, Milady, since you have proved yourself to be as skilled at hawking as you are with most everything, I felt it time to gift you with a special bird."

He proffered his gloved wrist upon which sat a breathtaking white gyrfalcon, hooded in white doeskin. "She is yours, my darling. Her name is Pilgrim. She is young, but well on her way to becoming a prized hunter. I wanted you to have a bird which would hunt with mine."

As Master Cheseman handed Henry his magnificent male gyrfalcon, Senator, also brilliantly white, I was well aware of the implications of Henry's generous gift. White gyrfalcons were reserved for royalty. He wanted to convey to me that my elevation to royal status was practically a *fait accompli*.

The field we stood in was known to be a nesting place for grouse, so we set Pilgrim and Senator upon the perch which the cadger had hammered into the ground, and removed their hoods. I was pleased to see that Pilgrim had been carefully 'manned': that is, she was very calm being close to me, and to Henry. Her sharp, intelligent eyes appraised me and scanned her surroundings. One of the assistant falconers mounted his horse and headed out into the field to flush grouse. I pulled on a leather gauntlet and extended my arm so Pilgrim could climb on my wrist. Holding her jesses, and moving out into the open space, I saw her become quickly attentive, with a piercing, scanning gaze, indicating she was keen to hunt. Henry stood alongside me with Senator. We removed the jesses from both birds, raised our arms, and they spread their impressive wings and soared into the sky. At that moment, the falconer gave a *Halloo* as he flushed several grouse from the brush. The birds circled and wheeled above, emitting their keening, whistling cry until they gained a wider perspective of the field and their prey. Without warning, one falcon - I could not tell which at such a distance - dropped from the sky like a stone, followed by its companion. A moment later and each had hit a grouse with a burst of feathers, and had its prey firmly grasped in sharp talons. With a call from Henry, followed by one from Master Cheseman, Senator and Pilgrim returned to us. At a command, the grouse were dropped, the birds landed on their perch, folded their wings and preened, and were forthwith fed choice morsels of raw meat and sweet comfits. They both looked about as they ate, and seemed quite pleased with themselves. I fed Pilgrim a sweet while stroking her softly, all the while marvelling that this magnificent bird was truly mine.

What an appropriate paradox she presented. Beautiful - yet altogether ferocious.

•

Though Henry and I rejoiced in the time we spent together in sport and other amusement, the spectre of the Matter could never be disregarded for long: particularly considering my anxiety at having to tell him about the purloined letters. I could not anticipate his reaction to this news, and I hoped I did not run the risk of angering him.

When the opportunity presented itself, I quelled my apprehension with several deep breaths and commenced my tale of the discovery of the missing coffer, and my theory about the maid who had been referred by Elizabeth, Duchess of Norfolk. To my dismay, he was clearly irked. He made it plain that the fact I had employed a maid referred by Elizabeth Howard disturbed him even more than the disclosure about the letters.

"But you knew, Anne, that the Duchess has been rashly speaking out in favour of Katherine, did you not?" Henry pressed with an unaccustomed sharpness to his tone.

"No, I did not!" I retorted, equally indignant. "I was unaware she was so set against me. I knew her to be a friend of Katharine's, but she is my aunt after all and I thought family ties would provide some sense of loyalty. And after all, it was simply the referral of a housemaid – not an act of Parliament! You cannot be angry with me for this, Henry! Can you not see it as an innocent mistake?"

Even as I spoke, I recalled the Duchess, a sharp, shrewish woman to be certain, positioning herself near Katherine at many events, stridently speaking out in her defence when the ladies'gossip took a contrary turn… which by default made my aunt an enemy of mine, I thought miserably as the pieces of the puzzle fit neatly together. "Then you think she directed the theft- so she could pass the letters on to Katherine?" The thought of Katherine holding my letters - poring over every romantic word - was almost more than I could bear.

"She may have. If Katherine has the letters in her possession and has read them, I will surely come to know it. She will be unable to hold her tongue. If they were not given to her, then I fear even worse - that they have been smuggled directly to a courier of Katherine's and are on their way to Rome and the Pope, no doubt to prove that my desire for a divorce is chiefly motivated by my love for you. If ever I discover who lifted that coffer from your chamber, their punishment will be swift and devastating. For now, Anne, there is very little we can do about it. If we stage a confrontation with Lady Norfolk, it will only serve to make others aware of the letters' existence, and that would serve Katherine's devious purpose just as well."

After only a moment's hesitation, he took me in a gentle embrace, and I rested my sorrowful head on his shoulder: my so forgiving sweetheart.

"At least I still have all the letters you wrote to me, my darling," he added grimly. "I have hidden them so secretly that no one will ever discover their whereabouts."

•

A message from Cardinal Wolsey was delivered on the day of our arrival at Grafton. The urgent request for an audience with His Majesty the King stated that a matter of great importance must be discussed without delay. When I heard this, I demanded to know how Henry had responded. He said quietly, "'I told him to write – and to make his statement brief." This pleased me, and I allowed myself a sigh of relief. It appeared that finally, Henry was becoming wise to Wolsey's methods.

On 14 September, the King was visited at Grafton Manor by the newly appointed Imperial ambassador, Eustace Chapuys. I was told Chapuys was a lawyer and a cleric; a native of Savoy. This meant he spoke French, as well as having fluency in Spanish. Of course, his main objective in service to his master, the Emperor Charles V, was to provide timely intelligence about the enterprises of the English King and his court, especially regarding plans to annul the marriage of Henry and Katherine of Aragon.

I looked forward to meeting the man to assess personally his manner and means of diplomacy. I determined to be wary, and not to let down my guard as I so foolishly had with the Duchess of Norfolk.

Henry and I sat side by side in the chamber used for receiving visitors in the hunting lodge. We had just finished our morning meal when Ambassador Chapuys was announced. A fine-featured, well- dressed man of about Henry's age entered the room and acknowledged the King with a deep, courteous bow. "It is a great privilege and a personal pleasure to meet you, Your Majesty."

As he rose, he faced me and bowed again. "… and to make your acquaintance as well, Madame," he said in the most soothing, elegantly accented voice. He glanced at Henry, but, covertly, his eyes lingered on me. Though I knew he believed his interest in me was undetectable, I was no neophyte at perceiving men's fascination, and I became quickly aware of his. I offered him a charming smile and a warm clasp of my hand and took my time to consider him. Everything about him spoke of affluence, education, and a well-honed ability for personal interaction. He could prove, I believed, to be a very clever adversary.

I did not remain to attend the meeting between Henry and Chapuys but instead took my leave to prepare for a hunt which was to take place in the early afternoon. The weather was too fair, and the hunting too good in Grafton Park for us to miss a day, new Imperial ambassador or not! We had but a short window until the season ended, having planned to rejoin the larger court to resume business as autumn approached. Henry and I agreed we did not wish to allow other concerns to rob us of our treasured time together; moreover, he had given me a beautifully crafted silver hunt whistle, and it was to be my honour to commence the hunt by sounding the whistle to call out the field and the hounds. As huntmistress, I would be entitled to ride at the fore with the King and his Master of Hounds. We were to hunt stag, and it was hoped we would bring one down to supply the lodge's larder with fresh venison.

•

I had been so enjoying my time at Grafton Manor with Henry that I'd found myself pretending the ugly Great Matter did not exist. By God's eyes, I'd needed a respite from constantly thinking about it and worrying about it. We both did. So I had found it quite easy to take each lovely day as it came, hunting, hawking, rambling with Henry and Jolie in the woods and fields … sitting in the rose gardens, appreciating the last of the summer's aromatic blooms in the setting sun.

We were doing just that late one afternoon when Henry announced, "Anne, tomorrow I will will see Cardinal Campeggio before he leaves England and sets off for Rome."

With a heavy sigh, I reluctantly drew myself from the pleasant thoughts and discussion we had been having. "I see. And what do you hope will be the result of that meeting?"

"I want to talk with the Cardinal to make it abundantly clear that he is to travel to Rome with all possible speed, provide his report to the Pope, and seek the Pope's approval to our desired end. Wolsey will be joining Campeggio and me for the meeting."

At this sound of the name Wolsey, resentment at having my delightful sojourn end gave voice to bitter sarcasm. "So then, we are to entertain graciously two men who have done absolutely nothing to deserve a welcome. Is that correct?"

"They will not be here as guests to be entertained, Anne." After betraying a sharp look, Henry replied with great deliberation. "It is a formal meeting. They will be questioned probingly by me. I will accept no excuses for their poor performance."

"That may be your plan, Henry, but I know very well how Wolsey handles you by making you feel sorry for him. He lies to you – lies to your face! You know how little I like or trust the man," I said, rising abruptly.

I kept my eyes firmly fixed on the ground as I stalked back to the lodge, not wanting Henry to see the extent of my disappointment and aggravation. Apparently, our pleasant retreat at Grafton had concluded.

On the following day, Sunday, I attended Mass in the morning then busied myself in my apartment, reading and planning the design of several new gowns so as to avoid any chance confrontation with the two cardinals. It was grey and raining, so at least I did not feel as if we had been cheated of a day's hunting. Furthermore, George had been asked to attend the meeting, and thus my brother would be my ears and eyes.

I dined in my chamber with Anne Gainsford, and we chattered and laughed to keep from imagining what might be taking place between Henry and Wolsey. The day wore on endlessly. Supper was served and cleared yet still I had no word. Finally, as the hour was late and I prepared for bed, a knock on my door revealed George.

We sat before the hearth, and he told me Wolsey had arrived that morning to discover, to his great chagrin, that no lodging had been arranged for him at the manor, and only due to the kindness of Lord Norreys, Groom of the Stool, who gave up his room, was he afforded a chamber to use as a changing suite.

"So far, so good," I thought spitefully. "One slight to Wolsey is worth a thousand disapproving eyes."

Seemingly, once Campeggio had arrived, the Legates were announced to the King, whereupon entering the presence chamber, Cardinal Wolsey had, with great difficulty, lowered himself to both knees and bowed his head before his sovereign, adopting a posture of great humility. Henry, whether from pity or long time familiarity, raised Wolsey to his feet. After that, commenced a long and engrossing conversation between Henry, Wolsey and Campeggio to which my brother had not been privy although he did say that Henry had raised his voice on several occasions, and at times waved a document in front of Wolsey.

That was promising. But what was not as satisfying - caused me the first glimmer of foreboding, in fact - was when I learned that after Campeggio's departure, Wolsey and Henry had continued their meeting long into the evening. Worse, according to George, the privy councillors who were Wolsey's opponents grew increasingly uneasy that he had restored his influence over the King. Hearing this, I found myself varying between controlled fury and a remote hope that Henry had not abandoned his resolve.

I went to bed that night in great disquiet.

The following morning, I was informed that Henry was again to meet with his chancellor. By now, my unease had mounted to outright alarm: that mood not being helped at all by a throbbing headache and the evidence of another month gone by without a legitimate pregnancy.

Just before noon, I was summoned to Henry's privy chamber. I did little to restrain my distemper.

I strode into the room. Looking squarely at him, I lashed out, "How could you, Henry? How could you have possibly betrayed all that we agreed? How, by God's blood, could you allow that man to control you once again?"

My voice grew higher and more shrill with each word. I heard myself but was powerless to stop. Henry stared back at me blankly, plainly aghast. He had never heard this tone in my voice, nor seen such anger on my face.

"Sweetheart," he attempted, "what causes you to think I would betray my intent in talking with Wolsey? How is it that you do not trust me?"

"Simply the amount of privy time you granted him tells me you also allowed him to fabricate tales of his dedication to you, as he has done for years!"

I felt perilously close to hot tears of frustration and bitter disappointment but did not wish for Henry to see me cry so I instead I delivered another vicious outburst.

"He is contemptible, Henry! He portrays himself as if he were the holiest, the most pious man on earth aside from the Pope. And, by God, we all know that not to be true. He is dishonest and full of vice. He has cheated you, lied to you, and robbed you. He has acted as if *he* ruled this kingdom, under the guise of allowing you time to enjoy yourself. But do not be fooled: he has been no friend to you - and he certainly has been no friend to me! Had he been so inclined, he could have secured your divorce long ago. He has no intention of delivering to you what you seek, don't you see? I cannot think of a greater enemy than he." I paced back and forth in my restless irritation.

Henry, not knowing what to do with a near-distraught woman, took cover behind his enormous desk, where he undoubtedly felt safer. With a level gaze, he said in a deliberately calm voice, "Anne, I well understand that you are not a friend of the Cardinal's. Regardless, you do not have liberty to attack me when you know not what was discussed. Cardinal Wolsey has been made well aware of my intense displeasure in his conduct and his failure to succeed. He has left to go back to London in disgrace. Campeggio is on his way to Rome."

At that, my deluge of woe was released, and the tears fell with abandon.

"I am sorry, Henry. Oh, I am sorry to have doubted you, but I am finding it so very difficult to bear up under the pressure of this never-ending situation. I fear you will allow Wolsey to convince you to be rid of me, or worse yet, you will return to Katherine, and I will be left alone and abandoned." I came to a confused halt, snivelling, unsure of which was more humiliating: my shouting or my crying.

Henry came quickly from behind his desk and hurried to me, encircling me with his arms. I wept for a while longer on his shoulder, then finally sniffed and mopped my eyes with his scented handkerchief. I knew I looked a mess but I lifted my face to his, and forlornly said, "Oh, I am such a trial to you. Could you possibly love me still?"

Henry looked at my red and blotchy features and drew me close.

"Nan, I love you still. I will love you always," he whispered. Then he kissed me as if I were at that moment the most beautiful woman in the world.

My state of mind improved greatly over the next days. I enjoyed the last of the hunting and the relaxed atmosphere at the lodge, along with the late summer warmth. We were preparing to continue on progress, and I would be accompanying Henry. I was excited to travel with him since this was my first journey by his side.

I was almost able to pretend we were husband and wife.

Progress
September 1529

OVER THE FOLLOWING ten days, we travelled from Grafton through Buckingham, then stayed for three days and nights at Notley Abbey. The yeomanry next headed southwest and arrived at Bisham Abbey in Berkshire on 28 September. Accompanying Henry on progress, I looked forward to greeting the townspeople and villagers who would line the roadsides to see their King and his courtiers, and cheer us as we passed by. How they hailed their King cheerfully! They were in awe of his magnificence, as well they should be. He was offered jams and cheeses - specialties of the region, which they had made. He always thanked them graciously, giving them the attention they craved and his good wishes.

When they looked at me, on the other hand, their response was markedly different. They did not know what to make of me, or how to react to the sight of me riding alongside Henry in my elegant attire, with royal equerries ahead and behind. Mostly, I was met with stares and blank looks. Some expressed their displeasure at the absence of their crowned queen, Katherine.

I was constantly aware of low hisses and unpleasant murmurs as I rode by. It was trying, at best. It hurt me, and I sorrowed because I cared about these hardworking, prideful people. After all, I was a country girl, myself. I could only wish they would see me as a supporter who had their best interests at heart. For the first time, I fervently wished I were their rightful queen. But it was not the case, and I bore up under the circumstances as best I could.

After spending the night at Bisham, we made our way south and east to Windsor, where we planned to remain for a while at least. I took advantage of our relative permanence to debate with Henry the ideology which fascinated us both. It had best been expressed in the treatise published by William Tyndale some months ago. Tyndale was considered heretical, having published his translation of the New Testament with a decidedly Lutheran context. These writings were banned in England but had secretly made their way into the households of many. When his *The Obedience of the Christian Man and How Christian Rulers Ought to Govern* was published, my sources in France supplied me with a copy. I found the writing to be exceptionally well thought out, and relevant to Henry's situation. It was, of course, Lutheran in its nature, considered blasphemous, and as such was one of the works which Wolsey had forbidden at court. It promoted the concept that a king is answerable to God and God alone. It succinctly denounced the artificial authority of the Pope and his selected clergy and stated that a monarch is the decision maker of his realm, trusting that his decisions will be in accordance with the laws of God. I notated passages for Henry, which I thought particularly enthralling.

The book was so explosive that it caused a great stir amongst the clergy and laity alike. I loaned my copy to my friend and waiting woman, Anne Gainsford, and one day while she read it in her chamber, it was snatched from her by her admirer, George Zouche. Zouche was a consummate jester, and I guessed he found the move funny and flirtatious but then began to read the book himself. But he was also careless, not having taken seriously the warnings against being caught with such writings, and was found absorbed in it by the Dean of the Chapel Royal, who promptly took it from him and reported the transgression to Wolsey. Poor Anne was nearly beside herself with worry, anticipating terrible things which might happen as a result, and came to me in tears of apology. While she was near frantic, considering what might occur, I must admit this situation worried me not a whit. I went directly to Henry and explained to him what had happened, and told him I had intended the book for him since there was no doubt but that he would find it enlightening. Without further ado, he retrieved the book from Wolsey and we spent many hours poring over its intriguing propositions. Reading this material encouraged us to know that we were not alone in our growing mistrust of the Papacy, and how it interfered with critical matters of state in England.

How could I possibly have foreseen, then, that the very existence of this book, with me as its acknowledged owner, announced to all that I had stepped beyond the standard?

That I, Anne Boleyn, had become a religious dissident.

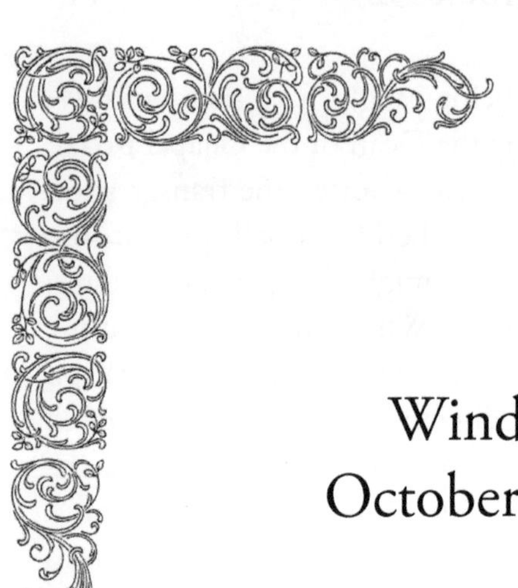

Windsor
October 1529

AT LONG LAST, I smelled a change in the wind, and that wind had now begun to blow in Henry's and my favour. Although Wolsey had been banished from court, he had still returned to London, somehow assuming all would be as it had been in his role as chancellor. I marvelled at his seemingly oblivious comportment: forging ahead with business as usual despite his most certain awareness that the relationship between him and the King had gone greatly awry. A profusion of his letters of entreaty had been received by many individuals including Lord Suffolk, Bishop Du Bellay, Henry, and most surprisingly, me. He had implored me to have pity and speak favourably to the King on his behalf. How absurd! To this request, I promptly and politely responded via messenger that I wished him well, but would never presume to interfere in the personal matters between him and His Majesty the King.

Equally encouraging was the introduction of Dr Thomas Cranmer to Henry and me. Cranmer, a theologian, and academic, had met the Bishops Gardiner and Foxe at

Cambridge in August. During conversation over dinner at the house in which they all happened to be staying, Dr Cranmer remarked that as long as the King intended to pursue his answer through canonical principles, he would remain frustrated. Instead, Cranmer avowed, it was a matter of theology and Henry's personal requirement to answer only to God which would ultimately lead him to the truth. When this opinion was reported to Henry by Dr Foxe, Henry was greatly impressed and called for Cranmer to come, as soon as possible, to court for an audience.

•

9 October was noteworthy. A lovely, crisp and clear autumn day, I had taken a long walk near the woods of Windsor Park. As I wandered with Jolie racing forward and back on the paths, I admired the Scottish thistle which thrived in the fields nears the woods' edge. Here, its leaves were a particularly dark green, and the crowning flower a brilliant purple tinged with blue. It was one of my favourite flowers, and its abundant growth gave the field a gorgeous, moody blue cast. I looked up when I heard the thud of horse's hooves from behind me, and saw my brother cantering toward me. He reined his horse to a quick stop and as he jumped down to walk beside me, said "Anne, I have news! The most intriguing - the most amazing news!"

"What is it, George?" I pressed, excitement growing.

For an annoying moment he quite deliberately hesitated, taunting me with that brotherly look of 'I know something - you don't.'

"What? George! Do tell me, you beast!"

"Today, in London, the formerly great Lord Chancellor Cardinal Thomas Wolsey was charged in King's Bench with the crime of *praemunire* … Anne – Wolsey is finished." His eyes were fervent. "We have succeeded in exposing his treachery to the King. Now – now the way is cleared for the King to appoint someone who shares the same ideology like so many of us who are enlightened, and it will release the death grip the Church has on him. It will pave the way for your marriage, Anne!"

My first reaction was elation. Yet, having been stung too many times, it was followed closely by a cautious sense of misgiving.

"George, what a relief! And thank you, my dear brother, for riding out to find me. This is such a promising step. But, let us be practical – as long as he and Henry breathe the same air you know there is always a chance that the well-handed Wolsey will find a way to winnow himself back into His Majesty's good graces. I dare not let down my guard. No, not for as long as he lives."

George and I walked slowly along the path, leading his horse, with Jolie following.

"This is such a hazardous game we are engaged in, George," I murmured reflectively. "'And not one for the faint of heart, that is the truth."

I shivered unaccountably. I wound my arm through George's as we carefully picked our way through the pretty blue thistle swaying in the cooling breeze.

Each lovely plant that lay ahead of us bore vicious, prickly thorns bestowed upon it by God to ensnare the unwary.

•

The remainder of October was marked by events of significance. By mid-month, Wolsey was no longer chancellor, having been required to relinquish the Great Seal, under his strident objection, to the Lords Norfolk and Suffolk. Possibly thinking it would help his eventual outcome, he pleaded guilty before the councillors and conceded all his many properties to his sovereign. Under the supervision of Stephen Gardiner, who had just been appointed Henry's official Secretary, and Sir William FitzWilliam, Wolsey's goods and belongings were removed from his houses and forfeited to the King. Wolsey, at the King's command, was escorted by William Kingston to

Esher, with just enough of his material items to make living tolerable. In total, it constituted quite a difference from the life of grandeur he had been accustomed to.

Henry engaged in earnest consultation with his privy council which resulted in Sir Thomas More being appointed Lord High Chancellor of England. I knew not how this appointment would affect me or the advancement of the Great Matter since I was well aware that More was a devout Catholic. He was reputed to be an honest man, and kind, and I believed he was truly devoted to Henry. But the fact remained that he was dedicated to the Pope and the Holy See. And by virtue of that fact, it seemed highly unlikely his allegiance would rest with me.

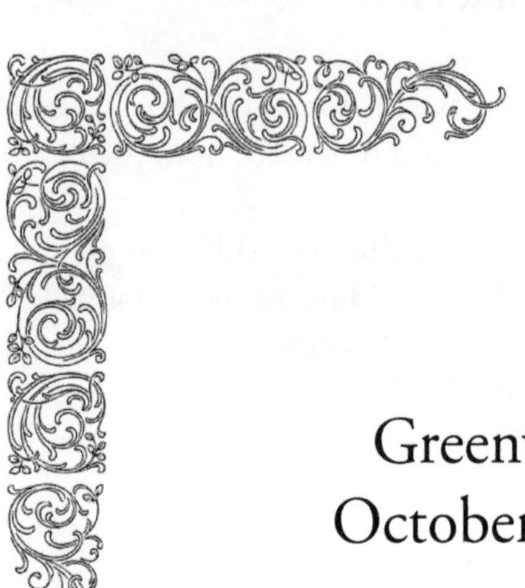

Greenwich
October 1529

TOWARDS THE END of October, the King and court returned to Greenwich. There, the first meeting took place between Henry and Thomas Cranmer to discuss the status of the Great Matter. Henry could not stop speaking of the fact that the erudite Dr Cranmer had shown him how the strategy he had been following to obtain a divorce was intrinsically flawed. In Cranmer's opinion, it was not a legal, but a moral issue. And only through a code of morality would Henry find his truth. Henry, inordinately grateful for some true scholarly insight and understanding, at last, appointed Cranmer to his court, requesting of my father that he invite the theologian to stay at Durham House.

It was what anyone would have described as a dank, chilly, and quite dreary late October day. The rowers were sculling the *Lyon*, Henry's royal barge, on the Thames to the measured sound of tambours and flutes. On board, wrapped in thick cloaks against the raw mist were Henry, my lady mother, and me. Our destination, downriver, was York Place at Westminster, one of Cardinal Wolsey's former residences. We were to inspect it in preparation for its complete renovation as a royal palace, and Henry had suggested that I might help him in defining the architectural plans for the new, magnificent structure. I was so thrilled and excited with the prospect that the day, although grey and raw, seemed to me to be full of sunshine and cloudless blue skies. We disembarked at the dock and walked toward King Street. From there we entered the building through the northern gate. I had never been inside York Place before, so I was greatly interested to see its current design, and how it might be suited for use as a primary residence for Henry and his court.

Once inside, we stood on a floor gorgeously laid in imported, painted tiles of striking colour. To the right of the entry staircase was the great hall with its glorious carved ceiling, gilded in gold, silver, and brilliant hues. Beyond the hall, exterior doorways led to a large open cloister which featured antique statuary and marble fountains. Stairs from the cloister directed one to a series of chambers, including Wolsey's former privy chamber, his bedchamber, and two presence chambers. From our entry point, and turning left, there was a large and beautiful chapel, ornately decorated, with a rich blue ceiling embellished with gold and silver stars, a fabulous altar with a crucifix of solid gold, and elegantly carved linenfold panelling on the walls. I looked about in amazement as I began to understand the extent of Wolsey's wealth, and his love of ostentation. Apparently, the priestly vows of humility and poverty did not apply to Thomas Wolsey.

Adjoining the Chapel we came upon a further courtyard - lushly landscaped, fountains splashing, and trees skilfully espaliered against brick walls, all overlooked by the guest quarters above. Walking south, we discovered a long gallery with official chambers leading from it. The gallery windows looked out to a large orchard, planted with many varieties of fruit trees and shrubs, all carefully cared for. Throughout the house was a magnificent collection of fine furniture, tapestry, and plate. All now belonged to its rightful owner, the King. Still, for all its grandness, it seemed stifling, oppressive. I was overcome by a sinister feeling, standing in the deserted hall, looking about and imagining Wolsey seated in command, as if he were king or Pope. In truth, I couldn't wait to escape and breathe fresh air.

We emerged, looking west towards King Street again, and I drew in deep lungfuls of air, shaking off the repugnance of the interior. I knew what it would take to transform the residence into a palace worthy of Henry and his new sovereignty. I looked to him to share my thoughts, and as I did, we spoke almost in unison, exclaiming, "We must expand!"

Completely in concert, we laughed and laughed.

"If this is to become a functioning royal residence," Henry mused, looking around, "it is much too compressed. There must be a way to incorporate the road, and include the property beyond. That will allow the palace private access to The Strand and directly into the city."

His gaze then rested on the narrow houses lining the road. "We will need to find a way to resettle the people living there before construction can begin," he said. "And first and foremost, Milady …" He reached to take my gloved hand, bringing it to his lips, "we will renovate the Queen's Chambers to provide you with the lodging you deserve."

I considered him with a look of love and gratitude. "I thank you, Your Majesty. Your kindness to me knows no bounds."

Henry's eyes sparkled, and his grin was jolly. "Oh, don't be too overly grateful - you will work for your reward, Mistress Anne. You will be responsible for overseeing all the designs and plans."

"It would be my greatest pleasure, Your Grace,' I said with a slight curtsey. "We will soon see how well our tastes intertwine."

Secretly, I delighted in the fact that there was no space now, nor would there be in any new design over which I had control, for Katherine or her pinch-lipped ladies. At York, I would have Henry all to myself!

Throughout November, Henry was kept busy with matters of state. He met regularly with the new chancellor, Thomas

More, as well as with Dr Cranmer, who continued to work on a treatise regarding the Great Matter. Parliament was convened, and in the speech customarily given by the Lord Chancellor on that occasion, More seized the opportunity to denounce Wolsey and all he had come to represent. More made it clear that, under his appointment, the clergy would act with propriety and Christian temperance. There would be a return to the Commandments, and the values Catholicism represented.

Taking yet another step toward their ultimate separation, Henry sent Katherine to stay at Richmond. Katherine's daughter Mary was instructed to go to Windsor, maintaining a distance between the two. I remained at Greenwich, and Henry travelled back and forth, conducting business from York Place while Parliament was in session.

At Henry's bidding, I began to establish a household of ladies-in-waiting. Of course, there would be Anne Gainsford, who had served me for some months already. I was pleased beyond words to include my friend, Maggie Wyatt, while I also sought Bessie Holland, who was known to me since she was the paramour of my uncle, Lord Norfolk. Finally, I included Mistress Elizabeth Harlestone, with whom I was not overly familiar, but who was recommended. I felt confident that none of these women were sympathetic to Katherine, had no disagreement with Henry divorcing her, and most importantly, would be loyal to me.

Henry returned to Greenwich to remain there through Christmas. I was overjoyed to see him again: this time after an absence of only a few weeks. Katherine had stated her desire and intent to oversee this year's Christmastide celebration, as was expected of the Queen. Since she was Queen still, there was no way to dissuade her. So I was faced once again with the unpleasant proposition that Henry, Katherine, and I were to be under the same roof. The situation was growing unbearable, but I worked hard at concentrating on other matters.

Since he had taken up residence at Durham House, I had become somewhat of a student of the very learned Dr Cranmer, and his tutelage largely consisted of engaging me in elucidating theological discussions. My respect and admiration for the man grew steadily, as did my knowledge of the movement which was destined to either reform the Church or prompt a separatist approach to religion.

•

Henry had come to my apartments one evening, bearing two parcels, and looking very pleased with himself.

"I have intelligence to impart to you, sweetheart, which you will find very, very pleasing," he said as he sat next to me on a bench. I inhaled his scent as he came close. It never failed to captivate me.

"Do tell me, Henry, I would delight in some good news," I said, nuzzling closer to him.

"Well, then, this is for your ears only. You may not share what I am about to tell you until I have done so first."

My curiosity was piqued, and I sat up, eyeing at him questioningly. "What could it be?"

"I intend, my darling Anne, to honour your family and your father by creating him Earl of Wiltshire in the English peerage, and Earl of Ormonde in the Irish. And I will do so in early December."

"Henry, that is magnificent of you. How generous!" I threw my arms around him in gratitude.

"And, Anne, here is something for you. We will celebrate the occasion at a grand banquet in York Place. You will hold the premier place by my side, and of course, you must be attired appropriately." He went to the table and retrieved the parcels he had in hand when he arrived. With his broad smile, he handed them to me.

"Oh, Henry! You give me too many gifts, my darling …" adding hastily, "I do love them all, though.'

Quickly I unwrapped the first parcel to find a bolt of exquisite deep purple velvet. I looked at Henry with curiosity. Purple was reserved for the royal family.

"I want you to use this when you have a new gown made for your father's celebration, Anne. The greatest nobility of the realm will be present, and I wish to have you appear as you should – as my wife, my queen, my love. It is but a matter of a short period of time until this will become reality and I see no reason to pretend otherwise … now open the other parcel."

That I did, and could not believe what lay inside: a circlet of diamonds, large and clear in the candlelight; a singular strand suspended from the necklace, ending in a large and rare diamond which would hang just between my breasts. I looked up at Henry, speechless.

But then, no words were needed. He gathered me to him, and we kissed: an ardent, sensual kiss which caused me to yearn all over again that he would soon be free so we could love each other as God intended us to.

•

I looked forward to the honour which was soon to be bestowed on my father, and to the celebration we would enjoy as a result. The design of the gown I would wear that evening was especially stunning, and I worked closely with the tailors who were making it. My family was elated once Henry had announced Father's elevation, and there was much discussion amongst the courtiers regarding this singular tribute.

I knew not when, or even whether Katherine had been informed of Henry's decision, but it became evident after a time that she had been. I avoided her as I always attempted to do, but my friends and allies told me she was anguished and doleful and took no pains to hide it from anyone in her company. I was aware that Henry was seen publicly with her on occasion. He felt it important to maintain convention while the Matter was still being debated. I did not agree, and had told him so, but had no choice but to defer to his way of doing things. I knew how much he now disliked being near to Katherine, and I assumed that if I but maintained my composure, and he suffered mightily being in her company, surely he would put an end to the pretence before long.

On St Andrew's Day, Henry had planned to dine with Katherine. They never dined together privately anymore, only when some ushers, stewards, and other members of the court were present so the word would be spread that the King honoured tradition. To finish the day, however, he had agreed to have a private supper with me, and afterwards, we were to play cards with some of our favourite ladies and gentlemen.

I was readying the servers for Henry's arrival, when he unexpectedly entered the room, looking ominously agitated. I took his arm and firmly led him to a seat by the window and out of earshot. "What is the matter, Your Grace? Your concern is alarming."

The tone of his voice invited close attention from the staff. Anxiously I stood and led him from the chamber into a smaller anteroom. With furrowed brow and reddening complexion, he vented that he had been in Katherine's company earlier in the day, whereupon the wretched woman had launched into a loud litany of grumbling and complaints, bemoaning that she continuously suffered the pains of Purgatory on earth.

"She looked upon me," he grated, "as if I were the Devil Incarnate, and accused me of treating her terribly because we never spent any time together – that we never dined together, nor did I visit her as a husband should, in her apartments."

"And what was your reply?" I asked, biting the inside of my cheek to remain in check. It was the first time in weeks I had been angered enough to resort to such painful self-control.

"I said she had no cause for complaint: that she is mistress of her household, and can do what she pleases. I told her that I am busy – busy with important matters of state which do not pertain to her. And finally, I said that, as to visiting her in her apartments and partaking of her bed, she should know I am not her legitimate husband, as innumerable doctors, canonists and theologians are ready to maintain."

"What else? What else did you tell her?" I asked between clenched teeth.

"That I am merely waiting for the opinions of the Parisian theologians, and that Dr Stokesly had been sent to obtain them. I advised her that as soon as I have those opinions in hand, I will forward them to the Pope, who will undoubtedly declare the marriage null and void. And if he does not, then I fully intend to denounce him as a heretic, and marry whom I please!"

And with that, he let out a pitiable groan and looked unutterably disconsolate.

"Anne, she looked me straight in the eye and said, as defiantly as you could ever imagine, that for my doctors and lawyers she cared not a straw; they are not her judges, and it is only for the Pope to decide. She then added that, as for the other doctors, whether Parisian or from other universities, I should know very well that the principle and best lawyers in England have written in her favour - and furthermore, if she were to procure counsel's opinion in this matter, for each doctor or lawyer who might decide in my favour and against her, there would be one thousand to declare the marriage good and indissoluble ..."

He shrugged helplessly. "At that, Anne, I stood and left the room without a backward glance at the damned shrew!"

My heart should have gone out to him, for he looked so unhappy. But the bile in me had risen, and my patience cracked. "Henry! Why did you give her so much information? Would you deem to provide a wartime enemy with your precise strategy for winning a battle? I have told you not to engage with her in an argument like this, for she unfailingly finds a way to contradict all you say. She's had a great deal of practice in garnering the upper hand from you in a disagreement, and she knows exactly how to make you feel wretched."

I arose and walked to stare out of the window in an attempt to control myself before my anger overflowed.

With my back to him, I watched the muddy river hurry on its course downstream. "If anyone has a legitimate complaint, it is I! I remain loyal to you, love and honour you when I have no guarantee at all that I shall ever become a wife, or a mother –nay, that I shall ever even have a *chance* to bear a child! It is *I* who may well end up alone years from now!"

My eyes burned with tears ready to spill. I spun to face him and with a release of vehemence let the words fly. "What reassurance do I have that you will not give up on this fruitless quest and simply go back to her, taking mistresses as you please?"

With that, to avoid being seen crying by the servants still setting the buffet, I ran from the room.

I'd hastened to my bedchamber, having lost all appetite. I needed to be by myself for a time, to deal yet again with the gnawing sense of bitter disappointment deep within. I longed just to curl up on my bed and cry myself to sleep, but I knew that would achieve nothing. Sitting at my *toilette* table, I put my head in my hands and wept. I had never felt so desperately sorry for myself. I abhorred wallowing in self-pity; it had never been my way. But I could not help but feel I had sunk into a quagmire which offered no escape.

I was so absorbed in my misery that I did not hear a soft rap on the door. With my head still buried in my hands, I felt a tentative touch on my back. Henry was standing above me, tears in his own eyes, his face a mask of anguish. I slowly stood, folded myself into his arms, and we clung to each other for a long time. No words were exchanged; they were not necessary. We shared the same feelings of despair, longing, desperate hope, and above all, love

•

The next day, desperate for some form of distraction, I asked Henry if we might go hawking after dinner, and so we walked out into the fields beyond the mews with our gyrfalcons, Pilgrim and Senator, accompanied, as ever, by Jolie. This was exactly what we needed: breathing in the fresh, biting air of late November, partaking of a sport we both loved, with a chance to clear our minds.

"I am sorry, Henry, so very sorry I lost my composure and my temper last evening. It was the last thing you needed to cope with after your meeting with Katherine." I cast a regretful glance his way as we walked, thinking once again how fortunate I was to be in the company of such a superb man. He looked arrestingly handsome today, garbed in deep green velvet and soft brown leather hose. His beard was closely trimmed and set off the angle of his strong jaw, which today, I could see, was set with determination.

"Henry, I need you to understand how I feel and why I cried such grievous tears last night." I took his arm and turned him to face me. "Surely I hurt because I hunger for you to be my husband. But even more than that – I chafe over those who treat you as if you were merely another nobleman, one of a group of well-born cronies angling for position. That is how you were dealt with by Wolsey, and it is Katherine's way, too. You are the King, and your subjects have an unconditional obligation to obey you - not the Pope, not the Holy Roman Emperor - you and only you, Henry! If such obedience is not brought to bear in this matter as well as all others, then what is the meaning of Kingship?"

Taking my hands in his, he gazed resolutely into my eyes and again I felt the intimate encounter of our thoughts in symmetry. "Anne, you are my soul and my very self. I honour and respect you beyond measure. We will triumph, after all, my darling. You will be by my side as my love, my wife, and queen; my soul mate before God."

"Then let us muster patience once again and wait for the scholarly treatise being prepared by Dr Cranmer. I am confident it will pave the way for you, Henry. You are the King of England, and able to create the prospects you desire and the ones you deserve. And once you have made your decisions, your subjects best abide by your command, lest they go the way of traitors before them!"

At this pronouncement, his slow smile of agreement matched mine. We proceeded to the open field, and there had a grand afternoon hawking.

York Place
Winter 1529

THE GREAT HALL of the Palace of York glowed with candle and torchlight and the warmth of hearth fire on the evening of December 8, 1529. I was not to forget that night because its light shone on my father and mother. The day before, Father had been created Earl of Wiltshire, an old and aristocratic title, as well as the Earl of Ormonde in the Irish peerage, nobility of the highest order. My mother, by association, became a countess. I was inordinately proud of both of them and so happy for their success. True, it was in part due to my relationship with the King, but my father had worked tirelessly over many long years to support His Majesty in all that had been asked of him. He deserved this honour in his own right.

On that evening, Father, Mother and I sat on the dais with the King, in the foremost places of honour, I sitting next to Henry in the place reserved for a Queen. Below me were to be seated the pre-eminent ladies in England, including the King's sister Mary, the Dowager Queen of France and Duchess of

Suffolk, andmy aunt, the Duchess of Norfolk. Henry intended to make it clear to all, that night, that he would have his way.

All eyes came to rest on me as I slowly proceeded to the dais on the arm of the King. I was gowned in a dazzling creation of deep crimson silk overlaying a kirtle of the purple velvet Henry had gifted to me. The purple had been intricately embroidered with silver floss complemented by further silver edging to the deep sleeves of crimson and purple. My hood was shaped like a crescent moon, with the back rim raised up from my head. Covered in silver tissue, its billiments had been outlined with rubies and pearls and presented the stunning illusion of a tiara. From the back of the hood draped a length of sheer silver tissue from beneath which my dark hair cascaded to waist-length. I wore the necklet of diamonds Henry had given me, my emerald ring as always, and a diamond ring on the first finger of my right hand.

The look I intended to display was nothing less than that of a queen soon to be crowned. I was well aware there were those present who did not approve and resented the position I assumed on Henry's right, and those of my mother and father to his left. I sensed the condemning stare of Mary Tudor, the woman whom I had served as a girl in France. Her dislike for me was apparent. Her husband, Brandon, Lord Suffolk, watched impassively, and I wondered how he managed, caught between the opinions of his wife and the greatest wish of his sovereign and childhood friend, the King.

Of course, the Duchess of Norfolk looked down her nose at me as well. She must have wanted to be anywhere else on that evening. It was now widely known that she was loyal to Katherine, and I could no longer encounter her without wanting to shake her and demand that my precious letters stolen at her behest be returned. True, she had her own problems, having been cast off by her husband in favour of a younger mistress, so I recognized that each time she saw me, it must have created an uncomfortable reminder of her marital humiliation. Regardless of how she felt, she was required to be in attendance that evening: her husband and my mother were brother and sister, and we all shared a Howard bloodline.

But that night was my parents' night, and such dark connivances should be set aside. I squeezed Henry's hand tightly under the draped white cloth, and proudly raised my golden goblet in a toast to the new Earl of Wiltshire. The music commenced, the wine flowed, and as the evening progressed we danced, ate, laughed, drank, and made merry until we were splendidly exhausted.

•

I had decided to remain at York Place over Christmastide, while the King would travel to Greenwich to provide the type of celebration, along with the Queen, that his court and guests had come to expect. Certainly, this was not the kind of Christmas I wished to have, but I was reluctantly becoming accustomed to the highs and lows which were a product of waiting for Henry to be freed from his marital captivity.

Anne, Maggie and I were planning our own Christmas celebrations; the first I would experience at York. We sat at a table in the library, quills and parchment arrayed before us, awaiting our ideas.

"We must indulge in some gaiety, Anne," Maggie insisted firmly. 'We cannot allow the joy of the season to be stolen from us by Katherine while she and her women smugly have a jubilant time, pretending you do not exist. Shall we plan a masque? We can have Sir William Cornish help us – his ideas are always exciting and unique. Or how about an evening of music and singing? We can each prepare a selection and have friends and courtiers perform instead of professional musicians. What would you like to do? You are not permitted to mope about because Henry is at Greenwich with Katherine."

"Well, I do feel like languishing. But you both know me better than that; I will not allow anyone to see me with a long face," I replied, then considered Maggie's suggestions. "A masque perhaps …? No, I think not. Oh, I am so undecided! It just feels as if we would be planning entertainment for no audience at all. Henry's bearing on our celebrations is so… so… immense. And his laughter so loud and infectious that it leaves a gaping hole when he is not around." I slumped in my chair at the expansive table, my cheek propped on my fist.

Anne Gainsford leaned across and placed a sympathetic hand on my arm. "It will be different next year, Anne, I am sure of it. In fact, perhaps we will be planning your marriage celebration. A Christmas wedding would be so lovely!"

I sighed, but then gave her a squeeze in return and smiled back appreciatively. "Thank you, my Anne. You always know how to raise my spirits."

"Oh, and by the by, Anne, I forgot to show this to you." Maggie reached for a book on the table and withdrew a piece of parchment tucked inside the pages. It was a poem, beautifully transcribed. "It is a piece written recently by my brother Thomas. This is a copy, and I wanted you to see it."

She handed me the sheet while Anne looked over my shoulder.

I read the script, mouthing the words to myself:

> Whoso list to hunt, I know where is an hind,
> But as for me, alas, I may no more:
> The vain travail hath wearied me so sore,
> I am of them that furthest come behind.
> Yet may I by no means my wearied mind
> Draw from the deer, but as she fleeth afore
> Fainting I follow: I leave off therefore,
> Since in a net I seek to hold the wind.
> Who list her hunt, I put him out of doubt,
> As well as I, may spend his time in vain.
> And graven with diamonds in letters plain,
> There is written her fair neck round about,
> 'Noli me tangere, for Caesar's I am,
> And wild for to hold, though I seem tame'.

I looked back to my dear friend and whispered, "This is me, Maggie. He has written about me. Truly, it is a beautiful composition. Thomas is such an insightful man: he, like no other, comprehends my plight. Indeed, I am Caesar's, and Caesar's I will be, nor anyone else's, for who would have me should this not work out?"

It was then that the full realization of what I had just said struck me. "Can you imagine? I will be one or the other - Queen or spinster! Is that not the height of irony?"

I laughed, too loudly, and my friends heard the undertone of fear.

"Anne, you must have faith that all will be well. Trust in the abilities of His Grace. The King will stop at nothing to make you his wife. You must not give way to constant worry."

Anne then looked at the two of us and smiled impishly. "My ladies, you should know worry does nothing for one's looks - just see what it has done to Katherine!"

There was nought else for it. We glanced at each other and burst into giggles.

On Christmas Eve, the King sent me gifts of sweets, fruit, and a large dressed and gilded deer for our table. We managed to have a merry time, but I missed him dreadfully.

•

Henry returned to me before New Yeartide, having sent Katherine and her covey of sycophantic crones back to Richmond. I was joyful and felt alive again.

Once the Monarch was again installed at York Place, the number of daily visitors increased dramatically. One afternoon, we received a visit from Guillaume du Bellay, Seigneur de Langey. The Seigneur was the eldest brother of Cardinal Jean du Bellay, our French ambassador. These gentlemen represented a very wealthy French family of the powerful Angevin line. It was a great advantage to the good relations between France and England to have the support of such noblemen. I had not met du Bellay's brother before that day, but I very much liked the Cardinal and, I truly believe, he me. We enjoyed conversing in French, and he had shared with me the witty and often bawdy writings of his close friend, François Rabelais. Seigneur de Langey had already sent me gifts at the New Year - quite exquisite jewellery which included two rings of opal, a gold link necklace and a beautiful rosary of gold, with pearl beads. I found the gesture to be charming and was looking forward to meeting him.

Seigneur de Langey had also sent a message informing Henry that he was in possession of some jewels which Henry might be interested in purchasing. Since Henry and I both had a love of beautiful gemstones, he had invited de Langey to meet us at Windsor so we could view what he had to offer.

We convened in the Windsor library one sunny morning in late January. Pale yellow light streamed through the windows and spilled across the massive oak desk over which the Seigneur had spread a bolt of deepest black silk velvet. It was a fine fabric of the richest quality, likely made in Brussels, and I noted de Langey's shrewdness with admiration, since its lustrous black surface would show off any gem to its best advantage. After we had exchanged pleasantries, and partaken of a delightful Bordeaux, the Seigneur placed a diamond on the velvet which took my breath away. It was huge – perhaps the largest diamond I had ever seen – and its surface had been planed perfectly flat and smooth with many facets polished underneath and on the sides which positively shimmered in the sunlight. Its broad upper surface looked like that of the clearest, coldest lake. Precisely positioned in the beam of sun illuminating the table, it possessed an incomparable allure.

Watching us closely and smiling, de Langey reached again for his bag and, with a flourish worthy of any magician, withdrew a sizable cross. When he placed it on the velvet, Henry and I gasped in amazement. Ornate but most tastefully designed, it was fashioned entirely of diamonds: each substantial in size, and glittering fiercely. I had never seen such magnificent work. Apparently neither had Henry, for he asked de Langey in awe, "Monsieur, where was this crucifix made? And who is the artisan?"

De Langey looked quite satisfied with himself and his ability to impress Henry, a widely recognized connoisseur of exquisite jewellery.

"Your Grace," he said with a deferential dip of his head, "*C'est magnifique, n'est-ce pas?* I knew that you, above all, *Majesté*, would appreciate its beauty and quality. This is a most special piece. *Il est trés rare* - a masterwork from the former studio of the great Giovanni delle Corniole of Florence. I am sure you have heard of him: he is acknowledged as one of the greatest gem engravers of all." He lowered his voice and said, almost reverentially, "His patron was Lorenzo de Medici - *Il Magnifico* - and he was a longtime resident of Lorenzo's court. His pieces are greatly prized, Your Grace, and rarely become available for purchase."

With a dramatic pause, he then added, "I thought it might be of interest to you."

I was enthralled not only with the jewel but with the Seigneur's masterful technique.

Henry scrutinized it, expertly using a jeweller's glass. I then squinted through the glass, marvelling at the workmanship, and wondering how anyone could so precisely polish a surface as hard as a diamond? Even more so - how could anyone summon the courage demanded in making the first cut at risk of shattering the gem into valueless fragments? I had heard that such craftsmen would spend weeks - indeed months - in considering the task before striking the irretrievable blow.

Henry leaned forward, resting his elbows on the table, and peered at de Langey over folded hands. I glanced from one to the other, thoroughly enjoying watching these two strong-willed men, who otherwise displayed every aspect of friendly respect for one another, prepare to play cat and mouse over the sale of these extravagant items.

"How did this rare and beautiful jewel come into your possession, Seigneur de Langey?" Henry asked.

"Ah, *oui*, Your Grace. It was brought to my attention by my brother, your ambassador. He was in attendance, along with Alessandro de Medici, at a dinner given in a noble's palazzo in Florence some months ago, where it was the topic of conversation. This piece had been commissioned by, made for, and personally owned by Alessandro's grandfather, Lorenzo *Il Magnifico.*"

It was obvious that the Seigneur had achieved the first *attaint* in the negotiation. Whether the French noble knew it or not, Henry had long been fascinated by the life and accomplishments of the great humanist, Lorenzo de Medici. The possibility of owning one of his personal possessions would be seductive indeed.

"And what are you asking for the purchase of this cross, Seigneur?"

"Your Majesty, if I am to be compensated in accord with what I paid for this precious item, its price would be no less than 12,000 crowns."

Henry snorted and shook his head. "It is a grand gem to be sure, Monsieur de Langey, but that is an exorbitant sum."

Never wavering from the coolness of his regal bearing, he waited for de Langey's response.

Seigneur de Langey hesitated for just the right length of time, then nodded in agreement. "*Vous avez raison*, Your Highness. It is a costly piece. And I am well aware that you have many expensive diplomatic and political missions underway. They must be draining your coffers considerably."

A further calculated pause. Then de Langey shrugged, "*Pas de problème*, Your Grace. Fortunately for me, I do have another interested buyer."

"Indeed? And who might that be?" Henry demanded with an imperious lift of his brows.

"Why, that would be your Imperial ambassador, Eustace Chapuys, Sire." Our artful salesman afforded Henry an indulgent smile. "He admired it just the other day, and indicated that he may purchase the jewel on behalf of his master, the Emperor Charles."

I credited the man for his boldness! Or perhaps he did not realize that he played with fire in baiting Henry so?

Henry kept his expression impassive, then surrendered. "In that case, *Monsieur*, I will purchase this item from you for the requested 12,000 crowns. And I wish to purchase the solitary diamond as well. And for that, I will offer you 2,000 crowns and not a penny more. Shall we agree to a total of 14,000 crowns with a handshake? I am certain such an arrangement will be pleasing to you - if ought else you will have the pride of seeing these very jewels on our person when you next seek to visit England."

A moment's equivocation was all it took, and then de Langey rose, swept his feathered hat from his head with a deep bow, and said, "It is my great honour, Your Majesty, to sell you both of these incomparable jewels for 14,000 crowns."

Henry stood as well and clasped de Langey's hand without rancour, delighted with his new acquisitions. As soon as the nobleman had departed, he slyly said to me, "A pleasant man but a brigand in negotiation none the less …These, my love, will be placed in safe keeping for a very special day. Do you know what day that will be?"

"I cannot fathom, Your Grace, what might be important enough for such extravagant and rare jewels. Unless they might be bestowed on the son we will have one day?"

"They will indeed belong to our son eventually, God willing. But before that day arrives, Anne, they will be worn by you on the occasion of your coronation as Queen of England and may that be imminent."

I went to him and kissed him, praying that with one kiss I could convey the promise of all which was to come.

•

While at Greenwich for Christmastide, Henry and his master builders had worked on structural plans for the renovation of York Place. He sent the plans to York, along with numerous books on classical buildings and structures. We spent pleasant hours together poring over those designs and debating what should be included and where, as well as discussing the style and substance of the interior and exterior decoration. I found myself particularly captivated by the structural drawings. They appealed to my sense of logic, and becoming absorbed in them offered a welcome respite from the emotional turmoil of the Great Matter.

The new palace was to be the epitome of luxurious city living, providing easy access for Henry and his Council to Westminster and Parliament, and leading directly into London's centre via The Strand. It would be a destination for entertainment and recreation, having advanced kitchens and baynes for bathing in comfort, with a network of privy chambers, even some secret chambers tucked behind the privy chambers which would be accessible only to Henry and his Groom of the Stool. This new design would allow the King his much needed and increasingly desired privacy.

A new and much more expansive quay on the Thames was to be constructed, along with a bridge and stair leading directly to the privy chambers reserved for the exclusive use of the King and his family. On the western side of the palace would be an elaborate tiltyard with an enclosed gallery for viewing tournaments while, of course, there would be tennis plays both small and large, a yard in which to play bowls, a pheasant field and fantastic gardens. King Street would divide the eastern and western halves of the palace. Spanning the road, a large and imposing gatehouse would be built, featuring a tower on each side. The brick towers were to be pierced by tall windows to flood their rooms with light.

Soon I was buried in textile samples, colour palettes, drawings and books from which I selected patterns, fabrics, designs for the creation of grotesques after the Italian fashion, mural ideas, and colours for the interior, beginning with the reconstruction of my apartments, which would then be enlarged into a maze of new rooms and galleries comprising the Queen's lodgings. I worked on this project with the happy confidence that I was designing Queen's apartments for myself, not Katherine. This was to be Henry's and my special residence. In fact, I secretly hoped Katherine would never step an unwelcome foot over the palace threshold.

•

Dr Cranmer had completed the book requested by Henry in October. Henry and I eagerly read through it, and I was imbued with a profound sense of calm upon understanding the reasoning with which Cranmer presented his various arguments in favour of allowing Henry to divorce Katherine and remarry.

In addition to articulating his opinion, Cranmer had excerpted sources as wide-ranging as Aristotle and Plato, Saint Thomas Aquinas, scripture, legal cases from England and abroad, and quotes from notable clerical and lay councillors. At last, in front of our eyes, was presented clear and irrefutable evidence impeccably assembled by a brilliant mind, that Henry, as a king ordained, was rightful in making his own decisions and had no obligation to seek the Pope's authority. Cranmer went so far as to postulate on the Pope's grievous error in contradicting Scripture, which was the rightful word of God. I almost cried with relief.

The next step was to gain support from the most learned minds in England and across the Continent. Thus, an operation was begun to provide the greatest universities with Dr Cranmer's findings, and seek their concurrence as indicated by affirmative votes. Selected to pursue this critical objective were Stephen Gardiner, Henry's Secretary, and Dr Edward Foxe, then Provost of King's College. Well schooled in his findings, they were to represent convincingly Dr Cranmer's position to the academics at Cambridge. Due to both Cranmer's and Foxe's association with that esteemed place of learning, it was believed by all that an affirmative reply would be forthcoming and rapid.

It was most disappointing, therefore, when the days and weeks dragged on without the anticipated outcome. I watched Henry restlessly pace the floors of the Long Gallery, awaiting from the Cambridge scholars the arguments for and against his Great Matter. His anxiety was palpable, and I knew just what he was feeling – each day a bit older; the imaginings of holding a baby son in his arms seemingly ever more remote. A letter, at last, arrived, which named the theologians chosen to comprise the voting body. Next to certain names, Gardiner had entered an 'A', communicating his knowledge that these men were already in agreement. It appeared there were enough annotated names to carry a majority vote and to position Cambridge in favour of Henry.

My father, who had been appointed Lord Privy Seal by Henry in January, was sent to Paris on an assignment to meet with the administrators of the Sorbonne and attain their agreement to Cranmer's position. Affirmation by the Sorbonne was critical in lending the kind of credence needed to gain the support of other major European universities. From there he would travel to the Auvergne region in south-central France where he would pay diplomatic courtesy to François while confirming his promised support. Following that meeting, Father was to continue to Bologna and, in an audience with Pope Clement and Emperor Charles, attempt to convince them of the verity of Cranmer's argument. The trip was daunting, and my father not a young man, but I knew he would use his mighty determination and all his skill to obtain the desired result for his King.

Leaving the relevant documents with members of the Sorbonne faculty for their thorough review, my father met with François, then made his way to Bologna to see the Pope and the Emperor. It was an exhausting journey, and we were informed that his health indeed suffered. However, true to my prediction, he completed the steps of his task as planned. But, it seemed, to no avail.

By the middle of February, Henry and I received word from Father that both the Emperor and the Pope were uncompromising in their disagreement with the assertions Cranmer had put forth. They were, and would remain, unyielding.

•

Henry stood in the library holding the letter, with his back to me. I waited long for him to speak. When he did not turn to me, I said quietly, "Henry. It is over."

At this, he whirled around and faced me with alarm. "What say you, Anne?"

"I speak of your relentless pursuit of the Pope's approval. Your futile desire that he agree with your decisions and your actions. Can you not see that the time has finally come to cast him aside? You must know now that he does not support you, and never will. He is not your 'Holy Father'. The word of Giulio Medici, elected Pope Clement VII by his fraternity of corrupt clergy, does not determine the fate of your eternal soul, Henry. You are a King born and ordained! That privilege belongs to God, and only to God. You *must* remove him from being an obstacle between you and the personal truths you reveal to your Almighty Lord." I spoke gently, but the intent of my words was unrelentingly clear.

I went to him, taking his hands in mine and, eye to eye, searched the core of his being.

We looked into each other's soul, and I knew then that he would stand on his own. I also knew the understanding which had been reached between us at that very moment would change the course of history for England.

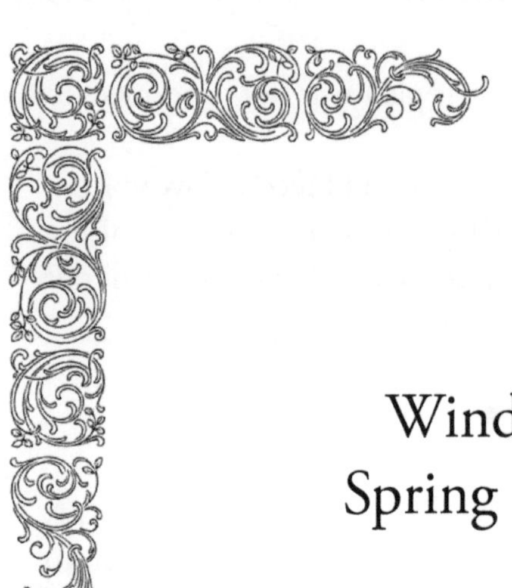

Windsor
Spring 1530

ONCE HENRY RECOGNIZED the complicity which existed against him between Emperor Charles and Pope Clement VII, I observed his attitude change significantly. On 24 February, Clement crowned Charles I of Spain as Holy Roman Emperor in an elaborate ceremony in Bologna. It was by then obvious that theirs was a political alliance every bit as much as a religious one - Clement would never oppose the Emperor he had just crowned. The longer Henry ruminated on these events, the more outraged he became. He threatened to withdraw his diplomatic ambassadors from Spain and blustered that he would be happy if Charles did the same since he had little liking for the unctuous Eustace Chapuys.

Dr Cranmer continued seeking approvals from the major universities in Italy while my brother sought them in France. As the weather warmed, so did our hope. Affirmative verdicts were received from Bologna, Ferrara, Padua, and Pavia, although not, it must be said, without difficulty. In France, another group of agreements was handed down from Orléans, Angers, and

Bourges. We were encouraged, yet most anxiously awaited a favourable verdict from the cornerstone, the Sorbonne.

•

"Anne, will you want to leave at least some of your hunting apparel here?" Maggie called to me from my wardrobe closet. I was in the adjacent room, selecting gowns and accessories to pack for our return to York Place. I had accomplished very little because Jolie had been doing her best to lure me into a game in which she liked to race back and forth and streak through the rooms of the apartment like a white arrow. It seemed the game was not fun for her unless I watched the entire thing.

Once the greyhound darting had subsided, I reviewed what Maggie had selected. She was an enormous help in organizing and cataloguing my growing collection of clothing and jewellery. Never would I have thought I would require help in keeping track of my articles of clothing, jewellery, and headgear! But thanks to Henry's incredible largesse, I needed a wardrobe assistant, and Maggie was the person perfectly suited to maintaining order. If ever I became Queen, I would ask her to fill an official position of Mistress of the Wardrobe.

"I think I will leave more garments behind than I have previously, Maggie. I know Henry will want to take advantage of Windsor Park in high hunting season, and by now I feel more confident that I will return here with him," I said.

"I could do no more than agree with you on that point," Maggie quipped, pointedly eyeing the magnificent riding kirtle and jacket Henry had just given me, which matched a gorgeous new black and gold saddle that had been delivered the day before, in advance of our trip. The saddle was a special one, indeed.

It was designed for two people to ride pillion.

•

On the cloudless morning of 9 May, Henry and I, flanked by assorted servants and courtiers, were ready to depart Windsor. The townsfolk had been assembling since daybreak in the hope of seeing the King in all his splendour as he rode by. None of them, I wager, expected what came into view once the standard bearers, equerries, and pages had passed. There were Henry and I riding together, our bodies pressed against each other's as we rode pillion on his big black warhorse through the town and countryside. I smiled to myself with great satisfaction: I had been reliably informed that Henry had never ridden this way with Katherine, even in their early years of marriage.

Oh, it surely was scandalous! The townsfolk's expressions were rich as they first delighted in seeing their Monarch, then saw me with my arms about Henry as he held the reins. For once, though, I did not care a jot. I intended to enjoy the ride. The heat of Henry's strong body next to mine, and our ability to talk privily with one another as we rode, to say nothing of the gorgeousness of my attire and Henry's - what damsel would not bask in such an experience?

•

It was delightful settling back in at York Place. In the time since we had last been at York, a great deal of progress had been made renovating our apartments. Because of my involvement with the design of the new palace, and because Katherine would have no residence there, it had begun to feel like home to me. The first week was filled with domestic matters, and Henry received few visitors. We moved into the newly refurbished apartments and talked endlessly about how it would look once all of the building and renovating were completed.

We installed new kitchen staff, including an inspired Frenchman as chief cook. He discussed with me his desire to create a cuisine which was *nouveau,* and I gave him permission to try his concept and see how it was received. With a grateful smile and a bow so low the flamboyant feather on the brim of his toque swept the floor, he rushed off to seek new and exotic ingredients for his menu. After that, on a daily basis deliveries were made, often fresh strawberries and herbs of all varieties sent by Jasper, the head gardener at Beaulieu. One day, Lord Berkeley sent Henry a gift of a freshly caught sturgeon. The cook was beside himself with joy at this addition to his kitchen's fare. He concocted a fantastic dish from the creature, with its roasted flesh finely chopped and combined with onion and *herbes fines*, mixed with butter, then brilliantly reformed in the shape of the fish. I will say we benefitted greatly from his skill since all his dishes were superb.

If I closed my eyes, I could indulge in the enchanting illusion of Henry and me living in domestic bliss. We took our meals together, read together, and enjoyed simple pleasures like gambolling with our dogs. Henry had called for his spaniel puppy named Cut to be brought to him from Greenwich, and two days later was much relieved when a yeoman steward also brought his favourite deerhound, Ball, back after having been lost in Waltham forest for several days. We laughed to ourselves about how we must have looked when we walked in the gardens, followed by a veritable pack of dogs comprising all shapes and sizes!

•

Came Sunday, the first day of June, and Henry and I were walking through the cloister after morning Mass. I was feeling somewhat melancholy because Henry planned to return soon to Greenwich and remain there for a time. He had much to attend to and thought it best if I stayed at York overseeing construction while he conducted affairs of state from Greenwich. I would see him whenever he chose to be rowed back to York, but the lovely fantasy of Henry and I as husband and wife had once again evaporated.

As we paused for a moment at the door to my apartments, he said, "Oh, Anne! I have something for you." And reaching into the pocket of his leather jerkin, he withdrew a splendid, small book. It was just large enough to fit comfortably in the hand and was gorgeously bound in soft white goatskin. HR was imprinted on the cover in gold amidst gold scrollwork.

"This has long been one of my favourite Books of Hours, and I would like you to have it, my love," he said, and with a departing kiss, I entered my chamber while Henry continued on.

Once at my desk, I inspected the book more closely. The binding was artistically done, and the pages of fine, smooth vellum felt silken to the touch. I had seen books of hours similar to this one when I was at the Austrian Court. The most beautiful and costly ones were usually made in Bruges, where the monks and the artisans were the most talented illuminators in the world. I pored over illustrations which were incredible in their intricate detail and dazzling colour. Every page seemed more gorgeously done than the last. Fanciful representations of Bible stories and proverbs leapt from the pages: brilliant with striking greens, deep blues, vivid scarlet, and liberal use of gold. Slowly I turned page after page, fascinated by the finely wrought paintings and beautifully done script. I was more than halfway through the book when I turned to a page on which a scourged and bleeding Christ kneeled before an open tomb: the Christ of Sorrows. At first, I was consumed by the heartrending sadness on the face of Jesus but, on scanning the rest of the page, I saw a notation in French at its foot. Looking more closely I saw it was Henry's writing, carefully and precisely executed. I took the book to the window and held it to the light. The notation read:

> If you remember me according to my love in your prayers I shall scarcely be forgotten, since I am your Henry Rex forever.

I studied his inscription for a long moment, then gathered the book to my chest and held it against my beating heart. This man – this marvellous man - for all his size, power, intellect and majesty, was the embodiment of the ardent romantic! I felt blessed for being loved so well.

It was evident, by the care he had given to his writing and the selection of the page which he annotated, that he had given much thought to this gift. I loved it especially because it was such a personal expression of Henry, the man.

I decided I would write a reply in the book, and slip it into his chamber where he would be sure to find it. But I needed to give my reply some consideration, so I could feel confident that it was worthy of such a precious gift. I put the book aside, this time very well hidden in my room, to inspect later.

•

On a fine balmy evening several days later, I sat by the open casement window of my receiving chamber conversing with Mistress Margery Horsman. Since she had joined my household, I had become fond of Margery. Especially since she proved to be a young woman who enjoyed, and was good at sport. As we talked, we thoroughly relished munching on fresh cherries, the earliest of the season, generously sent to me as a gift from Sir Thomas Pargeter, the Mayor of London.

"Then I will see you tomorrow, Anne, at the shooting range for some practice?" Margery inquired, rising and heading for the door.

"Yes! Let's hope the lovely weather continues so that we can enjoy a good afternoon for archery. William Brereton said he would accompany us and help by critiquing our form."

Margery shot me a cheeky look. "Yes indeed, I am certain he will do just that. My Lord Brereton is a man, and what man can resist an opportunity to 'critique' a woman's form?"

I doubled with laughter. "You are deadly quick, Miss Margery!" as she departed with a flippant goodbye wave. I fancied her shrewd humour. No one outwitted Mistress Horsman!

Once she was gone, I retired to my bedchamber. My maid had lit a fire in the hearth, and several lanterns were burning brightly. I went to a sturdy wooden chest and unlocked it with a key I invariably kept close to me. From it, I withdrew a smaller coffer and unlocked that as well. In the coffer was Henry's Book of Hours, along with his recent letters and some of the more controversial theological writings I had been given. Having learned the cruellest of lessons, I was exceedingly careful now about where and how I kept my most personal things.

I took the Book of Hours and sat at the table with the candle flame accenting the gold on the creamy binding, and flickering on the illustrations within. Again I slowly paged through, stopping to marvel at many of the renderings. I came to an illumination I particularly loved: that of the Virgin Mary sitting at a table by a window, wearing a glorious blue and gold gown. Leaning over her shoulder, the Angel Gabriel strove to gain Mary's attention since she, too, was absorbed in a book before her. He wished to tell her she was to have a son, the Son of God. Mary's face was radiant – peaceful, gentle and kind. A white dove, the Holy Spirit, blessed the scene from above. This beautiful work depicted a moment of great joy and wonder in the Scripture.

Then it occurred to me. This was the page on which I would reply to Henry!

From my writing desk, I removed a quill and a bottle of soft grey ink. The nib was cut broadly and would make a bold stroke, yet I thought it perfect for the brevity of my message. After scratching some ideas on a shred of parchment, at the foot of the page underscoring the Annunciation scene I wrote:

Be daly prove you shall me fynde
To be to you bothe lovynge and kynde

Anne Boleyn

I sat back in my chair and studied my inscription. The prominent letters jumped off the page, and Henry could not fail to find the message. I wondered what he would think when he came upon it. I wanted him to know how much I wished to make him happy by my dedication and love. And with the grace of the Holy Spirit, to make him the proud father of a healthy royal son.

There was no question. The positioning of my reply made a daring declaration.

I went in search of George Talbot, the Lord Steward, who was preparing Henry's suite for his visit to York. I explained to Sir George that I had borrowed the book and wanted to return it before Henry's arrival next day. He escorted me to Henry's privy study, unlocked the door, and I entered. Having a look about the room, so empty without his essence, my eyes came to rest on the corner where he conducted his personal devotions. There, I placed the Book of Hours carefully on his *prie-dieu* where he could not miss seeing it, then returned to my chambers with a gratified smile. I hoped Henry would find my reply pleasing; I hoped too that he would return the book to keep, for I would cherish it all the more with our inscriptions preserved within.

•

My newest fascination was archery. Henry had taught me how to hold a bow and arrow, and because my arms and shoulders were strong from riding, I was able to draw the bow well back and hold it steadily as I took aim. To my great delight I discovered I had a good eye, and when the arrow flew, it was well positioned. I could not help but let out a whoop of excitement every time my arrow hit its mark at the centre of the target while Henry guffawed loudly in chorus. To encourage my new interest, darling Henry provided me with an entire shooting ensemble including several beautifully made bows, arrow shafts with broadheads to fit them, decorative quivers for the arrows, and leather archery gloves.

I kept busy. So determinedly busy that I scarce found time to mull and fret over the resounding silence from Paris. The political intrigue in Europe was elaborate, and all the many distinctions impacted the delivery of a response. My father and Seigneur de Langey, who represented François, were both stretched to use every shred of diplomatic ingenuity they possessed to coax an affirmative reply from the learned doctors of the Sorbonne, and I worried that they would not succeed. This testament was exactly what Henry needed to bolster his growing conviction to relinquish his dependence on the Pope.

On a warm morning in July, Henry and I were at the archery butts at Greenwich, when across the lawn hurried a page with a small scroll for Henry. The young man deferentially announced that the message had come from the Earl of Wiltshire, with greater detail to follow soon. Henry broke the seal, unfurled the parchment and quickly read the contents. A jubilant grin spread from ear to ear, and he came to me, wrapped his arms around my waist, picked me up as if I were a child's toy and swung me about. The poor young page looked at the ground, uncomfortable and bewildered, until Henry dismissed him.

"Anne, look. Just look!" and he shoved the scroll under my nose. On it was Father's writing:

Your Royal Highness

Today was received the common seal of the university of Paris

Wiltshire

2 July

With an overwhelming wave of exhilaration, I blurted, "Henry, let us thank God! He favours our intentions. Now you are legitimately free of having to succumb to the commands of the Pope, and his accomplice, Charles. Oh come, do come. Let us hurry back and share the good news with our friends and supporters over dinner!"

Windsor
August 1530

THAT AUGUST THERE was to be no question – it was I who would accompany Henry on progress. We were ensconced at the royal hunting lodge at Easthampstead in Windsor Forest. Frequented by Henry's father, I was told it was here that Henry VII decided to offer his son Arthur in marriage to the Infanta Catalina of Spain as a part of the Treaty of Medina del Campo, so many years ago. I was not comfortable in that house; it smelt old and had an eerie, ghostly feel to it.

Gloomy house notwithstanding, the hunting was exceptional, and at this time of year, both game and the bounty of the gardens were plentiful. We dined on savoury dishes - fat partridge, sweets made from ripe, delicious pears and damsons, pies filled with fruits and filberts.

My father had returned home from his crushing travels on the Continent, and we celebrated at a feast in his, and Ambassador du Bellay's, honour. Though we rejoiced in the approvals from so many prestigious universities, we were nevertheless conscious of one shadow which hung over the proceedings. Upon Henry's demand for full disclosure, it was reported to him that there were, in fact, dissenting voters at the *Sorbonne*, the University of Paris. His disappointment at this news was obvious, having initially thought that the consent was unanimous.

After the banquet had ended, Henry and I were in his chamber.

"My darling," I said soothingly, "it matters not that some of those men voted against you. There were enough who agreed. Success was achieved. We are so close, Henry: I can feel it!"

He stroked my hair, sighed heavily, and said, "Oh Anne, what I have put you through. I often wonder that you have not departed me for a younger man, one with whom you might be married by now, and be expecting a child."

'Henry, never think that. Never utter such a thought! If I were to be burnt at the stake - if I were to be subject to death a thousand times - my love for you would not lessen one speck. I am yours, darling, and will be right beside you, always."

I said these words with a clear conviction, for I knew them to be true.

•

After my father had provided a complete discourse on the trip, Henry called on his closest councillors to join him at Hampton Court on 11 August. He wished to conduct a series of meetings to evaluate the results achieved in Europe. Katherine remained at Windsor, and Henry told me to be ready to travel with him and to stay at Hampton Court for a fortnight or more.

I sensed something momentous was about to take place. Henry's attitude was buoyant, yet resolute. I saw him little as we both readied for our move. He was busy preparing for the conference by reviewing documents and books brought to him from his libraries at Greenwich and Windsor. I believed I knew what he was intending, but kept to myself as he went about his business.

Hampton Court
Autumn 1530

WE ARRIVED AT lovely Hampton Court and settled in the residences which had been, and were still, under construction. There were few palaces frequented by Henry which were not being renovated. The man had a passion for architectural improvement! It did not bother me at all since I was used to the sounds and confusion of palace upheavals, York Place being a work in progress.

The newly constructed Bayne Tower, as Henry chose to call his new residential building because of his delight with the new luxurious bayne adjacent to his bedchamber, was simply beautiful. A three-storey structure, it was small, but a jewel of design. It was a perfectly private suite of rooms for Henry to live in and enjoy. My accommodations, which were connected to Henry's privy gallery and thereby to the Bayne Tower, were still being renovated, though my bedchamber, bayne, and presence chamber were near completion. The meetings were to take place in Henry's library on the third floor of the Bayne Tower.

Not only was I to remain at Hampton Court with Henry and his privy council, but I had been asked to attend the meetings as a delegate. I well understood that the matter pertained to the King, and only to me in an indirect sense, and so I was privately thrilled to be included in business of such importance, especially knowing I would be the only woman in attendance.

I took my seat at the long table in the library. Outwardly, I attempted to appear a study in composure. But my thoughts raced, and I will admit I was nervous. The other distinguished attendees took their seats: Henry at the head of the table with me to his right; my father, the Earl of Wiltshire, at the opposite end, with the Dukes Norfolk and Suffolk across from one another, Suffolk to my right. The erudite Drs Stephen Gardiner and Thomas Cranmer were across from each other, and the ageing Archbishop of Canterbury, William Warham, seated adjacent to Father.

While Henry spoke privately with the Archbishop, I seized the opportunity to scan the room - the handsomest library I had ever entered. Walls lined with dark, satiny wooden panelling which was beautifully carved but not overly ornate, furnishings of the highest calibre, many imported desks, comfortable chairs, and the magnificent long table under which were uniquely and cleverly constructed shelves holding stacks of books. All about the room were freestanding shelves with lecterns attached so one could easily support a book being read. The books lining the shelves were grouped by colour, which proved exceptionally pleasing to the eye. The top shelf held books with bindings of various shades of red: leather, velvet, even of embroidered satin; books on the second ledge were bound in black; the third in white; then there were those of tawny leather - all with lavish gold scrolling. Covering one entire wall hung a stunning tapestry in which a hunting scene was beautifully woven. The room enveloped one in a feeling of scholarly elegance.

As Henry called the delegates to order, I experienced a moment in which I felt as if I were observing the proceedings from outside of myself. It was a strange sensation to be sure, almost as if it were a moment frozen in time. I realized then, with a lump in my throat, one of the great wishes I had expressed to my mother – that of my inclusion in the coveted circle of those who make significant decisions concerning the Realm – had come true. That I, Anne Boleyn, sat at the right hand of the mighty King of England, preparing to discuss a matter which would have radical consequences now and long into the hereafter.

I pinched myself beneath the table and prepared to have my voice be heard: a female voice amongst those of powerful men.

For the next five days, Henry's most trusted advisors sat in council with him - and me - to debate the requirement of the King's assured allegiance to the Pope, and thereby the Church, in a country which considered itself Catholic. We discussed circumstances of law, of religion, of moral conscience. I contributed my views and held to my arguments when challenged. I knew how proud Henry was of me. He told me that these meetings were ample proving ground to convince all those present that I was well suited to be Queen.

Finally, we reached a consensus based on writings by French scholars who asserted that a King is equivalent to an Emperor in his realm, and no one can supersede him on any decisions which pertain to his realm. It was notably agreed in principle, though not without the evident unease of some delegates, that within his dominion Henry reigned supreme.

•

Henry had fallen in love with Hampton Court. His enthusiasm for updating the beautiful structure knew no bounds.

"Sweetheart, let us remain here through the autumn. Perhaps keep Christmas here as well!"

"You know that would please me greatly, Henry," I replied. "But what do you plan to do with Katherine all the while? Keep her confined to Richmond - and Mary at Windsor? If so, then I will remain with you. If, on the other hand, Katherine comes to Hampton Court, then I will make my departure. She and I can't live under the same roof any longer."

Henry hesitated. While he did not wish to be in Katherine's company, I could tell he was still not ready to banish her altogether, thereby invoking the further displeasure of those who supported her.

"We can spend the time we have together pleasurably, at least, my love," he offered tentatively, avoiding the question.

I took his hand, turned it palm up, and kissed it. His eyes glowed, watching me. "Let us go out for the hunt this afternoon, as we had planned," I suggested. "And then let us, you and I, share some of that pleasure this evening, shall we?"

I was certain all worries about Katherine would be banished from his mind as he looked forward to the evening to come. Hunting in the parklands surrounding Hampton Court provided good sport. On that afternoon, we were joined by the brothers William and Urian Brereton, Nicholas Carew, and Thomas Heneage. I had allowed Jolie to hunt with us several times over the summer, and though she was a bit unruly in the field, she seemed to love keeping pace with Master Rainsford's pack of hunting hounds. She had formed a close bond with a hound called Ghost, which belonged to Urian Brereton, and they often ran together.

The chase carried on for miles, as we tracked a fleet-footed buck. I began to tire, and was thankful when at last the hounds cornered the buck and held it to bay, and the huntsmen impaled it with their long knives. Henry ceremoniously stabbed it with his silver and gilt dagger, and we turned for home while the huntsmen dressed the carcass in preparation for carrying it back to the estate.

The hounds were whistled in by Rainsford, and, well trained, they moved as a collective pack across the countryside. Jolie and Ghost, on the other hand, ran about playing and chasing each other, frequently returning to check if we riders were still in their vicinity.

Henry and I rode together, talking. Our conversation halted in mid-sentence when from over the next hill we heard the unmistakable bellowing of an animal in agony. I looked about and did not see Jolie, and in alarm, I spurred my horse to a gallop and crested the hill. Laid out before me was a grisly scene, and at the centre were Jolie and Ghost. They had come upon a stray cow, and in their overexcitement had mauled it. Its pained bellowing was pitiful to hear. Thankfully Henry, Urian, and Rainsford arrived at the scene whereupon Rainsford leapt down from his horse, went to the cow and inserted his knife through its eye socket, instantly putting the animal out of its misery.

Jolie and Ghost, furiously called to by Urian, skulked back to us looking very miserable indeed once they had been loudly berated for their behaviour. As horrible as the scene was, I did have to bite the insides of my cheeks to keep from laughing to see Jolie, mere minutes later, filthy dirty and smeared with blood, blithely trotting beside us, head held high as if she was the best dog in the world. She was a wild thing, my girl.

One of the huntsmen went to seek the owner of the cow to pay him for his loss, with the regards of his King.

I was more than ready to return to the house, have a bath, and prepare for a romantic evening with Henry.

•

I was not at all surprised as rumours and various dispatches reached court about the suspect activities of the supposedly banished Wolsey during the summer and early autumn. I had believed for some time that the man would eventually incriminate himself beyond pardon. It was said that he still conferred regularly both with Charles V and with Katherine. I knew he would attempt to use empathy for Katherine's cause to try and manipulate his way back into a position of power.

Henry had been informed that Wolsey was trespassing yet again in affairs of state in which he had no place. It was reported that a series of letters had been intercepted which pointed directly toward Wolsey's treasonous communications with France and Rome.

Surely, now, the wretched man had undone himself, even in his Monarch's too-tolerant eyes.

•

I awaited news of Wolsey's arrest at the King's command. When it did not come, I simmered. The year 1530 was in its last months, and still I remained a maiden. Unmarried and a maiden at 29 years of age, while Wolsey, who had done nothing but damage in progressing the King's case, was permitted to conduct himself with great audacity, feigning piety, yet countermanding the King in the political arena. My resentment festered.

We walked in the gardens, and as Henry talked, I could not listen - I had no idea what he was saying. All at once it became too much to bear. Without warning I stopped, gripped his arm and turned him to face me.

"Henry – by God's blood! What *will* you do with Wolsey?" My voice sounded shrill; my throat constricted with tension.

Henry's eyes narrowed. He had encountered the look I gave him several times before, and he was forewarned.

'What mean you, Anne?' he said slowly.

'Why have you not arrested him? He is traitorous - malicious! He does you damage at home and abroad. What are you waiting for? If that be the concession for us to marry, it seems you will be waiting a long, long time. Oh, I see what lies ahead - you and Katherine still wedded; Wolsey reinstated to a position of power; and me - banished to a convent, childless, husbandless, and alone!" I started to weep. My tenuously held grip on the raw emotion I felt over our situation was in jeopardy of crumbling completely, in open view.

With tears flowing, I choked, "I just do not know, Henry, really I do not. I now think this must be a fruitless conquest. I think we should call an end to it. It is tearing me apart. I now have enemies! Never did I see myself as a person who would have sworn enemies! Your idea of us as 'second selves' is a delusion. Either Aristotle is wrong, or we are just not matched in that way. This clearly was not ever meant to be."

I slumped to a nearby stone bench and hung my head, tears dropping to my lap, glistening in the late afternoon sun.

Panicked by the tone of my voice and the fatality of the message, he came to the bench to sit close beside me. "Anne, darling Anne, you cannot mean that? Please do not say such things! It breaks my heart. Look at me Anne."

When I heard his voice crack, I glanced up to see tears streaming from Henry's eyes too. He took my hands in a crushing grip. "Do you not see that your pain is my pain? That I share your emotion as if we were one? This proves we are but one self! Please – never leave me or I should die, Anne. I cannot live without you."

With a long, rasping sigh of uncertainty, I allowed myself to be held by him.

•

On the morning of 5 November, I stood by a window in the Watching Chamber at Hampton Court, staring at the rain falling steadily from the leaden skies. George found me and led me to a more private location. This time, he dared not risk engaging in brotherly sparring.

"I have come to inform you, my sister," he said gravely, "that Thomas Wolsey was arrested yesterday, accused of high treason."

I stared at him for a long minute, hardly daring to believe what I had just heard. I grabbed his arm and steered him to a table set about with chairs. Even as we sat, I blurted, "George! Tell me what you know!"

"The Earl of Northumberland and Sir Walter Walsh were dispatched by the King to locate and arrest Wolsey. Since his eviction from York Place, he had been living at Cawood Castle in the north of Yorkshire. It was Northumberland who was instructed to inform Wolsey of his arrest."

I reflected on the irony of this royal command. Northumberland was, of course, Henry Percy; the young man who had loved me, and had been so publicly excoriated by Wolsey for his decision to do so. Upon his father's death three years ago, Percy had become the sixth Earl of Northumberland. I had not seen him in some time and wondered how satisfying it may have felt for Percy to be granted such a unique opportunity for revenge.

"How did it unfold, George? Do you know?" I asked.

Only then did George permit himself a smile of satisfaction.

"When Northumberland told Wolsey that he was there to arrest him, Wolsey replied with disdain, 'Arrest me? You have no such right! I am still a Cardinal and a Legate of Rome. No one with mere temporal power can arrest me!' Then the Earl showed him the commandment, signed by the King, and announced, 'By the King's commandment I urge you to obey!'"

Wolsey had no choice but to concede. He was ordered by royal guardsmen to gather his things, as he was to be escorted into the keeping of the Earl of Shrewsbury until the King should decide his fate.

I listened in wonder. "And what will that fate be, do you think, George?"

"I imagine he will be sent to the Tower. Whether he will be able to survive that ordeal will remain to be seen."

•

On the 22nd of the month, a brigade of Yeomen of the Guard, headed by Sir William Kingston, arrived at Sheffield to fetch the Cardinal and, to his great shock and dismay, transport him to the Tower. Despite Wolsey having taken ill before their arrival, either from poison or from food which was bad, he nonetheless commenced his journey with the detachment of guards. They arrived at Leicester Abbey on Friday 27 November where they stayed due to Wolsey's inability to travel any further. There he grew ever weaker.

On Sunday, two days later, he died at the Abbey.

•

Henry was circumspect about the former Chancellor's passing. I did not know how I should feel about it. On one hand, I was relieved that his demise represented the removal of a significant threat to my prospective marriage with Henry; on the other, it was a death after all. I was unsure of how Henry truly felt about the loss of someone who had been so close to him for much of his adult life. I decided to keep my thoughts to myself.

Wolsey was gone.

Now only Katherine remained in our way.

In answer to my speculation, Henry decided to leave Hampton Court and return to Greenwich to observe a suitably solemn Christmastide with Katherine in residence.

On 14 December, we parted: Henry bound for Greenwich and me for York.

York Place – Whitehall January 1531

I REMAINED AT YORK Place through Christmas, surrounded by my family and close friends. It was not as I would have wished. I should have been celebrating the season with Henry, and I resented his absence, placing the blame squarely on the self- righteous Katherine.

Henry promised to return to York following the Twelfth Night festivities, and by the second week in January, I eagerly awaited his arrival. I planned a special supper just for the two of us. Earlier in the day, Lady Guildford had brought one of the King's favourite dishes, baked lampreys, for his enjoyment upon arrival. I was so anxious to see him; our separation had felt like an age.

He swept me into his arms as soon as he entered the chamber. My passion for him was unabated, and, as ever, when he embraced me in that bold way I felt a weakening of my resolve to remain maiden till we married. I covered his face in kisses and pressed myself to him. I confess it was only the timely entrance of the yeoman ushers delivering our supper which saved me.

Later, as we sat at the table, talked and ate, Henry signalled one of the ushers. The young man left the room but returned quickly with a silver tray piled with gorgeously wrapped parcels and packages. Henry had the tray placed before me, saying, "My sweetheart – your New Years' gifts. Please open them."

I still was not accustomed to Henry's incredible generosity and began to open a profusion of riches. In one box lay a stunning, intricately wrought and weighty gold chain of Italian design. The next revealed a large, blood red ruby surrounded by pearls, all set in a brooch. A third contained yards of beautiful crimson tissue, of the finest weave, enough for a gown with a flowing train. Finally, I opened the largest package to discover the softest, most beautiful pure white ermine fur. Henry beamed, and cast me a significant look. Clearly he intended the ermine to be worn soon, upon our marriage. I was quite certain that Henry had never treated Katherine so well, not in all their years of wedlock.

"Henry, you are so kind to me and much too generous." I leaned closer, indulging in the scent of him. "Do you know how much I love you?"

"I do my best to imagine, sweetheart. But I suspect I shall never really know until we are in each other's arms with no impediments. I pray that will be soon."

"So do I, Henry, every single day," I said, thinking about how much I wanted and needed it to be very soon.

Again suppressing my desire, I offered, "While you were at Greenwich, darling, I had an idea. What if we were to host a grand party here at York, celebrating the new palace? What say you to that?"

"I would reply with a resounding yes, my love!" Henry chuckled delightedly. "The timing is perfect. We can christen the palace by its new name, Whitehall. It will no longer be known as York. The new structure, as it evolves, will be called the Palace of Whitehall."

"How wonderful!" I was excited to have again something creative to work on, to take my mind off of the interminable worry. "May I begin planning?"

"Indeed, you may, my sweet Anne. Let us show court and the world what you can accomplish as mistress of a household - on a grand scale."

I could not wait to begin.

•

I threw myself into the preparation for the banquet and ball. In addition to revealing the palace's new name, we decided to fête a new ambassador from France, Seigneur de la Guîche. This was the first event Henry and I planned together, and I loved it. It made me feel as if we were truly husband and wife, planning a great event for guests who would join us in our home. It would also afford me the opportunity to show Henry and everyone else what Anne Boleyn, England's next Queen, was capable of. I determined to bring a degree of discerning detail to this celebration never before witnessed at court.

With the help of my ladies, I decided on the theme of a magical winter garden. We worked with Master Lovell, the renowned head gardener from Richmond to create the fantasy.

Employing Master Lovell had been the brilliant idea of Honor Lisle. Honor Grenville had married Arthur Plantagenet, Viscount Lisle, over a year ago. Lisle, a tall, handsome man, extremely capable and refined, was Henry's Vice Admiral, and he had found a worthy wife in Honor. She and I had become great friends. I'd known her for ages and had always liked her, but with more time together, we found we were very similar in many ways. She was beautiful; small in stature, but with a soft roundness to her figure and face. She dressed well and was lively and witty with a great sense of humour. There were times when we melted into fits of laughter together, and I loved her for that. And when it came to running her husband's household and affairs while he was away on assignment – well, no one was her equal.

"Let us see what suggestions Lovell makes, Anne. We do know that we will need yards and yards and *yards* of gorgeous tissue fabric to make it appear as if a great white blanket of snow had fallen." Honor always used embellishments when she spoke – both in her words and her gestures.

"Do you think we will be able to fool the guests into thinking they are outside?" I wondered, hurriedly adding, "But of course the difference being they will be warm."

"With absolute certainty, we will. With you and me designing the decorations for the Hall, this ball will be magnificent … fantastic! Unlike any the court has ever seen."

•

The day before the ball, the palace was in chaos. Construction on the King's apartments was rapidly progressing, and dusty masons, carpenters, painters, and plasterers swarmed the chambers and corridors.In sharp contrast, the palace's impeccably uniformed house stewards and yeomen had no alternative but to work around the labourers, and they dashed hither and thither carting supplies for the banquet, all the while displaying their haughty irritation at the interference.

Master Lovell had proved to be invaluable in envisioning how we would bring our white winter garden theme to life. His assistants brought in cartloads of saplings, large and small tree branches of all types, and vast swaths of evergreens which he and his crew set up around the room to make it appear as if it were a forest clearing. Many branches had been brushed with white or silver paint to simulate a coating of snow and ice. Master Copeland, one of the royal mercers, brought us miles of gossamer silver and white silk tissue, which was artfully draped from the rafters and walls. As the men worked, with our guidance, my ladies and I looked about the hall with barely contained glee. It was being transformed from a room supported by carved wooden beams to an enchanted forest which lay serenely under a coating of freshly fallen, sparkling white snow.

My ladies' attire was as carefully planned as the rest of the setting. They were gowned in shades of silvery grey, from the palest shimmer to deep, lustrous pewter. The colour I chose for myself was an ice blue satin, very wintry, with a petticoat of cloth of silver. The trim on our gowns and hoods was done with silver thread, braided and embroidered to look like the tracings of frost on an icy morning windowpane. My jewellery was diamond: necklace, rings, bracelet, and the edging on the billiment of my hood. The design of all my French hoods now resembled a small crown, with the hind edge standing up from my head to feature the jewels which adorned them. I had taken especial, creative care with my *toilette*, wearing a new, opulent French scent which was a combination of jasmine and iris. I had accented my eyes with a silver powder mixed for me by the master painter at York. It looked exotic and fantastical, and I used extra kohl on my lashes, and then drew a thin line of kohl on the lower inner rim, a trick I had learned which lent an extra gleam to the eye. It being January, my complexion was as fair as ever it got, which for me was still the colour of honey and cream. I used a rose coloured powder to tint my cheeks, as well as to dust the swell of my breasts above my bodice.

Honor and Anne Gainsford came to my chamber once they were ready. They both looked exceedingly comely in their pearl velvet gowns. I was so proud of the ladies and friends who surrounded me! They stood behind me as we excitedly observed our reflections in the tall silvered mirror in my dressing chamber. The appearance we had achieved was ravishing, in truth. I hoped Henry would be captivated.

•

Even our *entrée* at the ball was theatrical. Just late enough to be certain most guests had arrived, we arranged ourselves outside the entrance to the great hall. The first to be announced was Honor. Next came Anne and Maggie Wyatt, both in gowns of luminous grey, a shade deeper than Honor's. Finally, entering the hall before me were Bessie Holland, Margery Horsman, and Elizabeth Harlestone, all wearing gowns of a rich smoke grey.

At last, the herald cried 'Mistress Anne Boleyn, Lady Rochford!'

I hesitated for the briefest moment, pulled my shoulders back, lifted my head high, and glided into the great hall. The guests had grown quiet enough to hear the soft swish of my satin gown as I slowly approached the dais where Henry and Ambassador de la Guîche sat. Even from across the room I felt the intensity of Henry's stare. I know I flushed in response but willed myself to remain composed as I passed through the enthralled crowd to assume my place at Henry's right. In an unprecedented gesture, he stood as I approached. Once I reached him, with grace and grandeur worthy of the theatre, he raised my hand to his lips and kissed it in full view of all present.

Only when seated at last did I have the opportunity to view the room and appraise how the hall had been transposed into a place of perfect enchantment. Silver and white tissue floated from the ceiling and billowed from the walls. With only the slightest imagination, one had the sense of being in a frosty landscape. Candlelight glimmered from behind tissue, affording the room an ethereal light. Everywhere, hundreds of white candles in clear and blue glass cups shimmered and sparkled. Saplings which lined the room were draped with the palest tissue and candles floated magically about in the trees, hung by invisibly thin wire. Lofty silver and white branches stretched skyward from silver urns on every table. At each turn, pine boughs appeared snow-covered, lightly swept with white and silver. The air was redolent with pine and rosemary incense burning in silver censers. The tables were swathed in pure white. I felt as if I were about to dine on a magical forest floor which had been cloaked in season's first snowfall.

Henry leaned into me placing his lips against my ear and whispered "My darling, you are a woman of rare beauty and even rarer talent. I am the envy of every man present, whether they wish to concede it or not. I am so proud of you, Anne."

My heart swelled with elation at Henry's approval. Nothing was quite so intoxicating as his extravagant admiration. I knew I would happily go to the ends of the earth to please this man.

As the music began, guests turned to each other in pleasured surprise. The esteemed virtuoso Alberto da Ripa played and conducted his musicians to produce a sound so superb that it lifted the soul. *Signore* da Ripa, from Mantua, was a famed lutenist and composer of enormous talent. King François I had persuaded him to join the French Court, but to our great pleasure, he decided to spend some time in England before leaving for Calais. At my personal request, he agreed to play for the King and our guests for the evening. He performed some of his lute fantasias, which were sublimely beautiful, and so apropos for the setting. He also, with several of his musicians, played the four-course guitar, which was uncommon, and greatly enjoyed by all.

Bessie Holland and I had conferred exhaustively with the head cook, and together we had devised an extensive formal menu. In the grand tradition, we agreed upon three courses of meats: suckling pig, then venison and bittern, and finally rabbit and snipe. At the conclusion of the meat service, the pastry cook provided a whimsical dish called a '*soteltey*'. This was a sweet, artfully made into an elaborate shape or design. The first *soteltey* of the evening was a marchpane in the shape of a snowflake, glistening with a shiny egg wash and sprinkled with minute flakes of silver. After the snowflakes had been consumed, an intermission was called during which the guests danced or simply mingled. We then began the fish course, once again made up of three dishes: spiced lampreys – a favourite of Henry's, roasted salmon, and flounder and sturgeon. The *soteltey* concluding the fish course was a golden jelly moulded to appear as a lion rampant.

Finally, the liveried ushers swept about the room, clearing food left from the previous courses and readying the tables for the sweets course, which was brilliantly executed by the pastry baker. Paraded in on silver trays held high overhead, they comprised a large sweetcake in the shape of a crowned eagle and sprinkled with gold shavings, a fruit and spice pie fashioned like a running greyhound, and a cake shaped to look like the sun, iced in lemon yellow with fruit and raisins studding it and, finally, dusted with gold.

When the fish courses had begun to arrive in such abundance, I'd caught the attention of Margery Horseman, and when our glances met, we completely gave way to fits of giggling. She rolled her eyes and mimicked a stomach ache, and at that we shrieked with laughter. So much food! But of course, we ladies could have scarcely more than a few bites, else our snug bodices would squeeze us like devices of torture.

The drinking and eating went on for some time until, eventually, my certainly replete Henry rose, not without a little effort, to signal the end of dining. He held his arm out to me, and I laid mine on his and we went to the dance floor to commence a galliard. I squeezed his forearm tight while we stepped and skipped, and winked at him each time he cast an admiring eye.

It was truly a most gratifying experience to watch the lords spinning with their gorgeous ladies, whirling brocade, gold, and jewels glinting in the firelight.

I danced with Ambassador de la Guîche and told him in French how grateful Henry and I were of his efforts and goodwill on our behalf. He reassured me that his support was mine alone, and he told me this as he gazed into my face with that fervent look I had come to know so well. I wondered if Henry had noticed the *Seigneur's* obvious devotion!

The dancing began to ebb, and we resumed our places at the table to sip some of the hippocras which had been served. I decided this was a good moment to amaze Henry with one more surprise I had awaiting him.

We sat at the table draped all around in white and silver cloth, talking with courtiers who were seated close by. I reached for Henry's hand under the table and placed it on my thigh. He glanced uncertainly at me from the corner of his eye, but I kept my attention focused on the conversation. Inevitably, Henry's hand began to stroke my leg. I guided his fingers upward and inward until they found the secret split in the fabric, carefully designed and sewn, hidden in the folds of my silver petticoat. My breath came quick with anticipation, yet I kept my attention on my guests. Off to the side, I saw Henry perilously navigating the boundary between regal behaviour and abandoning all sense of composure in full view of his subjects. More guests approached us as the hour drew late, expressing their gratitude for the spectacular evening. All the while, Henry's fingers slowly explored the extent of the split, only to realize that the thin silk chemise I wore as my undergarment also had an open seam. Beneath that, he discovered nothing but skin. Henry's face became ever more flushed. To be certain, the guests with whom he spoke thought it was from the abundance of wine. I knew otherwise.

It was no surprise that Henry could hardly wait to call the celebration to an end. He bid good night to his courtiers and other guests, as did I, and we left the hall to return to his privy chambers.

Once we were alone, his velvet cap came off, and I helped him shrug from his stiff doublet. He removed items of clothing and jewels until he remained in his hose and soft linen shirt. He looked at once so strong and masculine, yet tender. Oh, the way his eyes glowed with love and desire for me! He knelt before me, looking for the openings in my gown, and once found, his fingers, and then his tongue explored what he sought. I repaid him as best I could, but that beautiful evening in January belonged to me, from beginning to end.

Whitehall
Hampton Court
Windsor
Spring 1531

MY ENCHANTING REVERIE of early 1531 was short-lived. Another winter melted into spring and although the love Henry and I shared was as tender and beauteous as the snowdrops which dotted the April hillsides, we were no closer, in actuality, to being married than we had been the previous spring. By the beginning of May, my ever-changing mood had shifted from discouragement to hurt and despair, then to full-blown rage as more and more of those who we'd assumed to be Henry's closest advisors and friends defected and displayed support for Katherine. Sir Nicholas Carewe; Henry's cousin Reginald Pole; the Earl of Shrewsbury who was Henry's Lord Steward; and - unbelievably - Henry's closest friend and companion, the Duke of Suffolk, all took the opportunity to convey their objection to a divorce which was yet to be sanctioned by the Church.

Henry's elder statesmen had made another visit to Katherine, during which they tried one more time to plead with her to accede. After hearing that the result was as futile as expected, I received additional news which made my blood boil. I was informed by one of my ladies that Sir Henry Guildford was overheard saying he wished all those involved in arguing the King's great plan could be bound in chains and carted off to Rome. Not since before Wolsey's death had I experienced such a flare of fury at the brazen disloyalty of a man who owed his bountiful life to his sovereign - the King whose greatest desire he had just summarily dismissed. I rushed to find Henry.

"Have you heard what was said, Henry?" I felt as if I were choking. "Do you realize how many are against us? How can you tolerate it? If the decision were mine, I would sink every one of them to the bottom of the sea – starting with all Spaniards!"

At the ferocity of my approach, he eyed me imploringly, and not a little fearfully. "Anne, we simply must have patience. We will triumph in the end, and then we will surround ourselves only with those who have been loyal; this I promise you." He took on the soothing tone he used in an attempt to stave off the frenzy he knew was near.

In a shrill, reedy voice I heard myself say "Patience? That is your response? I have had the patience of Job, and it has proved of absolutely no use, Henry! None at all! I am thoroughly exhausted and sick of the entire issue. I simply can no longer abide it."

And then, precariously balanced on the very edge of hysteria, I spat, "This time there will be no reconsidering: our contract is broken!" I whirled about and strode from his chamber without a backward glance.

•

Once through the door I sagged against a wall. Oh, what had I done? God's wounds but this time I should have bitten my cheek until I fainted with the pain. Now my runaway emotions and overly sharp tongue had at last led me to ruin. My heart ached, and my spirit was crushed as I accepted the raw truth - I was a kept woman, and nothing more. My youth was gone and I did not know if I would be able to conceive a child even were I to be married on the morrow, much less months – or years – from now.

In anguish at the termination of our relationship, and of my life as I had known it, I went to my chamber and remained there in grievous seclusion all the next day.

•

That following evening, I was told that Father wished to see me. He arrived at my apartment, took one look at my forlorn, tear-stained face, then came to my side and put his arms around me to hold me as if I were still a child needing comfort from a hurt. I began to lose control, and the tears again rolled down my cheeks unchecked. I cried in my father's embrace for what seemed a long time, yet only when I was finished, did he release me.

"Anne, I have just come from the King. He is as full of sorrow as you are – perhaps more. I have never seen him weep, Anne, yet he laments for fear that you have abandoned him. You have not done so, have you?"

Lo, his voice was kind! So unlike what I would have expected from my father, and his gentleness towards me began to thaw my resolve.

"Oh Father, how can I be expected to withstand the defiance and condemnation of so many who are close to the King? All I yearn for is to marry the man I love - and I cannot. I feel as if I am juggling many balls, each one bearing spikes. One wrong move and I am sliced to the quick. I do not have the constitution to withstand any more!"

"Anne, my Anne. You are a special woman and a strong one. You are a match – the only match – for the King's courage. He needs you. And he loves you more than I ever thought to see him love anyone. You cannot forsake him! He has given up much for you, Daughter. Trust your feelings for him, and see this battle through standing firmly by his side. I promise you; he will be devoted to you forever."

An inconsolable, ragged sigh escaped me as I considered his words. I had been in this wretched place countless times before. What surety did I have that things would ever turn our way? I thought on my adamant decision, years ago, to never assume the role of Henry's *maîtresse.* Now, I could hardly remember why I had been so cock-sure that my situation would be different than Mary's, or Bessie Blount's. How naïve I was! Here I stood, as sorrowful as I had ever been, with nothing to show for my stubbornness but a wardrobe full of clothes and a chestful of jewels. The gnawing in the pit of my stomach felt unbearable.

Father looked into my eyes and softly said, "You are still young enough to have a son … many sons. Go to him, Anne, and tell him you remain his loving consort."

For minutes, I remained immobile. I knew him to be in the right. And what else was I to do? Separate from Henry, yet ache with longing whenever I thought of him or was in his company? Leave England forever? He had not been the only one who'd been struck with the dart of love those six years ago. Whatever potion had tipped that dart had infused me as well, and in truth, I could no longer fathom life without him. What that meant regarding my destiny, I did not know, and I realized that I did not care. There was little else I could do but to place the matter into the hands of God. So, with a heartfelt, soul-centred prayer, that is precisely what I did. And, thanks be to Almighty God, I was answered with a rush of renewed hope and strength.

I dried my eyes, squared my shoulders, and stepped forward, determined to resume my relationship with Henry – and leaving the need to control behind.

•

My renewed love and commitment was honoured by yet another dazzling gift from Henry. He had his goldsmith, Master Cornelis Hayss, create a jewel which could be worn on a necklace, on a belt, or as a brooch. I was dumbstruck when I beheld a cluster of golden roses intertwined with hearts, set with 21 perfect diamonds and 21 deep crimson rubies. Of the torrent of beautiful gifts Henry gave to me, this one was a favourite, and I treasured it.

Shortly after that, I caught sight of Guildford in the Gallery at Westminster. Even with my newfound sense of quietude, I could not let the opportunity pass.

"Sir Henry!" I called sharply to him. "May I have a word, please?"

Uncertainly he approached me and was just within earshot when, even before he could afford me the conventional bow, I lashed out furiously, "How *dare* you!"

He gave me a confused look. "Milady? To what do you refer?"

"I refer to the comments you have made which show a complete disregard for the King's greatest desire. I refer to your brazen disloyalty when it comes to repaying your Monarch – the man who has given you your position and your wealth! Not to mention his lifelong friendship! Have you no allegiance whatsoever?"

"Lady Rochford, I am as loyal to my King as any man living. You misunderstand my position. It is not that I disapprove of the King's desire for a new marriage and hence the chance to beget a son, it is that in all conscience I cannot accede to his intent to do so without the consent of the Pope."

"On the contrary, I am in complete understanding of your position, Sir Henry, and I think it wrong and narrow-minded. You can see as well as anyone that the Pope has no concern whatsoever for the English King's need for a son. Clement's obdurate stance serves his desires and no other. This is the type of circumstance which demands what *I* term loyalty

– providing unconditional support to your Monarch when it becomes difficult, no matter your private beliefs. Yet you have made it plain that you have no intention to do so. That said, Mr Guildford, you can be assured that when I do become Queen - which I will - there will be no official appointment for you! Loyalty works both ways, does it not?"

But his answer only served to emphasize further the depth of disapproval many of Henry's court harboured for me. I admit I felt a bit deflated when, almost without hesitation, he'd replied, "Lady Rochford, I will graciously save you the trouble, for I am happy to resign my post as of this very minute."

With a perfunctory nod in my direction, he turned on his heel and walked through the gallery and toward Henry's presence chamber.

Guildford did indeed resign after a struggle with Henry, who wished him to remain. He retired to his family estate in Kent. I was not a bit sorry about my altercation with him. Was I to smile prettily when I saw him and pretend all was well? That was not my way.

•

And thus, my curious lifestyle continued. Construction at Whitehall became so disruptive that Henry and I went to Hampton Court, where Katherine and some of her ladies were in residence. I kept myself as separated from her as I possibly could, and at no time did I look directly at her or meet her gaze. I did my best to pretend she was invisible. We never spoke to one another.

I observed that Henry's patience with Katherine had run its course. She, on the other hand, appeared to assume that since they were cohabiting once again, his position was softening. Playing into that misguided hope, she suggested that perhaps it would be pleasing if their daughter Mary might spend the month of May with them, as a family. Henry flatly refused, and replied that Mary might visit her mother, but it would not be at Greenwich while he was in residence. On hearing this, Katherine quickly recanted, and replied that she would forego a visit with her daughter if only to remain with Henry. She proudly stated that she would never wish to give anyone the idea that she was separated from her husband.

These infuriating behaviours of Katherine's caused Henry to writhe in vexation. Yet she persisted with them.

From Hampton Court, the three of us – Henry, Katherine, and I - moved to Windsor. Spring was in full flush, and I kept Henry completely occupied by losing ourselves in the hunt. He had acquired several new horses, and we rode out daily.

The domestic situation had by now become intolerable. Continuously frustrated by all previous attempts, I determined to put an end, once and for all, to the awkward and embarrassing sight of Katherine and I both accompanying Henry from location to location. I asked Henry if we might hunt Ditton Park, which was well stocked with deer and had a lovely, rolling landscape. He agreed with enthusiasm whereupon he and I set out - without Katherine - to stay at Chertsey Abbey, our home base for almost two weeks. We took with us only the smallest of retinues: Nicholas Carew to manage the horses, William Brereton, and William Compton. We had a wonderful time; the weather was fair, and we brought down deer and other game which were prepared for dinner the following day.

It was at supper one evening that a courier from Windsor delivered a letter to Henry. As soon as he opened it, I knew it was from Katherine. Henry read some of it, the colour rising from his neck to his hairline. Finally, he exploded in a tirade of anger, throwing the letter on the table. Growling that he needed air, I let him stalk from the room, thankful I would not be in his proximity while he cooled his temper. Once he was gone, though, I picked up the letter, and after only an instant's hesitation and a glance about began to read. Like Henry, I could scarce believe the tactics this … this *crone*… had now resorted to in her vain attempts to gain his attention. Her whining was nothing but self-serving. She complained that he had left her without saying goodbye. She asked why she could not accompany him. Why had he not given her even the most basic consideration of allowing her to bid him farewell? Finally, she had the gall to ask solicitously after his health just as if all were fine between them!

I replaced the letter just as Henry returned from his fulmination. He groaned as he sat down heavily in a chair across the table from me. Slowly and pointedly, I looked at the letter. Then I raised my eyes and met his gaze. We said nothing, yet I knew Henry understood. And I knew he agreed.

The Vyne
Windsor
Autumn 1531

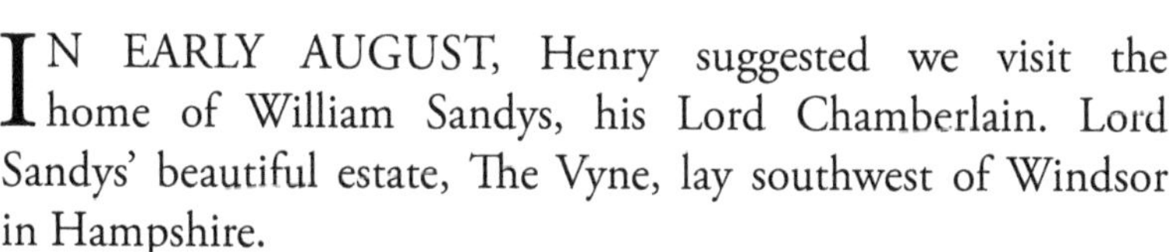

IN EARLY AUGUST, Henry suggested we visit the home of William Sandys, his Lord Chamberlain. Lord Sandys' beautiful estate, The Vyne, lay southwest of Windsor in Hampshire.

The elegant brick structure was nestled adjacent to the flowing Shir tributary in Sherborne St John. Little expense had been spared in its recent refurbishment which had been completed by this, the third William Sandys. The current Lord had added elements to enhance the graciousness of the house and had improved its gardens and grounds to a level of astonishing beauty. It was surrounded by thick woods, rife with game. The wetlands bordering the Shir were home to flocks of cranes, whose shrill, piercing cries were to be heard when they took to the air. Ducks and waterfowl were plentiful and had become a specialty of the Vyne's chief cook. It was an estate to be envied, and I was so very pleased to have been invited.

We had a most enjoyable stay; Lord Sandys' hospitality was unequalled, and we met and were entertained by many of the wealthy landowners in the vicinity. Above all, I was relieved and quite elated that everyone was cordial to me and respectful of my place beside Henry.

Refreshed by our excursion, and also well bolstered by such support, we made preparations to return to Windsor. We were both acutely aware that Katherine remained there. I had no wish to see her ever again, so concerning the subject, I merely said to Henry, "What do you plan to do, Your Grace?"

With an impassive expression, he replied, "She will be gone before we arrive."

Indeed, upon Henry's command, Katherine was removed to the Manor of the More without delay. The More was Wolsey's former residence near St Albans. Katherine's daughter Mary was ordered to go to Richmond, separating the two.

Henry's conduct made it abundantly clear, perhaps for the first time, that his marriage to Katherine was well and truly over.

•

The political and theological churn created by Henry's open challenge of the Church had become turbulent. Strident speeches were the norm. The most learned, the most prestigious, the most respected of Henry's advisors and councillors were locked in a battle over that which each side felt was morally right. Personal bitterness became ever more the emblem of what had previously been scholarly and erudite conversations. Thus was the backdrop against which Henry and I waited – and continued to proclaim our love to the world.

•

My mother visited Windsor in early November. We spent the afternoon with the dressmaker, Master John Skut, and ordered several new gowns each, with a hoped for delivery before the Christmas season.

Once Master Skut had wrapped up his patterns and designs along with samples of silk, lace, and satin and taken his leave, Mother and I sat for supper. We were alone, and I was glad because I needed her supportive ear and her wise advice.

I could feel the tension threatening as if it were a band gripping my forehead. "Mother, my thoughts are so entangled I hardly know how to sort through them. My life is anything but straightforward. As well you warned me."

"That is a truth which cannot be overstated, surely." Mother reached across the table and patted my hand with hers. Her touch comforted.

"I strive to maintain composure, yet there are many times when I am anything but. I must hide my uncertainties from Henry. Also from Father, and even dear George! They expect me to be strong and have foresight when all I want to do is curl up and pull the blankets over my head like I did as a child on summer nights when booming thunder rolled across the Eden Valley, and I was so frightened."

Her concern was apparent. "Anne, I do so want to help. Are you completely unhappy, then?"

"No, no, that isn't it! Not really. I am not unhappy – on the contrary, Henry and I are so very content together. My love for him grows and knows no bounds, while I truly believe his does for me, too. No, it is more about what the love we share portends for England – and even beyond. There are so many whose lives are being turned askance by the decisions Henry is taking. John Fisher, Sir Thomas More, Archbishop Warham, Henry Guildford, and scores of others who were a part of Henry's trusted circle now have become akin to enemies because they threaten his plan. And the separation of Katherine from her daughter Mary? I well know they pose a great danger to me, especially when they are permitted to commiserate, yet I cannot help but take pity. I can only imagine how I would feel were I not permitted to see you or speak with you. All this - to simply marry a man I love and who loves me …" I paused, considering what I had just said, then added, "… but then I guess Henry is anything but a simple man!"

At this, my mother and I looked at each other and dissolved into laughter at the thought.

We continued our talk long into the evening. By the time I watched my candlelit reflection in the mirror, the maid brushing out my hair and readying my chamber for bed, my soul felt restored. My mother had, as usual, buttressed my resolve. Again I was prepared to ignore the cynics, and step confidently forward into my future with Henry.

•

We kept a quiet, reverential Christmastide at Greenwich. I did not miss the celebrations this year; it was contentment enough that Katherine and Mary were banished from court, and I did not worry about having to see them.

Out of sight must surely mean out of mind.

Greenwich 1532

THE BEGINNING OF the new year found me looking eagerly ahead. During the Christmas season, my thinking had begun to shift. At thirty-one years of age, I found that all I wanted was to savour every aspect of my relationship with Henry. In accord with my surrender of the matter into God's keeping, I relaxed my watch over every detail of the proceedings and felt much happier as a result.

New Year's gifts were distributed, and though the entertainment had been more reserved this year, Henry's generosity abounded. Silver and gold cups, goblets, bowls and larger vessels were common gifts for his courtiers and their ladies. Several days after New Year, a messenger arrived at Greenwich to deliver a package to the King. He inspected it, and I knew from his look of dismay that Katherine had sent it. The package contained a gold cup accompanied by a short note. Henry had forbidden Katherine to communicate with him and was infuriated that once again, she had tried to insinuate herself into his daily life, using a traditional gift as the guise. Waving it away, he instructed that it be returned post-haste.

For me, though, Henry could not do enough. My New Year's gift was unsurpassed. In Greenwich, Henry lodged me in the Queen's former apartments. He'd reconditioned the chambers completely. New furniture had been ordered, featuring a magnificent bed, and he had provided draperies and bed hangings of cloth of gold, silver, and crimson satin. The walls were hung with precious tapestries which I took great pleasure in studying. My reciprocal gift was much more modest and certainly not as spectacular. I had commissioned, some months prior, a set of elaborately carved boar hunting darts from the Basque in France. It was always difficult deciding upon a gift for Henry since there was little he did not already have. I hoped the spears would provide him an enjoyable challenge on the hunt field.

•

George grinned triumphantly at the King and Sir William Compton, both of whom he had just bested in a game of shovelboard. "Your Grace," he bowed reverentially to Henry, "My Lord," nodding to Compton, "If you gentlemen would be so kind, I shall collect my winnings now." Then, clearing his throat, "of course, should you find it a personal hardship to empty your pockets at the moment, I would prove most amenable to affording you credit."

I thought how saucy George had become with Henry. They did like each other so much and had a grand time competing and betting with one another. I believe Henry looked forward to having a brother-in-law, a younger male sibling of sorts. As George collected his winnings, I interjected, "I am returning to my suite, my lords, to ready myself for the supper this evening."

Henry looked up, "I look forward to seeing you later then, my darling. A ravishing sight I know you'll be, as always."

I met Honor Lisle as I headed back to my chambers, and she walked with me along the privy gallery. "Look at you, Anne! You look radiant. Anyone can see you are a woman in love – in love with a special man. I truly am so glad for you."

I placed my hand on her arm and gave her an affectionate squeeze. There was something about Honor which was so affirming – quite reassuring. I felt as if everything she said must be true because she was so sensible.

"Thank you, Honor, and you are most perceptive. I am happy, and indeed, I am in love with an extraordinary man. I feel quite blessed, and am doing my best to dwell on the happiness Henry and I share, instead of being weighed down by the travails of the politics surrounding us. At times, it is anything but easy, but I am doing better at remaining at peace."

"You deserve tranquillity, my dear. And now we will enjoy ourselves this evening at the welcome banquet for Monsieur de la Pommeraie. I cannot wait to see what you will be wearing."

With a cheerful wave, Honor left me at the entrance to my apartments and continued on her way.

•

My maids assisted me in finalizing my *toilette* and fastening my jewellery. I spared one final look at my reflection, assessing the allure of the deep blue silk gown with its gold embroidered bodice and kirtle - the hood set with blue sapphires - and sapphires and diamonds about my throat and on my fingers. One glance at my face was enough to confirm what Honor had seen that afternoon. I did indeed appear radiant. My eyes sparkled, my lips curved sensually, my skin glowed, and my brow was as smooth as a baby's. Love certainly provided its enhancement to beauty!

I went to the presence chamber to meet my ladies. Giggling and chattering, we proceeded through the Queen's Watching Chamber, down the staircase, and into the hall. The court crier announced us, and we approached the banqueting table where

I took my place next to Henry at its head, with Monsieur de la Pommeraie on his left. The new French ambassador rose to bow charmingly, taking my hand and placing upon it a most delicate kiss.

Seated amongst the nobility that evening was Thomas Cromwell. Cromwell had been Wolsey's lawyer, and perhaps his closest advisor. Through planful, bold contriving, his career had remained intact after Wolsey's fall from grace. He had the growing reputation of being both diligent and adept, and now he was a Member of Parliament for Taunton. I had been told that Cromwell was a talented negotiator and shrewd spokesman who supported Lutheran ideology. This intrigued me, and I found it even more compelling that he openly supported Henry's right to supremacy, and thereby his right to dissolve his first marriage. Quite a departure from the position taken by his former patron! The Parliamentarian had shown himself to be solicitous of me, and courteous to my family. It became increasingly evident that his beliefs, and aptitude for detailed hard work, made him someone of great potential value to Henry. In fact, Henry had appointed Cromwell to his privy council just before Christmas. He was, though, a person whom I would watch closely, and consider well before trusting completely. But it did seem possible we might have a clever ally in Master Cromwell.

Our guest of honour, Monsieur de la Pommeraie, was an important player in the political arena and was not to be left to the devices of our adversaries. I paid him considerable attention - we danced, conversed in French, and toasted François and Henry with French wine. I invited the Monsieur to join us at the hunt as soon as grass season commenced, and he was delighted. By the end of the evening, I believed I had him firmly in my camp.

•

The month of May was tumultuous. A collection of petitions filed against the clergy were being used to leverage their agreement to Henry's position as Supreme Head of the English Church, but there remained peevish resistance from some on whom he'd formerly depended.

Two of Henry's previously most trusted advisors refused to accede to the supremacy. When the King was informed that, after all his service on behalf of the Great Matter, Bishop Stephen Gardiner stood staunchly in support of the Pope and his determination, Henry was consumed with anger. Perhaps more hurtful yet was the unwavering refusal of Thomas More to align with Henry's position. This decision was not taken without obvious personal anguish on More's part, since it was plain the two held each other in high regard. Even so, More refused to relinquish his stance on the side of the Church; never to agree that Henry's marriage was invalid, nor that the Monarchy reigned supreme in all matters of state and of theology. With sorrow, he recognized the breach which existed between them was irreparable, and he resigned his position as chancellor. Gardiner, not the most daring of men, proved less confrontational, quickly removing himself from Henry's sight and keeping as low a profile as possible.

•

But things had changed for me, too; about this, there was no doubt. I had somehow become able to watch such proceedings as if from afar. I remained passionately, delightfully entangled in a love affair and, with the onset of spring, I could not bring myself to care about the legalities of Henry's marriage to Katherine, or even about the Church. I did not care if I was wicked or impious. All I wanted to do was to take pleasure in my love for and with Henry, and I did it for all to see.

And because of that new-found calm, I had come to yet another decision …

Of late there had been much discussion about the marriage prospects for the young Henry Fitzroy. He was now in residence at Hatfield House in Hertfordshire and made appearances at court on occasion. These occurrences gave me the opportunity to observe him closely. A Knight of the Garter, Fitzroy was Earl of Nottingham and Duke of Richmond and Somerset, with precedence over all other dukes of the Realm. At thirteen years of age, not only did he bear all of these illustrious titles, but he was also Lord High Admiral of England, Wales, Ireland, Normandy, Gascony, and Aquitaine, and then he received the commission as warden-general of the marches of Scotland. He had certainly been endowed with great riches, and several years ago, Henry had awarded him the lord-lieutenantship of Ireland, with the intent to some day make him king of Ireland. His prospects for an impressive marriage union were bright. He was excellently educated and had grown altogether pleasing and well-mannered.

Looking on this handsome young man as he made his way about court, my thoughts then rested on his mother, Henry's former mistress, Elizabeth Blount Talboys. She was a baroness, with sons and rich lands. Her husband had died two years previously, and since that time, it was said that she had been consistently wooed by Lord Leonard Grey. Bessie, however, chose not to become Lady Grey, and gossip revealed that she was instead in love with the handsome younger Baron Clinton, her neighbour, Edward Fiennes. Henry had ensured that Bessie's life - the life of his former mistress - after bearing him a son, had been one of peaceful wealth and comfort.

Why, I wondered, had I been so adamant? So staunchly inflexible? Was the life of the King's mistress, and her fair son, so abhorrent after all?

•

So, on a soft, fragrant evening in late May, I awaited Henry's arrival in my chambers at Whitehall. I had thrown open the casement windows, allowing the perfume of lilac to drift into the room on the light breeze. The flames from the candelabra fluttered and flickered, and the fire in the hearth was softly reflected in silver vases holding bunches of spring blooms placed about the chamber.

Full of nervous expectancy, I picked up a silver-backed brush and played with the ends of my hair for the tenth time. On hearing the sound of Henry approaching, I quickly replaced the brush and turned to face him as he dismissed his esquires at the door and entered the chamber. Once within he blinked, then ever so softly closed the heavy door behind him. He looked at me without speaking, his gaze traveling the length of my body.

I allowed him to look for as long as he liked. It was the reaction I craved, for, on that evening, I wore something special for Henry alone. It was meant to be a part of my *trousseau*, but I chose not to wait for him to see it: a black, liquid-satin nightgown, simple and close to the body and only partially concealed by a black satin cloak edged in deep black velvet. My dark hair flowed to my waist, and about my throat hung only a fine chain with a single diamond.

He came to me, encircling me in his arms. All nervousness banished, I moulded my body to his as we kissed. His touch was gentle as he slipped the cloak from my shoulders then stood back to study me in the gown. I breathed thankfully, unencumbered by bodice, stomacher, or undergarments. The satin felt wickedly smooth against my skin. I sensed it slide transparently over every curve. It was a fabric made to be touched, and Henry's fingers most urgently conformed to its sensuous invitation … our time had come.

I helped him undress, snuffed the candles and, in the ebbing light, let the satin gown fall to the floor. We came together, and he led me to the bed, soft with pillows. We lay together, wordlessly looking into each other's eyes.

I was ready: I would wait no longer to consummate the love I had known for seven long years. And just as I hoped and dreamed, our union was exquisite; boundless. I was transported as if I shared Henry's mind and soul, as well as his body.

I lay in his arms, my breathing deep and steady, not having experienced such serenity in as long as I could remember. I nuzzled my face beneath his chin and pulled him even closer.

Nothing, now, could draw us apart.

My bliss was complete.

Greenwich
Summer 1532

In the lush fullness of early summer, no two lives could have been more entwined than were ours. I knew his moods: the changeful look of his eye and the sinuous curve of his mouth foretelling his every action. He knew me as well; knew that his intrepid glance would fill me with courage when I grew uncertain and that his warm grasp on my arm would palliate my most irascible moments.

We were lovers now, in every sense of the word. Yet I hesitated to allow him into my bed night after night, still hoping that when our son was conceived, we would be man and wife. And marriage was an objective which had yet to be fulfilled, although having known him and loved him for seven years, in my heart, I felt as if it had.

Yes, it had been seven long years from the moment at which my destiny became one with that of Henry, King of England, by a sublime exchange of glances. From that instant, nothing had been, or would ever again be commonplace in my life, and I could scarcely give rise to a thought without considering

Henry's opinion of the same. He was, as Aristotle had foretold, my second self. And I was his. And since we were like the same being, I would achieve all that was good for Henry, and he would do the same for me.

Fiercely did the arguments surrounding the Great Matter swirl. Henry's demanded divorce from Katherine became the linchpin in all that was transformative in England and Europe in that year of 1532. The growing acceptance of Lutheranism, pitted against a continued resolute allegiance to Roman Catholicism caused many a bitter standoff between countrymen. Henry's battle with the Pope and the Holy See over his divorce, and his acknowledgement of the logic in many reformist writings of the day caused him to consider breaking from Rome and the Church, although he had been thus far loath to do so. I firmly believed this to be the only way forward, and encouraged him to that end. And significantly, my views and visible role as Henry's beloved and his intended wife positioned me in the eyes of many as the emblem of all that was wrong in the realm.

•

Strong alliances between countries were of paramount importance, and Henry was keen to nurture the accord he had carefully built with François I of France, especially in light of the bond between Charles V of Spain - the Holy Roman Emperor and nephew of his estranged wife Katherine - and Pope Clement VII. The ambassadors of François, who were envoys to the English court, were given great access to the King and his council and were frequently fêted at dinners and banquets. The French ambassador of the moment, Giles de La Pommeraie, gave early indications were that he would be a helpful courier of information and builder of good will between the powerful monarchs of England and France.

Progress
July and August 1532

AS PREDICTED, MONSIEUR de La Pommeraie did prove a true ally. He used his considerable skill as a statesman to gain François' agreement to a new treaty Henry greatly desired between England and France, ensuring their united Christian front against a potential attack from the Infidel, the Turk Suleiman. Henry was well pleased, as was I, if only because it deepened the bond between the two countries – both of which were home to me. I considered myself as much French as I did English.

Since the degree of affinity between France and England was of concern to Emperor Charles, his man in England, Eustace Chapuys, was on point to make sure his master was regularly and thoroughly informed. It was fascinating, then, to observe Ambassador Chapuys' mad scramble in an attempt to uncover the details of the proposed treaty.

To reward La Pommeraie for his success, Henry invited him to join us on summer Progress across the bountiful royal hunting grounds north of London. He was honoured by the invitation, accepted graciously, and in early July, a small band of us departed for Waltham. We resided at Waltham Abbey for about a week, then set off for Hunsdon, where we planned to visit my new Manor of Hanworth.

What a splendid summer I had. After supper, Henry and I would meander, enjoying early evening on the grounds of Hanworth and listening to the lyric songs of thrushes, dunnocks, and nightingales; admiring the precisely trimmed lawns, shimmering emerald in the deeply slanting sunlight; the formal gardens immaculately groomed; the endless rows of strawberries warmed by the day's sun and affording a soft, sweet aroma delicious enough to make one's mouth water. By day, we hunted in the adjacent woods and park. Departing the manor, we then travelled northward, towards Nottingham.

Monsieur de La Pommeraie was a capable rider and sportsman, and often after the hunt had concluded and we were headed back to the manor house, I watched him deep in conversation with Henry, their big bay hunters walking almost in tandem, tails switching.

One evening over supper, Henry told me he and La Pommeraie were working on plans to meet with Francois – on French soil.

"Remember, Anne, I told you I had several surprises in store for you?"

I could not contain my anticipation. I did not dare breathe. I yearned to go to France again. "I do, Henry. Can that possibly mean you will take me with you?"

"It does, sweetheart."

I jumped up from the table with a shriek of delight, twirled about joyfully, then hugged Henry around his neck with such fervour that I near choked him.

He grinned. "I cannot wait to show you off to François and his nobility, my special beauty. He will rue the day he allowed you to return home to England those years ago."

"Henry, how I do adore you! Thank you, my darling."

My lips curled in a smile, not at all unlike the cat that stole the cream.

•

The very next afternoon, I rode out with Monsieur de La Pommeraie. We paused on a hillock, shading our eyes from the hot sun with our hands, watching a parcel of deer leap and bound across the field below.

I leaned towards him in my saddle, affecting an air of familiarity. "Monsieur, you do know that I have been asked by the King to accompany him on his diplomatic trip to France?"

"*Oui*, Madame, I am aware of this, and could not be more delighted. What a wonderful addition you will be to the event. My King will be greatly pleased to see you once again, *je suis certain.*"

I smiled sweetly in response, well aware that the Monsieur was an ardent admirer of women. "Then, Monsieur, may I request a favour? Or - perhaps two favours, if you would be so kind."

I lowered my voice and came closer to him. His thin, groomed moustache quivered slightly. "Will you see to it that a special person joins François' retinue? Will you have François' sister, Marguerite de Navarre, join the guests? I was, as a girl, influenced by that great lady, and I would be overjoyed to see her again. And Monsieur, I would be ever so grateful if you might persuade your master, *le bon Roi François*, to personally extend me an invitation – one of a more formal nature?"

"*Bien sûr*, Lady Anne," he swept a gallant bow, well executed from the back of his horse. "*Certainment,* it will be my pleasure to do as you ask."

"Oh, and Monsieur ... just one more *tiny* favour, if I might be so bold?"

"Madame?"

"I would not wish to be in a position to have to entertain the Queen – Queen Eleanor. I would not want her to feel awkward, you understand, since she is, after all, Katherine's niece. I feel sure she would have no desire to see me, either. You, ah … do follow, do you not, Monsieur?"

"*Absolument*, Madame." He gave me a knowing nod. I returned a smile of great warmth, and lightly touched his arm as a gesture of thanks before we rode on.

•

By the beginning of August, the King's progress had become more about hunting and planning for the visit to France than creating the expected royal pageantry for the locals as we moved from town to town. Nevertheless, Henry continued to meet his subjects and bestow great generosity upon them. Especially kind to the poorest of country folk, Henry had his special apothecary make up some medicines and deliver them along with much-needed foodstuffs to the parents of an ailing child who were beside themselves with surprise and thankfulness.

From a stay at Grafton Manor, we rode to Woodstock, and a few days later, on to the Palace of Langley.

On our first evening's stay at King's Langley, Henry and I supped alone in his chamber. Ravenously hungry after our long, hot ride, I was relishing the baked artichokes, salad of herbs and cucumber, and roast chicken the cook had prepared for us.

I had a bite of chicken halfway to my mouth, when Henry quietly asked, "Would you prefer to be addressed as 'Madame Marquess' - or simply 'Lady Marquis?"

Not being sure I had heard correctly, I put down my knife with the chicken still impaled upon it. "I beg Your Majesty's pardon? I do not understand."

An enigmatic smile played about his lips. He lingered, enjoying the moment. Then – "I have decided to create you Marquis of Pembroke, my lady, and wish to know how you will be addressed thereafter." He watched while my expression slowly changed from confusion to wonder, then astonishment.

"Could you mean you wish to convey me with a title? On my own account? I am confounded, Henry. There are no women who hold such titles in their own right."

My uncertainty was apparent, for he responded, "You, Anne, are not simply any woman; you are a special woman. You are my other self. Thus, you should – you must – have a title, and an important one, with great meaning. So, yes, that is correct - I intend to create you a Marquess fully in your own right. You will hold the title once held by my great-uncle, Jasper Tudor. It is the Earldom in which my father was born. It is a title befitting a great lady."

"I am at a loss for words, Your Grace. Your generosity astounds me."

"It is an honour you deserve, Anne. Cromwell is already hard at work planning the event. The ceremony will take place on the first day of September, at Windsor. You, my dear, must now work purposefully to prepare your attire for that day, and for our trip to France. Make certain your ladies look glorious as well."

Tears of love and gratification brimmed, then spilled to drop onto Henry's hand, which I grasped as I knelt before him. Slowly, I turned it over and kissed his palm, then said, "Your Majesty, I cannot wait to give you a gift of great joy; the one you most deserve – a handsome, healthy son."

The King lifted my chin and looked into my eyes. "I have no doubt whatsoever that gift – that day – will come soon, Anne."

•

The last two weeks of August flew by. We progressed from King's Langley to Abingdon Abbey. There, Maggie Wyatt, my Receiver-General George Taylor and I met with mercers, silkwomen, tailors, furriers, goldsmiths and jewellers in a flurry of activity to create the wardrobe I would need both for my creation ceremony and the visit to France as Henry's consort. Between meetings and fittings I hunted with Henry in the forests of Wychwood, and though the sport was fine with both stag and boar being plentiful, I was elsewhere: completely absorbed in anticipation of the imminent ceremony, and our trip.

The array of fabrics from which one could choose was astonishing. There were textiles imported from Italy and France, Belgium and Persia – a heavy bolt of leaf-green velvet patterned with embroidered chestnut branches on ivory silk with silver thread; a luxurious violet damask with a gold-woven lattice pattern enclosing dragons framed within laurel wreaths; delicate silk *ciselé* velvet in black and gold with silver; damask brocaded with brightly coloured silks in a pattern of parrots with bunches of flowers in vases and crowns … The dressmakers jabbered while they pinned and stitched patterns on me, holding the extraordinary bolts of cloth against me and each other to determine the best selections. I had requested that the seamstresses use patterns from the most current designs in the French Court. Frenchwomen might be fashionable, but I had no intention of being outdone.

Windsor
August and September 1532

AND, OH, THE jewels!

It is quite impossible to describe the brilliance, the variety - the sheer luxury of such a collection. Because he decided to have many of his gems reset, Henry felt it a good time to review the royal collection in total, and acquire new pieces.

Henry summoned me to the library where he and his royal goldsmith, Master Cornelis Hayss, were reviewing designs for an important new jewelled collar to be worn by the King on our trip. I looked over the drawing, and thinking how stupendous it would look on Henry's impressive chest and shoulders, approved robustly. The collar, a wide, thick and ornate rope which, once draped over his shoulders would encircle his chest, was to be made from the glowing, ancient gold from deep within the ancient Dolaucothi mine, in the county of Carmarthen, Wales. The collar was to be inlaid with seven sizable blood red balasses, interspersed with large round diamonds set in twos. Its appearance would be astounding, for it would take a man of Henry's stature as well as endurance to wear it for more than mere minutes, for it would be as heavy as a thick vest of armour.

My uncle, Norfolk, had been sent on the unpleasant mission of reclaiming the Queen's jewels from Katherine. As I predicted, he returned empty-handed, with an account of her indignant defiance, and her refusal to relinquish anything – most especially anything for my use – me, whom she called 'the scandal of Christendom'! Upon hearing this, Henry growled, "Norfolk, you tell her she is to release the royal jewels to you immediately, at my direct command, and without further comment, or suffer the consequences." I opened my mouth to vent what I intended as a biting remark about Katherine's Spanish insolence, but on second thought, clamped it shut. Oh, how good it would have felt to air my contempt in a verbal assault! Instead, I came upon a more diabolical idea – one which pleased me. Once the Queen's jewels were in my possession, I would savour the supreme satisfaction of wearing her favourite, most recognizable, most personal jewel to the grand banquet for François I when Henry- my betrothed - and I were in Calais.

With the Queen's jewels retrieved and added to the collection, it was immense in scope. One would have thought the task of examining many of the most precious gems in the world would be a heady pleasure, but I found it overwhelming. In a heavily guarded inner chamber at Windsor, Henry, Thomas Cromwell, Master Cornelis Hayss, and I silently stared at two long tables, draped in black velvet and laden with jewels of every description.

There were twenty stunning table-cut rubies and two large diamonds which Henry had set aside for me. Equally enticing were emeralds of varying sizes and depths of green; aquamarines which looked like chunks of the bluest sea; more than fifty diamonds, cut in the newest style, two large rose-crimson balasses and a vast assortment of milky, radiant pearls, some loose, and some set in gold … hundreds in number. My eye was quickly drawn to three cabochons of the Persian stone, turquoise. I had seen but one piece of this stone before, in a brooch owned by Queen Claude in France. I found its colour to be heavenly: the shade of a brilliant blue sky, but the stone was not clear; it did not shimmer in the light. Instead, its silken smooth surface pulsed with an intensity of colour I found irresistible.

Henry saw me, enchanted, and broke the silence. "Hayss, what do you propose to create with these pieces of turquoise for the Lady Marquess?"

Master Hayss promptly replied, "I think they would look best set into a golden coronet, Your Majesty, which could be worn alone or might well be attached to a hood. Then its colour will often accent the Lady's lovely face. Do you agree?"

"I do, indeed, Hayss. You are a man who both creates, and appreciates great beauty. I will look forward to seeing your handiwork."

I knew it would become one of my best-loved pieces.

•

In preparation for the ceremony which would create me Marquess of Pembroke, my mother and sister Mary arrived at Windsor. The ladies' apartments being now filled with family and the women who made up my growing household, I was in exceedingly high spirits. In the warmth of late summer, my ladies and I partook of an afternoon outing on that last day in August; rugs with wine, delicacies to nibble, cards and games spread on the lawn at the base of the lower ward of the castle. As Jolie and several other dogs gambolled, chased, and snapped at each other, then came panting to flop down beside us, the ladies laughed and joked, sang, danced and fluttered about me in anticipation of the events planned for the next day.

I did not see Henry at all that day or evening. Unusually, I was glad of this, since I wanted him to be surprised and dazzled by my appearance at the ceremony.

•

Early on Sunday, the first of September, I was awakened by Maggie. While the chambermaids set a table with ale, fruits, cheeses and bread I rose, shrugged my dressing gown over my shoulders, and went with Maggie into the wardrobe where my ceremonial gown and cloak hung, waiting. We both drew in our breath upon seeing the ensemble in the clear light of morning. It delighted the eye. Both the gown and cloak were made of the softest, deepest crimson velvet which gave off an opulent sheen. The kirtle was cloth of gold, and the bodice completely overlaid with gold embroidery. The neckline was trimmed with rubies, pearls, and diamonds, and the sleeves were slender, straight, and long, ending in a point set with pearls. The surcoat was a marvel. Crimson velvet lined in crimson satin, with a flowing train bordered entirely by the most sumptuous pure white ermine. I could scarcely believe I was to wear such garments.

My *toilette* began with a warm, scented bath. My ladies' maids brushed out my hair, drying it afore the hearth fire, and applying a touch of lemon oil to enhance its shine. I took care with my cosmetique, not applying much, as I wanted my face to be unadorned.

I was laced into my chemise, petticoat, kirtle, and bodice, the beautiful sleeves attached, and my hair brushed loose, glistening while flowing to my waist. Finally began the task of donning the jewels which had been selected for this day. I wore the emerald ring Henry had given me for our betrothal, the thick ropes of gold which had been part of the Queen's jewellery, diamond rings on the first and last fingers of my left hand, a carcanet of gold studded with rubies about my neck, and a girdle about my waist of woven gold, each tail embedded with diamonds.

My ladies accompanied me to the watching chamber. There my mother came to me, stroked my cheek softly once, and murmured, "Anne, how proud I am of you. You look regal, and you carry yourself with dignity. I congratulate you, my daughter."

I could not allow tears to ruin my appearance, which had taken so many people a long time to achieve, so I swallowed the lump in my throat. I grasped her hand tightly; gratefully. "Thank you Mother. I could not imagine this day without you."

We stepped into procession formation. The Dukes of Suffolk and Norfolk, attired in doublets and gowns of Tudor green velvet, led the way. Following was my father, the Earl of Wiltshire, accompanied by the French Ambassador Gilles de La Pommeraie. And behind them trailed an assemblage of earls and viscounts.

We began our stately approach through the long gallery and the King's waiting chamber. Suddenly I had the most extraordinary feeling of watching the procession from above. It was so strange, and I recalled another occasion upon which I had experienced the same notion – just before the meeting of Henry's advisors at Hampton Court some time ago. It was so very peculiar; as if I were looking down on myself, and for a long moment it seemed as if this ancient rite was for someone other than me. I took a deep breath, and as I slowly exhaled, regained my counterpoise while Bishop Stephen Gardiner began his walk toward Henry. Garter King at Arms carried the patent, beautifully illuminated on vellum with my new badge: a crowned white falcon, hooked talons dug into a tree stump from which bloomed red and white roses.

Elizabeth Manners, Countess of Rutland, and Dorothy, Countess of Sussex, preceded me. They looked beautiful in splendid gowns of tawny velvet traced with gold embroidery. Slowly we approached the presence chamber. The room went silent, and the sound of my slippers against the polished wooden floor rang loud and echoed in my ears. Following me and bearing the crimson velvet mantle, heavy with ermine, and the delicate gold coronet was my young cousin, thirteen-year-old Mary Howard, the daughter of the Duke of Norfolk.

The room was not a large one and was filled with people. Henry stood, waiting for me at the head of the chamber, between two tall windows; the light at his back making him appear even more majestic, more powerful, and more daunting than ever I had witnessed.

I approached the King; eyes cast down. Just before I knelt at his feet, I glanced up, and his eyes met mine. He did not need to speak to tell me how proud he was of me that day. The Letters Patent of Creation was delivered to me, read by Stephen Gardiner, Bishop of Winchester. The King laid the mantle about my shoulders and gently placed the golden coronet on my head.

He said, "Anne Rochford, I invest in you the Patent of Creation as Marchioness of Pembroke. And I hereby grant you and your heirs an annuity of one thousand pounds for life."

I arose, heart tripping, and looked long into the King's face. As slowly and as deeply as I could, I curtsied and said in a clear and distinct voice, "Your Majesty, I swear to you my eternal fealty. And I humbly offer you my immeasurable gratitude and steadfast loyalty."

With a nod, Henry released me, and I stepped back to depart amongst the congratulations of the many witnesses. The Countesses accompanied me as I returned to my apartments, where I removed the mantle of estate, replaced it with the velvet surcoat, and was escorted by royal guardsmen to the Chapel of St George for High Mass.

•

I was seated beneath the oriel window in the Quire of magnificent St George's, with Henry near me in the Sovereign's Stall. The intonation of the Latin Mass, the pungent scent of burning frankincense, the profound significance of the morning's events all encouraged scenes from the past six years to twist and spiral, unbidden, in my mind. At once marvellous and grievous, the mélange of my life with Henry seemed to mirror England's turmoil, conveniently hidden from view by the serenity of the chapel. I reflected on the study in contrasts. There stood Bishop Gardiner, the celebrant – I wondered just how reluctant he must have been to participate in honouring me that day, since, despite his efforts on behalf of the Great Matter, I knew he was not in favour of my relationship with Henry. I looked upon Mother and Father beaming with pride and satisfaction at the family's continued ascent. I thought of the angry refusal of my aunt, who had become my enemy - Elizabeth, Duchess of Norfolk - to carry my train even though royal protocol demanded it of her as the highest ranking woman in England, aside from the Queen. Across from me sat the studiously reverential Thomas Cromwell, who had so deftly organized the events of the day – I observed him for a time, thinking on the strange dichotomy of opinion in which I held him: so capable yet inscrutable. I recalled the angry public outcry at the recent hanging of a young priest for the crime of filing down gold angelots and reselling the gold: most believing he was hanged at Cromwell's instigation, simply because he was a cleric in an increasingly anticlerical milieu. My thoughts came unwillingly to rest on Katherine, banished to the More, while her daughter Mary languished at Richmond and their many supporters protested. And this very Mass, being sung in all its glory; while Henry now stood in open defiance of the Pope and the Church.

I was pulled back to present, hearing the choir sing:

Te Deum laudamus: te Dominum confitemur.
Te aeternum Patrem omnis terra veneratur

We praise Thee, O God: we acknowledge Thee to be the Lord. All the earth doth worship Thee and the Father everlasting

Finally, I contemplated the visit Henry and I were to make to France: a visit designed to introduce me as his future wife and queen. My thoughts lingered there, picturing my meeting with François, and the consultor of my youth, Marguerite, now the Queen of Navarre. The Mass drew to a close, and as it did, I determined to remain lodged firmly in the present, and to enjoy every aspect – nay, every minute! - of Henry's and my journey together.

I decided that only after its completion would I allow myself to be again concerned with more troubling matters. Those who continued to threaten our happiness.

●

I was gladdened to learn that my good friend, Seigneur Guillaume de Langey, would be visiting Henry and me at the Manor of Hanworth. Ever the charming Frenchman, he brought a present and made a great show of delivering it to me: one far better than the jewels he had given me previously. This time, it was the greatly desired official invitation from his *Souverain*, François I, that I accompany Henry to France for a visit. Reading the letter, beautifully written in French on creamy vellum, I was so elated I wanted to jump for joy, shout and clap my hands like a little girl. With some effort, though, I regained control and resumed the behaviour befitting a noble lady, rewarding the Seigneur with my sweetest expression while allowing him to press my hand to his lips for an extra long moment so he could fully enjoy my costly French *parfum*.

My disposition was so cheery, in fact, that I invited the French ambassadors, La Pommeraie and de Langey, to a festive supper in Henry's honour at Hanworth, my beautiful new estate. The evening was well timed, because, as we eagerly consumed the mouthwatering delicacies concocted by my master cook newly arrived from Lombardy, the table was alive with animated conversation finalizing plans for the trip. My excitement was almost impossible to contain as I sat at the table with Henry, de Langey and La Pommeraie, Master Cromwell, Arthur Plantagenet and Honor Grenville (Lord and Lady Lisle), and others who would be a part of the group travelling with us to France. Seigneur de Langey revealed that the meeting between the Kings would take place on 20 October in Boulogne, with final preparations by the Duke of Norfolk and the grandmaster of France to be completed a week prior.

De Langey instructed us that this meeting of the Kings would be quite different from the lavish Field of Cloth of Gold twelve years ago; the presumption being that both monarchs had matured and grown confident in their sovereignty. Hence, there would be no need to compete in wealth or supremacy. Employing his biting and irreverent wit - sharpened, no doubt, by his friendship with the devilish Rabelais – De Langey pronounced while looking directly at Henry, one eyebrow cocked, that the apparel worn at this meeting was to be as modest as possible, with no cloth of silver or gold – and there he paused dramatically – save for that worn by His Highness and the ladies, and only if they must! How I loved watching these two spar with one another. Clearly they enjoyed such exchange as well.

In response, Henry slowly drew himself to his full height and breadth in his seat. "*Seigneur, ni argent, ni or soient nécessaire*!" I chuckled to myself when I heard Henry brashly declare that neither silver nor gold were necessary. *Au contraire*; I knew the depth of his penchant for self-adornment!

Not only in attire, but modesty was also to be strictly maintained when it came to the size of each king's retinue. De Langey continued, "Your Majesty, he who keeps to these rules most precisely will be henceforth known to the other as the undisputed master at commanding order!"

At this, a hoot of laughter escaped me while others at the table did their best to cover their mirth. A moment later, an unexpected and especially loud guffaw from Henry had us all in uncontrolled giggles as we recognized how droll the challenge: a competition between two famously ostentatious monarchs in which the victor would be awarded the title of Most Modest!

•

Churning unrest in Scotland was proving a distraction for Henry. His nephew, James V, threatened to wage war unless Henry complied with his wishes; among them the release of the body of his father for burial in Scotland. Henry deftly handled the posturing of the young King James, and we continued our preparation to depart for Dover and our crossing. I determined to be a model of constraint, at least when it came to the number of ladies who would accompany me, and selected only twenty-seven of my favourites as traveling companions. Indeed, there were some gossips who tittered about the fact that not all the premier English noblewomen would be a part of my escort, but truly - did I care? Not one whit. It was important to me that this adventure be shared amongst my most loyal friends and family. I was not about to tolerate jealous, disapproving, vicious glances or comments by anyone. No one would discourage my pleasure of this visit.

Henry had been attending to affairs from Greenwich while I was making ready at York, where my lodgings were well nigh complete, and Henry's nearly so. Just a week before our departure, my chambers were humming with people delivering items which had been ordered. My chief mercer and dressmaker, Master William Locke, fluttered importantly about the apartments, with his bevy of young apprentices scurrying closely behind, to deliver gowns, cloaks, and hats which they had so beautifully constructed. Master Richard Gressam arrived, bearing a collection of ravishing silk dressing gowns edged in glossy marten fur. These particular gowns were of the utmost importance to me. They were to be worn and admired by Henry, but only by Henry, and only on the most personal of occasions.

I had determined that it was time to live with him as if we were husband and wife. This was something he had hoped for - longed for - yet he did not know of my decision. I planned to surprise him with the news once we set sail.

•

A knock at the door of my inner chamber late one afternoon in the first few days of October revealed a messenger advising that the King would be joining me for supper in my apartments that evening. Since we had been in separate locations for several days, I was excited as a foolish young girl to see him again. My heart skipped happily, thinking about him and his magnetic gaze as he would observe me from head to toe. I scrambled about in preparation, my maids and the ladies who were attending on me rushing as well.

At six o'clock, Henry was announced, and he and several of his esquires swept into my suite. He looked superb – perhaps more so than I remembered from just days ago if that be possible. One glance confirmed my decision. It felt completely right, and there would be nothing that would dissuade me.

Henry signalled to me, and we stepped into an inner chamber where we slid our arms about each other and enjoyed a sensual kiss. "Anne, I cannot wait to start our travel to France. I feel as if it will declare a new and positive direction in the long road we have travelled."

"Oh darling, how I do agree. Our visit to France must be a foreshadow of what lies ahead for us, Henry. Nothing but happiness - and children!"

I believed every word.

"Speaking of children, Anne, I have a gift for you."

I protested weakly, not knowing anymore how to respond to the embarrassment of riches Henry had already bestowed upon me.

"This, sweetheart, is different. You will love it, I know."

He summoned his esquires to bring the gift into the room. I saw immediately, although it was draped with a swatch of velvet, that it was a painting. A gilt frame peeked from beneath the cloth. It was set on a chest, velvet draping still in place. "When I first saw this, Anne, it felt very special to me. I believe it will do the same for you."

Henry lifted the cloth, and I drew in my breath. Before me was an artwork of such heart-rending beauty that it brought tears to my eyes. I looked at Henry, questioning.

"It is by the Venetian master Giovanni Bellini. He painted this work seventy years ago, and it was one of his first depictions of the Virgin and Child. They say, even after his death, his painting school in Venice rivals those of Florence and Rome. Bellini painted many Madonnas during his life, but this is widely acknowledged to be one of his most beautiful. Do you like it?"

Truly, it was so moving I found it difficult even to reply. The top of the painting was arched, framed in a simple golden band, the sky a celestial blue. In the foreground, the Virgin Mary gazed down and to the right, but not so much that one was unable to see her clear azure eyes – such expressive, fine, melancholy eyes. Her face was realistic and astonishing in its delicate beauty, with a deep flush to the cheeks giving her a high colour. The dark hair was covered by a black veil, and she protectively held her son close while He stood on a parapet before her – a babe of robust beauty and delicacy of features equal to hers. In a childlike gesture, He had His forefinger in His mouth but looked steadily at the viewer.

To own such a treasure!

"Henry, I cannot possibly know how to thank you. I will cherish it. It will forever be an inspiration to me."

With his arm about my shoulders, we silently contemplated the masterpiece.

As we did so, I sent a silent prayer heavenward that its subject represented a prophecy for me, soon to be fulfilled.

•

"This hand must surely bring you a turn of luck, cousin."

Sir Francis Bryan gave me a roguish wink with his good eye as he handed cards about, two by two; first to me, then to Henry at my left, then George and, finally, Maggie. Bryan was bold and irreverent, always peppering his conversation with witty double entendres which amused Henry as much as did the jokes performed by Will, his fool. Sir Francis's wit seemed somehow accented by the eye patch he wore to cover an injury received in a jousting accident some years ago. Perhaps, though, it was just his angular good looks. Henry and Sir Francis were great friends, and laughed and laughed together raucously; it was no wonder that Bryan was Chief Gentleman of Henry's privy chamber. A quite shameless flirt, he paid me and Maggie constant attention during our game of Primero.

I gathered my cards and was pleased to see a two of clubs, three of diamonds, four of spades, and the King of clubs. Keeping my expression unaffected, at my turn I stated, "Primero forty-nine."

Henry gave me a smug glance before throwing in his bid, accompanied by a hearty wager, "Primero fifty-nine, at two crowns,"' whereupon George, knowing when he had been beaten, grumbled, "Pass!"

Maggie interjected with a change of subject. "Your Grace, I have heard tell that a great deal of work is taking place at the Tower. I was told the place is packed with labourers both night and day. Are you building a new structure there?"

"Not entirely new, Lady Margaret. New rooms, though, within the royal palace. The entire building was in dire need of repair and refurbishment, so it is timely. I expect it to host an important guest in the very near future," he added with a sideways glance in my direction.

I knew Henry was readying the royal apartments and the great hall in the palace within the Tower for my stay on the eve of my coronation as Queen, having previously conferred with me regarding the style of decoration and furnishings. Maggie observed the tender unspoken exchange between us and gave me the warmest look – one that conveyed 'I share your joy'. It was the look of a true friend, not the false panderings of those who were secretly jealous. I did love her so for her generous nature.

A fist slammed on the table. "Enough drivel! The Tower has stood there a long while already; I expect it will wait 'til we finish this hand."

Bryan had been impatiently awaiting his turn. With typical bravado, he released his cards on the table for us to see - and envy. "Maximus!" he announced, beaming triumphantly. "At six crowns, a raise from your paltry two, Your Grace."

With an ace, a six, and a seven of clubs, it did indeed seem as if the pot would go to Bryan this round.

We nearly overlooked Maggie's turn to show, being too busy griping over Bryan's ongoing lucky streak. Until that was, she said quietly, "Chorus."

We all turned her way, whereupon, with an almost-diffident shrug of her shoulders, she spread before us a hand displaying four kings. "Thank you most kindly, Sir Francis," she said most politely, and neatly gathered the chips she had won to swell further her accumulating pile...

Greenwich, Dover, and the English Channel October 1532

THURSDAY 6 OCTOBER was a day of final, frenzied preparation. The royal apartments at Greenwich became Bedlam as palace staff topped off trunks and crates with items needed for the trip. The kitchens were equally frantic as many foodstuffs were to be taken with us, rather than be acquired on the journey, or once we reached Calais. I sat at a circular table with George Taylor, Maggie, who had become my *de facto* Mistress of the Wardrobe, and several chambermaids, reviewing lists of clothing, jewellery, cosmetics, furs and other adornments I planned to wear throughout the visit. Such comprehensive organization was required – not my strong suit. Thank heaven for Maggie's ability to tend to detail. My ensembles must be packed together, or I would spend the entire trip rummaging about searching for a certain hood to wear with a particular gown or the correct surcoat for an outdoor event. When all was ready; the last trunk lid closed with the lists of items carefully stowed within, the crates and trunks carted off to be transported to Dover, and my travelling attire set out I fell, utterly exhausted, into bed. The soft linen sheets felt smooth and cool against my skin, and I drifted off into a blissful, dreamless sleep.

By seven of the clock the next morning, we set out from Greenwich on the royal barge *The Lyon* and were rowed downriver to Gravesend, where we boarded the King's ship, *Minion*. With an air of great celebration, we sailed in her to the Isle of Sheppey where we were to be hosted by Sir Thomas Cheyne and his wife, Anne, in Queenborough Castle, for several days.

We docked at the mouth of the River Swale and were rowed by barge along the creek to the approach to the Castle, its towers and turrets illuminated by the late afternoon sun. I felt a pang of recollection at the sight – it reminded me of many of the chateaux in the Loire, in France. It was an impressive fortress. My excitement grew as we crossed the drawbridge spanning the moat, pages and yeomen scurrying to carry the baggage we would need for our stay. The castle was unlike most in England, it being of a circular design. The moat surrounded the curtain wall, with six mighty round towers stretching skyward, their decorative pointed caps each brandishing colourful standards which whipped in the sea breeze. Once inside the keep, we faced a rotunda of white stone. The massive doors opened, and we were beckoned within to centre court, a round room with soaring ceilings, adorned with paintings, ancient armoury, tapestry, and long tables. This chamber served as the great hall, but what was unique about it, other than its circular shape, was the well located in the centre of the room. The servants were able to draw fresh water from below to use in the chambers which ringed the rotunda. Henry's face was alive with interest as he explored the space with Lord Cheyne.

Our supper presented another surprise – we were served fresh oysters: raw, which Henry and Sir Thomas slurped happily, and baked – which I enjoyed far more. They were a specialty of the castle's cook, being readily available from the sea. At the conclusion of the meal, we all stepped out into the keep, and from a viewing platform near the curtain wall, we watched a sunset wash the sky with primrose, and peach streaked with violet. Eventually, an immense orange moon rose slowly over the water, and we were enchanted. Our trip was off to a perfect beginning.

We had a marvellous time at Queenborough with Sir Thomas and Lady Anne, who had had gone to great effort and expense for the honour of initiating such important travel for Henry and me. We were entertained with feasts and games which included the wealthy local merchants and their wives, and the nobility from the area. I was treated as if I had already been crowned, for Sir Thomas could not have been more solicitous, and her Ladyship constantly curtsied before me until, finally, I asked her to stop. She calmed somewhat when we spent the afternoon at the shooting butts together, practising our archery. It was great fun to enjoy friendship with another woman so enthusiastic about sport. While we sat and shared refreshment, she thanked me effusively for the intercession I offered several years prior when first her father, then her brother, died, and her wardship became a matter of argument between the then-unmarried Cheyne and Cardinal Wolsey. Wolsey of course, ever the arch manager, had wanted to be in control of Anne and her sister - and thus their sizable inheritance - but upon adept political handling by Cheyne, supported by my poignant appeal to Henry, Anne's future ended up being determined by Cheyne, and her sister's by my grandmother Howard, to the girls' great relief. Shortly after that, Anne married Sir Thomas. To me, they seemed a most happy couple, and I envied them, just a bit.

On 10 October, we parted from the Cheynes with great thanks for their hospitality and headed for Canterbury where we would meet with the majority of our traveling party to hear Mass in the Cathedral and pray for a safe, successful voyage. It was thrilling to see the throng of Courtiers and servants awaiting us as we arrived in that most revered of cities, and a great cheer was raised as Henry and I came into view.

Following Mass, the King and I, the nobles and the yeomanry all proceeded to Dover. Approaching the great fortress, with its imposing tower looming at the top of the bleached cliffs, I cast a glance round about me. There I surveyed the peers of Henry's realm, gorgeously bedecked, horses elegantly caparisoned, accompanying us to an ancient fortress which overlooked the sea, and all that on the eve of a triumphant return to France - the beloved home of my youth. I was filled with wonder at my good fortune.

It had been some years since I had last seen the sea, and when we crested the hill giving rise to the castle, we all stopped and simply stared, enthralled by the dark blue expanse in constant motion, frothed with whitecaps, extending as far as the eye could see beneath the cliffs. That day the sky was clear and cloudless, yet a sharp wind buffeted us as we paused. I dearly hoped for such weather on the morrow to speed us to our destination and said so to Henry, who agreed wholeheartedly.

We stayed that night in the castle, in lodgings on the second floor of the keep. I recall it being quite damp, musty and odorous from the constant moisture, and not at all warm. But I cared not, for we were to board ship at three of the clock in the morning, so there was little time for sleep anyway.

Wrapped warmly against the cold and stinging sea spray, I hurriedly gathered my belongings as we prepared to leave the castle and descend to the dock in the deep of night. Torch bearers fore and aft led us through the dark stone corridor until we emerged to confront steps leading down to a lookout terrace. The night being clear, the stars formed a blanket of brilliance which ended abruptly on the horizon where, near invisibly, the sky kissed the sea. I caught my breath and uttered a little cry as I scanned the heavens. Bright and resplendent in the east hung a great comet, its fiery tail splayed across the sky. I tugged silently at Henry's sleeve, and we observed it together, marvelling at its spreading silvery wake: God's firework, in truth. I tucked my arm through Henry's and squeezed. We both sensed it to be a powerful auspice and meant especially for us.

Descending the spray-treacherous steps toward the dock, I kept my arm closely wound through Henry's, both to steady myself on the descent and to share his warmth. The cold wind coming off the sea sliced through my heavy cloak. The dock was brightly lit with many torches, and it seemed there were servants and seamen everywhere, running loads of baggage and goods into the hold of the ship. While our fellow travellers assembled, hunched and discomfited against the blow, we were immediately guided by the captain to the plankway to board ship first.

The *Minion* rocked in the swell. She was a graceful vessel, a four-masted carrack. Not one of Henry's greatest warships but, still, she had made many voyages, not merely back and forth across the Channel, but also to more distant, exotic ports to trade in silks and spices.

With us was Henry's son, Richmond, now thirteen years of age, tall, angular of limb, and awkward. One could tell he felt very important, accompanying his father on this journey. I was amused to note his diffidence as he was saluted by the ship's crew – he was, after all, their Lord High Admiral, appointed by Henry when only six years old. I knew my naysayers hoped the inclusion of Henry's bastard, but beloved, son would cast a pall on the trip for me, but it certainly did not. His mother, the former Bessie Blount, was enduringly married to Gilbert Talboys and had been so for ten years, at the King's arrangement. I had nothing to fear from this engaging young man - only the promise that since Henry had once got a son by Bessie, surely he would beget one with me.

•

We were escorted to our staterooms, small though they were, and my stomach turned slightly from an unmistakable whiff of decaying mice, ever present in the holds of ships - but at least the tiny chambers afforded us privacy. I shrugged from my bonnet and cloak and joined Henry, Richmond,

Suffolk and Lord Lisle for refreshment in the officer's mess. While the remainder of our fellow travellers gratefully boarded, accompanied by seemingly endless streams of baggage, we drank ale, ate manchet and cheese, and waited impatiently to set sail. I partook of little, not knowing how the sway of the ship might affect me.

At last, we were respectfully invited to make our way to the aftcastle, and beneath the slowly brightening sky, with the royal standards snapping and cracking under the press of the still-stiff wind, the rowers moved the great ship out from the dock. The deckhands hoisted sail with such rapidity and skill that I was amazed, and when the keen blast filled them, we were off, heeling and skidding across the dark water.

Cloaked in furs, Henry and I sat on deck, watching the sunrise and enjoying the thrill of sailing. Thankfully my stomach had proved as steady as a rock, and we'd held each other snug under the furs, savouring such warm intimacy while talking and laughing.

Carried away by the moment I placed my lips close to his ear. "I, my darling Hal, have an announcement for you," I whispered.

At once Henry looked at me sharply, expectantly, and I realized I may have been less than adept at broaching the subject which so preoccupied me. For a heart-stopping moment, he must have assumed I would tell him I was with child. It was possible, I guessed, since we had been intimate, albeit merely a few times - but no, that had not been my intent.

Suddenly taken by remorse over my clumsy approach, I hugged him tighter. "Henry, I understand what you hoped I was about to say, and although that is not my news right now, it will be soon ... No, it is that I wish to begin living as if we were husband and wife. I want to be with you every waking moment, darling - and every night as well! Why should we wait any longer? You know the gossips say that you are taking me to Calais to marry me. So let us live as if our joyous union has already taken place."

I held my breath, then, before looking into his eyes. "What say you, my love?"

He leaned down just a bit so he could give me a tender, lingering kiss, and with both his look and his touch he gave me his answer.

•

By midmorning, we spied the coastline. I trembled with excitement. Approaching shore, we could see a sizable crowd assembled to greet us, looking almost like an army, with knights and dignitaries on horseback and flags and standards held aloft.

Once the ship was docked and secured and the deckhands had placed the plankway, the Dukes of Norfolk and Suffolk disembarked to cheers from the French party there to greet us. They were followed by the Bishops of Winchester, London, Lincoln, and Bath. Next to leave *Minion* were the Marquess of Exeter, the Earl of Derby, the Earl of Arundel and the Earl of Oxford, the Earls of Surrey and Rutland, and Viscount Lisle. Sadly there was one prominent figure missing from that grand lexicon of nobility: my father, who remained at home in Kent, ailing. I felt badly for him, knowing just how much he would have enjoyed this trip.

Henry, Richmond and I appeared at the top of the gangway and were met with a salute of cannon. We disembarked to huzzahs and waves from the large crowd. I was delighted, even though we were not yet in the French territory. Calais was part of the English Pale, lands, and marches which encompassed almost thirty parishes, all belonging to the English Monarch. We assumed our place in the procession which travelled through Searcher's Tower, then through Lanterngate and on into the town proper, which was surrounded by thick stone walls. The parade paused in the busy, central marketplace, giving me a chance to inspect the square. It was lined with stone and timbered buildings which were clearly the nave of commerce; and merchants, barristers, and military officers hastened to and fro between them. Through narrow, cobbled streets we travelled, to arrive at the pretty Church of St Nicholas where we heard Mass, sung in French and English. At length, we stepped back out into the bright sun of midday and continued through the streets to a timber-framed building located well behind the market square: the Staple Inn, which was to be our residence while in Calais. Although my smile had not wavered as we walked those seemingly endless streets, I was mightily relieved to reach our lodging. I desperately needed a bath and a nap!

Much to my pleasure, I discovered that my apartments were directly adjacent to Henry's, connected by a series of small closets. I thought the arrangement would work very nicely. The rooms were most pleasing. Usually reserved for the governor of Calais, they had been thoughtfully decorated for our visit; Henry's having a massive carved bed, with opulent hangings, as the centrepiece of his innermost chamber.

That evening after we had been comfortably settled in, and supper served and cleared, Henry and I retired together. We neither drew attention to our exit nor did we hide it from those who were to stay in apartments close to us. It was a perfect opportunity to commence our new cohabitation, since the building was small by palace standards, thereby harbouring fewer prying eyes.

In one of the wardrobe closets which adjoined our rooms, I slipped into a green silk damask chemise and dressing gown, had my hair brushed out, and then glided noiselessly into Henry's fire-lit chamber. To say he was delighted to see me thus would diminish the truth of his reaction. His face slowly broke into a grin, and he came to me and gripped me in an embrace so tight I near suffocated. He had reigned over the pageantry of the day - the all-powerful commander of his territory - with shouts and cheers and cannon fire, but at that moment I looked into the shining face of the young man he was to me: that vulnerable, captivating, familiar face which I had come to know so well and love so much.

I rejoiced in the chance to share with my Henry – my King - the passion and lust I had for him, held so long in check.

Calais
October 1532

SEIGNEUR DE LANGEY greeted me with a nod followed by a courteous bow, *"Madame la Marquise de Boulan …"* I took note of his expression and saw that it did not reflect his usual joie de vivre.

"Good morning, Seigneur Guillaume," I replied. "To what purpose do I owe the pleasure of your visit this morning?"

"Most unfortunately, Madame, I bear some less than happy news."

I detested bad news and looked at him guardedly. "And what might that be, Monsieur?"

"The Lady Marguerite d'Angoulême has taken ill, Madame. We hope and pray she has not become ill with plague. You know it runs rampant in Paris, as well as in London, at this very moment. I am sorry to say, Madame, she will not be able to meet with you in Boulogne, as you had so wished. She is filled with regret since she had greatly looked forward to seeing you once again, as you did her."

"Oh, Guillaume! I am so disappointed! Yet even more, I worry for her. I pray she will recover. I am heartbroken because I may never have another chance to see her, mostly to offer my thanks for everything she so generously taught me. I wish to write and tell her how much I will miss her company and how I wish her a speedy and complete recovery. Will you convey a note from me?"

"Of course, I will, Madame. I know it will cheer her to receive a letter from your own hand."

"Then I will have the letter delivered to you as soon as it is completed. Thank you, Guillaume."

As soon as he had departed, I sought Henry, who was preparing for a tour of the garrison.

"Henry, I am disconsolate. My Lady Marguerite will not be able to make the trip to Boulogne. And she is ill, possibly to her death! I know not whether to be more disappointed or more fearful for her life. I pray for her well-being, but, Henry, I am so dismayed!"

My lips trembled as I held back tears. Was this to portend the tone for the entire trip?

"I am sorry to hear of her illness, Anne." Henry stood while his grooms arrayed him with the equipment and attire necessary for the military inspection. When he finally looked up and saw the depth of my sorrow and my tenuous hold on composure, he waved them away and came over, drawing me to an upholstered bench where he took my hand. He was apprehensive, I could see.

"Sweetheart, you know that without a woman of appropriate rank to greet you, you will be unable to accompany me to Boulogne to meet Francois, do you not?"

He peered at me hesitantly with his lips pressed together, fearing an uncontrollable outburst, while I studied the floor, trying to regain some poise. Finally, I looked Henry straight in the eye and lifted my chin bravely.

"So be it. If I cannot be received by a noblewoman whom I respect, then I will be greeted by no one. I will remain behind, here in Calais, and pray for Marguerite's recovery."

Henry smiled at me with admiration - and not a small amount of relief at my measured reaction. "Anne, when François and I return together after completing our state visit, you will reign over the celebrations as if you were my wife and queen. While I am away, please oversee the plans so the French will not soon forget their stay in Calais, as hosted by the English King and his Queen-in-waiting. I trust in your style and eye for detail, and with Master Cromwell to assist you, I can be certain that Francois and his nobility will be duly impressed."

"I will do precisely as you have asked, Henry. You will be most proud of your court and me in Calais."

I laid my hand on his cheek. "Do not tarry overlong, my darling, for I will miss you."

"And I you, my love. And I you."

The King and his company of noblemen took leave to meet with François and his courtiers for a stay, hosted by the French, in Boulogne. The remaining English company looked forward to reports forwarded from the meeting of the great Kings. We knew it was attended solely by men, and that there were frequent pauses in conducting business to allow for entertainments which included bull and bear-baiting, cards and gambling. There was ceremonial giving of gifts – fine horses, jewels, and clothing – and the awarding of honorary titles. The sons of the respective monarchs were officially presented each to the other King, being admonished that they now had a new royal 'Father', and must always honour, respect and obey him.

•

On Tuesday 25 October, I anxiously stood, along with my ladies, at a vantage point along the route which would be travelled by the English and French Kings upon their joyous return into Calais. Just inside the Mile Gate thronged soldiers of the garrison and the entire remaining English force; on their toes, necks craned, to gain the first glimpse of the glittering parade of French and English nobility soon to arrive. With soldiers lining one side of the street, brightly clad in crimson, blue and yellow uniforms, and the English serving staff on the other, in coats of French tawny, we made quite a welcoming sight. Every man present wore an identical cap of jaunty scarlet, with a white feather waving in the breeze. I shifted nervously from one foot to the other, feeling as if I could not wait another second to see my Henry come into view. Suddenly, a deafening roar of cannon and the stinging smell of gunpowder filled the air, and when the smoke cleared, there he was, riding majestically at the front of the brigade, with François by his side, both dressed in gleaming white. He was gorgeous – grand beyond description! And I was enraptured. Despite having been so curious to see François again, at that moment, I had eyes only for Henry. He spotted me; our glances met, and I was filled to bursting with pride and happiness.

Henry and François, with a select group of French nobles including François' sons, the Dauphin and the Ducs d'Orleans and Angoulême, rode to Staple Hall on the market square, in which lodging had been prepared for them. I knew Henry would be pleased when he toured the housing readied for François and his sons, since I had personally reviewed every detail during the King's five-day stay in Boulogne. The rooms were lavish; François' chamber being draped with fantastic fabric of golden damask, embroidered with silver and colourful silks to emulate flowers and vines growing from the floor. His presence chamber was hung with silver tissue, his cloth of estate finely wrought with red roses trimmed in pearls. The privy chamber, grandest of all, was a vision in green and crimson velvet embroidered with branches, flowers of gold bullion, and noble beasts and golden coats of arms. Throughout the room, the drapery was adorned with precious stones and pearls. It was apparent that the call for modesty had been left at the entrance to the royal lodgings! I would not have Henry outdone by the King of France under any circumstance.

I awaited Henry back in our apartments within the Exchequer, the Staple Inn. When at long last he arrived, he was accompanied by Monsieur Pierre Viole, the Provost of Paris. Monsieur Viole presented me with a gift from his own King.

The note accompanying the package said, "*Madame la Marquise, j'attends notre réunion.*"

Within the perfectly presented gift was an ice-white, impeccable diamond. The largest I had ever seen.

•

My wardrobe chamber in the Staple Inn was alive with chatter and laughter that Sunday evening. A select few of my circle and I donned costumes for the masque which was to take place after the grand banquet in François' honour.

"Madame Anne, you would decide well not to feast too avidly on the tempting dishes served at the banquet!" As we were being swathed in crimson tinsel satin, I peered over my maid's head at Lady Lisle. I saw by the teasing look on her face that she likely had a crafty follow-up brewing in that clever head of hers.

"Why so, Honor?"

"Well, since your garment is so lustrous, and it hugs your body *just so*, a large meal would surely be misinterpreted as a baby, boldly showing himself on the evening of his mother's presumed marriage. Just *imagine* how quickly the gossip would reach Dover and beyond!" came her pointed reply.

I let loose with a volley of laughter, hindering the maid's attempt to swaddle me in silk. I did adore Honor, and only she would be audacious enough to joke so about the persistent rumours that Henry and I had secretly planned our wedding for that Sunday, instead of a masque.

"You know, I am tempted to pad my stomach so that we might measure the speed of the spoken word."

Honor winked at me, and we continued to be adorned with the gossamer silver cloaks which would only partially conceal our crimson undergarments. The diaphanous capes were to be drawn together by a delicate cord of gold, which was woven loosely in a sensual pattern, leaving enough of an opening in the front that the body-tight crimson tinsel could be observed.

To add a final and vitally important touch to my costume, I ducked into my suite and retrieved from a chest a single piece of jewellery. As I placed it around my neck and saw my reflection in the mirror, I smiled wickedly to myself. Just for this evening, I planned to indulge in a personal act of revenge. I stepped back out to join the other ladies and was met by wide-eyed stares. Hanging prominently between my breasts was the Occitan cross which had been Katherine's favourite jewel from the Queen's collection. It was made of heavy gold, with dark rubies in the centre and on each of its four points, and suspended from three of those points were large, pear-shaped pearls. The piece was not at all to my personal liking, much too heavy and ornate, but it was instantly recognizable as the royal jewel Katherine wore constantly. I smiled coolly back at my ladies – and swept from the chamber with a flourish.

•

While we waited outside the doors of the banquet hall, my sister Mary; Agnes, Lady Darby; Margaret, Lady Fitzwalter; Jane, my sister-in-law; Elizabeth Harleston; Lady Wallop; Honor Grenville, Lady Lisle, and I completed our costumes by raising glittering masks to our faces, and having them fastened behind our heads with satin riband. The masks had been specially made by a master craftsman in Venice and were indeed a sight to behold. Covered in gemstones and exotic feathers, they completely disguised all distinguishing features of the wearer save the eyes, creating an alluring air of mystery, particularly when combined with our daring and enticing costumes.

At a signal, we slid into the banquet chamber to the plaintive beat of a single tambour. All conversation stopped abruptly; every eye fixed upon us as we sinuously wound our way about the head table. From the notable guests there, we each selected a partner and silently motioned for him to join us on the dance floor. The Kings were bewitched, and every man who was selected as a dance partner grinned blissfully as he came side to side with his mysterious lady. I, of course, beckoned to François, who was only too happy to oblige, and who wound his arm snugly around my waist. Agnes chose the King of Navarre, and Honor selected the English King - my English King, the cheeky little strumpet!

Barely had we completed one galliard, when Henry, filled with exuberance, danced over to me and whisked the mask from my face, revealing my identity to François. Following his lead, the other dancers removed their masks as well, and Henry crowed, "*Voilà mon frere François!* Stunning feminine beauty is not the sole dominion of the Frenchman!'

With that, he pointedly traced my cheek with the back of his forefinger, and with one last, lingering look, released me back into François's company.

François took my arm and guided me to a small adjacent chamber for some privacy, where, relaxing on thickly padded chairs and sipping cups of spiced wine, we laughed and conversed in French for over an hour. While we spoke, I watched him assess me thoroughly. There was no question but that he found me pleasing, and I knew, were it not for Henry and the recommitted brotherhood between them, François' attentions would have been distinctly more purposeful than he presently allowed. Eventually, our discourse turned serious, and I was gratified beyond measure to hear, quite directly, that he not only understood Henry's desire and need for a new wife, but that he believed me to be a superlative choice. François, too, operated under the belief that, as monarch, he was absolute ruler of his realm; that his decisions were irreproachable. Not an advocate of Pope Clement, his religious views leaned decidedly in the same direction as Henry's. This was anything but a surprise, I thought, since he was a compatriot of some of the finest minds promoting the reform of the Catholic Church. And if their writings were not enough to persuade him, he was certainly subject to the lecturing of his sister, Marguerite. I asked after her health, and told him how much I had missed seeing her, and François expressed his appreciation, advising me that it seemed she fared better and had thankfully escaped the plague. For that glad news, I was greatly relieved.

The exhilaration I felt on that glorious evening was just what I needed. For the time, I had vanquished my rival Katherine and had been the object of desire of two kings.

•

Late that night, after the entertainment had concluded and the house had at last grown quiet, we took to our marvellous bedchamber together. I lay abed with Henry, and having told him every scrap of my conversation with François, continued to prattle on about the events of the day, till I heard him yawn hugely. I grew quiet, and he pulled me to him, curling his strong body securely around mine. I sighed in absolute happiness. My thoughts drifted pleasantly, occasionally broken by Henry's snore, and I wondered if it was possible to be more content than I felt at that very moment. Queen or no queen, I was nestled next to the man I adored, held in esteem by the two greatest monarchs alive, and had the entire world at my feet.

I could not fathom anything but joy ahead.

•

On All Hallows' Eve, the two Kings rode from Calais to Sandingfield, where they shared refreshment and final conversation. They bid each other the warmest of farewells, deeming the meeting a success, and parted at the border of the French-English Pale.

There was well-nigh as much commotion created by the packing and moving of goods for departure as when we prepared for the trip. Henry and I, however, intended to remain in Calais at the Exchequer for a while yet, with a greatly diminished staff.

I savoured the thought.

Picking my way through a tangle of crates, coffers, trunks and busy stewards, I was on my way to the long gallery to seek respite from the din and confusion. Glancing up, I found myself unexpectedly face to face with one of Henry's premier ambassadors in Rome. Gregorio Casali was an important advisor to Stephen Gardiner and Edward Foxe, as they laboured to convince Clement to grant Henry an annulment. Signore Casali was knowledgeable in the conventions of the Curia at the Vatican, and the instruction he provided to Foxe and Gardiner, combined with his personal efforts, had been intended to secure the long-desired outcome. To date, of course, his contribution, however conscientious it may have been, was not marked by any movement at all in Clement's opinion. I had met Casali at court on those occasions when he returned to England, but most of his time was spent either in Rome or in meeting with individuals elsewhere who might advance Henry's cause.

Plainly taken aback at our chance encounter, he bowed low, saying, *"Bonjour, Madame la Marquise. C'est mon plaisir de vous voir aujourd'hui!"* in his heavily accented French. His native language was Italian, and his English was poor. Although I had witnessed conversations between Henry and him in Latin, he mostly spoke French at the English Court. It took me a mere second to recall that I had little liking for Signore Casali, whose nervous glance darted to and fro, and never came confidently to rest on the person with whom he was conversing. Inherently, I did not trust him.

"And to what do we owe this great honour, *Signore*? I have not seen you for some long while. Nor …" I added with a healthy dose of sarcasm, "… have we heard much from you, or about you. I presume you are here in Calais to provide His Majesty with wonderful news - the news he has sought from you for, oh … several years?"

Casali's bearded chin twitched, and his eyes narrowed and rapidly scanned the room – landing anywhere but on my face. The man knew he had confronted the wrong personage by accident as he went about his errand. Others in the vicinity pretended to work at their tasks, but they had caught the tone of my voice and were curious, so they lingered, waiting to hear what would next happen.

"Madame, I come seeking an audience with His Royal Majesty. I have been greatly concerned. I have not had any communication from him in over four months. I became anxious that he might not be in good health."

"Well, well - how kind of you, *Signore.*" My voice dripped with disdain and grew louder. Anger bubbled as I thought of the money, the privilege, and the trust Henry had placed with this little man in the hope that his case would be successfully represented. And all for naught. "His Majesty is quite well. Quite well indeed. In fact, his well-being grows greater by the day, thank you. I believe his pleasant state of mind is because he will no longer require the Pope's approval for aught that he does. And, just consider, if you will, this curious and interesting concept, *Signore* – if His Grace no longer needs the Pope or the Pope's approval, then should it not follow that he no longer needs you? Would you not agree with my simple logic?"

My gaze was direct and unsparing.

"Madame, truly, progress in the Great Matter is being made, even at this very moment! I merely need to speak with His Majesty to convey the detail and acquire one further small payment with which to persuade those few cardinals who remain obstinate. Thereafter, I promise you, the news I will bear to the King will be joyous."

"Spare yourself the effort, *Signore* Casali. It is a matter of too little, too late. You have failed in your assignment."

Seething, I paused, "…and I shall not forget it!"

Brushing past him I continued on my way.

I would have enjoyed a backward glance to witness his embarrassment, but would not allow him to think I had reconsidered.

•

In the span of only a few days since the final meeting between Henry and François, the previously humming household at the Exchequer became almost abandoned. Most of Henry's retinue had packed up and left to sail back to Dover. Cromwell had been sent home, with instructions by Henry to attend to what matters he could, and defer to Norfolk and Suffolk when needed – and only to contact him if the situation became dire. Remaining were a scant few of Henry's closest companions and members of his privy chamber, and to attend me, Anne Gainsford, Lady Margaret Fitzwalter, and two of my most trusted chambermaids, Lucy Holbrook, and Emma Potter.

On the first of November, as if on cue, the previously mild, sunny coastal weather took a vicious turn with the approach of a storm which blew in from the northwest. The temperature dropped precipitously; a cold rain fell unceasingly, and the wind keened day and night. We were told that those who had set sail for Dover were driven back into Calais harbour, and some were blown off course as far as the coast of Flanders. I pitied the men and women who had no choice but to remain aboard ship, docked in the harbour and in great peril, waiting for the storm to subside. It continued for days, raining and gusting. The winds swept townsfolk off the streets of Calais, and the cracking and booming thunder made all but the most stouthearted among us anxious.

As for me - it was quite extraordinary- the worse the weather became, the more appealing I found my situation, ensconced as we were in the cosy lodging, secure within the sturdy town walls, with few others. Removed from the garrulous court, the politics and diplomacy of the previous two weeks and the worries of everyday life back in England, I basked in the contentment of being house-bound with my love. Finally! I found myself, quite literally, to be at home with Henry, who had, after all, become my long-desired port in the storm. I was never happier in my life than during those wet and wild days in Calais.

We were never bored or discontent. We walked in the long gallery and watched, enthralled, through the windows overlooking the gardens as the winds bent mighty trees till they near snapped in two. In the evenings, we feasted on the delicious local pheasant, cheeses, grapes and pears, then retired to our inner chamber, where, before a warming fire, we played endless games of Pope Julius with Francis Bryan, Francis Weston, and Anne Gainsford. We were completely absorbed in this newest card game, and I became quite skilled, often taking the purse to the grumblings of Bryan and the King.

Once the evening's entertainment had drawn to a close, Henry and I were left blissfully alone in our bedchamber. With the wind wailing about the eaves and the windows rattling in their leaded frames, we exulted in sleeping together and loving each other, naked under the silken sheets and soft, thick coverlets.

Henry and I were so besotted with each other that rarely were we apart. But by the tenth day of November, we reluctantly readied for our journey home. We were drunk with love and grateful to our Almighty Father that he had given us, finally, the opportunity to be together after so many years of patient waiting. We determined to show our thanks by generously giving alms on our way back to London, and we provided money and medicine to the poor folk who waited just outside the town walls. Henry also generously rewarded all of those who had enabled his travel.

Sunday the tenth dawned fair and still, and we sent forth most of our belongings, hoping to set sail before sundown. As the afternoon wore on, though, a mist folded in from the sea, until it became so thick that one could not see a hand in front of one's face. So we remained, fogged in for yet another day, until on Tuesday 12 November, we boarded ship just before midnight.

This time, though, the crossing was not so pleasant as it had been some weeks before. I huddled within that creaking, noisome carcass, smelling the foul air beneath deck, and with every roll of the ship, I thought I would die. I hid from view, keeping my sickness to myself, and vomited until there was nothing left inside me … and then vomited again. My head ached unmercifully. Vaguely, I wondered if my sickness could have been brought on, or made worse by pregnancy, but I was too wracked with nausea to ponder the thought for long.

The voyage took what seemed an eternity. I finally ceased heaving, and was able to rest, though fitfully. I somehow pieced myself back together to disembark and make our way to Dover Castle, where we were able to stay for a night on blessedly firm ground.

We took our time returning to London, staying in manor houses throughout Kent. Our merry band of travelers: Bryan, Weston, Henry and me and my few ladies, at last arrived at home in Greenwich on the twenty-seventh day of November.

We had been away for almost two months, and in that span of time, the relationship Henry and I shared had become, we agreed, *immutable* – exactly as he had presaged in one of his letters to me so long ago.

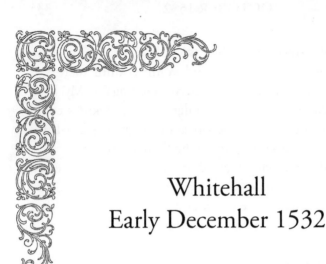

Whitehall
Early December 1532

HOLBEIN STOPPED PAINTING, his brush waving in mid-air. "*Dame Pembroke! Sit bitte noch!* Please! Remain STILL!"

"I will do my best, Master Hans," I said, duly chastised, and tried to settle myself on the uncomfortable stool such that I would not need to adjust myself again for a few minutes. "If only this stool were a bit more friendly to the *derriere*!"

I gave voice to a hearty sigh, resuming my former pose.

"As I have said, *Dame*, the stool raises you high enough that your face catches the best of the morning light from this excellent window."

"Your work is so extraordinary, Master Hans, that the result will be well worth my stiff back and the crick in my neck," I chuckled, then, at sight of his expression, hurriedly rearranged my face into the serene, graceful look Holbein and I had decided upon as appropriate for my portrait. I was not very good at sitting still for any period of time, and while I was excited about the prospect of having a portrait painted for Henry, the time did drag.

Smoothing my black velvet gown, I idly played with the pearls which trimmed the sleeves. It was a truly splendid gown, after all, in which to be immortalized. Rich, deep black velvet cut low through the bodice, edged in Belgian lace, then trimmed in an alternating row of double grey pearls and carved gold buttons. The velvet sleeves had wide, silky bands of sable fur which encircled my arms above the elbow, and my hood was simple, but elegant – a narrow French design, completely outlined in grey and black pearls with a billiment of crisply pleated gold-hued taffeta peeking from underneath. The sable fur, taffeta, and the buttons all matched the colour of my hair, which was smoothed from a centre parting to each side of my face and was visible enough to make its own statement. And, of course, I wore the pearl necklace with the "B" which had been given to me by my mother. I was to sit up straight, arms bent at the elbow but resting on my lap, and gaze at the viewer with a knowing look in my eye and just a hint of a smile on my lips. No doubt the final product would be striking if I could just manage the pose for the required length of time.

… and if Master Holbein didn't, in error, capture the contortions my face assumed as pins and needles prickled my stiff back!

At last, released from my morning's prison of sitting, I had my maid Lucy fetch me a cloak, and pulling it about me against the air's sharp bite, wandered out into the gardens beyond my apartments at Whitehall to stretch my legs. We had been back in London for one week, and Henry was constantly occupied in meetings with ambassadors and dignitaries who had been awaiting his return and was daily rowed to the Tower to inspect progress on the construction projects. Unrest in Scotland continued, and his attention to this and other pressing matters had kept us apart for the better part of that week. His attention had begun to wander, which I disliked. As I walked, I hatched a cunning plan to remedy the situation.

First, I sent a message inviting Henry to come to Whitehall from Greenwich for a special evening. Then I set about my preparations. I requested the cook prepare a light supper I knew Henry would enjoy, but made certain it would not be laden with heavy dishes. Spiced wine would be served, with a selection of sweets, including his favourites, lemon and orange suckets. About the privy chamber in which we would dine, I had silver lanterns placed, with candles twinkling through tracery to produce a beguiling light. More lanterns were added to my bedchamber, with a censer, ready to burn rosemary and lavender incense. As a final touch, I requested that Mark Smeaton play his lute for us as we dined. Master Smeaton, a young and talented musician, played the lute and other instruments with sensitive touch and was rapidly becoming the most admired musician at court. His was just the sound I desired for the evening ahead.

We enjoyed a lovely supper together, and the alluring environment I created had begun to work its magic. Rarely did Henry take his eyes from me. We conversed, jested, and wittily teased one another, all in low tones as we sat side by side at the table. Smeaton's music was the perfect accompaniment, and I flashed the young master a warm smile of thanks. He blushed, and bowed in acknowledgement.

When I felt the moment had arrived, I excused myself, encouraging Henry to finish his sweets without haste, pay Smeaton and dismiss him, then join me in my bedchamber. I quickly slipped into my closet, where Emma assisted me in divesting myself of my constricting gown and hood. I then donned a special dressing gown which had been made according to my direction. It was of gold tissue; a free flowing gown which skimmed my body, and was held together by a single satin tie. I am quite certain it must have been thought scandalous while it was being sewn, and it amused me to think of the eyebrows raised amongst the seamstresses. Emma helped me loosen my hair and brush it out, arranging it both front and back, so it fell past my shoulders, and hid my breasts. For I was naked under the gown, and it was so sheer that all it served was to add a mere shimmer to my nude form beneath.

Emma let out a nervous giggle at my audacious attire, but in the next breath, said, "Madame, you look exquisite. Like a golden fairy who is about to seduce a warlock in a fanciful tale. The King will not be able to resist you."

I gave her a smile and a wink. That was exactly my plan.

•

I went to my bedchamber and arranged myself near the hearth with the fire to my back. Eyes downcast and apparently deep in thought Henry opened the door and entered the room, then glanced up and caught sight of me. I knew my body was clearly visible through the gossamer gown. He froze, dumbstruck, and I approached him, bare feet making no sound on the soft carpet. I stopped just beyond his reach and allowed him time to regard me fully. Henry was a man who was exhilarated by visual beauty, and I was not about to hasten the moment. I had carefully planned his seduction, and it was to be enjoyed.

I waited while he removed his doublet, shirt, and hose, and stood before me, an incredibly virile sight at forty-one years. I hesitated only a moment more, went to him and, lowering his face to mine, we kissed with a heat that sent a thrill through my entire being. I caressed him, my hands softly traveling the length and breadth of his body. Quickly, then, with a single movement, Henry pulled the lacing of my gown, allowing the garment to whisper to the floor in a golden cloud. Now both flushed with desire, he lifted me so easily, carried me to the bed, and placed me upon it. He lay next to me, and I made him remain still while I continued to fondle him. When I saw he could wait no longer, I climbed atop him, and we breathed and panted together. Both my body and my mind were filled - were consumed - with Henry. His passion stoked mine, and we dissolved into a single entity, exploding mightily as one.

At length, I tumbled from him, and we lay gasping, soaked in a sweet pool of intermingled sweat. How was it possible to conjoin so totally with another human being? As my breathing slowed and my thoughts cleared, I understood that something different – and quite profound – had just taken place between us.

"Henry," I said, stroking the sweat-soaked hair at his temple, "we are each part of the other, just as you have told me so many times, my darling."

He murmured sleepily in my ear, "I know, Nan. You are my heart and my soul. There is no height we cannot reach together."

He pulled me to him, and we fell asleep, entwined in each others' arms.

Greenwich
Christmastide 1532

HAD I THOUGHT previously that His Majesty the King fawned over me, I would evidently have been mistaken. For in the days which followed our magical evening, he followed me everywhere, petted and kissed me constantly, looked after my comfort, 'til I felt I had never witnessed a man so idolize a woman. Neither I nor others of his close circle had ever known him to be this radiant and lighthearted. He took me with him on an inspection of the new building projects at the Tower. The great hall was noisy with plasterers and carpenters; the magnificent hammerbeam ceiling took shape as we watched.

Eyes shining, Henry then led me to the Jewel House. I was completely unprepared for the sight which greeted me when the massive oaken doors were unlocked with the great brass key, creaking loudly as they swung open. I recalled feeling overwhelmed that morning in the library at Windsor upon viewing so many gems. Nothing, though, readied me for the imposing opulence of the Jewel House. Laid about on tables, in casks, and on shelves were gemstones in staggering abundance, stacks of gold bullion, bricks of silver, and piles of gold, silver and enamelled plate. All lent an unearthly glow to the darkly panelled room. The sharp smell of rich metal filled my nostrils, and for some reason, we all felt it appropriate to speak in whispered tones.

While I goggled at its entirety, Henry made a sweeping motion indicating a corner in which a massive pile of treasure had been set aside from the rest. Every item had been neatly catalogued by Thomas Cromwell, and the open ledger was on a lectern sitting atop an impressive desk.

"This will be yours, Anne, to furnish your household when you become Queen," he said. "New pieces will be smithed especially for you, to bear your own badge and devices. I hope you approve of what I have chosen for you."

As if on cue, Cromwell stepped smartly to the fore. Quickly he located the pages in the ledger which pertained to me. I scanned the list:

A gilt cup with a cover, Spanish fashion, chased with "holines leaves," with a tower on the top

18 gilt trenchers of Flanders touch

A cup with a cover, of Almain making, and on the pomell of the cover a man holding the King's arms

A pair of covered gilt basons: one chased wreathen, the other upright with beasts

A round bason of silver for a chamber, and a silver pot with a lid

Three goblets chased, feather fashion, having a boy bearing a shield with the King's arms

A pair of flagons with roses embossed upon the sides, with plaits in the midst, and therein the King's arms

A pair of gilt flagons or bottles with the arms of France

Twelve gilt spoons with half knops at the end

2 gilt cups of assay with the King's arms in the bottom

A great double cup, gilte arsed, of Almain making ...

...and the sequence of costly and sumptuous items went on and on. I could not possibly comprehend owning such a mountain of valuables. Though, apparently they were now officially mine. I had just become an extremely wealthy woman!

•

Stepping out of the Jewel House and into the thin December sunshine, I squinted up at Cromwell.

"Madame, would you kindly accompany me to the apartments being constructed for you? I have some questions I wish to ask you concerning the planning of the rooms."

"Of course, Master Thomas. Henry, will you be joining us?"

"No, Anne. You and Thomas resolve whatever building questions he has. I plan to meet with Suffolk for a time. I'll rejoin you later, and we will be rowed back to Greenwich." With that, he tenderly kissed me goodbye before setting off in the direction of the Wakefield Tower.

I caught Cromwell's droll look as he witnessed Henry bidding me *adieu.*

As soon as Henry was out of earshot, I turned to Cromwell. "Ah, Thomas! I see you find the King's attachment to me entertaining," I said, dangling a bit of bait to see if he would grasp it.

"Quite the contrary, Madame," came the quick and artful reply. "I sincerely could not be happier than to observe the love between you two. It does my heart good to know of His Majesty's joy. And, to be honest, I am a bit envious."

"Is that so, Thomas?" I raised a brow and eyed him carefully. Although it was true he had become increasingly indispensable to Henry, still it was not to be forgotten that he was Wolsey's right arm for a long while before the Cardinal's death. I could not help but feel wary around him.

"After I lost my wife five years ago, Madame, it has not been my good fortune to find another woman willing to put up with my penchant for work in service of King and country. My time and dedication, I have concluded, are best spent in Parliament and handling the King's business, as opposed to my own."

"I am most sorry about your wife, Thomas," I said, meaning it. "I know Henry does indeed value your ethic when it comes to work, and especially your efforts on behalf of issues which are critical to him."

I paused, wondering just how far to go in probing Cromwell's philosophy and motives.

"It is a comfort to me to know you are a believer in the King's authority to rule, and to determine his course of action as he sees fit - a right bestowed upon him by God," I offered.

"I have been of that mind for a long while, Milady. As you might imagine, it did not behoove me to express such thoughts while in the employ of Cardinal Wolsey. I am, and always have been, an independent thinker, and even while assisting the Cardinal, I avidly read and was influenced by the treatise *'Defensor Pacis'*, by Marsilius of Padua. Have you read it? If not, I have a personal copy which I would be quite happy to loan you."

"Thank you, Thomas. I have read it, and found it to be clear and concise in its argument that there be only one ruling power in any kingdom, and no mortal has the right to interpret or dispense with divine law. Only the body of Christian people can do so. What a brave soul Marsilius was, to openly state what was complete heresy in 1324. Would you not agree?"

"Absolutely, Madame Marquise. I believe that we are greatly obliged to thinkers and writers like Marsilius and Tyndale for providing the fodder needed to stimulate progress."

We walked across the common and arrived at the Queen's Apartments which were connected to the great hall by a series of small chambers and corridors. Cromwell and I picked our way through the building materials and arrived at the suite of rooms which would be my privy apartments at the Tower. We conferred about the number of windows to be placed in each chamber, all of which would overlook the formal gardens. As we spoke, I studied Cromwell's fleshy face. His lips were thin, perhaps from continuously pressing them together to hold back thoughts which were better left unspoken. His eyes were small but intelligent and keen, and not altogether cold or aloof. As I had noticed before, his manner of dress was understated, usually consisting of a black ensemble, covered by a black wool surcoat modestly trimmed in fur. His complete departure from the ostentation his former master displayed appealed to me. I liked how his expression flashed warmth and humour, though he never appeared to seek to entertain nor be the centre of attention.

I decided I would give Master Cromwell a chance to prove me his worth.

•

Of a late afternoon, Anne, Maggie and I were walking and conversing in the long gallery. We needed to stretch our legs, albeit indoors, after three days of continuous rain. Deep in discussion we suddenly broke off, rudely interrupted by a frenetic scrabbling on the polished wood floor behind us. Turning, mystified and not a little put out, we saw a tiny puppy, long ears flailing and sweeping the floor, rushing headlong toward us.

"Where in heaven did this little creature come from?" I laughed, watching the pup work his way toward us with great determination.

Anne stooped to scoop up the silky, tawny wagging ball of fur. At that moment, Lord Westmoreland followed around the corner and into view. "Sir, is he yours?" Maggie called out.

"No, he is not, ladies." With a respectful nod, he added, "It seems that he belongs to all of you!"

My friends and I glanced at each other in confusion, then with a smile, he handed me a note on parchment, with the seal of Calais affixed. I opened it quickly and read the script written on behalf of Honor, Lady Lisle, who thought this lovely little spaniel would be enjoyed by me and my ladies, and might be a companion to Jolie. The pup was a gift to me, Anne, Maggie, Bessie, and Elizabeth!

We giggled with enchantment as Lord Westmoreland looked on. "He has been sent to you as a gift from the Lady Lisle, Mistresses. She thought you might all take pleasure in his frolics."

"We are certain to do just that," I said. "And thank you most kindly, my Lord, for bringing him to us. Does he have a name?"

"Not as yet, Madame. That is something you can decide upon."

As we talked, from his vantage point in Anne's arms the little dog looked raptly from face to face. Each time he turned to watch one of us while we spoke, he tilted his little head as if to try and understand. When he gazed curiously at me, head askew, I looked right back and blurted "*Pourquoi*? Why?" It seemed exactly as if this is what he wanted to say.

Maggie chuckled with delight. "That's it, Anne! Little Purkoy! What a perfect name for him!"

And so Purkoy he became, and loved nothing more than to snuggle on one of our laps whenever he could.

Life at Court was nothing if not tumultuous that Christmas. It was a joyous time – perhaps the most celebrated season I remember. In contrast, though, anxiety was high, at least for Henry and me. It was all too apparent to Henry that he simply must bring the Great Matter to fruition, and rapidly. He and

I lived fully as husband and wife, and we shared each other's bedchamber almost nightly.

•

The Great Hall at Greenwich was bedecked for the Christmas banquet, preparations for which, this year, I had overseen; thus it promised to be a grand and gorgeous affair. Gold and red were the colours I chose as the decorative theme throughout the palace. We wove holly and winterberry with ribands of gold and placed these arrangements around golden candlestands burning brightly, and the rooms and hallways simply glowed with a festive light. My ladies and I planned to repeat that theme in our dress for the evening; my gown being red satin with yards of gold tissue forming a train. I had planned excellent entertainments for the guests, with the best music, a skit to be performed by an acting troupe, dancing, and of course an elaborate menu full of the most pleasing dishes. The King had received a sizable delivery of oranges just ten days prior, so the master cook was engrossed in creating a pudding worthy of such a treat. Every member of the palace staff was excitedly busy as we anticipated a glorious Christmastide.

In the days leading up to Christmas, Henry was rowed to Westminster, where he, Norfolk and Suffolk, my father, Thomas Cromwell, and Sir Thomas Audley, Keeper of the Great Seal -and the likely next Chancellor- met during a prorogued Parliament to conduct critical matters of state. There was one party whose opinions and views would have been indispensable, but he was absent. Thomas Cranmer had been sent months ago on a diplomatic embassy to Emperor Charles. Now he was much needed back in England - at court - to help direct the concluding steps in the nullification of Henry's marriage. I had the greatest of confidence in Dr Cranmer, and admired him enormously, so I encouraged Henry to stop at nothing to retrieve him. The former Archbishop of Canterbury, old William Warham, had died over the summer, and the position was vacant. I remembered Warham's disapproving look and lack of support when the meetings at Hampton Court had taken place some time ago, and now that he was gone, there was an opportunity to fill the esteemed position with someone aligned with Henry's increasingly reformist views. Cranmer was the obvious, and perfect, choice. We waited impatiently as he travelled with difficulty from Italy, through France and across the Channel, from Dover to London, but the weather worsened daily with layers of snow and ice, and by Christmas Eve, we had only a message that he would hope to arrive 'soon'.

•

I looked forward to the Christmas banquet with excited anticipation, and on that evening, made merry with Anne and Maggie, Honor and Margery, Elizabeth and Dorothy – all my favourites, while we dressed and embellished ourselves. We made our entrance after the others had assembled, and upon stepping into the hall, my senses were assaulted by the riot of colour, bright torchlight, the din of sound, and the heady smells. Suddenly I felt dizzy and gripped Maggie's shoulder to steady myself. After a moment, the feeling had passed, and I assumed my place next to Henry at the head of the room on the raised platform which held our table. The evening drew on, and though I did enjoy myself, especially basking in the radiance of an exuberant Henry at my side, I did not feel my best. I had not eaten much throughout the day, and should have been hungry, but was not. In fact, the smell of some of my favourite dishes did not appeal to me at all, and when the Christmas Pie was served, I was surprised to find that the sight of it turned my stomach. I hoped I was not coming down with an illness which would keep me abed for days.

I smiled and danced, but finally pulled Henry aside, and telling him I was tired, made an early retreat to my chamber and went directly to bed. I must have been soundly asleep when Henry came to the room and climbed in beside me, for I do not remember. What I do recall, though, is being awakened early the next morning with nausea which prompted me to jump from the bed and run to a basin in the room to be sick, a condition which both Henry and I attributed to overindulgence on the prior evening.

Oddly, though, for the next few days, nausea came and went. At times it overtook me, and I had to find discreetly a place to vomit, or to merely heave if I had eaten nothing. My initial panic at this pattern was only slightly mollified when I did not come down with a fever or the ague: I would never forget my encounter with the sweating sickness. But the ailment persisted, and it seemed very strange indeed; I had never felt that way before.

We received regular reports from Cromwell as to the approaching whereabouts of Dr Cranmer. On 1 January 1533, the court New Year celebration was held during which gifts were distributed to all, including palace staff, and a great many poor folk were given alms. I surprised Henry with the now completed, and exceptionally masterful, portrait of me painted by Master Holbein. To say that Henry was delighted with its realism would not nearly describe his zeal for the painting. He spoke bandog and bedlam about it to anyone who would listen, and presented Holbein with an extra large stipend, along with the promise of many more commissions. He stated resoundingly that he wanted a life-sized portrait of himself, with me painted by his side. At this news, Holbein thanked Henry most graciously – but as he bowed, I caught a roll of his eye at the thought of trying to keep Henry and me captive long enough to paint even a reasonable likeness!

Well over a week into January, Dr Cranmer arrived at court. He and Henry met shortly after he settled himself at Greenwich, and Henry wasted no time in telling Cranmer he was to be appointed Archbishop of Canterbury. Surprisingly, Cranmer's reaction to that news was not one of pleasure or grateful enthusiasm. He was of the mind that the requirements of the position of Archbishop ran counter to his views of

Rome and the Papacy. Henry, though, was not going to permit anything to stand in the way of having the trusted Cranmer in the highest clerical position in his realm, and so after consultation with some of the best legal and canonical minds in England, a solution was devised – a disclaimer which would allow Cranmer to accept the position with a clean conscience. At this conclusion, my relief, as well as Henry's, was palpable. Dr Thomas Audley was then named Chancellor, and with these two supporters in the positions of power, the obstacles to my marrying Henry were, at last, falling away.

•

Emma and Lucy bustled about my chamber, straightening, organising, lighting candles and adding wood to the hearth fire, and preparing to assist me in dressing for the Twelfth Night banquet and amusements. My gown had been selected and laid out on the bed, with the kirtle, sleeves, bodice and stomacher close by. Once I had completed applying my cosmetics and my hair had been woven into a riband, I stood for Emma to help me into the bodice and stomacher. I was to wear a gown which had been made for me upon my return home from Calais, in November. I had worn it once, and loved it – deep sapphire blue, with gold and silver embroidery – it was very flattering. Emma tugged and tugged at the bodice, which for some reason would not encompass me. "Emma, are you certain this is the right piece? It looks as if it is, and I believe I have but one deep blue bodice shot with gold and silver, but why doesn't it fit?"

"I have no idea, Madame," Emma replied, quizzically peering into the mirror's reflection which captured us both. "I am certain this is the very same bodice you wore in November. Let me try again." And she yanked the laces together, resulting in a right ample bosom spilling from the neckline of the gown.

I gaped at the sight, thinking it looked so unlike me that something must surely be amiss. And at that instant, it dawned on me. Holding on for support, I slowly sank into the chair in front of me. Nausea; the vomiting; the loss of appetite for familiar foods – the bosom! I quickly made note of what had not appeared for well over a month: my menses.

By God's great grace! I was pregnant! A sublime joy filled my soul and caused me to spill tears of elation. Emma and Lucy, concerned by my reaction, rushed to help, looking questioningly. I smiled through my tears and gazed back, cradling my stomach. No words were necessary – they immediately understood - and Lucy murmured, "Oh, Madame! How wonderful! Our lips are sealed until you deliver the news. We will care for you most tenderly, though, dear Madame."

My sense of exhilaration carried me through the evening as if I floated on air.

Oh, how I wanted to shout the news from the palace turrets! I so wanted to tell Henry – and every moment I was near him caused me a struggle to maintain my silence. As great was my desire to share the miracle with him, even greater was the need to be certain – to be absolutely sure – before I told him that I carried his child. And so I waited.

With each passing day, I knew. There was to be no doubt. How curious pregnancy was, I thought to myself. The most subtle but undeniable changes took place. Nausea remained, especially upon awaking, but was manageable if I nibbled some manchet and sipped weak ale. My dukkys were now clearly increased in size, and I would very shortly need to have all my bodices taken out to fit properly. In the afternoons, I became so sleepy! Naps were a must, and I was glad it was January, and not hunt season so my absence would not be noticed.

By mid-month, I could wait no longer.

I planned a private supper and evening alone with Henry. He was pensive while we sat at the table, and I presumed he was musing on the many state details which had concerned him of late. He sat gazing steadily at the hearth fire, lost in thought. I placed my hand gently on his face and turned it, so we were eye to eye. "My love," I said, my voice thick with emotion. He smiled in return, but I could not avoid seeing the weariness etched around his eyes. How long, after all, could he be expected to wait to fulfil his desire? How many obstacles must he cross? When something we seek evades us continuously, do we not finally, from sheer exhaustion, turn away and give up?

This child has come not a moment too soon, I thought.

"Henry," I said, so softly. "I have something to tell you. I first thought to present it in a special way – an elaborate enactment. And then I realized that nothing in the world could render these words more beautiful than they, themselves. Your Majesty, I am with child."

He was impassive. No expression of surprise registered on his features. I held my breath. Then, great tears welled in his eyes, spilled and splashed onto the tablecloth below. His face crumpled, and he enfolded me in his arms and wept on my shoulder. And I wept, too. Our long, long wait was over.

Whitehall
25 January 1533

LUCY WOKE ME, and it was dark as pitch. My sleep-heavy eyes searched the shadows, and for a moment, I was not sure of my whereabouts. But as she lighted candles and stoked the hearth, all came flooding back to me. I was in my bedchamber at York Place. Henry was not beside me.

If ever there was a morning to lay abed, burrowed deep under the coverlets, it would have been this one. Freezing cold it was, and when I pushed open the window casement for only the briefest moment, snow swirled thickly just outside the window and did its best to invade the room. I jerked the window closed as tightly as possible and then went to stand, shivering, in front of the hearth which was now comfortingly ablaze, to begin to dress for my wedding day.

Lucy and Emma helped me on with the petticoat, kirtle, bodice, and sleeves. We giggled excitedly about how cunning my ensemble – the entire gown created in luxurious white velvet, with a white satin petticoat beneath – in matching the weather for the day. The only jewellery I wore was a large diamond, given to me by Henry, dangling from a golden chain around my neck – and my emerald betrothal ring. My hair hung loose, and my face was devoid of cosmetics, save for the tiniest bit of rouge to my cheek and lip, just to offset winter's pallor.

Anne Savage came to my chamber. She was to be my only attendant at this, the quietest and most secretive of weddings. At one time I had envisioned myself at the centre of a spectacular wedding celebration. But after the interminable wait for release from Rome, which never came, Henry had taken the Matter into his own hands. And now that the longed-for day had finally arrived, such a display mattered not at all to me. I was aglow and thought the pre-dawn rendezvous to marry my love the most romantic thing I could ever have imagined.

I pulled an ermine wrap tightly about my shoulders, and Anne and I hurried silently through the shadowed halls of the sleeping palace to the northern gate, which connected the two new towers spanning King Street. We wound our way up the spiral stair till we reached the uppermost chamber. Brightly candlelit, with braziers in each of the four corners radiating warmth, the room seemed to me dreamlike. It was simple, but beautiful, with a soaring ceiling, a stunning marble hearth ablaze on the courtyard side, handsomely carved wooden panelling all around, and a bank of eight stained glass and mullioned windows, four up and four down, overlooking King Street.

Anne and I approached the others already present in the chamber: Henry, Henry Norreys, Thomas Heneage and William Brereton. The officiant was to be the King's chaplain, Dr Rowland Lee. These few people would be witness to the most significant day in my life.

I waited, holding my breath, while Henry assured Dr Lee that the marriage licences were in order, but the hesitation was plain to see in Lee's expression. I knew that no licence existed as yet, and it was to be Cranmer's mandate to ensure all would be in order with immediacy. Lee asked Henry to please show him the licence, and at this, I watched Henry's face begin to darken. I worried that an altercation would again postpone what had now become the most urgent of matters. With a look of absolute command, Henry told Lee the paper was in a protected place – one he did not intend to reveal by retrieving it at that moment. He glared at Lee and growled menacingly, "Go forth, then, in God's name, and do that which pertaineth to you!"

We assumed our places.

Henry stood to my right, I to his left, both facing Dr Lee. Our witnesses stood to the side, and when Lee recited the marriage banns, asking thrice if anyone present knew of an impediment to this marriage, all eyes in the room were lowered discreetly to the floor. No one uttered a word.

Lee asked Henry and me if we were willing to proceed with the ceremony, and as is traditionally done, we both answered '*Yea*'. Then Henry took my right hand in his right hand and held it – warm, steady and strong. Prompted by the Chaplain, Henry said, looking into my eyes, "I Henricus Rex, take thee, Anne Boleyn to my wedded wife, to have and to hold from this day forth, for better for worse, for richer for poorer, in sickness and in health, till death us depart, according to God's holy ordinance, and thereto I plight thee my troth."

Trembling, my voice not nearly as strong as I would have hoped, I squeezed Henry's hand and said, "I, Anne Boleyn, take thee Henricus Rex to my wedded husband, to have and to hold from this day forth, for richer for poorer, in sickness and in health, till death us depart, according to God's holy ordinance, and thereto I plight thee my troth."

The delicate golden band which was to be my wedding ring was offered on a plate of gilt for Dr Lee to bless. Henry picked it up, and I placed my right hand in his. We met each other's gaze and at once I felt like a stream cascading wilfully toward a flowing river. It was as if there was no one – nor anything – around us: only Henry and I. For a moment I heard naught but the sound of rushing water, and as the stream and the river merged, surging forward as one, I saw Henry's lips move, and the image abruptly vanished. He said, slowly – deliberately - "… with this ring I thee wed and this gold and silver I thee give; and with my body I thee worship and with all my worldly wealth I thee honour." He carefully held the ring on my thumb: "in the name of the Father," then on my second finger saying, "and of the Son," then the third finger, "and of the Holy Ghost," and finally situated the band on my fourth finger, "Amen."

As snow softly blanketed the awakening city of London on that January dawn, I found myself unable to tear my eyes from the simple golden ring on my hand.

I was wed.

SOURCES

Contemporary Accounts:

Brewer, J., ed., *Letters and Papers, Foreign and Domestic, of the Reign of Henry VIII*, Volume 4, 1875

Brown, R., *Calendar of State Papers, Venice*, 1867

Cotsgrave, R.,ed., *A Dictionarie of the French and English Tongues*, London: Adam Islip, 1611

Gairdner, J., ed., *Letters and Papers, Foreign and Domestic, of the Reign of Henry VIII*, Volumes 5 through 10, 1880 – 1887

Gayangos, P.ed., *Calendar of State Papers, Spain*, Vols. 3 and 4, 1873-1879

Grose, F. Esq and Astle, T. Esq., ed., *The Antiquarian Repertory: A Miscellaneous Assemblage of Topography, History, Customs and Manners*, London: Edward Jeffrey, 1809

Hall, E., *Chronicle Containing the History of England During the Reign of Henry the Fourth and the Succeeding Monarchs to the End of the Reign of Henry the Eighth*, London, 1809

Hinds, A., ed. *Calendar of State Papers and Manuscripts in the Archives and Collections of Milan - 1385-1618*, 1912

Mayhew, A. ,ed., *A Glossary of Tudor and Stuart Words*, London: Oxford Press, 1914

Nichols, J.G. ed., *Chronicle of Calais*, London: Camden Society, 1846

Nicolas, N.H. Esq. ed., *The Privy Purse Expences of Henry the Eighth*, London: Wm Pickering, 1828

Phillips, J., ed., *The Love Letters of Henry VIII to Anne Boleyn, With Notes*, Watchmaker Publishing, 2009

St Claire Byrne, M. ed., *The Lisle Letters, An Abridgement*, Chicago: University of Chicago Press, 1983

Wriothesley, Charles, *A Chronicle of England During the Reign of the Tudors*, London: Camden Society, 1875

Secondary sources:

Carley, J., *The Books of King Henry and His Wives*, London: The British Library, 2004

Cressy, D., *Birth, Marriage, and Death – Ritual, Religion and the Life-Cycle in Tudor and Stuart England,* New York: Oxford University Press 1997

Drummond, J., and Wilbraham, A., *The Englishman's Food – A History of Five Centuries Of English Diet,* London: Readers Union, 1959

Emerson, K., www.kateemersonhistoricals.com/TudorWomenIndex.htm, 2008 - 2013

Fletcher, C., *Our Man in Rome, Henry VIII and his Italian Ambassador*, London: The Bodley Head, 2012

Fraser, A., *The Wives of Henry VIII*, New York: Vintage Books, 1994

Ives, Eric, *The Life and Death of Anne Boleyn 'The Most Happy'*, Blackwell Publishing, 2004

Jokinen, A., www.Luminarium.org, 1996

Mikhaila, N. and Malcolm-Davies, J., *The Tudor Tailor – Reconstructing 16th century dress,* Hollywood: Costume and Fashion Press 2006

Starkey, D., *Six Wives, The Queens of Henry VIII*, New York: HarperCollins, 2003

Thurley, S., *The Royal Palaces of Tudor England - Architecture and Court Life 1460 – 1547,* New Haven and London: Yale University Press, 1993

Discover Book Two...

TRUTH ENDURES

The Palace of Whitehall
February 1533

LO, HE WAS something to observe - as observe I did, with pride and pleasure: my royal consort in resplendent authority, impeccably groomed and luxuriously draped in burnished sable, his broad chest weighted with a golden, gem-studded collar. He was radiant! Flush with health, his resonant voice echoing as he paced the length of the new gallery in Whitehall with his councillors. The events of recent weeks had steeped him in vigour and confidence.

No one wore an air of aplomb as well as did my husband, Henry VIII of England.

Unconsciously I placed my hands on my gently swelling belly. The gesture had become a habit for me of late. With a contented smile I reflected over the months since late autumn, when Henry and I had travelled to Calais to meet with the French king, François I. It had been a triumphant visit for me - Anne Boleyn - the girl who had spent her youth at the royal court of France, being groomed in the ways of royal demeanor, Christian humanism, and womanhood. Now I returned in splendour as a Marquess in my own right, accompanied by my betrothed, His Grace the King. We enjoyed a most pleasing and very successful stay, and an even more romantic trip homeward, taking our time crossing the English countryside, revelling in each other's company before – very reluctantly on my part - returning to London just before Christmastide. Even that sojourn had been an unexpected pleasure. The winter season spent at Greenwich was jubilant despite our increased disillusionment with the Pope and his obstinate refusal to align with Henry in granting him his rightful divorce from Katherine of Aragon. Regardless of that cumbrance, I basked in the adoration of a man with whom I now lived as if we were husband and wife. Yes, I had decided before we departed for Calais to abandon my dogged stance to remain chaste before we wed. The resulting fulfilment of living as a couple was rewarding and we were happy and content with one another. Indeed, it was a Christmas to be remembered.

During that halcyon period, I did admittedly experience one cause for anxiety - it seemed I had the beginnings of a nagging illness which I could not identify. I had eaten less and less yet remained nauseous throughout the day while feeling overbearingly tired in the afternoons. Only when my maid, Lucy, tried valiantly to lace me into the bodice of a new gown, resulting in the spillage of an unusually ample bosom from its neckline, did I finally perceive the exultant truth - I was pregnant with Henry's child! Please be to God, with his *son*? Never again will there be such a gift for the New Year as was that realization. The tender scene between us when I told him the news will be forever etched in my mind's eye. Occasionally I had allowed myself the luxury of imagining a time when I might announce a pregnancy to the King – I would create a gorgeous, elaborate tableau in which to unveil the news. The moment came, however, when Henry's exhaustion and melancholy over years of thwarted effort to gain his freedom to marry me were etched deep in the lines on his face. In truth, at times, I had wondered why he persisted in his intent to have me – to marry me. Was it not possible with the very next obstacle thrown in his path - one more denial from the Pope - he might just give up, even though we loved one another? But then! *Sweet Jesu*! The pregnancy I had suspected became certain, and while we dined together alone one evening, I tenderly turned his tired face to mine, and in a voice thick with emotion, told him, simple and plain. At first, he was devoid of expression, and I held my breath, fearing he had already determined to abandon me and our hopeless suit. But then his face crumpled, and he had clung to me, weeping into my shoulder. I held my strong and powerful King and felt his shoulders heave with quiet sobs, overcome with relief and joy at the news he so desperately wanted: had waited an eternity to hear.

The next day and those that followed were imbued with the exhilaration of an expected prince.

In late January, then, urged on by the great blessing the Almighty had bestowed upon us, His Grace the King had taken decisive action by designating Dr Thomas Cranmer, our staunch supporter and friend, as his choice for the vacant position of Archbishop of Canterbury. This step placed in Cranmer's capable hands the task of acquiring licenses necessary for our very secret marriage. So in the dark pre-dawn of 25 January 1533, Henry and I were wed in the northern tower of Whitehall Palace. While snow softly cloaked London's rooftops, we had stood in the fire-lit chamber with only the fewest witnesses, looked into each other's eyes and, prompted by the Reverend Rowland Lee, stated our vows to remain together 'til death us depart'.

And thus did I find myself impervious to all previous misgivings. No less powerful a man than the King of England had promised, even before God, to become my sworn protector.

Pregnant, married at last, with a husband who doted on me?Life could not be more blissful. More secure.

•

Here were now three highly competent men operating from the leading positions of power in Henry's Council, all of them motivated to present His Highness as the ultimate determiner of all matters, political and theological, pertaining to his realm. His word would thus be supreme, and the dependency on the Church of Rome and those decisions previously considered the prerogative of Pope Clement VII conclusively broken.

I observed with satisfaction the culmination of what had been a long and arduous campaign to gain Clement's agreement to annul Henry's marriage to Katherine of Aragon. Despite many setbacks, a combination of brilliant logic, practiced crusading and, ultimately, sheer force of will, had brought us to the present status: Henry firmly in control, and me a married woman, expecting a fully legitimate prince, heir to the throne of England.

Before me strode the ingenious lawyer Thomas Cromwell, who, by demonstrating cunning and dedication to the King's service, now held several illustrious titles including Master of the Jewels and Chancellor of the Exchequer. Beside him walked Thomas Cranmer, Henry's personal nominee as the new Archbishop of Canterbury, and - of no lesser stature - His Grace's recently installed Lord Chancellor, Thomas Audley. They, along with Henry, would appear before the House, make their case and subsequently, following negotiation, payments, and politicking would confidently await an acknowledgement from Rome on Cranmer's appointment to the highest clerical office in the land.

Undeniably, the tactics this trio had devised to gain victory were worthy of the master manipulator and Florentine statesman Niccolò di Bernardo dei Machiavelli himself. We had heard much of Machiavelli and the crafty principles he espoused. Cromwell was an enthusiast of Machiavelli, and for that matter, all things Italian; especially the barbed offensives so aptly utilized by the powerful families who ruled the principal city-states. And of course, Henry had long been an admirer of the great Lorenzo de Medici and a student of the humanism flourishing in Florence. I was aware that the Florentine principles of leadership were exacting a great influence on Henry's newfound determination to grasp and direct his destiny.

Once formally sanctioned by the Church in Rome, it was intended that Cranmer would immediately use his newly appointed authority to exercise the conviction that the King of England was now Supreme Authority of the Church in England and that his previously held jurisdiction was no longer the privilege of the Pope. The premier directive? To officially pronounce Henry's long marriage to Katherine of Aragon null and void, and let the Pope be damned!

With that act of defiance, we would be sure to hear the bell toll for the Church of Rome in England.

Until Dr Cranmer's new position was confirmed, which would then allow him to create the necessary official documents for certification of our marriage, I was obliged to keep my two 'secrets', albeit there were a few in my closest circle who did know the truth … that I was the wife of the King - his new Queen - and I carried his child. Oh, how difficult it was to remain circumspect when I wanted to shout the news from the Palace towers!

I resigned myself to maintaining the privacy of my condition, but at least felt able to share the joy with my family. My mother and my sister Mary proved great sources of comfort and advice as I became accustomed to life as a pregnant woman. It proved helpful, being able to discuss the peculiarities and subtleties of what I experienced as the early days of sickness began to wane, and other cravings took precedence. Particularly I delighted in being included in that special clan of women who smiled knowingly when pregnancy was discussed.

My queasiness did subside, and in its place, I found I had little tolerance for meats but had a great urge to eat fruit, especially apples. I delighted in how my belly had become firm and had begun to swell as the babe within me grew and flourished.

Admittedly there were times when my resolve to remain discreet faltered. Rapturous over my new and treasured position as the King's pregnant wife, and simply itching for some jovial mischief, one wintry and bleak February afternoon I mingled with the usual groups of courtiers clustered, talking and passing time in the Presence Chamber. While conversing with Thomas Wyatt and the newly married Anne Gainsford Zouche I'd first looked artfully about to assess the crowd within earshot, then, during a lull in our discussion, had selected an apple from a porcelain bowlful which sat upon the sideboard before calling loudly and playfully, "These apples look delicious, don't you think, Thomas? It is quite strange because, of late, I find I have an insatiable hankering to eat apples such as I have never experienced before."

I waited for my words to register, and then widened my eyes in mock disbelief. "The King tells me it must be a sign that I am pregnant. But I have told him I think he *certainly* must be wrong …!"

Then I laughed loudly, thinking this little scene terribly humorous, prompting heads to turn and everyone within range of hearing to stare. Gratified with the reaction thus generated, I stood, gathered my skirt with a flourish and swept coquettishly from the room, leaving all in my wake wondering what had just taken place.

Not that Henry, either, could contain our joyful secret entirely. He was giddy with unbridled elation at being a new husband and father-to-be. And although no official royal announcement had yet been made concerning our matrimony or my condition, he became less and less concerned with guarding the news. And how rightfully he deserved to proclaim the reasons for his exuberance for, I thought, no man had ever shown such patience, such loyalty, such *dedication* to any woman as did my Henry to me.

To provide him with just the smallest demonstration of my gratitude and devotion, I planned an elegant banquet in his honour, which was to be held in my beautiful new apartments in Whitehall on 24 February; the Feast of St Mathias. I invited all of the great personages of the court, and personally attended to every detail, as was my wont, to ensure the room looked its grandest. With fine arras lining the walls, masses of glowing gold plate on display, and spectacular dishes presented in elaborate style, my position and wealth were now evident to all. The ladies whom I had assembled as members of my household were all present, gaily bedecked, looking stunning, and in high humour. On that evening, Henry had chosen to partake of *aqua vitae*, or as its distillers called it - *uisge beatha* - the wickedly potent spirit produced by Scottish monks. He quickly became flush with the drink, jesting and flirting madly with me and my ravishing companions. I found his boisterous, ribald jokes and silly levity to be completely endearing, thinking how much he deserved an evening of release after the tensions he had endured. At one point he gave me a staged wink so noticeable that anyone in view would have wondered what was to come, then moved close - *much* too close - to the very proper Dowager Duchess of Norfolk before blurting loudly, with a noticeable slurring of the tongue, "Your Ladyship! Doth you not think that Madame the Marquess, seated right here next to me, has an exceptionally fine dowry and a rich marriage portion as we can all see from her luxurious apartment?"

He gesticulated wildly with his arms to indicate the scope of my possessions, nearly knocking the goblets from the table. "Does that not make her an excellent marriage prospect, hey?" Then, as I had done just a few days prior, he exploded in raucous laughter at his drink-fueled sense of comedy. The Duchess, stony-faced, leaned as far back in her seat as was possible in an attempt to escape Henry's liquored breath while those observing tittered behind their hands. Watching my beloved sway while he roared with amusement, I couldn't help but enjoy my hearty chuckle.

The celebration did not conclude till early the morning next. From the room littered with the debris of gaiety, I saw the King off. Henry Norreys, his Groom of the Stool, had his arm firmly about the shoulders of His Majesty as he guided him, staggering amiably, toward his chambers. I suspected I would not see Henry at all on the morrow since there was little doubt he would remain abed till he could recover from the effects of the *uisge.* Smiling happily as I took myself to bed, I reflected on the entertaining moments of the evening, and mostly on what an irresistible drunk my husband had been.

•

Maggie Wyatt, Anne Zouche, Nan Saville and I sat at a polished table in the well-appointed Queen's Presence Chamber at Whitehall. Sipping small ale, piles of letters and personal references strewn before us, we reviewed the lists of maids and ladies who had been proposed to make up my retinue: potential appointees to the household of the Queen. Glancing up from a sheet of parchment, Maggie looked at me inquiringly. "How well do you know Lady Cobham, Anne?"

"I know her scarcely. I have met her on several occasions but can't say I have ever had a conversation of any depth with her. Do you know her, Maggie? How is her temperament? I daresay I am not keen on having those unknown to me as a part of my close personal circle. But then, I am not permitted to make strictly my own selections." Eyeing the stacks of letters from noble families all imploring for a position for a daughter or niece, I added, "His Grace the King owes many a favour, and I conveniently provide a solution by taking daughters of those so favoured into my household." I paused then, sniffing, "… even though it is of considerable concern to have someone unfamiliar serving in such proximity."

Indeed, I believed I was well justified in feeling irritated by this requirement. With a sharp stab of anguish, I remembered the incident of my stolen love letters. I recalled, as if it had happened only yesterday, my panic at the discovery and resulting despair which flooded me when I'd realized that someone – a spy; a secret enemy within my closest personal space! – had stolen the locked casket which concealed the letters which I had carefully kept together, and out of sight, over the years. I believed the miscreant was a maid employed to serve me in my privy chambers. She was recommended by my Uncle Norfolk's wife, but at the time I was unaware of the extent of Elizabeth Howard, Lady Norfolk's animosity toward me. So I fell into the Duchess's vicious trap and naively exposed my greatest treasure to an individual who had been hired by a detractor to steal evidence of Henry's love for me. They were intimate and immensely personal: gorgeous letters full of the romantic expression of a man deeply in love - missives composed by Henry throughout the beginning years of our courtship, mostly while we were apart, I having been at Hever while Henry remained at court. Every scratch of the quill, each splotch of ink smeared by his big hand had drawn me closer to him. He had revealed his wit using clever wordplay, and his bawdy, waggish self when he described a beautiful gown he had had made for me – one that he longed to see me in – and out of! Mostly, I ached to see once again those sweet and wistful drawings of a small heart, etched around my initials at the close of an especially endearing letter. I pored over them often, running my fingers over his writing, knowing he had meant them for my eyes only. And then, in a trice, they were gone, never to be returned or seen by me again. My heart broke every time I thought of it.

I was pulled back to the business at hand as Maggie shrugged, "I too, know her only superficially even though she is sister-in-law to my brother Thomas … or *was* when Thomas was married to that little scandal, Elizabeth Brooke. But the few times I have been in her company, she seemed quiet. Or perhaps simply exhausted, seeing as she has seven children!"

"That I cannot even imagine," I rejoined, wryly patting my stomach. "I am happy to be working on just one."

Anne smiled indulgently at me. My dear, close friends were treating me with such loving care. Then, narrowing her eyes and peering again at the list, she questioned, "And what of Mistress Seymour? Do either of you know much of her? She has been at court off and on for years since she served Katherine yet still I have never talked to her about anything of consequence."

I could not resist the temptation to be waspish about a woman of questionable allegiance, for whom I cared little anyway. Arching one groomed brow, I sneered "Why, is that not simply characteristic of Mistress Seymour? And the reason is that she appears to hold naught in that empty little head of hers which *is* of any importance ..."

Hearing myself, I ruefully observed that my pregnancy had somehow stripped away a goodly layer of the discernment needed to avoid saying whatever came to my mind, no matter how cutting. But I didn't care so I added smugly, "Forsooth, ladies, her intelligence mirrors her looks - quite common!"

Anne and Maggie looked at each other and pressed their lips tightly in an attempt to suppress their laughter. Apparently they found my unchecked outbursts entertaining.

"WELL ... Am I wrong?" I demanded with mock severity, my probing glance shifting between the two. "Speak out - what *do* you both think of her?"

"You are by no means in the wrong, Anne," Maggie hastily allowed. "She is quiet and dull as a tiny titmouse. She will offer no hardship as a member of your household because she will provide no opinions, and no one will even notice her."

Mollified, I grumbled, "Well then, that should be acceptable to me," and continued to peruse the lists.

The assembling of ladies who would make up my household neared completion, with many well-liked appointees and some about whom I was indifferent but whose appointments served their purpose. My closest confidantes had already been included, and then we added to the total number Nan Cobham and, somewhat grudgingly on my part, Mistress Seymour. It only remained, then, to confirm positions with Jane Ashley; Margaret Gamage, who was betrothed and set to marry William Howard in the spring; young Mary Norreys, who was the daughter of Henry's Groom of the Stool; the very pretty Grace Newport; Eleanor Paston, Countess of Rutland and a mother of six; Mistress Frances de Vere – at sixteen already wed to Henry Howard, Earl of Surrey. There then followed Elizabeth

Browne, Lady Worcester, and my sister-in-law Jane Parker, Lady Rochford. All were possessed of a singular degree of beauty - apart from Seymour. It was important to me that my ladies present an exceptional appearance and, furthermore, conduct themselves with unblemished gentility, and I fully intended to duly instruct them once they were all in place.

As for the men of my royal household, there were to be numerous trusted advisers. Thomas Cromwell, already indispensable to the King, was among those whom I considered beneficial, and he would serve an important place in my retinue once I was Queen. George Taylor would continue his good work as my Receiver-General. William Coffin, long in the King's service, would assume the position of my Master of the Horse; Thomas Burgh as Lord Chamberlain; and Sir Edward Baynton as Vice Chamberlain. Perhaps most important to me were those selected to be my personal chaplains. These brilliant men would confer with me and preach on our shared reformist views, a mission which would demand keen intelligence, a broad knowledge of theology and, perhaps above all, courage. We selected Hugh Latimer, a Cambridge scholar; Matthew Parker, another Cambridge theologian whom I had liked and trusted from the first time I met him; William Betts, who had already proved his mettle several years prior when found to be one of a group of scholars boldly circulating books deemed by our opponents to be heretical; and the redoubtable John Skypp. Skypp could be almost too resolute in the expression of his views, but I admired that about him. All in all, I intended to surround myself with a strong, outspoken assembly who would advance the cause of reform and unfailingly support Henry's right to supremacy.

Yet there were many in and around court who remained sources of great frustration to me. My abiding perception that Henry's chosen ambassador in Rome, Sir Gregory Casale, was apathetic had proved all too true when, late in January, we were given letters he had written boasting his self-described 'advancement' of Henry's cause. After years of fruitless negotiation on the Great Matter, Casale still considered it acceptable to present letters to the King, that laid out numerous additional conditions demanded by the Pope to pronounce in Henry's favour. First, Henry must send a mandate for the remission of the cause, along with a newly appointed legate and two auditors. Then, he must persuade François to accept a general truce for three or four years, even amongst other ridiculous requirements. This contrivance was in complete opposition with Henry's instructions to Casale and did the Ambassador's credentials no service in my view. Henry however, always the gracious Sovereign, still responded politely to his man in Rome, advising him to thank the Pope, and discreetly tell his Holiness that the overtures were taken in good part, and trusting the Pope would concur, only by 'will and unkind stubbornness, with oblivion of former kindness, which be occasions of the let of the speedy finishing of our cause'.

I had looked on Henry's temperate reply in amazement, and with no small measure of cynical admiration. It made me realize I needed to learn all I could from him, seeing that soon I was to be Queen, and would often be required to respond well and fairly to vexing situations. Learn I must, because had this particular matter been left to me, I would have delivered a tongue-lashing to Signore Casale that he would not soon have forgotten!

On occasion, I would think back - oh, not so many years - to my life in France followed by my early time in the court of Henry and Katherine, and marvel at how my existence had changed so dramatically. Upon reflection, those days were so easy and light-hearted in their simple pursuits: maintaining a young lady's proper demeanor; hunting, dancing, playing at witty pastimes, dallying with the most handsome men and adorning oneself to play the coquette ... the threads weaving my life's tapestry had long since become much more intricate indeed.

Ever conscious of the new life – the all-important life – growing within me, I was engaged from morn 'til night. Details concerning the establishment of my household called for my attention; audiences were requested by those who sought my support in pleading matters to the King's Grace; there was constant worry about the increasingly intense skirmishes between Scotland and England while the tentative relationship with France was always of concern. Above all hung the palpable hostility of my opposers. Those critics – I had begun to think of them as enemies – were becoming ever more brazen, and openly included some who had been previously close to Henry and me: his sister Mary chief amongst them, with her husband Charles Brandon, Duke of Suffolk, who precariously balanced between the opinions of his wife and his King … even my Uncle Norfolk, surprisingly – whose position could only be strengthened by the Howard bloodline on the throne, yet who openly disapproved of the dire measures being taken with the Church to achieve that goal.

•

At times I did wish for a reprieve, just a simple moment in time when I might revert to being Anne from Hever – but, of course, it was not to be had.

I could do naught but rejoice, however, when, in March, Cromwell delivered his carefully crafted *Act in Restraint of Appeals* to the Commons in Parliament, urging them to approve the statute which would enforce Henry's supremacy in all things pertaining to his realm. Both Houses approved the Act, and on 10 April, just before Easter, a definitive blow was delivered to Katherine. She was informed by a deputation comprising Norfolk, Suffolk, Exeter, Oxford, and the royal chamberlains that we had been married and, on direct orders of Henry the King, she was no longer Queen but would henceforth be referred to as the Dowager Princess of Wales. Her daughter Mary, whom I had not seen – or frankly, even given much thought to - in many months, remained apart from her mother with a diminished household.

True, the mere fact of their continued existence presented me with a vexation - but how good it was to think no longer of Katherine, or the former Princess, now known simply as Lady Mary - as active threats to the happiness I shared with Henry!

And happy we truly were.

Sandra Vasoli, author of *Anne Boleyn's Letter from the Tower*, *Struck with the Dart of Love* and *Truth Endures*, earned a Bachelor's degree in English and biology from Villanova University before embarking on a thirty-five-year career in human resources for a large international company.

Having written essays, stories, and articles all her life, Vasoli was prompted by her overwhelming fascination with the Tudor dynasty to try her hand at writing both historical fiction and non-fiction. While researching what eventually became the *Je Anne Boleyn* series, Vasoli was granted unprecedented access to the Papal Library. There, she was able to read the original love letters from Henry VIII to Anne Boleyn—an event that contributed greatly to her research and writing.

Vasoli currently lives in Gwynedd Valley, Pennsylvania, with her husband and two greyhounds.

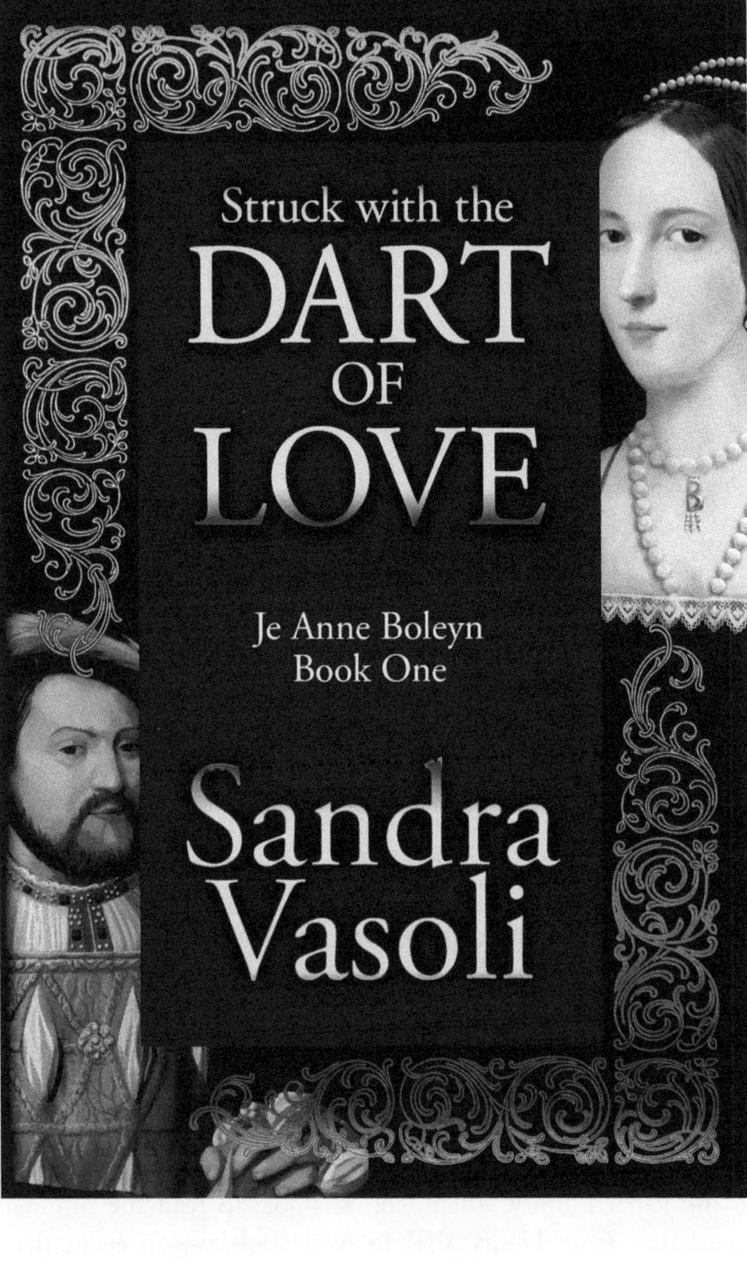
Struck with the
DART
OF
LOVE
Je Anne Boleyn
Book One
Sandra
Vasoli

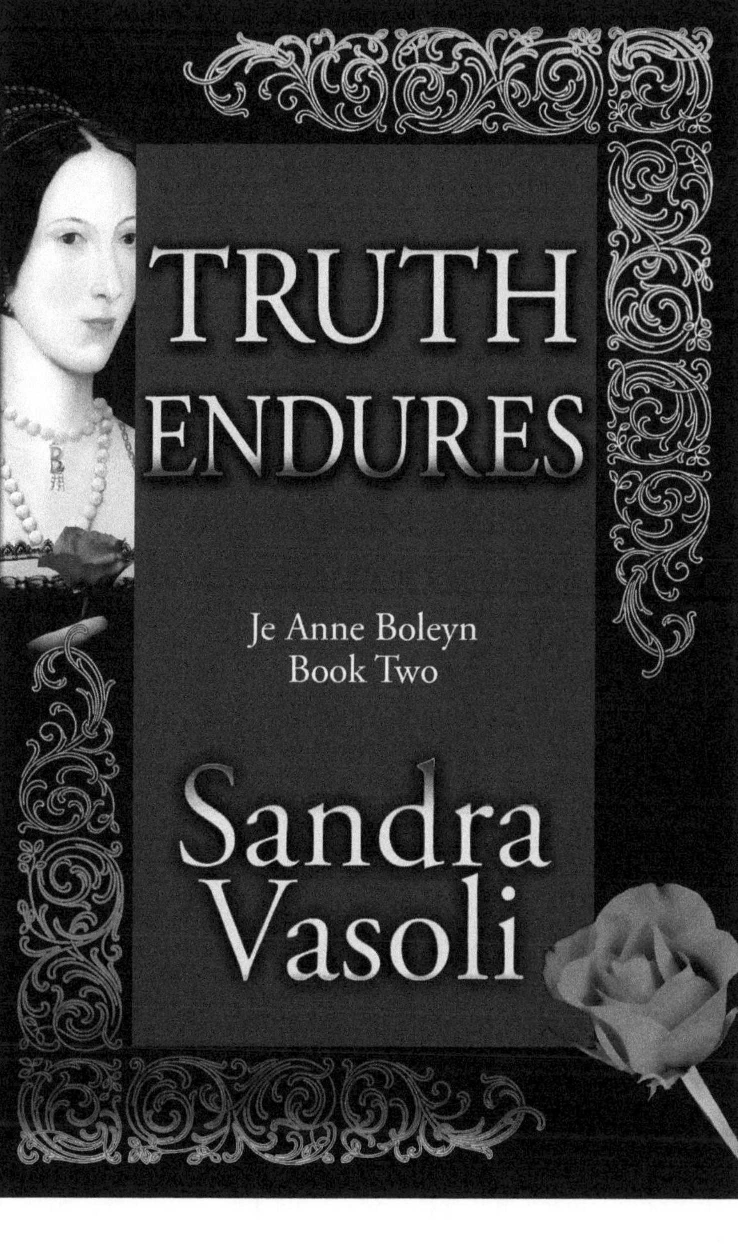
TRUTH
ENDURES
Je Anne Boleyn
Book Two
Sandra
Vasoli

Sandra Vasoli

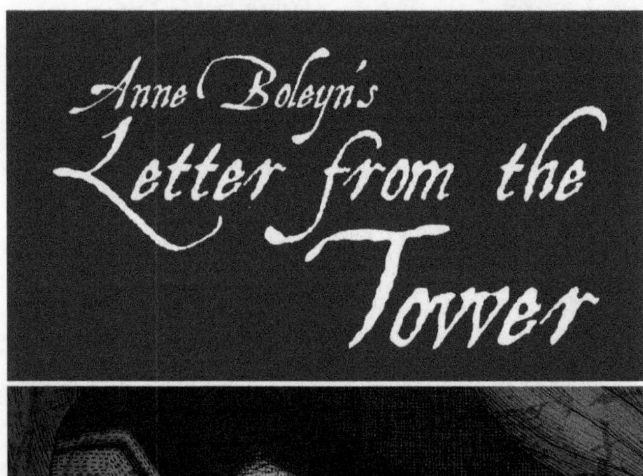

A New Assessment

ISBN: 978-84-943721-5-5

"Sir, Your Grace's Displeasure and my Imprisonment are Things so strange unto me, as what to Write, or what to Excuse, I am altogether ignorant."

Thus opens a burned fragment of a letter dated 6 May 1536 and signed "Anne Boleyn", a letter in which the imprisoned queen fervently proclaims her innocence to her husband, King Henry VIII.

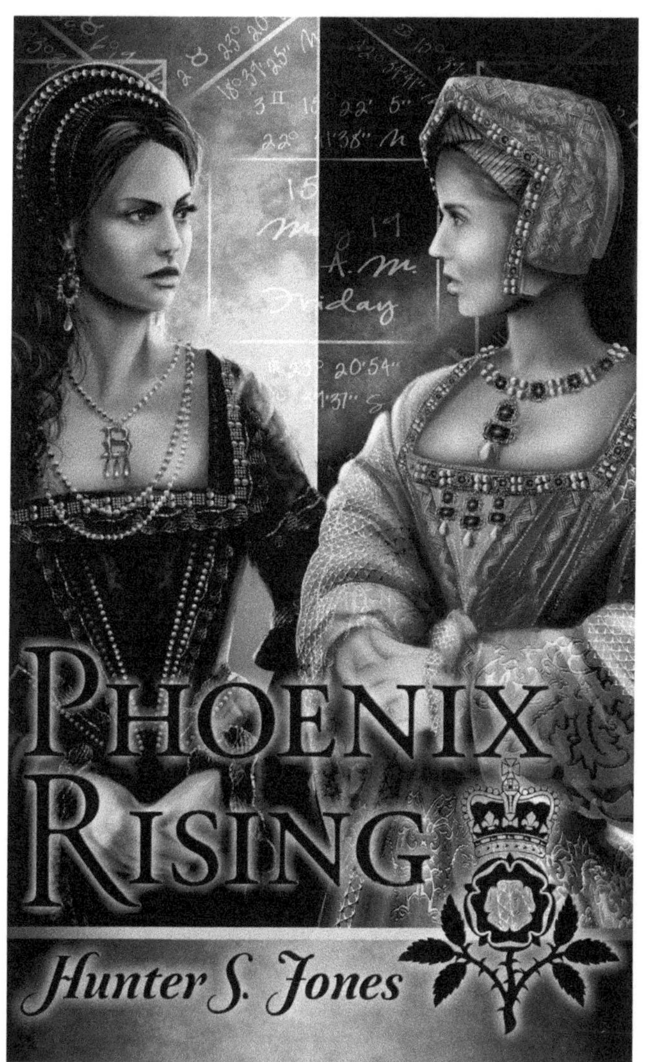

ISBN: 978-84-943721-4-8

The last hour of Anne Boleyn's life...

Court intrigue, revenge and all the secrets of the last hour are revealed as one queen falls and another rises to take her place on destiny's stage.

A young Anne Boleyn arrives at the court of King Henry VIII. She is to be presented at the Shrovetide pageant, le Château Vert. The young and ambitious Anne has no idea that a chance encounter before the pageant will lead to her capturing the heart of the king. What begins as a distraction becomes his obsession and leads to her destruction.

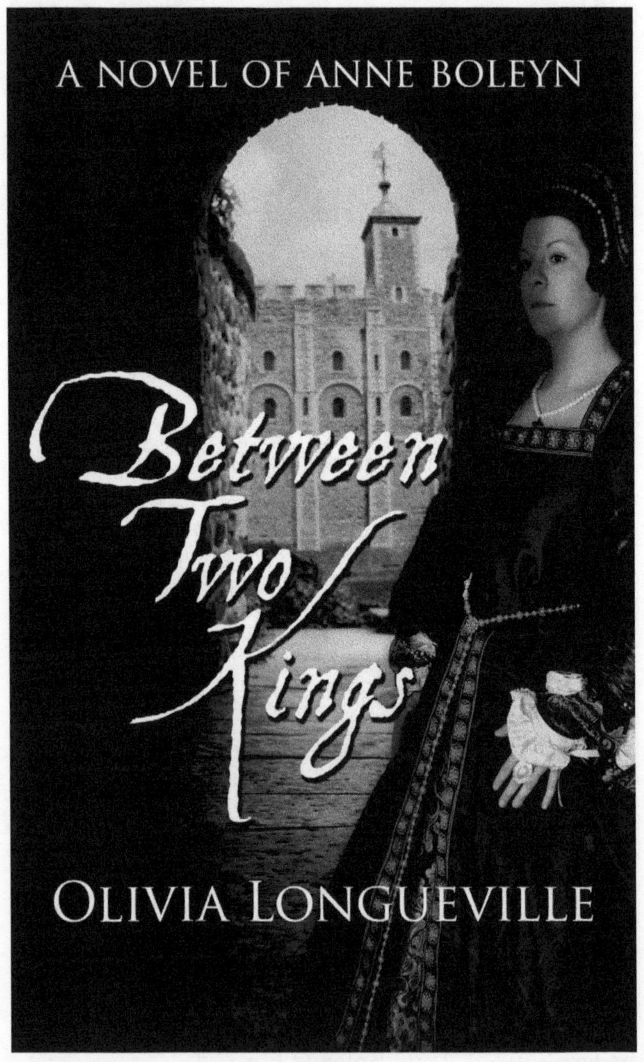

A NOVEL OF ANNE BOLEYN
Between Two Kings
OLIVIA LONGUEVILLE

ISBN: 978-84-944574-9-4

Anne Boleyn is accused of adultery and imprisoned in the Tower. The very next day she is due to be executed at the hand of a swordsman. Nothing can change the tragic outcome. England will have a new queen before the month is out. And yet...

What if events conspired against Henry VIII and his plans to take a new wife? What if there were things that even Thomas Cromwell couldn't control, things which would make it impossible for history to go to plan?

TONI MOUNT

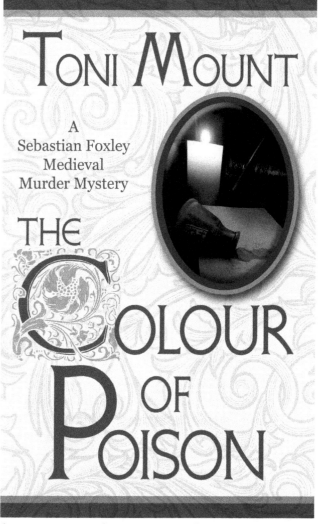

A Sebastian Foxley Medieval Murder Mystery

THE COLOUR OF POISON

The narrow, stinking streets of medieval London can sometimes be a dark place. Burglary, arson, kidnapping and murder are every-day events. The streets even echo with rumours of the mysterious art of alchemy being used to make gold for the King.

Join Seb, a talented but crippled artist, as he is drawn into a web of lies to save his handsome brother from the hangman's rope. Will he find an inner strength in these, the darkest of times, or will events outside his control overwhelm him?

If Seb can't save his brother, nobody can.

Non Fiction History

Anne Boleyn's Letter from the Tower - **Sandra Vasoli**
Jasper Tudor - **Debra Bayani**
Tudor Places of Great Britain - **Claire Ridgway**
Illustrated Kings and Queens of England - **Claire Ridgway**
A History of the English Monarchy - **Gareth Russell**
The Fall of Anne Boleyn - **Claire Ridgway**
George Boleyn: Tudor Poet, Courtier & Diplomat - **Ridgway & Cherry**
The Anne Boleyn Collection - **Claire Ridgway**
The Anne Boleyn Collection II - **Claire Ridgway**
Two Gentleman Poets at the Court of Henry VIII - **Edmond Bapst**
A Mountain Road - **Douglas Weddell Thompson**

"History in a Nutshell Series"

Sweating Sickness in a Nutshell - **Claire Ridgway**
Mary Boleyn in a Nutshell - **Sarah Bryson**
Thomas Cranmer in a Nutshell - **Beth von Staats**
Henry VIII's Health in a Nutshell - **Kyra Kramer**
Catherine Carey in a Nutshell - **Adrienne Dillard**
The Pyramids in a Nutshell - **Charlotte Booth**

Historical Fiction

Struck with the Dart of Love: Je Anne Boleyn 1 - **Sandra Vasoli**
Truth Endures: Je Anne Boleyn 2 - **Sandra Vasoli**
The Colour of Poison - **Toni Mount**
Between Two Kings: A Novel of Anne Boleyn - **Olivia Longueville**
Phoenix Rising - **Hunter S. Jones**
Cor Rotto - **Adrienne Dillard**
The Claimant - **Simon Anderson**
The Truth of the Line - **Melanie V. Taylor**

Children's Books

All about Richard III - **Amy Licence**
All about Henry VII - **Amy Licence**
All about Henry VIII - **Amy Licence**
Tudor Tales William at Hampton Court - **Alan Wybrow**

PLEASE LEAVE A REVIEW

If you enjoyed this book, *please* leave a review at the book seller where you purchased it. There is no better way to thank the author and it really does make a huge difference!
Thank you in advance.

Lightning Source UK Ltd.
Milton Keynes UK
UKHW01f2338010618
323613UK00001B/109/P